CREMATION

CREMATION

Rafael Chirbes

*Translated from the Spanish
by Valerie Miles*

A NEW DIRECTIONS
PAPERBOOK ORIGINAL

AC/E   Support for the translation of this book was provided
ACCIÓN CULTURAL   by Acción Cultural Española (AC/E)
ESPAÑOLA

First published as New Directions Paperbook 1518 in 2021
Manufactured in the United States of America
Design by Erik Rieselbach

Library of Congress Cataloging-in-Publication Data
Names: Chirbes, Rafael, 1949–2015, author. | Miles, Valerie, 1963– translator.
Title: Cremation / Rafael Chirbes ; translated from the Spanish by Valerie Miles.
Other titles: Crematorio. English
Description: New York : New Directions Publishing Corporation, [2021]
Identifiers: LCCN 2021037305 | ISBN 9780811224307 (paperback) |
ISBN 9780811224314 (ebook)
Subjects: LCGFT: Novels.
Classification: LCC PQ6653.H6 C7413 2021 | DDC 863/.64—dc23
LC record available at https://lccn.loc.gov/2021037305

10 9 8 7 6 5 4 3 2 1

New Directions Books are published for James Laughlin
by New Directions Publishing Corporation
80 Eighth Avenue, New York 10011

CREMATION

YOU'RE LAID out on a sheet, a metal table, maybe a slab of marble. I can picture you. Again, I picture you. I'd forgotten about you while I was talking to the Russian in the café first thing this morning, watching, through the window, the tourists lounging in the patio chairs outside, another cluster of them a few more feet along stretched out on the sand, frolicking in the water. He drank a pair of bourbons. I had an iced tea. Don't like to start so early. Though I kept a restless eye on the two tumblers the waiter set on the table in front of him. If it weren't for him, if I'd come on my own, I might have been able to relax in that spacious, empty salon (just the two of us there) with its beachfront view, so green along the shoreline rising into a deep band of cobalt at the horizon, the barges already moving, the sailboats, the catamarans. Traian, the Russian, drank both shots of bourbon. First one then the other, an almost continuous motion. I glanced back at the café as I turned the key in the ignition, thinking why not go back in, why not hang out for a while under the jet of air-conditioning, read my newspaper and enjoy the view, by myself now, with my own bourbon in hand, two rocks. I picture you laid out someplace. Who knows where? But there you are anyway, lying on a steel table, a sheet, a cold marble slab, under a jet of air-conditioning. Truth is I don't like seeing you that way. The engine turns and I press the button beside the steering wheel with my index finger to switch on the radio. The sudden commotion, the sound of the motor, they displace you, leaving me alone; I concentrate on the movement of my hands now, gripping the wheel, the movement of my right foot, stepping on the accelerator. The car's wheels crunch across the sheet of sand blanketing the ribbon of asphalt along the beach.

Little granules of it dust the sidewalk, framed by fences and trellises sprouting with leafy flora: hibiscus and oleander slowly drift past the car window, bougainvillea, green hedges of thuja, rows of cypress trees. Black, pink, and blue trash bags are piled beside the dumpsters and hanging from apartment railings, like another species of blossom. They impregnate the musty iodine breath of the sea with their tang. The car rolls sluggishly forward and I forget about you, Matías. I stop seeing you. It's sweltering even at this early hour. I push the button to close the window and isolate myself in the vehicle's interior. Finally alone. It's five past ten in the morning; the little green numbers on the dashboard flash thirty-four degrees centigrade. Consecutive foggy mornings and high levels of humidity had made the air grow stagnant, muggy, and oppressive—what the French call *marais thermique*—but a rough westerly kicked up on Tuesday afternoon that dried the atmosphere out, stoking the mercury an asphyxiating three or four degrees higher. Come afternoon the scorching winds stir up again. The branches of shrubs sway to and fro as the oven door opens in an incandescent yawn somewhere behind the mountains, its afterglow deepening as dusk settles in. The local radio DJ is talking about the heat; Misent's climate records tell us there hasn't been a heat wave like this since the fifties. It's the second one this summer. The first (not quite a wave, more of an *episode* the meteorologists say) peaked at the end of June: the thermometers spiked unpredictably, hitting maximums of over thirty-six degrees for eight or nine days straight, eighty percent humidity and higher, before temperatures plunged again in the following weeks. Now the *episode* is repeating itself, but more savagely. The radio says to expect temperatures to soar above forty degrees inland, and none of the satellite images forecast an appreciable shift. The tiny arrows dotting the maps on the television news predict continued sweltering, sand-laden winds. Cars parked outside overnight are covered in a film of reddish dust by the morning. I had to ask the gardener to wash mine before I left home this morning; I forgot to park it in the garage last night. A new Heat Task Force was announced on the news, with an emergency hotline. The broadcasters are constantly warning everyone to keep hydrated, stay out of the sun in the merciless peak hours, wear a hat and light clothing so the body can perspire—cotton, linen—and slather on the sunscreen; but mostly they recommend water and more water: drink several liters a day, splash a little on the wrists and nape of the neck. The broadcaster repeats the Heat Task Force number, reminding us it's toll-free, one eight hundred. All this harping seems ridiculous to me. In Misent, in Xàbia, in Calp, in Benidorm, summers have always been sweltering. But the broadcaster and all the guests on his program babble on about the advance of climate change, how the rapid depletion of the ozone is wreaking havoc and they support their assertions with data and statistics that invite pessimism: the mounting thermal oscillations are melting the ice caps in the Antarctic, causing chunks to break off and create drifting icebergs (dangerous for ocean fauna, for navigation); the Alpine glaciers are thawing (danger of avalanches this winter in the Swiss ski stations), and the snows of Kilimanjaro are vanishing (inevitably causing droughts and new famines on the dark continent: the death knell of the great African lakes, reduced to mudflats. Kilimanjaro, Africa's highest summit, crowned by the perpetual snows and immortalized by Hemingway, is now scantily clad in tiny patches of ice. Africa's ceiling is no longer white, the broadcaster cries excitedly). Where Spain is concerned (how will climate change affect us?, a listener asks), the talk show guests discuss how the drought threatens at least one third of the Iberian Peninsula with desertification over the next few decades, including the landscapes I'm driving past right now; all the orange plantations peeking out from behind the dwellings and condominiums will vanish, the sea will eventually swallow up the waterfront properties. None of it matters to you anymore, Matías, and I've just about had it with all this squawking. I push the button to change from the radio to a CD, and music spills over the car's interior. I need to find calm now, break the tension built up during the conversation with Traian. It's done, I told him, Collado's been taken care of. He tilted his glass toward me for a second. Motionless. Sarcós called me first thing to confirm. Talking to Traian always aggravates me. Cheers, he says, clinking his glass against my outstretched teacup. The music is soothing, lending a sense of unreality, of somnolence. I need my composure on a day like today. I'd planned on meeting several foremen at a few building sites scattered around Moraira, in Xàbia, in Altea, the ones that were supposed to be done before summer, but probably won't; not even by Christmas. I'd spend the entire day in the car, most likely, and don't feel up to it. Might just skip the three morning appointments. Do what's best for me, stop for lunch somewhere, maybe even go home to eat. I don't have anyone to answer to. I'm on my own. I enjoy spending these days on my own, no chauffeur, no yapping guests tying me down to a schedule. My mind works better when I'm alone. Just me, humming along to the music, whistling the tune, moving my head to the melodies. Music helps me think. That team of architects pops into mind, the one helping me design the project in Benidorm to rework the poolside restaurant into something more formal, more exclusive, more private, with the cool slip of water *sans* swimmers (I envision the type of place I'd take a client for lunch, or Monica for dinner, or a lady friend), I like the pool view, but don't want to share it with random bathers, these are my thoughts at ten minutes past ten in the morning, while in some other room, some cold basement, I imagine, they're dressing you, applying foundation, powder, rouge; but I don't want that in my thoughts right now; I'll think about it later, when you're in front of me, and I'll think about you when you no longer exist, when you're nothing but smoke, and even then I won't be free of you, you're with me, Matías. Like it or not, I'm going to think; I'll have him with me. The problem is that even now you get into my thoughts when I don't want you to. There you are laid out, projected like a transparency between my eyes and the cars in front of me. Something external, but inside of me, too. Like a spiderweb in my head that leaves very little space to think. I try to shake the image, and concentrate on the day's work, on what I'm doing right now, on the brake lights of the car in front of me, on how the car behind me accelerates suddenly, on the man's face I see reflected in the rearview mirror. I look out the window and survey Nido Beach, already teeming with early morning beachgoers, as the car rolls forward slowly, stopping every couple of meters in traffic that's blocking the access road leading to the highway. The traffic on my left, heading in the opposite direction, is at a complete standstill. I watch the cars idling, trying to make their way downtown. Many have their windows rolled down, the elbows of their tanned and sweaty arms hanging out. Everything glistens in the sun, the surface of the sea, the glass of the buildings, the metal of the cars, the skin of the people inside of them. I keep the windows shut so the cool of the air-conditioning can't escape. I feel sheltered, like other times when I've sat here with the music just beginning to play (*Schubert. The Late Piano Sonatas. D 958– 960. Andreas Staier, Fortepiano*, the CD cover reads), in the crisp cubicle that acts like a barrier from the summer bustle outside. I'm amused by watching what's around me, what I'm slowly but surely leaving behind each time I take my foot off the brake. I catch glimpses of the palm trees between buildings that climb high on my right; there's the azure sea, and the thin yellow strip of Nido Beach. I used to spend time there as a boy, as a teenager, but I wouldn't think of setting foot there now, the dubious hygiene of the water, the congested beaches. For years the inside of my car has been my favorite summer spot, my own private Nido, but it's not a bird's nest, for something snug and warm-blooded; it's more like the cool, clammy den of a reptile brumating in the rocks. I laugh at the idea (a reptile in the rocks) and glance at the skin of my hands, all rough and liver spotted: lizard skin, a little more saurian than reptilian, and it takes a few seconds for the irony to fold in on itself and bring a stab of despair, which I struggle to contain: furrowed hands that no lotion can smooth, dappled arms, necrotic skin in the cycle of decay, face covered in spots that no cream can blanch, no youth-preserving moisturizer like the ones Monica lightheartedly applies to my skin at night; spa sessions, water therapy, essential massages of grapefruit, carrot, wine, chocolate, or mud. Think about other things, better things, or better yet, don't think at all, live the happy moment inside this car, the cool air expanding, the fresh, welcoming vessel that shelters you from the metallic light, the aluminum glare outside. A reptile's den. The air-conditioning, climate control: it makes the air characteristically humid and cold, makes your nose prickle in that particular way like it does when you're in a cave, among the rocks, that in-the-bilge kind of cold, wine cellar cold, or saltpetered-walls-of-a-dungeon-in-a-castle-by-the-sea kind of cold. So I think heat, I think oven, and Matías is back. I think dungeon and there he is again. He's here. He reads aloud so I can hear him. He reads about Edmond Dantès suffering locked away in the cold, dank rocks, a reptile's den, a damp dungeon, a capsule frosted with saltpeter and quarantined from the sun of Marseille, his prison cell in Château d'If, where he hears the sea breathing outside the walls, sees the hoary white blisters of saltpeter filtering through them. Matías reads me chapters from *The Count of Monte Cristo* under the garden trellis of our house in Pinar. He says: "I want to be Providence, because the thing that I know which is finest, greatest, and most sublime in the world is to reward and to punish." I must be eighteen, Matías a little over ten, or maybe not—no, he hadn't turned ten yet, he must have been eight or nine, but he reads well, haltingly, using different levels of stress in the sentences to tickle out meaning: the finest, most sublime thing in the world is to reward and punish; he modifies his voice, changes timbre and tone for the dialogue: neutral for the narrator, more affected for the different characters. He says: Let's go down to the pond and read another chapter, and as soon as he falls into the hammock he starts reading again. I doze dreamily, think about my things (what am I thinking about?), Matías's voice still has a child's pitch; its musicality drives my thinking. They say the first thing you forget about a dead person is their voice, but if I concentrate, I can still hear his voice when he was a boy, or maybe I only think I can hear it: I want to be Providence. To reward and to punish. I must've been about eighteen. I hadn't gone to college yet, or maybe I was already in my first year as an architecture student, and back for vacation. The light breeze made the leaves of the lemon tree shiver, the laurel leaves, the eucalyptus, a breezy commotion of leaves in the back garden: it sounds like the tide, the sea sucking at stones, rubbing the pebbles against each other, sucking at them again. Memories: the fuchsia bougainvillea blossoms, translucent, as if made of silk paper; the wisteria curling over the garden wall like a spongy blue wave; the fleshy leaves of garden plants, the sun aglow, and the boy who is Matías reading to the teenage Rubén. The table is set, the maid's voice can be heard from the terrace above, the house invisible behind the vegetation, the two of us hidden in a vegetable labyrinth with the muted crepitation of the breeze and the deep sound of the motor that spurts a jet of cold water to nourish the irrigation pond—it's a world that's mine alone now, nobody else's. I'm the sole proprietor of those memories. Safe in my refrigerated car, I preserve it. The bluish-gray tinted window increases my feeling of isolation, of being protected. Nobody else remembers the old garden anymore, the voice, how the sun reverberates on the pond's basalt blackness, shimmering, like a colossal petrified flower with four curled stone petals; wasps gliding over the water, red dragonflies levitating, the wind rippling its presence across the surface; a few devil's darning needles, green and blue, iridescent, glimmering electric carapaces, their wings moving like fizz in the air. The maid calls. Lunch is ready. Go on now, time to wash up. There's soap in the bathroom. Matías, I want those hands smelling of Heno de Pravia soap—if they don't there's no dessert for you, and no snack later, either. And for your information there's vanilla ice cream in the freezer and chocolate sauce in the jicara bowl. Summer. The table is set. Nobody else remembers this. Only me. And when I'm no longer here to remember, it will no longer exist. Silvia's been to the garden, the pond, she'll have her own memories, similar memories (our childhoods were alike), but not this one, not this vegetable tableau, not these words spoken on this day, in that place, the asthmatic rustle of the air breathing among the trees, stirring the old eucalyptus's canopy into a rasping, resonant backdrop. I think about it all and it seems like such a wasteful thing: to have lived and then to stop living. To have recorded all of this somewhere, and then conceal it forever. What I'm looking at right now in Technicolor is furtive, what I hear, what I smell. The music in the car playing quietly: the pianist's fingers describing virtually imperceptible filigrees on the keyboard to transmit feelings of serenity, of distance, and the beach jam-packed, observed from behind the tinted glass, filtered through an invisible curtain of music, there's something strange about it all, as if summer were being projected on a screen in an air-conditioned cinema: the scenography, the representation of heat that's somewhere else, people fully dressed inside—it's absurd, like a silent movie. Matías says: Let me read another chapter. The wings of the devil's darning needle shiver, vibrate, and then buzz against my fingers when I catch one. I hold the little blue body up, the wings are transparent, fragile as silk. They shiver, hum. Flutter only slightly. Here, Matías, look what I caught for you, I tell him. I hand the little blue-green creature to Matías, its body is twisting and doubling itself, the creature opens a tiny mouth to bite only when it's trapped in the glass jar, a harmless little mouth opening and closing, wings beating desperately now. I stare at the luminous orbs of its eyes. I can hear its wings, only now a dryer sort of thumping because they're beating against the glass of the jar Matías is holding. To reward and to punish, be Providence. The insect is captive in a luminous dungeon like Edmond Dantès in his miserable cell. Is it a prize or a punishment? Matías: A prize, because now it's my friend. Summer advances. I liked summer when I was young, the constant hustle and bustle of friends coming and going, looking for the scene, the place to be, crushed ice in our glasses (*frappé*, we used to say back then, *peppermint frappé*, to the sounds of Lorenzo Gonzalez's bolero; or later, a few years later, even tackier, we adopted a lounge English to sound sophisticated and ordered our drinks "on the rocks," a "*güisgui own di rrocs*," we would say, and dance in the sand to Peppino di Capri's "Saint-Tropez Twist," like in that Vittorio Gassman flick), skinny-dipping at night, quick, casual hookups with the first tourists who came to town before the real estate boom (I was already married by the "Saint-Tropez Twist" craze, and had already started building), all the necking, the sex in the water, or in the cordgrass that grew in the still empty dunes back in the day, or in some rinky-dink hotel room: French women, Germans, they had no inhibitions. That was a long time ago. And yet it's summer again. The effervescence of those summers, the buzz, because now

I spend my time avoiding the sun, the heat, stuck in a nodal grid of climatized capsules: the office, the car, restaurants, cafeterias, the hillside house on Montbroch hermetically sealed and air-conditioned all day (I endure enough heat each time I visit one of the construction sites); but I haven't completely given up the occasional afternoon dip in the pool—I still relish them—a glass of crisp white wine, an occasional vermouth, and every once in a while an indulgent poolside gin and tonic, sipped while still dripping and a towel around my neck. I like to catnap on the patio chaise during sea-breezy afternoons, in the shade with my car, yachting, or travel magazines; a book on art or architecture; a novel; but no economics or politics, I get enough of that on the radio throughout the day, or in conversations with partners and clients. I read something light and stare at the palm fronds swaying in the breeze. I breathe in the fragrant grass as the afternoon glides by, the soil drenched by the sprinklers; the scent of jasmine and lady of the night (here we call it lady's man of the night), whose perfume grows lustier as dusk steals closer. The moon above, like a lighthouse, like a slice of ripe melon. I ask Monica: Why don't we eat out here tonight? And I continue reading while I wait for salad to be served the way she likes it, with little crunchy things: some bacon, pine nuts, or toasted almonds. Not on your life would we venture into the city to sit in some crowded patio under the old sycamores on Avenida Orts, no seaside dinner in a windowed restaurant overlooking the cliffs with hordes of people milling about and kitchen staff rolling out orders double time and waiters taking an age and a half to serve your dishes, all those strident people, all the fracas and shrill music. I dutifully grunt through it when I have a business lunch with partners, clients, or suppliers. But I can't suffer crowds anymore. Silvia makes fun of me when I complain: Don't cold-shoulder them, these people are your clients. She speaks softly, Silvia's voice is whispered and wounding—yes, it is—like a serpent slithering among the sea rocks. She's used that voice since she was a little girl: it's something that slinks along the ground while threatening you from above. My first wife is more than a little to blame for Silvia's slippery aplomb, and it isn't something transferred through the genes (Amparo was made of a different clay, more benevolent, though equally uptight), but in the classroom, it's an entire school of behavior; she was sent to demanding French schools because Amparo felt the Spanish educational system (heir to Franco after all) was, besides more than a little uptight, lousy. She said they don't teach philosophy in literature departments, or how to order one's mind, and instead it was pure rhetoric, variants of scholasticism, redundant languages (she had studied at Madrid's Universidad Complutense and considered herself a victim). As a result of her painstaking education, to which Matías contributed a few of his own Jacobin notions, Silvia doesn't really even try to communicate (no rhetoric) and then only in whispers; and for me, being hard of hearing especially on my left side (my car speakers are customized to a volume setting accordingly) means I have to bow my head and lean in close to hear the not always veiled barbs my daughter tosses my way, put on a façade of staunch attentiveness, which I find particularly humiliating since with my head lowered like that, it looks as though I'm conceding victory even before I've heard what it is she has to say. That's how you make your living, Papa, by packing all these nice people in, Silvia says, whenever learning about one of my new building projects, or when the company purchases a property: I read it in the paper yesterday, she says. Bertomeu buys, sells, develops. She always sees it in the paper, hears it on the radio, while out shopping somewhere, always by chance, not that any of it interests her one bit. She carps: Misent is looking a lot like Dayefe, she says, which is what she calls Mexico City, as if she were so familiar with the place, with Mexico D.F.

14

Concrete and rubble everywhere, she says. I've never figured out whether her allusions to my development projects are meant to criticize their negative impact on the environment, or to recriminate me for getting so rich (I make a note in my little pad: write her another check, buy a stereo system for Miriam, remind the secretary to book hotel rooms and flights for the trip to Saint Petersburg with Juan in the spring to celebrate his birthday). When I look at my grandchildren, Miriam and Felix, and my son-in-law (Juan, why don't you stick around and watch the game with us? Plasma screen, forty inches, HD), it makes me realize nobody ever raises their voice in my house—you can be wounding without ever raising your voice: my mother, my wife, but above all my mother, knows how—so I repeat the lesson in my patient voice, the same lesson I've been trying to teach my daughter for thirty-odd years (now I say it so my granddaughter can hear me, and so the same old tune can start boring a hole in my grandson's skull. I like to think: before you retire, your grandchildren will be working for you, you'll watch them prance into the office every morning, hang their jackets and bags on the coatrack). I explain it very serenely, very deliberately, it's not the builder's or the real estate agent's fault that half of Europe wants a Mediterranean vacation, or wants to spend their retirement years here (not me, though: I peer sideways at my bubble gum chewing granddaughter, what's she eating, what's she putting in her body, those bloodshot eyes, that croupy voice when she comes over on a Sunday afternoon; my grandson, a little doll dressed up in his homespun Spider-Man costume, snot-green pajamas, mask and cape). I ridicule her, hoping the kids will eventually figure it out, even if only by the tone, the inflection, the air of the old song and dance: In Mexico Dayefe not many people can put up the thirty-some million pesetas it now costs to buy even the crummiest condominium, the kind you like to call "shitty" (I still can't get used to talking in euros, I earn in euros but speak in pesetas). People were dying of hunger here not so long ago. I saw it. I saw folks rummaging, salvaging, pulling up the grass from the sides of the roads. I saw men calling at the house in Pinar to ask for three pesetas against future work, women sobbing to my mother who would shout for the maid and tell her to serve a plate of leftover potatoes in the kitchen from the batch she'd boiled yesterday, the mangy urchins with their heads stained with iodine or sulphur against ringworm, mashing potatoes with a spoon, adding a little water from the bottle the maid set in front of them, cold potatoes watered down with cold water, not even oil. I'd leave the kitchen unable to stomach the scene. Not a red cent, my mother would say; the men drink it all away. Charity: a concept that's all but disappeared. Nobody's in need of bread anymore, or oil, or even kids' clothes. Look around at how people live nowadays, how much has changed in just a few years—make a list of my own cars: a Citroën 2CV, a Simca, a Peugeot 507, the used Mercedes 1, the Mercedes 2, Mercedes 3, a Volvo, the BMW 1, and the BMW 2. A chronological list of the cars a person's owned over the past twenty-five or thirty years is enough to measure the size of the jump; thirty years of everyone trading their cars in for better ones; and me, thirty-odd years arguing with city counselors, deputies, the director of the zoning commission (clever guy, a real fox: same background, former leftist militant alongside Matías, I helped a little too, some money, times were different then: life is a merry-go-round), with landowners, architects, construction workers, painters, welders, drywall installers, ironworkers, machine operators, plumbers, electricians, landscapers, plasterers, designers, decorators; I had to pressure people into modifying the plot development plan to rezone an area that somebody had had the big idea of trying to keep rural and protected; get the license; get the certificate showing it's fit to be inhabited; negotiate power-line supplies with the hydroelectric agency, cabling with the phone company, the art of persuasion and calling in favors; though the toughest battles of all are the ones unleashed in the offices, the office wars as they're called, right?—the bloodiest, the ones that go something like this: if you buy a plot, it's zoned for agricultural or social use, tertiary, undevelopable, whatever; but if I buy it, first thing tomorrow the permit will be signed by the municipal architect for seven or eight floors and an illegal penthouse—to which they'll turn a blind eye in city hall—garages, and commercial sites. It's a matter of receding the floors a few centimeters, setting it back structurally in order to eke a few extra meters of height: and then there's the kickback, again the briefcase, the plastic bag, the regular bag, the man purse, the sports bag like the ones bricklayers use to carry their change of clothes at a building site. As I said to Collado a couple of years back, when it still seemed like Collado might be capable of learning a thing or two: it's a question of tact, and you need to practice; here, among the cranes tickling the sky, booms and jibs, container trucks, dump trucks and those earsplitting backhoes, stealth is an asset; ceremoniousness, ritual, know when to raise your voice and when to lower it to a whisper; when to use the art of seduction, caress the nape of a person's neck, speak softly in his ear so your lips just slightly graze the lobes, grab him by the kidneys, give him a bear hug, a pat on the shoulder, a little slap on the back and a rub while you're talking; know right when to drop that nice little tailor-made phrase you know fits just there between his two worst fears, and work it like a lever, like the ice that seeps into the fissures of a block of granite and ends up cracking it open. Business to me is like those retractile flowers whose pincers close ever so coyly when a shiver of air suggests the imminent presence of an insect. You have to know exactly where the equator cuts, the precise pressure point that can shatter the glass. Collado never got that through his skull. I told him over and over again: Be careful that your strength doesn't turn against you.

Strength pushes you forward, but you have to know how to focus the momentum to avoid crashing. When you're strong, you fall harder. It's easier to crack your skull open. For Silvia—unlike with Collado—you have to convince her that not everything in life is a minuet. Silvia has always considered me the most fragile filament, the easiest person to break. Matías's shadow hovers over all of us, a shade among us, engulfing us, obscuring us. Red-eyed Matías tapping the countertop with his glass, a liquid ring on the marble. We'd argue. If she was present, she'd always take his side. Silvia would spend entire Sundays in Benalda cooking, talking with Matías, walking out into the sown fields with Matías, but she and the kids only come to my house once in a blue moon, they all sit with the tips of their asses balanced on the edge of their chairs and jump to leave as soon as dinner is over, using any lame excuse on hand. Silvia, Juan, and the kids; Silvia and Matías. My mother and Matías and Silvia. Silvia builds a common front with Ernesto, Matías's son, even though she hates him, just to prove that despite being my daughter, she's conscientious about things like the so-called environment. She's jealous of Ernesto for being Matías's son and wants to prove that she and Matías are connected through a different type of filiation, *disons que* intellectual or moral. She's always concocting new ways to aggravate me; she'll look me straight in the eye and say: The buildings around here are so tacky. There's not a single country house left, which European architects study for their balance of harmony and functionality (Le Corbusier himself came to study the old Mediterranean houses. Sert brought him to Ibiza to see a *casament*, a typical Ibizan house, which are canonical examples of local architecture and used to be all over the place before you starting razing them). She knows Ernesto spends a lot of time in Santander and the Basque Country, where the climate imposes different building conditions, and praises him, fishing for his complicity: Everything's so two-bit here. Now I'm the one looking at Ernesto. I'm convinced his views are closer to mine than to my daughter's. What he does in Santander and the Basque Country, he says, isn't so different from here. I jump in: Silvia thinks the local construction companies are to blame, since a hundred years ago it occurred to someone to invent reinforced cement, what the Yanks call concrete, or the French *béton*, and on top of that they realized its advantages over other materials, for example, its strength, its durability, its reduced cost and ease of production. My encyclopedia at home goes into greater detail: the component materials of reinforced cement can be found everywhere, within arm's reach; it's easy to work with, requires no specialization; it's highly ductile and adapts to a wide variety of forms; it's stronger than natural stone. It resists corrosive conditions, particularly in marine environments. Arguing with my daughter is so boring. What do you think Le Corbusier planted in the bucolic landscapes of Provence and outskirts of Marseille, if not concrete? Those *villes radieuses* he designed. Don't they say that concrete was last century's flag for architectural progressivism? What about Niemeyer in Brasilia? Frank Lloyd Wright said thanks to the invention of reinforced concrete, a building could be designed to look like a flag held in the fingertips of outstretched arms. He proclaimed a new era of freedom. So, in freedom we stand, Silvia. New York is nothing more than a big block of concrete, or *béton*, or whatever you want to call it, with thick macadam on the streets where not a single blade of grass can grow. Maybe this place is tackier than New York, you're right, but only because we're poorer. It's a matter of scale. Nothing else. You like cities that are richer than this one (personally, I like Paris most of all), that's your real problem, but don't go on some moral tangent, some swerving moral clinamen. You're looking down your nose at the penny-pinching middle class who built all of this. And now you want something better. That's what happens when you travel first class and stay at fancy hotels from a young age: you admire what's above you and despise the shabbiness below. I've never heard you say that Manhattan is congested; that its streets are a mess of tar and potholes. That it's filthy and noisy and that even in the poshest neighborhoods the homeless rummage through garbage during the day, and as soon as dusk falls the rats come out, slinking around the cracked sidewalks. Never in my life have I seen so many rats in one place as in New York. And yet you find it so exhilarating. You go, you come back, you tell everyone you were there, what you saw, what you bought. And I always agree with you. We never fight then. Jünger, the German writer, said he was particularly sensitive to concrete architecture (he hated bunkers, casemates) and for that reason he never thought it strange when he fell into the deepest depression of his life precisely in New York. Not the Ukraine, not the Caucasus, where he witnessed unbearable things during the war, even cannibalism. I don't share his view, but at least it's coherent. If you hate concrete, then you hate New York more than anything. But, ah, yes, who's going to sniff at a loft on Madison Avenue? The first time you went there was with me; we had to wait in those endless lines to go up the Empire State Building. But I wanted you to realize that we were right smack in the center of the world. If I were to take you to the center of the world today, we'd have to go to Shanghai, Tokyo, Singapore, or Hong Kong, where Jünger also lost his mind (*totum revolutum* he called it. His favorite city in the world was Paris, and I have to agree with the old fascist on this point). Obviously, you were too young to appreciate anything on that first trip to New York. You were homesick most of the time—all you wanted to do was go back to Misent. Probably some new boyfriend, or some plan you were missing out on with your pals. The whole time, Ernesto looking on, smirking complacently. I think he enjoyed watching me scold Silvia. Like I said, they've never really gotten along. I'd shoot her a scowl and say: It's tiring to constantly be explaining the world to Silvia. I'd say to her: Take a photo and look for yourself. The world is what it is. So why not drop it, and let's make do with what we have, which is not nothing. Your grandfather used to say this was the closest he'd ever come to paradise. He roamed a lot when he was young, got as far as Buenos Aires—a vague, youthful adventure he never cared to talk about, planting orange trees in Argentina like Blasco Ibáñez's settlers in New Valencia, or something like that—but as an adult he resolved to never again set foot outside the county and shut himself away in the Pinar house, with his music and his records. He would stroll through the orange groves and go fishing with his friends. It may not be a paradise. But it's certainly not the worst place I've seen. What neighborhoods in Dayefe did they show you, Silvia, that make you want to compare them to this? I admit we put up with some violence these days, a few gangs, express kidnappings, but how could you have missed seeing the tens of kilometers of slums there? Where is there anything comparable around here? Our main problem is that everyone wants a more luxurious apartment than the one they already have and a second home in some exclusive neighborhood with views of the sea or a snowcapped peak. Ernesto suggested we toast to celebrate his imminent trip to New York, and then Mexico (the trip is what started the argument in the first place). You'll be on my mind when I'm at the Empire State Building, he said, and especially Uncle Rubén, the Concrete King; I'll think of you two (addressing Felix and Miriam in the voice of a kindly schoolteacher) when I cross the Brooklyn Bridge, which you're going to see over and over again on television and in movies; and I'll raise a cold Coca-Cola to Silvia's health in the ferry passing by the cast-iron Statue of Liberty. *Salud*, cousin! The glasses clink. Silvia can barely contain her anger. So, think you'll have time to see it all? she asks. She knows Ernesto's itinerary is too ambitious and he's only making a quick stop in each of the cities he's planning to visit. I hold my tongue, and think gloomily: I've made the best world I can for you, my little dove, and I can't make it any other way. I wouldn't know how. I'd like a different one for myself, but can't seem to find it. Oh, it doesn't exist. Yes, call her little dove, the same term of endearment Dostoyevsky's characters give to their daughters, girlfriends, or Chekhov in his plays, one of those sweet nicknames Russian authors place on their characters' tongues. A character in *The Cherry Orchard* calls his beloved his "little cucumber." Yes, I like that. Addressing her with words that make you feel so tender, so sad, things like: I'm only your father my little lettuce, not God the father. I've made some blueprints, yes, but not for the world. I gave you baths when you were a baby, I gave you your pacifier and took it away. I changed your diapers when they were dirty and smelly. This and that. The daily rituals, same as everywhere, same things parents have been doing since time immemorial. This is the world, big and little all at once, so wildly different and so fucking the same. Life. Now, as I inch forward in this line of traffic thinking about these things, I feel a warm wave of nostalgia wash through my body. Silvia, my little lettuce: I imagine my little lettuce as something tender and crunchy; the moisture between my teeth when I bite is innocent and clean. I could never have said such a thing to Silvia. Ever. Or her mother. Even in the privacy of our bedroom it was hard for me to tell Amparo that I wanted to fuck her, that I wanted a good solid poke. I always had to beat around the bush, as it were—why don't we lie back for a bit, come now, let me give you a little kiss: never telling her what I really wanted to do to her, never telling her I wanted to fuck her nice and hard. Fuck you right here like this, baby, like that. Not being able to say that to your own wife—what kind of a goddamn marriage is that? How could anyone find it strange that you'd look elsewhere for those

22

things, outside the marriage, to say the kinds of things a man needs to say? To feel like you performed it all, said it all, touched it all. Sex is spoken, too. I had to wait for Monica to come into the picture before I could feel that way at home, and now it's really too late. Now the words are stronger than the flesh, and words alone only go halfway, to say them without being able to act on them is pathetic. Look at her, fondle her. The urge to fuck so strong it makes you want to cry. I say to Silvia: I liked Notre-Dame du Haut when I visited it with your mother in Ronchamp, but I got there too late to build it myself (tell her about the last trip I made with her mother. Try to stir my daughter's emotions by trafficking in memories). In my time, things like that weren't built anymore. Or maybe I just didn't know how. It wasn't as easy as you think. No matter what your Uncle Matías tried to claim (Ernesto pricks up his ear, Silvia doesn't love me; Ernesto and I don't love Matías: he doesn't love his father, I don't love my brother, that's just life: asymmetries), even capitalism needs its portion of heroes, martyrs, the ones who are condemned to silence. Contrary to Christianity, no one should try to imitate the martyrs of capitalism. The fiascoes, the bankruptcies, the insolvencies that leave creditors in the lurch, the outstanding payments, the debt. Capitalism turns its martyrs into outlaws. I told her as much one day: Your husband has a good subject there, he's so interested in realist literature, the social novel: Misent's martyred bourgeoisie, people wiped off the map, ruined by gambling, whores, drugs; who live in hiding in Brazil, in Argentina; who put a bullet through their temple or who hanged themselves because they couldn't get free of their creditors. The martyrs of capitalism fall into a dark well of silence. He should pay attention to this subject, he should write his own novel already, instead of trawling decades-old working-class novels. The working class is no longer a protagonist of anything, or a subject of history. It doesn't even exist. It's dead. What's more, this region never had a working proletariat. The transition from impoverished peasantry to small-business class happened too quickly. Most of the parents of Misent's business class had been simple peasants, mule drivers, shepherds; even immigrants: shrewd newcomers who knew how to exploit the relatives they brought with them from the south or the plains. Juan agreed, saying I was right. But I don't know why I even care about these sorts of things, they're as boring as a weatherman who won't stop blathering inane details. Forget about them, focus on myself. The piano is still playing. Andreas Staier, etc. I stopped listening to the music for a minute. Didn't even hear it. The CD was playing, but I got distracted by the chatter in my head (landscapes have soundtracks my father used to say: I learned the music of landscapes with my father; the cities, the ports, the mountain ranges, each place its own score; it's been a while since the only sounds in my head are voices tripping over each other). So, there's the piano again, and someone honking a horn behind me. The sea sparkles in the sunlight, raising an expanse of what looks like molten steel just above the water, diffusing the landscape through the haze into a single, sticky mass. The metallic gleam is reflected on the bodies of the cars. It flashes across the windshields, the side lunettes, the rearview mirrors, glints of white fire, white sparks, white-hot steel, lightning in a dry storm (Staier's piano). A blazing oven and a traffic jam. Luckily, I can turn right at the first light and probably escape the cacophony. I change over to the radio to hear human voices, to distract myself. I press the button beside the steering wheel and the pianist stops short. As if they'd cut off his hands with a guillotine. The newscaster comes on. I turn up the volume. I'm going deafer by the day. I have trouble making out the DJ's words, chattering about everyday things: a car bomb hitting a military barracks in Baghdad, the massive arrival of refugees in rafts (this year they're calling rafts what last year they called *pateras*, trends in journalese, like climate change), more than a thousand sub-Saharan Africans have descended upon the beaches in the Canary Islands over the past three days, taking advantage of the fair weather of the Atlantic summer. The newscaster tells of a Toyota Corolla exploding into flames on the outskirts of the city, near the parking lot of a bar along Highway 332. The firemen were called to the scene. Minutes earlier, someone pulled a man from the vehicle, whose initials are R. C. V.—he was rushed to the hospital in Misent with third-degree burns, he's in serious but stable condition. The police are investigating the cause of the explosion, the newscaster continues, while I tell myself that Sarcós is as big a brute as ever. I'll talk to him tomorrow, to find out how he did it and I'll have to call Collado, too. Ask the wounded man: What happened, what'd you get yourself mixed up in, son? What did they do to you, who did this; nothing to do with why you called the other day, right? Got yourself into some real trouble, huh? I hope you learned your lesson this time. Give me a call next week. If things go south, maybe I can figure something out. Talk to him again like father to son.

MONICA WAS up by eight, she doesn't like spending all morning in bed during the summer, it depresses her to see the light filtering through the slits of the venetian blind. Brushing her teeth, she considers how, finally, the oppressive shadow that had been hovering around her house had dissipated, it had been seeping into the furniture, stealing into bed between her and her husband, an invisible gauziness, an unpleasant, viscid presence. Matías died. When Rubén finally got home, distraught, he went straight to bed. He barely uttered a few sentences. Monica didn't like that. She would have liked to talk to him, console him, share in the difficulty of these moments with him. But it didn't happen that way. And when she laid down beside him and put her arms around him, cuddling herself up against his back, he moved away from her and toward the edge of the bed (he always sleeps in the middle, face up, hogging even the space on her side), and he didn't touch her again for the rest of the night. Monica sleeplessly waited for Rubén to respond somehow, a word, a nuzzle—but nothing ever came. She found his behavior beyond inexplicable, as if his distress, instead of bringing them together, was pulling them further apart, turning them into strangers, confirming something she had long intuited or suspected: for however much Rubén complained about him outwardly, Matías governed Rubén's inner world: he exerted a lot more influence than what was immediately noticeable, and she could never fully shake a lingering concern— what if she isn't all that Rubén says she is, the most important thing in his life, but someone to spoil and flatter, to lavish treats on as if she were a child, but one who could be cast aside in the telling moments. That's why she'd been in such a miserable mood all night long. And first thing she had Silvia on the horn, sobbing and stricken: Matías died, Monica, he died, she repeated three or four times. You can't imagine how Silvita bawled into the phone before leaving for the airport, asking for Rubén, who wouldn't take the call. Tell her I already left. That I'm in the office, or she can call my cell, and if it's off, leave a message, I'll get it. I'll see her later at the funeral parlor. I'm in no mood for a scene, Rubén answered. We've already said what we had to say. Hearing the sounds of Silvia sobbing, Monica is reminded of that passage in the Bible when Moses strikes a hard, dry rock with his staff and a gush of sweet water springs forth. The stone in the desert is shedding tears, she thinks. From out of those parched holes water doth flow. Welcome it, let it soak the arid fields of affection through which we all wander, aimless as zombies, Monica says to herself. Through these once barren fields, the soothing water of sorrow flows, after months without a single drop of rain. She wonders: how can her husband—so even-tempered, so sure of himself—be related to such a hysterical creature, always dressed in shabby-chic, those faded shorts and loose-fitting blouses, all puffy-sleeved and over-sized, so impromptu, so Ibizan hippy, but oh so pricey, and oh so phony, because beneath that outwardly carefree Mediterranean spontaneity lurks a little animal chomping at your neck and who won't let you go because its jaws are locked, isn't that what happens with Rottweilers? Or maybe it's pit bulls? She read about it in some magazine, or maybe it was on television. Some dogs when they bite aren't able to let their prey go. Murderous dogs. Was it something genetic or a result of training? (She shivers at the first possibility, that somehow Rubén, with his calm strength, could have a cruel gene tucked away like that.) But today the little animal is crying, crying and baring a mouthful of bloody teeth. Apparently, Silvia's damp inside too, like everyone else. Her body is largely—like other humans—composed of water, nothing more and nothing less. Like other women. Who knew? Monica smiles at the reflection of herself in the mirror as she brushes her hair. She looks at herself, grimaces, makes funny faces baring her teeth, opening her lips like theater curtains pulled back by cords at the edges of the stage, she pouts, making her mouth into a trumpet-like shape, like some sucking insect; she passes the pillows of her index fingers along her cheekbones and pinches them a few times: she calls this her program of facial gymnastics, something she learned at the bodybuilding center, exercises to keep the cheek-bones taut, to keep the contour of her face in a nice curvature, no puffiness. There's not an ounce of fat in her face, it's a perfect, porcelain oval even though she's never had any work done on it. Her butt yes, her hips have been nipped just a little bit, not that she was ever overweight, but it seemed to her that despite all her care she was on the road so common among Spanish women, like her mother, like her older sister Rosa (she looks at herself once more in the full-body mirror instead of the one in the bathroom, she's naked, the shower has stimulated the flow of blood and her skin has a delicate, pinkish flush), the road that leads not toward fatness, per se, more like a certain portliness, amphora, Mediter-ranean, Latin, wider and rounder in the hips: that's what attracted men back in the day, a seeming disposition toward maternity, but nowadays it's more of a deterrent. A feminine trait they used to say, her mother said: wide hips, a good mount, cushioning, like a waterbed, or a box spring, or a mattress filled with wool or feath-ers, jellylike, so men would feel like lying on them. It's the lay of the land, nature's wisdom that stimulates and pursues procreation, the strategies of a species to avoid extinction—them on top, us below (she and Rubén do it the other way around, him below and her on top, his belly is the cushioning, like quilted padding, ge-latinous), an excess of femininity. Her mother used to ask: Who wants to lie on a bag of rocks? Northern women, Aryans, they're not only taller, their bodies are more angular and they're bigger-boned. Thinking back on her mother's words, she's reminded of the tall, broad shoulders of Greta Garbo, Marlene Dietrich, and other actresses in the classic films that Rubén watches at night. Though not all of them are so lissome and elegant, they're the minority, the top of the top, because—Monica likes to say—you see them by the ton around here, and there is no lack of female tonnage up there, either, those plump waitresses carrying half a dozen mugs full of beer in each hand in the Munich *Biergartens* that Rubén took her to. Just goes to show, she concludes, that there are both fat women and thin women in Central Europe and the northern countries, and it's the buxom ones who are so much more conspicuous here than there, because a good lot of them add height to their volume and stand like quivering towers of flesh, erect, massive mammalian strongholds. To summarize Monica's thoughts as she goes through her facial bodybuilding session in front of the mirror: there, like here, fat women are mostly poor, slatternly working-class women like the ones you find in train stations; or those dowdy housewives you see eating candy on the sidewalks with a pair of cranky kids in tow looking as scruffy as she does; waitresses in bars and restaurants along the highway; supermarket cashiers. The upper classes—and girls who work for them, who are in that atmosphere—take better care of themselves. Class. Monica likes to draw a relationship between her own aesthetics—the ability to turn your own body into a work of art—and Rubén's, of looking for art in the things around you. Monica shares this idea with her friend Menchu, because Menchu's husband hasn't got a clue about art, he buys it in places like the antiques section of the Corte Inglés department store, so his house looks like a junk dealer's depot, full of high-priced pieces in vulgar taste. It's Monica's defect. She'll talk about something nonchalantly, as if it doesn't really matter, though what she's really doing is jabbing her finger in an open wound. All too often she tries to downplay her own lack of self-confidence by poking at her friends' insecurities. She never tells them how nice they look without a meticulous counterpoint analysis (balance the scale with an equal or greater weight in the opposite pan). It's her way of proving she's now allowed to put on the airs of class; it's not so easy anymore—it's rather difficult in fact—for someone to pull the wool over her eyes. She tells herself: class, who are we without a little class, you have to search it out, a poor person can still have more class than a rich one. It's hard, but conceivable. She said as much to Menchu: Without a sense of class we'd be a pair of klutzy hens; class shows you how to walk, how to dress (and she relished watching Menchu peek sideways at her own legs, at her shoes, how she had trouble performing the once simple act of standing up from the couch and walking across the living room with poise: she was self-conscious now, aware that Monica was observing her every move and it upset her, turned her into a klutz), class shows you how to move your hands properly, how to hold your head; class to just hang out. She knows that—like it or not—Mediterranean women tend to be ovoid and womanly: soft, rounded shoulders, shapely backs. Women from the north are manlier, swimmer's delts peek from their décolletages. Her father—who worked as a plumber in Germany and Switzerland before marrying—always said that Central European women were equine, though nothing like Andalusian mares, not elegant mounts (this is what the Spanish were), but cobs, plow horses lacking the natural elegance of southern women, even the ones from the underclasses who keep from going to ruin. His point of view was of a man educated after other tenets (and, let's be honest, from a different class), who found it awkward to talk about women who weren't Spanish, a man for whom French women's style was pure whoredom; who died young and before Spain went through its revolution of the body these past ten years.

What would he have said about all the skin care clinics, the gyms, the new procedures like liposuction and lifting and peeling: high-tech refining, or refilling done by injecting fat; belly and hip reductions; breast implants; the fight against cellulite on thighs and buttocks; open war against saddlebags? Of course, her beer-bellied father wouldn't have been ill served by a tummy tuck and a little time at the gym: weight lifting, crunches, push-ups, pull-ups, rowing for the back muscles. He had been strong, but misshapen. Monica was mortified to think she might have inherited her father's irregular physique and shot a suspicious glance at her stomach. Silicone implants were just beginning to make the rounds among celebrities when he died: a duchess here, some popular entertainer there, four pitiable transvestites pumping themselves with hormones to look more feminine, a pair of overstuffed balloons for breasts, cruising in wigs and five-o'clock shadows, gravelly voices as if they'd been binge-drinking grain alcohol, imitating divas and pop stars. It was still considered against nature to take that much care of one's physique. That modern idea of civilization hadn't yet taken hold, the newfangled cult of the body and improvement of one's appearance: now your body is a responsibility, it's a natural resource, a raw material, it requires work and attention: to form it, to sculpt it, to mold it, like Play-Doh. The awareness of one's body as an artifice, as an idea, it hadn't sunk in yet: the body as matter given to each of us—by God, by nature, by whatever—to create the best possible version of ourselves. People hadn't yet rid themselves of a sense of resignation, of accepting one's lot in life, of the inevitable pessimism of acknowledging that the way of all flesh is decay, a resignation in Christian garb (it's in the hands of God), but we know, now, that resignation is more animal, something left over from what the scientists call the pre-hominids, when people feel zero responsibility for their own destiny; barbaric fatalism, or lack of ambition, or lack of faith in

Linksley, E.
(201) 321-0301

****

Transit to: GARDINER
Transit date: 3/13/2022,
13:22
Transit library:
VALLEYCOTT
Item ID: 32841010563566
Call number: CHIRBES
Title: Cremation
Transit reason: HOLD

*
*
*
*
*
*
*

Due
4/9

*
*
*
*
*
*
*
*
*
*
*
*
*
*

themselves and their own potential. If mankind has learned how to cultivate the land, or how to make shoes to protect their feet, and clothes for their bodies, then what kind of vile idea could make a woman think she should resign herself to not keeping herself up, not cultivating and transforming herself, not taking care of the most important thing she has, her body, because for however important everything else is—the house, the dresses, the furniture—they are mere accessories for the body, adornments, instruments that protect whatever it is that you are, the only thing you are. This idea of resignation has been a very Spanish trait, especially during some of Spain's darkest years, the years of the dictatorship, because if you look back you'll find that throughout history, everywhere, human beings have cultivated their own bodies according to whatever means they've had on hand: the Egyptians used cosmetics, add-ons, prosthetics; the Romans wore carefully concocted hairstyles, in locks or severely and elegantly separated into parted halves, delicate earrings hanging from their lobes, dusted with jewels, posing for portraits that can still be found on the walls in Pompeii, in museums, presenting or simply showing carefully fashioned bodies, well-oiled, curly-haired women fresh from the hairdresser, bejeweled, collars encrusted with stones of all colors around long, stylized necks. What these women wouldn't have done to their bodies given today's opportunities! It had been lost in the folds of time; now it's coming back as if it were a novelty, and most people have a hard time trusting what's new. It's that way with everything. Why else is she so tired of reading articles about all the people who have qualms about marine farming. Even her friend Menchu, who considers herself so up on all the latest trends, so ecologically minded, so environmentally friendly, says she can't stand farmed gilthead or cultured sea bass, something the ecologists also fiercely reject. It comes down to the same thing: Menchu, the ecologists, all the people who think they're so hip and informed are basically afraid of anything that's new. Monica argues the point: They've been keeping animals in corrals and cultivating them for thousands of years and it's never been a problem, and for ecologists and progressives there's nothing worse than hunters—yet they're outraged by farmed fish when the truth is it helps prevent us from plundering the ocean's resources. I just don't get you or the ecologists. Licensed fishing, with nets, boats, sailors, is just another form of hunting. Going out in the morning to see what the catch will be: like savages, it's prehistoric. How many thousands of years have passed since that's been allowed on land? People hunt for sport, for the thrill of it, same as with sport fishing, they go out on their little yachts like Rubén and his friends, booze in the fridge, *pata negra* ham, just to spend a morning out because—and she's so tired of arguing about this—we buy our fish in the supermarket, along with the lettuce, the tomatoes, and all the rest. Menchu digs in: But how can you even compare the two, no farm-raised sea bass can rival the taste of a wild one. Wild sea bass is natural, it's what we've eaten our whole lives, what our parents and grandparents ate, it's "ours." That's when Monica has a conniption: "Ours," darling? How can you qualify something like that as being "ours"? I understand when you say "our" fruits and vegetables, the varieties grown by local farmers. That's how the posters advertise them: homegrown vegetables, organic, from our own backyards. But apply that to fish? It's exactly the opposite. The only fish that are truly "ours" are the farm-raised ones. The ones you have to go out and fish as if it were an adventure, the ones that have to be tracked and caught, are nomads, drifters, stateless. They're anything but "ours." They come from the Sargasso Sea, or the North Atlantic and pass through here completely oblivious to us or our sense of place. Menchu thinks it's hilarious to hear her reasoning like that: You go ahead and eat all the farm-raised sea bass you want, my dear, just bring me a nice fresh-catch grouper steak. Rubén won't budge on the subject, either. He won't tolerate farm-raised fish under his roof, reprimanding her later if he ever hears her broaching the subject with others. They're going to think you're nuts, he says. She defends herself: Just tell me it's not true that the tuna they fish by the *almadraba* come from anywhere else but here? He'll glower at her for the rest of the evening. All of them, Silvia and her husband, Matías, her friend Menchu, Rubén, they're all against farmed fish, yet all they do is brag about being environmentally conscientious. So, what's it going to be? Monica wonders; it's there, in that little nuance she doesn't quite understand, where the slippery fish of class swims right through her fingers. She sustains the thought as she looks at herself in the mirror: she's doing what nature, ever stingy and ever lazy, won't do on its own. Imagine if the only thing we had were chickens provided by God, or nature, or whatever you want to call this thing we supposedly all belong to that is everything and nothing at the same time. We'd eat chicken once a decade, and at fabulous prices. People would scour the mountains tracking the chickens with dogs, shotguns slung over their shoulders. Journalists would write long articles in gourmet magazines singing the delicacy, the enigmatic flavor of chicken flesh, its aroma, as they do in that wine club magazine Rubén subscribes to, *Sobremesa*, touting the marvels of animals that won't be domesticated and how few of them there are left: the woodcock, of course, the red partridge, the ortolan bunting. People would describe their first experience savoring chicken by jotting it down in their diaries, knowing it could very likely be their only time eating it, and the story would be passed down from generation to generation. By the time Monica has reached this corner of her musing, Menchu interrupts with a guffaw and says: Your reasoning always tends towards the communist, doesn't it? Myself, feed me some game. I know what I like. Poor folks eat what they eat. Monica is not amused by the remark. As if Menchu were alluding to Monica's humble origins. Communist: common stock, that's the gist. There's resentment in Menchu's words, Monica senses. She brushes her cheeks softly with the palms of her hands, then her chin, which she massages several times before continuing down her neck (how dangerous the neck is, ghastly when the skin starts sagging like a turkey's wattle, little hollows like an empty bag). In truth, it's Silvia whom Monica looks to for lessons in class. Silvia (who hates farmed fish and scowls whenever anyone talks about body wellness) represents that class of people who pretend not to notice social differences, a class Monica will never be able to access. Silvia, her husband (you can see the fox's little paw in him in the way he hides his parents, the same way Monica hides her mother), their social groups, they all take for granted that it's a matter of genes, something intrinsic, so much a part of them that there's no need to invoke it, so they lose nothing when using foul language, or when they dress sloppily, or pull vulgar gestures; they're people who spend their days trying to show how little they care about the most valuable thing of all; how everything just falls into place naturally for them, what else can they do but take advantage of what they have because they do have it after all, and they're so nonchalant, even though they wouldn't last a minute if it weren't for the things they find so terribly unimportant; and when they finally do go legs up because of it, they just run off to Paris, blow through stores haggling and harassing the personnel, wearing what they purchased as if somehow it'd fallen from the sky. Monica is aware that materially she's got everything a woman could want, but knows that she lacks those tiny pleats in her soul, that glimmering flame and warmth of spirit that comes from a genealogy of class, a process of cultivation that has been passed down through at least three or four generations, growing up in a house with mahogany bookcases lining the walls in the library, a collection of Vivaldi and Bach recordings beside the record player, signed paintings gracing the living room walls, ever a book on the bedside table, a collection of verse, food for the soul, and another, a big fat novel, an English whodunit in its original language, something to keep you amused till sleep comes. Silvia and her friends have always had these things, and so they pretend they're nothing special, but boy can they sniff out someone who hasn't grown up that way, who lacks the subtle refinements (this is what she'd like to talk over with someone, her mother, Menchu, her sister, but it's precisely what she's not able to talk about at all); Silvia and that daughter of hers, who's even worse: a wave of anger clouds Monica's eyes whenever she hears the buzz of the girl's scooter, Miriam's scooter, Miriam coming up the driveway, peevish, helmet lodged between hand and hip, which she carelessly drops onto the first chair she walks by, not worrying whether she's soiling it; Miriam shooting a glance over her shoulder as she pulls a peach from the tree and nibbles at it half-heartedly, Miriam resting half a butt cheek on the arm of the sofa, the juice of the fruit about to drip on the upholstery, Monica, on edge, anxiously watching the flow of nectar, Miriam asks: Grandpa's not home? Then I'm outta here. She turns around, giving Monica her back; even when Rubén is present and watching she won't give Monica more than an air kiss, and when he's not, she doesn't give as much as her cheek, she's always surveying Monica with that kind of distance one keeps from someone who has the flu, who's infectious, and sometimes she just yells in from the doorway not even bothering to come in, standing in the gravel outside as if she'd arrived too soon, Monica's still there, she hasn't yet packed up her things and vacated the premises once and for all because Monica's only there provisionally, she's a trespasser, and Miriam is waiting for something that will expel her, something unduly delayed and long overdue; or better yet, waiting for someone to be no longer, an absence that will spur her departure thanks to a marriage regulation called separation of ownership. Miriam views everything through the eyes of proprietorship, as if someone had entrusted the estate's maintenance to the staff while she's off on vacation, or a trip abroad; yes, that's the crux of it, ridiculing someone with a mere glance, no need even to raise an eyebrow, there's a certain twinkle of the eye, a glare that takes at least two or three generations to cultivate, otherwise you overdo it, use a baser, Venezuelan soap-opera version of that telltale look, like in those afternoon shows that air just at the time when housewives have cleaned up the dishes and are sitting down to a cup of coffee, a smoke, the kids finally back at school, or doing extracurricular activities, dad still at the office, and it's finally time to relish a moment of privacy, but that's just when everything starts to collapse, when the housewife realizes she has no way out, that she is nothing, she'll never amount to anything, their house isn't worth a bean and they'll never be able to afford a bigger one, they'll only have more space when the kids grow up and move out; truth reveals itself, they'll never be able to travel to this place or to that one, to Cuba or to Rio de Janeiro, like she'd talked about that morning with the neighborhood ladies while out grocery shopping, those early hours when she's still sure that this is just an interim life, she's going to buy a designer coat and a new flat-screen television before Christmas. Miracles are marvelous things, only nowadays miracles don't happen very often: that's what Rubén says, her husband, and what housewives think when they're finally home alone, their kitchens tidy, their favorite soap on TV; and they realize there's one more errand left to run, to swing by the lottery seller they'd bypassed in the morning's euphoria, sure that tomorrow the life they've been waiting for will finally arrive: she'd seen it in her mother, her older sister. She'd seen it circling her, and saw herself about to fall into the same rut, and fled, as if from some kind of genetic decree. It's not inevitable—she told her mother—you can escape it, it's your duty to get up and get out. Her mother wept: I have no idea who put this foolishness in your head, but if he's old, if he's older than what your father would be if he were alive, older than me, so old even I'd have to think twice about marrying a man his age—I'm not saying he's not a good man, that he doesn't love you, but that you need to think it through, money is everything when you don't have it, but when you do, it only highlights the things that are missing, and don't doubt that with a man like that, there will be plenty of things missing. The life she leads now scares her mother and older sister, all the security a rich, seventy-something husband can give: like it or not, you think he won't swap you for another, but think again, he's terrified that you'll get bored with his money and want to swap it for a stronger body, a younger and fresher body (or let's say a younger and more ardent one?).

HIS HANDS and head are bandaged and he can hardly move without feeling a wave of excruciating pain. The hospital won't release him for several days and the doctor already warned him that it'll be at least a few months before he'll be able to work again. The fire had caught up with him, finally. He thinks: I am the earth that is scorched, the horse that is gutted and soaked in gasoline; but what he's really thinking about is his cell phone, what'd they do with his phone, it must've burned with the car. What if Lola's trying to call, he thinks, and he isn't able to answer. He panics. The thought that she might be calling and he's not answering overtakes his thoughts and leaves no room for anything else, not even the physical pain, which is growing more and more intense. He thinks about her, about the other evening when he said he would be by to pick her up today. He thinks about the money he left with her, a sign that he would keep his promise, but she doesn't know he's there, in the hospital, and he isn't able to call her. He can't even pick himself up out of bed. Maybe tonight, when everyone has gone, he'll get some nurse to lend him a cell phone and dial her number since he can't do it himself, with his hands in bandages and set into a splint. Punch in her number and hope she answers, talk to her and explain. It might scare her to know he's in the hospital now, and the circumstances that put him there, she might want to leave him, saying: I'm scared, I don't want anything to happen to me; and one thought leads him to another: hands in bandages, head in bandages, the entire right side of his face, his left leg, what will these parts of his body look like when the bandages are removed, lesions, damaged tissue, possibly revolting to look at, monstrous, how can he be with Lola looking like that; the thoughts accrue in his mind until everything goes dark, the fuse blows and he drowns as he's lying there. He wants to get up, move around, he feels like screaming, telling everyone to leave him alone, but who exactly would he like to leave him alone? He can't even make it to the door. It's not the nurse's fault he's there, the nurse who brings him a pill and a glass of water, or the woman who tidies his room, or the doctor who shows up with three young interns to discuss his condition with them, explain the therapeutics, the prescribed medications. If he sits up a little, he can see all the way over to Bertomeu's estate, there in the distance, on the far side of the valley. He watches the machines at work, the cloud of red dust hovering in front of the mountain. He was there just three or four days ago, when they told him the machines had arrived, and lickety-split the rickety riding pavilion had been demolished, and now the backhoe was excavating where the stables had been. Thanks to the machines' brute force, an entire segment had toppled practically in a single piece and lay there like a colossal lizard in the sun, there on the ground with the skin of its back bowed, as if struggling to get up. Chunks of wall, bars of twisted iron, others still rigid like great fish bones. They'd piled up a few horses' carcasses and parts of skeletons on the right side of the property. He'd watched it all from his car. If anyone had asked him why he'd gone there he wouldn't have known what to say, though he suspected it had something to do with a sense of order, seeing it all come down, it helped put things back in order, or so he imagined: he parked his car along the road leading up-mountain and saw—from an angle along the wire fence surrounding the property—the mounds of earth, the shovels driving their metallic fingernails into the red soil, into the bones. He went back again later that afternoon, when the construction workers' shift was over, and looked out over the fields, smoking a cigarette. He saw how they'd piled up the horses' bones, protecting them with fluorescent bands. Someone had lined up three human skulls beside the mounds. Nothing out of the ordinary, it wasn't very unusual to come across human remains in the municipality's urban construction sites: Roman necropolises, Muslim cemeteries, the city was riddled with them. They'd dig a trench and pieces of the old city wall turned up, ancient loading bays in the port, olive presses, ovens for ceramics or lime, the ruins of an Arab hammam, mosques or Visigoth churches, Roman civil edifices. Brigades of workers would show up, brought in by archaeologists, and spend months digging, storing the relics of tableware, weapons, coins, bones of people who had lived a thousand, two thousand years ago. Even the stonemasons knew more or less how to classify findings. If the cadavers had coins in their mouths, it was a Roman cemetery, the departed soul needed a coin to pay the boatman to be carried across the river, when the empty eye sockets were looking out over the sea, they were Muslim cemeteries: and in a snap they'd be back to construction again, filling the spot in with concrete, raising the structures of buildings that in a few short months would house new residents from all over Europe. In the restless succession of digging up and refilling, the city seemed to be freeing itself of its past in double time. Contemplating the excavation site, he too felt as though he were ordering, classifying, and storing things from his own past to free himself of them. He got out of the car and leaned up against the fence, smoking. It smelled of damp earth. The red clay was compressed beneath the crust left by a dry summer. Perhaps the water had collected over decades of irrigation by surface flooding; maybe there was a natural spring somewhere nearby. The area's hydrographic profile is a tricky one; there's more water than there appears to be. The limestone mountains filter and store water for centuries in hollows and ponds; from there it travels through capillaries toward the earth to form underground rivers. The freshly turned earth almost smelled like rotting flesh. He gagged, felt like vomiting the way one does after eating something that has gone bad, when the body wants to cleanse itself, getting rid of what is making it sick. From there it was easy to see the steepness of the mountain slopes, the darkness deepening as the sun disappeared behind the peak, a few yellowish rays still cutting crosswise through the fields, though up along the silhouetted bulk nothing at all shone, there were no glimmers of light along its inclines. Down on the far side of the valley, beyond the slopes, however, the orange trees and buildings shimmered in a golden light, as if sprinkled with glitter. Lying in his hospital bed, Collado conjures the vision and is transported back to the years when the riding stables were up and running, when he was Bertomeu's guy, his deputy, his right-hand man, and remembers the arguments he used to have with the foremen, the sales manager. Back then, building was at the center of it all, the backbone, even sales felt like an encroachment, the outside coming to meddle into the peaceful progression of things. Bertomeu said: You leave the thinking to me; I'll think for both of us. Collado is called to action whenever Bertomeu has a scrape with someone, some Black Hand, paralyzing a construction site, interfering with an acquisition, canceling a rezoning scheme that'd been in the bag. Collado is pure action; he knows how to pop these kinds of corks, he knew how to shout down the three foremen assembled in an office, how to send Sarcós's goons to visit a dogged property owner determined to cause problems, or nocturnally accost the site of some meddlesome developer trying to get a piece of the pie at a banquet no one invited him to; he knew how to purify by fire, the same fire somebody used on him yesterday. Rubén enraged and Collado leveling the road for him. Once, in a meeting, Rubén started choking after taking a swig of water from a little bottle he had in front of him. He'd unscrewed the cap, made as if to pour the water into a glass, but instead brought the bottle to his lips, swallowed hard and started choking. His face went red; he spit some of the water into his glass and coughed and coughed, touching his neck with his hand, his chest, the top of his stomach. Collado, seated on his left, considered slapping him on the back, but as he confessed later to Eladio Sarcós on their way out of the meeting, he didn't have the nerve. Eladio Sarcós was the serious security guy. What is he up to now? He hasn't seen Sarcós for ages. Now there's a brother-in-arms who could sing a few lines about the tough old days. Sarcós respected Rubén almost to the point of what seemed like fear. Collado could never figure it out. Rubén used to talk to Collado about everything, but never about Sarcós. He would talk about his wife, his daughter, the building engineers, the architects, and Monica, yes, he even talked about Monica, how they would see each other here and there, even while his wife was still alive. But never about Sarcós. For Sarcós, Bertomeu was authority. All caps (he had the same attitude as an ex-boxer who was hanging around the office for a while, Del Moral, a snarly, slobbering dog). Sarcós said that Rubén had married a lady, not a whore (wouldn't say the same thing today, though). That day he explained: anyone's guess how the old man would've reacted to being slapped on the back, even if he was choking to death. Old man, he said. A matter of authority, surely. What Sarcós liked to call respect. He said: Important to know your place, and keep to your own territory. Who'd have dared give Rubén Bertomeu a slap on the back on a day like that, when someone contradicted him out of the blue (it was Mañez, threatening to talk if Bertomeu didn't accept his conditions, I have recordings, he said) not once or twice but with a kind of skillful resolve. Thinks he can fuck with me, Bertomeu said before bringing the bottle of water to his mouth. He was still coughing as he walked out of the office. And he didn't come back. The two of them stayed there waiting for him, but he didn't come back. He called Collado's cell about a half hour later to tell him he was waiting for him at La Xarxa for lunch. You by yourself?, he asked. Yeah, Collado answered, even though he was still in the office with Sarcós, who was talking on the other phone and wouldn't have been able to hear Rubén's voice anyway. Son (he called him that sometimes), not a word to Sarcós about us having lunch together. Sarcós did all the dirty work, so it had to be something pretty special, Collado figured, if Bertomeu was keeping him out of the loop. They didn't say much over lunch. Bertomeu ordered vegetables and a piece of grilled tuna (not seared, no, no, not cooked on a dirty griddle making it smelly and overcooked; I want it chargrilled, Rubén insisted), rare, flash cooked on each side, which he wolfed down as soon as it arrived, as if he was trying to choke all over again. Or afraid he might choke all over again. I don't want to see that asshole ever again. Call the Russians. Collado dialed the number every fifteen or twenty minutes, each time the metallic click of an answering machine picked up. The intervals between calls got shorter and shorter as the hours slipped by and Collado's sense of unease mounted. At nine p.m. a voice with a foreign accent finally responded, and Collado asked for an urgent meeting: tonight, whatever the time. He'd been hanging out in the living room the whole time, waiting, hadn't even taken off his shoes. Forty-five minutes later, he parked his car looking out over the sea, on a beach road whose last bits of asphalt were slowly but surely engulfed by drifts of sand till it finally vanished altogether. The radio was tuned in to a sports program. The anchors were arguing about soccer, the lights were off. The last of the streetlights glowed behind him, allowing its halo to fall across the hood. There were no signs of life in any of the chalets bordering the street. He waited for about ten minutes before a Peugeot drove up beside him. A tall, lanky man got out. The streetlight gleamed over his pate where a few long, scraggly hairs grew in a loop around his ears and the nape of his neck. His face was long and horsey (Traian had a horseface too, this man was like an ugly brother), and so pale it almost seemed phosphorescent. Collado got out of the car and stood beside him. He handed him a folder: It's all there, Collado said. Photos, home address. The maid and the gardener take off first thing, and I've noted down the times when the others leave the house and return, though they're not very regular in their habits. Except for the morning. They always leave around nine, nine thirty, in time to have breakfast out somewhere, then there's banking, or shopping. But they get back at very irregular hours. Each one follows their own schedule. He goes for a drink here and there, she goes to stores in Valencia, in Madrid, maybe Barcelona, that's what she says, but who knows, she travels a lot, outside of Spain, too. Before you do the job, these papers have to disappear, vanish, up in smoke, so I'll need them back tomorrow morning. I'll burn them myself. He considers the word *burn* and tries in vain to move his fingers, locked immobile in the splints. He says to himself again: The fire caught up with you now, and his eyes start to water. He feels sorry for himself, someone did something to him that he didn't deserve. The smell of smoke permeates the inside of his room, the smell of singed hair and skin that his own body is giving off, the smell of rubber and paint, of scorched cables, odors stuck to him since the night before, and thinking about the Russian brings that odor of char back to the fore, of smoke and paint and plastic; Lola comes back like an ache in his chest that takes his breath away. In his mind's eye, he sees Bertomeu's offices over time, one after the other, each one bigger than the last, each one more sumptuous, the first one a table among piles of tools and supplies, a cork board stuck to the wall with invoices hanging by thumbtacks. He closes his eyes and describes the offices to himself, the furniture, the view outside the window, where the bar was located, the door and the secretary's desk. He still remembers the business calendar stuck to the frosted glass window of the engineer's office. Strange how his first tough job was fire. Collado thinks it's all a nightmare: returning, recurring, fire. It happened years ago—dirty money, as if there were such a thing as clean money, the grimy coins of his childhood, the worn-out bills, stained, blackened by use; he torched the folder and photos the Russian gave back to him, and within a few days fire tore across the hillside, flames engulfed the roof of the house in ruins, igniting the nearby pine forest, scaling the top of the mountain. He shudders thinking of fire. It finally caught up with you, he thinks. He imagines his face among the photos in a folder clutched under someone's arm yesterday, photos of his wife, his children. He wants to cry. The bandages. The burn unit. The first phase of the job is complete, Rubén had said, rubbing his palms together. First there was a silent explosion, like an artillery shell, then tongues of flames started licking at the pine trees, lazily at first, more and more eager as the hot westerly fed them that day. Leveling, clearing. Rubén: Plants need manure to grow, fertilizer, mulch, urea, ash—ash is an excellent organic fertilizer, the primitive towns used to burn the fields, the Castilian peasants burned the underbrush; ash and shit, best there is for growing things. Weed, hoe, fertilize. Ask the Chinese, they're the master agrarians. Everything grows bigger and better in shit. Chinese peasants used to buy the city's excrement, carrying it off in huge barrels from the public latrines; the barbers kept the hairs they shaved from their clients' beards and sold them to the peasants for fertilizer. I read it in a book. We too started to thrive when we got into waste; the most valuable thing a human has is not what he consumes but what he excretes, what he throws away (Bertomeu made a deal with Guillén at the time, and took over the local government's waste management contract). Soft, spongy land, nutrient-rich. Only later did Bertomeu start saying that nothing's black and white. Bertomeu told him: Collado, any man who can't discern

shades of gray is lost. Yeah, that all came later. Before that, he and
Sarcós would joke around driving down the highway before going
tight-lipped in some private room in a restaurant or chalet surrounded by security cameras and lawns guarded by dogs; negotiating with a briefcase in hand, the other guy packing a pistol.
Those were the years when we worked the stables, the early years
when you could get away with doing business that way. The times
were rough and tumble but exciting too, a happy chaos, lots of
booze. Looking back, there was a sweet dose of truth to it all; he
feels nostalgia for those days, the way old folks do when they
watch kids play. That's what he's thinking, he's thinking his photo
is in a folder someone's hiding somewhere, he's thinking about
fire, and doesn't know what to think, he looks at the bandages
around his hands, the traction splints like two white shovels. He
thinks about her friends, Lola's friends, Irina's friends, he thinks
he's alone and feels like crying. He wasn't alone back then: the
network of contacts was well oiled. He and Rubén, so intimidated,
running around the streets of Mexico City, the Zona Rosa, Cabal-
lito, sipping sangritas and tropical juices in Guadalajara's Camino
Real Hotel, nights at that place they call *el parián* at Tlaquepaque,
the songs of the mariachis, *tres cosas te pido y nada mas*, more tequila and sangritas with a tapa of beans and bacon, some snacks,
killer spicy, the mariachis belting *alma para conquistarte, corazón
para quererte y vida para vivir junto a tiiiii*; he remembers the long,
restless wait with those fellas who brought them to Tehuantepec,
some shithole place stuck up the world's ass, in Salina Cruz, scared
shitless, but afterward lounging poolside in Acapulco, playing
some blackjack in the hotel casino. The shipment of horses landed
in Barajas and we had to transport them to the riding stables. Driving the trucks down the country road that snaked through the
parched Manchegan fields, the frost, the coffee stops along the
way, the animals on edge, whinnying in their boxes. Like they

were breathing down your neck through the window between the cabin and the trailer. But Rubén broke off those contacts, washed his hands of them—times got softer, or the roughness went elsewhere. No politician would have your back nowadays, not in an operation like that; even the higher-ups supported you back then, and not just the local dogs, the ones in Madrid, too. Collado knows that times have gotten tougher here again, not just the police but the patrons are sleazier, more brutal, gratuitously violent, there had never been this level of violence back then, you could teach someone a lesson (the thought makes him shudder, he looks at the bandages covering his hands: they taught him a thing or two), there's something dirty in the atmosphere, contaminating everything, a change of character in the bottom rungs, the ones above are haughtier than ever: as if the new rich aren't about to make no room for new arrivals. Rubén Bertomeu: We played it dirty for a time, Collado (not "son" anymore, not Ramón, no more hand on his shoulder, no more soft palm on the nape of his neck), we did what we had to do given the circumstances, what those classical economists used to call primitive accumulation of capital, the country had to establish a new class after Franco, but didn't have the resources to do it; and now that class is closing its borders, the quota's full, now it's time to hinder social mobility, no more shimmying between classes, no more permeability. Absolute porousness is confusing, and a confused society is condemned to bankruptcy. To being eaten up by something else. Those dirty times are over, now it's time for purity, it's time for well-being, as they say on the television. All that is healthy, all that is clean, correct, no tricks up this sleeve, nothing up that one. We're in old Europe now and old Europe is, on principle, squeaky-clean. They're all dirty, the people who come knocking at the door, who didn't take advantage of the first stimulus and are still at the bottom rungs (Collado thinks about himself running around in vans, overseeing work crews, underpricing quotes, all the shoddy work, never taking off). Let them do all the dirty work, the nasty jobs: they're pus, lymph nodes that inflame Europe's armpits and groin. Their cash, those still-sticky bills they use to pay for things, only make us sick now, they're sickening. Make a name for yourself, a position. Was it back in ninety-five when Bertomeu broke it off with the Russian? Election year. Ninety-five, and in ninety-six the new ones showed up. Time to get out, I'm not about to be gored by an unfamiliar bull, we don't know it, it doesn't know us. So he broke it off with the Russian. It's over, he said. One morning he woke up in a good mood, came to the office whistling, called for him and Sarcós—follow me, he said. And one more time, the last time, the two strongmen of Bertomeu's circus, Sarcós and Collado, escorting him to that last meet-up with the Russian, where he said: Same thing will happen in Russia, I guess, and all the nations of the ex-Soviet Union. They're still in the primitive accumulation phase, when corporations have to devour everything. The cannibal moment. The universal stew, the *potpourri*. But leniency will come to an end. Then the public morality phase will kick in. At first you have to gorge, lickety-split, devour as much as you can in three or four gulps before they take the plate away, but as you slowly become more civilized, you have to learn other things, how to put on a proper banquet, use the right silverware and linens, organize things, know where to seat each guest, learn the name of the chef who prepares the menu, the order in which the dishes should be served, the types of wine for pairings, the best vintages. How to hold your knife gracefully, your fork, your fish fork, the asparagus tongs, or that other awkward utensil for the *escargots à la bourguignonne*; the sauce spoon, the tiny coffee spoon: stir the tiny spoon with refinement (that little spoon that disappears in those chubby Russian fingers). It's a rudimentary principle, there can't be a majority of rich people; no ruling class can include half the country, an economy ruled by assembly. That's a poorly scripted scene. When a lot of people have a lot of money, its value declines; it becomes worthless. Money has value when it's scarce, and when the little there is accumulates in just a few hands. If not, it loses value: to come home from the store brandishing a stick of butter, you have to leave home with a basket of bills, contrary to what the economic world supposes, where money is but the summation of the merchandise it represents. The madness of Germany between wars: it took a Hitler to show up and put things in order, rebuild the ruling class. He overdid the purging because ultimately, he was not a politician, not a statesman; he was a predator, a butcher. An elite is finite by definition. It aspires to exclusivity. Privilege can never be shared all around, wealth is not something quotidian, that would be humanly unfavorable. The upper class exists because there are lower classes, anything different would bring us back to communism, which I don't think truly lasted anywhere in the world for more than three or four years; it was Lenin himself who brought in the New Soviet Economic Policy, NEP, to encourage the emergence of an upper class: and the traffickers materialized, the amassers, the antique dealers, the new suzerains of style, and almost instantly the bureaucracy was instated, I mean just look at you, Traian, and tell me there aren't classes in your country. In the wake of the French Revolution a new, more demanding class emerged, more stylish than the fusty old aristocracy: *la jeunesse dorée*. That day, Rubén resolved everything with the Russian tastefully. No more than a friendly parting of ways, you know, you follow your own path, I'll follow mine. I'm here for you though, if you need anything. Handshake, hug with pats on the back, sonorous kisses. He said to Traian: Work with Guillén. You can keep at it with Guillén, he has the politicians, nobody's going to peek at his underwear. Not the socialists who've been in power in Madrid, not the conservatives who still hold the reins here. He takes some of them yachting, makes secret deals with the others, finances campaigns on either side, subsidizes their vices—whatever takes financing. He knows them inside and out. He's amphibian: I'm just your garden-variety bricklayer (Rubén always liked to refer to himself that way: I'm a bricklayer whose head happens to be a little more organized than others', I'm all about building, the rest of it is only what I need to do to make it happen, nothing more). Rubén's new office. I can picture it now. The intercom, the fancy paintings, the frosted designer glass—his last office. No more nudie calendars. Now it's what they call *minimalist*. A Japanese air. Meant to be relaxing, to transmit feelings of peace, order, with light colors, straight lines, muffled footsteps, not a folder out of place, not a voice raised above the rest, a soft buzz, and Rubén, pushing the button on the intercom, saying: Julita, bring us some coffee; Julita, a few glasses of champagne. Of course it's *Champagne* champagne. Mumm, Roederer, Dom Pérignon, Pommery, Veuve Clicquot. A few years ago, he'd say: Bring us some champagne to freshen our gullets, boy did I break a sweat with this guy, what a trader, hard-nosed, no-nonsense. He'd say it in front of the other person to flatter him, to make him feel respected, pulling out a cigar and offering him one: Collado, son, study this man's face, commit it to memory, and don't even think of buying or selling from him, no deals, what a shark, sucked the wind right out of my sails. In a theatrical flourish he'd pull the lining of his trouser pockets out, see, nothing left, nothing here, nothing there, this guy took it all, even the spare change. He called it champagne when it was only cava, maybe even cider, and the real celebration was how he'd just scalped the chump with a sharp, shiny blade, that hard-nosed wheeler-dealer, gutted, the whole thing a big game at the sucker's expense, he'd just pinched millions of euros by convincing him that two-thirds of the land Rubén was taking off his hands were zoned exclusively for agricultural use, undevelopable, protected, useless, when three months earlier Rubén had closed an urgent rezoning deal with the local government to make the plots 100 percent developable, and had designed a suburban expansion project of one hundred new homes to begin within a few months, a colossal get-rich-quick scheme, and there's the big sucker toasting with a flute of El Gaitero cider—world-famous, with bubbles!—sure he'd just divested of a few barren almond trees, rickety orange groves whose yield didn't even cover the cost of the pesticide and the picking cycle—bring on that champagne! Those were the easy years, now it's nearly impossible to pull off a scheme like that, the rednecks have grown long ears, they're accustomed to land trafficking, they sniff around now, smell a rat, figure things out, they're in contact with the local authorities who whisper, drop hints, everyone's in the know now, common knowledge that no plot of land eyeballed by a contractor won't sooner or later be developed, no one can be duped into believing you're buying just for the hell of it. Only thing left now is what they call direct action. You get the mayor to rezone that public mountain, the mayor will sell it to you after a quick million is pinched and deposited into a bank account and the sale takes place as he simultaneously rezones it. That's the real champagne. And dinner in a Michelin-star restaurant while you're at it, you betcha. Back in the day, when they first got started, you'd be hard-pressed to find a bottle of champagne anywhere in the entire county. At best there was a local variety of bubbly, what today we call cava, Freixenet, Gramona, Cordoniu, Juvé y Camps, and cava was pretty exceptional in those days. Most of the time it was El Gaitero cider. At least it had a little foam and sparkled. Bubbles express joy, like seltzer water and wine, sangria: seltzer with some nice dark Jumilla wine and some banana slices, peach, even a few chunks of pineapple. A jar of sangria and a little paella at a shack overlooking the sea cliffs. What an amazing view you have here. It

all fascinated Collado because he was still just a kid, barely twenty
years old, he'd never seen anything like it before, the girls, especially the girls, nowadays you find girls like that in the bordellos,
but back in the day those girls with their big tits looked like millionaires, dressed in designer clothes, towering five-nine, some
even taller, everything matching, everything in proportion, blond
hair and foreign accents, French, German, Italian, they'd get down
on all fours to blow a twenty-year-old, that silky skin, that pussy
squeezing it in French and you coming from behind—if that's not
glory then what is, admit it, they were the best years of your life,
in Misent, in Madrid, in Cartagena de Indias, in Mexico, we fucked
everything, they fucked everything, and me, well, I snorted everything, Collado thinks. Not Bertomeu. Bertomeu would say: Either
you're doing business or you're a client, and we're doing business.
He'd go insane if he found out I'd done a line, if one of the whores
would tell him: the kid fucks and snorts everything in sight, he's
got more room for coke in his nose than I do for dick in my pussy,
and Rubén would lose it: like he was jealous, like we had some
kind of intimate relationship, Collado thinks, like the coke made
him jealous, those sudden mood swings weren't normal. Never
really minded all the fucking, though. But he couldn't stand it
when Collado behaved with that kind of happy-go-lucky coke euphoria. Cut the yakking already, you're giggling like a retard, he'd
warn. Well, no matter, those were the best years. Other ones can
come now, that's what Collado hopes, though not today, not this
morning, now there's another crook in the road, he came into the
fire that clears the way, clears the weeds, his mouth full of ashes,
the horizon clouded in black smoke, though for a while he had
been sure that the tides had turned back in his favor, better times
were just around the corner. He'd started playing the lotto again
these past months, the sweepstakes run by Once, the association

for the blind; lady luck would be stroking him again soon, he was
sure of it. Convinced. But fire came instead. Lola. Irina. Lolairina.
Let's set up shop somewhere far away from here, be rid of the
great, viscid octopus that's held him, trapped, in its suckers for the
past few years, since he left Bertomeu and starting working odd
jobs for the Russians, when the spring started drying up, just repairs, patch-ups, some home maintenance out in the boondocks,
social security admin always biting at his heels, environmental
protection and the tax agency chasing behind, laborers not declar-
ing, unlicensed construction, invoices without local taxes, dirty
money, always waiting to be audited, more anxiety than achieve-
ment, cut the legs off the monster that's sitting on your chest and
devouring you bit by bit, get out unscathed, stop fighting the octopus from the puddle your life has become, raise your head above
the surface and breathe, breathe in deeply, go back to the old
times. Things are never easy at first, it was hard back then too, at
least in the beginning. It's not the struggle that scares him though,
what gets to him is the stress of having to do all the shit you don't
believe in and never what really matters to you, knowing that if
only you could do that one thing that matters, you'd finally become who you were meant to be, and with a bit of luck, you'd be
able to give the best of yourself. You'd be happy regardless, or at
least satisfied, because you'd be yourself. He'd got off on a few bad
starts, and it didn't matter. That's why the champagne scene, he
says, wasn't where it all started, that was the second phase: encounters of the second phase (Rubén Bertomeu loved dividing
everything into phases. That was the first phase, this is the second,
this the third). Describe the pool table he'd installed in the office
to help him relax when things weren't going well, when he'd get
so bent out of shape when someone dared say no to him, or left
him in the lurch, pool and classical music as a remedy, to take the

edge off. The balls gliding this way and that, falling into the trap, the hole, the pocket. Why bother trying so hard to avoid it, I wonder? At the end of it all, into the hole, Rubén would say laughingly. Billiards is like life, too, all games are a metaphor for life, he'd say. Rubén played like a maestro. It was a matter of honor. When you're around other people, only do the things you know you do better than everyone else, he always said. In private, practice the things you don't know how to do yet, until you learn how to win. Only compete when you are sure you're going to win. Not when you *might* win, but only when you know you'll win for sure. If you say you don't know how to play, nobody's going to help you learn, they'll just make a fool of you. They'll pretend to pity you, but they're really making fun of you. I don't know anyone who's aware of their own strength and chooses not to wield it, who knows they're superior to someone else and doesn't feel tempted to crush. And once the temptation exists, who's above it? Papa Rubén, at first, he was like a father. Maestro Rubén. There he is with his gravitas, talking to you about architecture, telling you about his trips, what he's seen, the names of the architects, the buildings, the museums—we went here, we drank this wine, we ate in this restaurant with so many Michelin stars, we saw this painting, everything so serious, you'd never imagine, how could you ever suspect that between all the bottles of vintage wine, all the Renaissance this and that, all the Baroque and Rococo, his hand would weasel its way into your pocket. Who'd ever think, Rubén, that in a different time you and I were equals. You the dad; me the son, like family. Other times. Think: I have to call him. I'm going to have to call him. Let him know what happened. Tell him about Irina. I wouldn't bother you if I didn't need to, Rubén. You were like a father to me once, more than a father. Back in the day. Sounds like a drunkard's song. The olden days, way back when you ran around in the wee hours with the headlights off so the police couldn't see you from the mountain roads. What the horses were carrying in their bellies. That was a different kind of power. Rubén was able to close down the racetrack. Turn it into a warehouse for receiving merchandise; keep the horses there, isolated, drumming their restless hooves. You could hear them neighing in the stalls at night over the sound of the waves, gorgeous animals, most of them condemned to death. Years earlier, his father had told him about all the beautiful horses prostrate over the ice in the Russian steppes. Rubén told him: As if McDonald's wasn't worse than any drug out there, Big Macs, big Big Mac and cheese, mustard and glops of ketchup, laboratory french fries, dressings for plastic salads, paper napkins, read this label, here, read that one, look at what they're giving you: sorbates, glutamates, stabilizers, antioxidants, ascorbates, nitrates, nitrites, diphosphates and dipolyphosphates, carrageenans; check out this hot dog: it has cochineal dye—what the fuck is that? I think it's a red dye the Phoenicians used for their clothing, he said: Rubén knew a shitload about paints, cobalt blue, Prussian blue, malachite green, verdigris, his daughter restores paintings. Though—Collado considers—so much more difficult now, tighter regulations, everything's shittier quality. There's more of it around, but not as good. It was so delicious back then (is there anything in this world better than good coke?—the thrill, time outside of time, the world is your oyster, though everyone else has to suffer the effects, you get that zing, and get hyper: virtue is yours, punishment for the next guy), it's been years since that good stuff has trickled down to the masses, now the rich kids snort shit in beachside bars, clubs, after-parties, shit for weekend lowlifes who come out in a blaze, ready to torch it all, burn the house down (fire again, agony in his hands, his face burns beneath the bandages, shooting pain) for a buzz, whatever it takes, amphetamines, acid, ecstasy in pills or crushed, alcohol, Red Bull, Coca-Cola, poppers, glue, shit, junk, rat poison. Surefire migraine

come morning. Take whatever's there, jump and twirl and feel the
blood rushing under the waves of white laser bathing the dance
floor: all I snort is shit now, Collado thinks, crushed aspirin, glucose in the best-case scenario, powdered lime, that's what most of
any line of so-called coke is nowadays. The clubs. The young girls,
your granddaughter, Rubén, your little granddaughter who likes
to play with adults, I see her in the club, back and forth to the
bathroom, touching her little strawberry nose. And to think
Rubén used to get so pissed at Collado for snorting coke. Just
before they parted ways, Rubén told him: When are you going to
get it through your thick skull, we oversee the merchandise, make
sure it goes from here to there, but we don't get cozy with it, it's
other people who do that for Christ's sake, we're not the ones consuming it in toilet stalls. When you consume, you cross over to the
other side, you turn into one of them, then you're the one in the
stall. Tie yourself to the mast like Ulysses, you remember that,
right? Tie yourself to the mast, listen to the mermaids purring,
then go home peacefully. That's what you do. As if Rubén didn't
know whom he was dealing with, the Russians. Collado had to
hang out, to work with them: always up to their eyeballs with coke
and whisky (only vodka when they wax nostalgic) till they fall
backward. A sleuth of bears strung out on the living room floor,
in the bathroom, log-legs jerking and flailing like overturned
cockroaches. The shipments would arrive in the stables. He hated
the stables. He couldn't stand it when Rubén sent him to stake out
the stables. He would ask Sarcós: You take care of it for me. When
Rubén sent him to the stables it felt like his father had returned to
punish him again, thank God it ended soon enough, it brought
back too many childhood memories: his father chasing him
around the house, him hiding in the stables, the dankness, the
animal noises, their breathing and shuffling. It was cold in there,
but he was always sweating, trembling and sweating, his feet stuck

in the hay, the hay scratching his ankles every time he moved his feet, like a rat scratching against his legs, closing in with its teeth, he nearly died of fright, he always hated rats, it was a primal fear, a phobia that must have come from his mom, for sure. What is truth, father? Truth is authority. The world is a pyramid, it exists because of authority, because some people have command over others, a chain of command. The military is a metaphor for the world. Collado's father would have liked him to go back to the military once his conscription period was over. But it didn't happen that way. Rubén pulled a few strings so he wouldn't have to go beyond boot camp. His father always considered himself a military man, though he never ranked higher than corporal, a military bricklayer in the Corps of Engineers. His arms and chest were covered in tattoos. We all have a particular time in life that makes us who we are. Collado's best times had been spent with Rubén and he thought they were coming back again, then it all went south. His father's greatest moments were spent in the two wars (the Ebro Front and the Stalingrad Front). Orders are supposed to be brief, categorical, precise. Atten-hut, har, fire, har, FOR-waaard march, left, left, left-right-left. In the military, clarity is truth experienced every second. You accept unreservedly that there are commanders above you, and submit without inhibitions. Everything is clear-cut, everything transparent, no doubt, no questions. There's greatness in the act of obedience. Everyone obeys and there is no belittlement in it. He who serves is of value. Each one bears his glory, it lasts but a second, burns like a match, and there's nothing left but ashes, but it's a luminous flash, worth a lifetime. His father used to tell him: That white world, the earth, the sky, the horizon. The endless expanses of snow where the dead horses lay, the dead men. The blood, the fat gleaming over the snowy plains: black and red over an infinitude of white. Nearly half the company perished. The rest of us were taken captive.

Horse-drawn carriages heaped with families, suitcases, cauldrons, and teakettles drifted across that white blanket, sinking into the snow. Shacks set aflame over the whiteness of the snow, the blackened trunks of birch trees smoldering, the billowing smoke. His father was twenty at the time. It was 1942. That's glory, the flames of valor illuminating your world for an instant, giving you a reason to persevere, to twirl a few times more. Truth is staring into the jaws of death. His father would finalize his wine-induced binges, which were what spurred these exalted words, by rising up tall, all voice, frightening even though he was not a corpulent man, his body no more than a stingy thing, hirsute, but not with the kind of hair that sprouts from a vigorous body, expressing its potency, his was coarse and scraggly, as from a childhood of paucity and malnutrition, and all the hungry, bellicose years in the Nationalist army, followed by the Soviet steppes with the División Azul; postwar starvation, then the years selling trinkets door-to-door, till he finally found work in construction. His violence—his father's brand of dry violence, pure nerve and bone—needed little encouragement, it snapped fiercely out of nowhere, then would peter out, something like a stone and the hole it leaves when it's pulled from the damp, squishy soil, the bone of an animal long dead and the sticky little pit it leaves when you dig it out of the mud. He'd be out drinking until late, then come home completely pickled and wake him and his mother up and make them march around the dining room table, down the hall to the door leading outside and back to the dining room and back around the table again. Then he'd collapse onto the sofa and start snoring, or on the bed and his mother would ask him to help her remove his father's shoes, his shirt, his pants, his scrawny, woolly legs, at times the dark shadow of his member peeping out from his underwear. His father plunged from being a hero to an insect, the kind you swat at or squish with a flick of the wrist. That disgusting fly that keeps coming back, over and over again, no matter how many times you swipe at it— that sticky body, back again. He was an insect who couldn't afford to educate his only child, the child of an older man who didn't even care about his own future because life was war, battle, the daily fire (his father was over forty when he was born), and he wouldn't let the boy pay for his own schooling. He had wanted to become an engineer, but no, not an option. His father sent him off to work as a low-skilled apprentice before he'd even turned fourteen. It's the builder who builds the house, not the one who imagines it, or draws pictures of it. There's pride in bricklaying, it's building as war. There's order. An unskilled laborer is like a foot soldier, then there's journeymen, foremen. Look at my hands, now look at these tools, here's the trowel for laying brick, here's the one for plastering. They's mine and nobody else can use 'em but me. They's custom fit, so no one else can use 'em. The person who imagined, drew, sold, and got paid for the house was Rubén. It was Collado's job to build it. He was one of a dozen other guys who kept an eye on their tools, their bricklayer's trowel, plasterer's trowel, tools whose edges were custom fitted to the curve of each hand. And there's Rubén eating, arguing with this one or that one, gorging on brasserie shrimp, king crab (and oh how size does matter when talking crab, my friend), grouper, slow-roasted Castilian lamb with a Ribera del Duero wine glaze in Asador Arandino, decapitating fleshy langostinos in La Xarxa, smacking his lips, scarfing, slurping; and there, managing a gang of cranky foremen who say to you, first thing out of their mouths, nobody told me nothing 'bout that, not in my fucking life. You calling me stupid? Only idiot round here's you, asshole. Sourpuss grunts say that kinda shit all day, going home to houses they don't like, shacking up with women they don't love, having kids they don't want. Only song they know: nobody told me nothing 'bout that. They're afraid of words, a word can knock you out quicker than a left hook, words cut, they wound, they crush, they're sharp as a knife, blunt as an axe. They're guys corroded by bitterness and resentment. Either they aren't getting laid or they don't know how to fuck; they fuck whores because it makes them sick to do it at home, they think they're not worth a nickel, so no matter what you say, what they hear is that you're trying to fuck them over, pull a fast one because you think they're idiots and assholes, you're calling them good-for-nothings, less than men, whatever they consider the worst possible insult; and so they shout at you, because they know they're a bunch of assholes, that as men they aren't worth a nickel, and so they snarl, convinced it'll all stay secret if they snarl enough, because nobody'd dare say it to their faces, nobody'd dare think it, though they do think it, everyone thinks it, they think it about each other, they think it about themselves; the whole bunch of them ready to pounce. Lessons, the dismal legacy of a father who died a bitter man, penniless, alcoholic, an unhappy man who made everyone around him unhappy: that's how you man up. Stand on your own two feet. Know when, how, where, and against whom. That's the rule book his father bequeathed. And after hitting someone's car, you're the first to offer to drive the other person home, or let him use your phone to call a twenty-four-hour garage. You're the one who has to understand that they defy you because they're afraid of being eaten up. They threaten you with violence because they're intimidated. And they're way more scared than you are, they too have a mortgage to pay, and kids' tuition, and a wife who has whims, and they know if they get blackballed, they're done for. They bare their teeth, maybe even a little knuckle, but they can't show their asses because they're full of shit. They whine and swagger and threaten because they're shitting their pants, a steamy chunk of it gluing their underwear to their asses. They find their strength in work. Where else? Protecting their job, their position, grabbing the officer who wants to take their job away by the neck, same as the officer who bares his teeth at the laborer sucking up to the developer, trying to convince him he's better at the job than what the others say, that he can outperform the rest. There's discipline in work same as in everything else, authority, chain of command, orders by cascade. The officer is your captain. Orders: his father was a bossy insect who had nobody to boss around. That's the very definition of a loser. A bully who has no one to bully around. All the orders that were barked at him throughout his life grew into a poisonous stinger inside of him, a stinger that stabbed into his own guts, hurting him, and infecting him. The only way of easing the pain was by letting it loose on everyone else, on his son; where the strength comes to make a son. The drip that escapes you, it's nothing, nothing. Collado had to learn everything on his own, had to find his own books. His father used to make fun of him: All that reading. He sang the old song, same as Rubén, but from the bottom of the pit: A real man only bets when he knows he's going to win. Collado couldn't resist: Yeah, like you, he said, and that drunken pussy of his father beat the shit out of him and he couldn't fight back. He'd learned that lesson: a son can never strike his father. Chain of command. So he left home. He'd admired Bertomeu back in the day, a reasonable father, but Bertomeu was the type who'd go on a bender with you, hit the bordellos with you, but you were always left wondering whether he really wanted to be there, be with those people. Cultivated people always had the kind of shifty vibe that women have (Rubén's first wife, who was a lady, and even Rubén always listened to classical music in the office, in the car). More patience than verve, more cunning than drive. Their words always keeping you at bay, nullifying you. The spider spins its web with the thick saliva of words. Words sewn into a netting that keeps you separate from them, one you can't puncture, so you'll never be able to touch them, there's no contact. Lull

Samson to sleep and cut off his hair with two swipes of the scissors. He was Samson, stumbling feebly as he wakes, Delilah having shaved his head clean. This was one man's truth. In the beginning it was constant motion, building sites by day, meetings in the evening, shipments, never leaving Bertomeu's side, him and Sarcós; Sarcós was the machine, he was the son (or did Bertomeu, when they were alone, tell Sarcós that he was like the son he never had, and Collado the machine?), but that's all over now. Collado watched helplessly as Rubén Bertomeu got away, as if the thief Collado had been chasing were Rubén, who suddenly jumps into the basket of a hot-air balloon. You stand there looking up, arms hanging by your side. You stare at the balloon as it gets smaller and smaller until it's no more than a pinprick, though it's a false perception because the balloon is the same size as before, only it's rising higher and higher and impossible to reach, and the one who has shrunk down there is you, while others can touch the sky with their hands. Rubén avoiding him in the boardrooms, in meetings, barking orders at him more than asking his opinion, a few terse words instead of saying: Come to my office and let's talk. Calling him Collado instead of Ramón. All feminine spirit now, all excuses, niceties that widened the distance between them. It's not that Collado doesn't like to read. He likes to read books about things his father taught him, firearm magazines, military magazines, humans are the only animal to invent instruments of murder, the most refined; well, there's the spider too, the spider spins its snare, and if you stop to think, there are plenty of other animals who trick and deceive to capture their prey, and many are cleverer than humans. He tries to remember some of them now, lying in his hospital bed: he inherited these notions of manhood from his father, one inherits a genetic makeup (though his body is more like his mother's) but what you really inherit is a certain view of the world, you may not even realize it yourself, his father said, but that's what you inherit, you inherit a way of looking at things, like bees inherit their compound eyes, that's what you get from your father, because it's when you're young that you learn how to look, to notice certain things and not others, and though you may think the eye sees everything, it's not true, all things are made up of an infinity of details and you cherry-pick, you only pay attention to a few of them, and that frames your version of things, his father's eye is anchored in this notion that humans kill to live and that death takes certain forms, and that this is the eternal work of mankind, the artisan of death. There's nothing wrong with being afraid, it's neither good nor bad. It's merely a state of mind. Your father: Things won't go better for you because you're afraid. The book of life is already written, you can't change what's already there, and mine was written in black ink. Though I think things may go a little easier if you avoid being afraid, because fear excites evil, haven't you ever noticed? When evil senses fear it starts licking its lips, starts slurping and sucking. In the absence of fear, if you aren't afraid, evil gets bored. He knew it: evil is confused when you're not scared, it feels out of place. It becomes like a butcher in some dull municipal market selling insipid meat products to clients; one who kills out of boredom; who clocks in to the job before doing the killing, puts on his leather apron, a hat, a mask if necessary, half-heartedly sharpening the knives, checking his watch between one cow and the next to see how long till his sandwich break. A pitiable man. The killer, the rapist—those guys need extra pulses. Evil grows in the place where fear stirs the body. Even ordinary things can become evil when there's fear in the other. A dry, motionless, mute sex isn't usually what draws the rapist's attention, it's a trembling sex, one that screams no, don't, hands hiding a head or a mouth, shrieking over and over no, no, no, one who defends herself, that's what the rapist loves, that's his natural medium, that's where he grows—fear is a biological tiller of evil:

please don't hurt me, and evil swells; in the name of what you love, and evil grows, ever bigger, ever stronger. That's how it goes, the plant can't grow roots if it's neglected, in the quiet of the morning the sun shines overhead, yawning rays that are blind, deaf, and dumb. Ever stopped to think about it? They say that animals and plants can feel an eclipse before it happens, that nature panics, and that's where you find fear, in that broken routine, in what steps outside of the everyday, your ability to laugh or to suffer. Human beings are the only animals capable of laughing and suffering, they alone sigh to think of the future, nothing else can—no mineral, vegetable, or animal—fear is a vision of the future, and only humans can do that, nothing else is able to calculate his or her own future, no other animal, and it's the future, fear of the future, that's the root of all suffering. In documentaries, you see people panic when an air-raid siren goes off, even when there's no plane in sight. People run around terrified, screaming, looking for refuge even under a calm, blue sky. His mother encouraged him to say his prayers as a boy, even though his father didn't like it. Devotion makes me sick (his father said). Taking advantage of the fact that his father stayed out till late, his mother would have him kneel at bedtime, hands folded below his chin. It doesn't matter if sometimes you have doubts, even if you stop believing in God, or think there's no meaning or order to life. It doesn't matter. Never stop praying because it's a way of finding the good that's inside of you. He looks inside himself, really searches, but can't seem to find anything good; what he finds is sadness, maybe sadness is good because it helps you understand others (to know others look inside of yourself, his mother said), but it's bad too because it makes you vulnerable. If you carry sadness inside, anyone can hurt you. His mother was a robust woman, and kind; from her he inherited a body he had to control so as not to scare people, take care with his gestures and the way he moved, his tone of voice, to keep his body from striking fear in others. His body was his mother's, but he hadn't inherited her kindness. His father turned to alcohol and those books he read to compensate for the energy and corpulence that nature had taken away, while his mother found in religion the best way to knead her doughy, authoritarian shape. She swore it wasn't about religion, not that kind of religion, but instead prayer, pure prayer, the kind that's free of expectations. I'm not talking about religion. It's prayer that helps circumvent the kinds of things all mothers want their sons to avoid, life's bitterness, life's sugarless coffee. There are two kinds of fruit that grow on the tree of life: cynicism and bitterness. You just pray—and I'm not saying these things will suddenly vanish into thin air—but praying helps bring clarity, praying helps alleviate the headache, the migraine you've had for days. Prayer had never unburdened him, had never eased his migraine.

SILVIA COULDN'T find anyone to take the boy to the airport so she had to do it herself (hard to imagine her sending him off without being there in person, anyway), so she wasn't able to swing by the hospital to see Matías one last time before they transferred his body to the funeral parlor. She called Angela's cell as soon as she was in the car, asking for news or instructions, but her call went straight to voice mail: the phone was off or out of range. So, she tried the hospital and asked to be connected with reception or someone who knew the extension where Angela or Lucía were, they must be sitting on one of those benches by the glass windows that separate the patients and the visitors in the intensive care unit, though they may have left, maybe they were already in the morgue, or outside of the hospital, in the funeral home, the hotel, resting after the stress of the past forty-eight hours. The receptionist's voice told her that it was impossible to connect her with anyone at the moment because the phone company was changing the cable structure and only the outside lines were working. Everything else has been disconnected, she said. Then can you tell me whether Matías Bertomeu is still there, please, she snapped at the receptionist, she of the incommunicable telephones. I need to know if Matías Bertomeu has left the hospital. We don't have the admissions list at the main desk, the woman's voice responded. Now she wonders whether a cadaver removed from the hospital would appear on the admissions list. The voice had a whiny lilt (though it was a clear-cut voice, metallic, a mature woman accustomed to addressing strangers, giving bad news, cutting the speaker off briskly if necessary) and announced: The whole system will be out of service today and tomorrow, until

66

they've finished laying the new cables. She could tell the authoritarian receptionist was on the verge of cutting her off, so she quickly snarled: I want to know where to find someone who is dead, who died last night, find out where he might be. Her words spilled out so quickly they must have been nearly indecipherable. Asking some stranger, someone you can't see or have never set eyes on, for information about one of your own dead. It made her feel awkward, the tears began to well, and deep inside she hoped the despotic voice might say something to console her. The word *dead* persisted, hovering in the connection like something indecorous, a cadaver lying in a ditch that shouldn't be within sight, that should be removed. She muttered a quick apology and hung up the phone between sobs. Once she regained composure, she tried Angela's cell again, maybe there'd be luck, but once again it went straight to voice mail: Hi, this is Angela, please leave a message and I'll get back as soon as I can (she was getting accustomed to Angela's voice again, after so many years). She thought: They don't approve of people using a cell phone in the hospital's terminal wing, they interfere with the machines and the ringing can upset the patients. Shouldn't be using a cell phone in the morgue, either. It's a lack of respect toward those who can't hear anymore. She has no idea where the cadavers are kept after a person dies and before they're sent to the funeral parlor. She imagines some refrigerated room under bluish neon lights, or greenish ones, as in a photo lab, or an aquarium, or maybe that hospital with the busted telephone system doesn't have a real morgue, they probably just store the cadavers in a room like any other, thick and heavy in the summer air (rickety air-conditioning incapable of lowering the room's temperature), a windowless room, or windows that are closed airtight, the corpses marinating for hours, their textures and colors subtly changing like slow-roasted food. She hung up before the voice message recording ended. Nothing is going according to the plans she'd laid out with Angela and Lucía, they hadn't accounted for the contingency of Matías dying in the hospital. They'd arranged all the necessary authorizations to bring the patient home. They wanted Matías to die there, in his bed—that's what he would have wanted. To die at home, to be cremated and have his ashes spread below the carob tree in the garden. The simplest and most natural way possible. But the doctor emphatically rejected the idea. Just do me a favor: don't intensify this man's suffering, there's no way I can condone such a thing, it's cruel. He's fine here, he's comfortable, you'd be upsetting him. Lugging the machines around, the IVs, the mobile intensive care unit, transporting him by ambulance, it's a waste of time and would cause the patient unnecessary suffering, it's just cruel. He showed them X-rays, talked about metastasis, deployed his index finger over the shadows and wide surfaces that were Matías's liver and lungs; the hollows, the noticeable cavities, tumors that had grown out of shape. It's beyond treatment. All that's left is to sedate him. He won't suffer too much. I doubt he'll make it to next Sunday. They'd resigned themselves to seeing him die in the hospital, but not so quickly, the doctor had guessed wrong, Matías didn't even make it to Wednesday. A vein burst unexpectedly, or an artery, just a few hours after their conversation with the doctor. He's clinically dead, the same doctor said a little while later, an aneurism, a stroke. Meanwhile, in an inverse sort of reaction, the nearly dead Matías seemed to come back to life, he started moving, moaning with his eyes open, as if he wanted to speak, as if he were waking up, as if he were returning from somewhere and not departing; yet he was still inside himself, closed in there, as if he were using an unintelligible language, prehuman, like an animal moaning more than a person trying to communicate something. It was heartrending. That was the last she knew. Her father had checked his watch, bid a quick farewell, and practically run out of intensive care. Silvia went out after him but couldn't find him. He wasn't waiting by the elevator doors or in the stairwell. She wasn't sure why she ran out after him, why she didn't stay there, waiting a little while longer. Go on and get some sleep, Angela had told her, take care of your boy and rest, you have an early drive tomorrow. Take the boy to the airport, we'll see you when you get back. There's nothing to be done here. She hadn't wanted to leave yet, but when she saw her father run off, she felt the urge to follow him. Angela had made all the necessary arrangements ahead of time, all she had to do was give the order: the funeral home, the transport, the announcement in the newspaper with a hammer and sickle instead of a cross and a phrase that went something like "your fight was not in vain." Silvia thought: You're someone's wife for a while, then you're not, yet when all is said and done, when your husband is no longer here, you feel, or need, to be that again; she realized that all the negative feelings she'd projected against Angela as an adolescent were resurfacing. She wanted to catch up with her father, telling him: Let me drive you myself, leave your car here in the parking garage; we'll pick it up later tonight, or tomorrow morning, let's have a chat, just the two of us. Bring him to a bar and spend some time talking together in a cozy place. Have a few drinks and reminisce about Matías. Tell him: He's gone now. He's at rest. Say: It's such a pity he never had the chance to see the new olive groves in full production, the excellent foreign strains he brought in, the ones the nursery procured for him, plantations of Frantoio, the finest Italian variety, which produced the great Tuscan oils, green, piquant, grassy, the kind they press at Poppiano Castle near Florence, the descendants of the Guicciardini; of the Frescobaldi and Marchesi and *tutti quanti*. Say: How unfortunate that Uncle Matías will never taste the oil from these olive trees; that he left this earth just prior to the first Italian crop, when his only glimmer of hope, he said, was here, in these lands, in this new Middle Ages he called them, a rebirth of religions from out of the pit of the desert, the depths of the sarcophagi (Matías said: The Enlightenment's unburied dead are coming back). We could talk about Matías's shoes, his shirts, his three-pack-a-day Ducados habit, and his Larios gin. Joke around with tears in our eyes. Say: We should put him in the box with a bottle of Larios and a pack of Ducados, no cold turkey while waiting to be cremated. We should drizzle some alcohol over the cadaver before sticking him in the oven, *flamber* his marinated liver. *Flamber* the quarry. *Flamber la palombe, la bécasse*; cook up an *oncle au rhum*. Matías *au fine liqueur, rôti au Père Magloire*. Laugh with her father between tears, between sobs. Isn't that how families are supposed to do these things? Pay homage to their dead by talking about these kinds of things, by talking about their loved ones? The psychologists say it's important to symbolize the pain, the funeral ceremony, the grief, the mourning, all the psychologists say so, they recommend it, because by representing pain you displace it, or more precisely you transform it into something else, into a different form of suffering because closure offers a sense of consolation; when it's shared, pondered over, pain seems to feed into something else, pain transforms into something useful. It goes from being a creature eating your guts out to a little pet you can stroke and talk to. One that likes to sleep at your feet, or on your bed. Talk about the dying person as a child, as a teenager; reminisce, remember some story that includes all three of them, Uncle Matías, her father, and her, or one that takes in someone else in the family, grandma or grandpa, her mother. Mom and Uncle Matías, did they get along? As if she didn't already know they had a lukewarm relationship, there wasn't enough getting along done to know. But with Grandma yes, since he was a baby, he'd always been the apple of Grandma's eye, right? Tell me about it, Papa; and there goes Papa telling me about how naughty Matías was, all the boyhood mischief he got up to. That one time when he crossed the line and got into real trouble. Was he a rascal? What was he like as a kid? Pure chitchat that waxes moral, becomes a mood: what they call a family lexicon, a shared vocabulary, rites that may seem tacky to those outside of the nucleus, but necessary to separate those on the inside from the others, to strengthen their difference from others, protect them from the others, the nucleus of the family. But even now her father didn't seem to have anything to say about Matías. If her father had nothing to say, she should have stayed at the bedside of the person who was already clinically dead and not run out, not said goodbye to Angela, their tears mingling when they touched each other's cheeks, not kissed Lucía telling her: I'll call in a little while. She should have stayed by his side even if only to tell Matías, no longer conscious of anything, that she never considered herself one of his women. One of my girls, my little niece, part of my tiny harem, what an exclusive club, he used to say laughingly. Lies. Describe to the deceased her distress as a young girl, a sort of monkey abandoned by a family whose members cared very strictly about themselves alone: Papa's silence, Uncle's lies. Cry because now it can no longer be fixed. Lucía and Angela were the true women in his life. Now they stand like sentinels over his cadaver. Silvia belonged to other people's lives. She had a different father. A different husband. Another man's children. Other children. She's not one of Matías's women. She's Juan's wife, his girl, she's been with other men at times, too, she's also José María's woman in a way—they fuck now and then, vigorously, hurriedly, intercourse that doesn't last too long, sudden explosions, all fire and ash—and she's also Felix's woman, her son. She carried him inside her body, and he hasn't had the chance to be inside another woman yet. For the time being, she's little Felix's only woman. That'll change eventually. Felix will become a man, he'll belong to other people, but this first mark will never be erased. As she drove through a congested Misent by night, passing in front of the rows of music-filled terraces or other cars cruising with their windows down and their music at full blast, nearly blinded by tears, she thought: You're only someone's woman when they've been inside your body, and they profane it (profane the temple of the Holy Spirit, a Christian would say), and turn it into—the word that came to mind scared her—a drainage for its own tensions, its own flow. Not a very encouraging vision. But tonight everything is making her sick, everything seems like a lie. Right now, she sees everything in a different light, with more resignation: she's Felix's woman, she thinks, watching over his luggage, buttoning his shirt. Felix had been inside of her, his fluids had seeped into her interior: and now Silvia is in the airport because he's her little man, she's waiting in line to check her son's baggage, the son that had been made by a man who is not Matías, while Angela and Lucía, as it should be, are beside the body, accompanying it down hallways, through the corridors one imagines in hospitals where cadavers are covered by sheets, their nostrils stuffed with cotton balls. Each woman, her man. As soon as she sees that her son has passed through security, she'll head straight for Misent and back to the hospital, as soon as his belongings have passed the screening process, the long, sluggishly moving line, where guards are endlessly stopping the machine, asking people to open their bags, their carry-on luggage, those little suitcases with wheels that people pull around. There's a proliferation of security checkpoints these days. The most innocuous things have become suspicious vessels now since the most recent attacks, high-risk items, lighters, liquids, gels, aerosols, even bottles of water and breast milk are regulated following directives on European flights. How inconvenient airports have become in the wake of the Twin Towers, all the screening and more screening. Later came the Madrid attacks, then London, the threats to other European airports and German trains. Exactly what was needed to make any trip just a bit more aggravating. Especially traveling to England, where every little thing is scrutinized and checked. Silvia finds all the fuss unbearably tedious, but she'll stick around for a bit, she thinks: I'll stay in this waiting area with runway views until my son's plane is air bound. She's irked by not being allowed to board with him, say goodbye once he's seated, buckle his seat belt herself before disembarking, then watch his face in the window, her hand intermittently crossing before her face as she waves. At the very least, she'll make sure her son's plane has taken off before she departs the terminal. Though nobody can raise a finger and point toward a specific taxiway and say it's that one over there, the one taking position on the airstrip, advancing like a stroppy bird, running, accelerating, that one taking off, air bound, leaving a streak of smoke in its wake, the magnificent one now glistening in the sunlight, that's the plane your son is on. An endless number of flights are displayed on the monitors of the congested airport. You can't trust the letters decorating the fuselage, or the logo of the airline that Felix is flying with, a budget company. And there she is now, standing with the director of the agronomy school who organized the trip, telling her that she doesn't trust these budget airlines and the director is assuring her that the company is fully certified. The rumor about budget airlines being less safe than Iberia, Air France, British Airways, or Lufthansa, the woman says, are spread by the established companies themselves, the pricey ones who think their oligopoly is being threatened, the old state-sponsored companies with their senior workforces, unions, privileges, and high salaries. Silvia acknowledges the accusation with a wide, toothy smile that seems to express candor, but is really only masking a sense of panic and as her son approaches the door through security, she casts a sideways glance at the director. Tragic scenes pass through her mind, the plane crashing, a flaming airstrip, tarmac melting, a fiery bird sinking into a puddle of black pitch and she is overwhelmed with guilt, consumed and destroyed by self-reproach, held captive by it for however many years of life she has left: she left the boy alone in the hands of a budget company. She glances at her watch. Almost forty-five minutes before takeoff. She'll have to wait to make sure the flight isn't canceled. It's the least she can do. Wait until the 11:35 to Edinburgh disappears from the departures screen. Doesn't look like there'll be any problems: more than a dozen kids are on the same flight, on their way to the same camp, there's a teacher accompanying them and a ground crew assistant too, a girl dressed in company uniform who will take them through security. She had to park in an improvised lot nearby, partly because the airport is crowded and partly because it's under construction, and then she'd had to walk to the bus stop that connects it to the terminal (a shuttle the sign says, not a bus) lugging Felix's suitcase and her own purse. Felix carried a sack and his backpack. It's her fault he's bringing so much stuff, as if they didn't do laundry in Scotland. The boy is traveling with more luggage than an opera diva on tour, thanks to Silvia's insisting that he pack clothes for bathing, clothes for any weather or climate, clothes for the remote possibility of an unseasonal cold snap. You never know, she thinks, what the weather is going to be like in the northern climes of Scotland; clothes for mountain hiking, a dressier outfit for a day trip to the city, to a museum or the theater (the itinerary they got says there will be field trips to cultural events). How's he going to get around with all that gear in the Edinburgh airport? They assured her that someone from the school would be there to pick everyone up, no worries, but, she wonders, what if something goes wrong? Felix, so helpless, so little. She'd kissed him half a dozen times, shed a few tears, clamped his shoulders again when he started to move toward the gate and kissed him one last time, pressing his face up against her own.

Kisses and tears (she who has never been very effusive). Mom, he groaned, you're embarrassing me, and he pulled away from all the clutching and smooching, self-conscious in front of the other kids who were watching the scene. Silvia thinks: My little man is leaving me on my own. When she finally separated from him, she felt like sobbing, the need to was vague and not only because Felix was leaving, but also for something barely perceptible that was enveloping her, enveloping all these sweaty people dressed in garish colors, a kind of sorrow like a shadow covering the building and the palm trees and the dusty cars flattened under the sun. She chose not to tell Felix about Matías and now she's sorry he's leaving without knowing, without the awareness that Matías passed away. Felix had stood by her side to the last minute, she had to nudge him toward the ever more raucous group of children. Now she's watching the kids pass through security and she blows Felix one last kiss before he walks through the metal detector. Onward to the boarding gate: Silvia isn't allowed where Felix is now and he can't come back to where she is. She contemplates the frosted glass windows, behind which are the invisible boarding lounges, the shadows crossing from one side to the other. The boy is so close, but inaccessible now, and the tears well, again. It's the first time Felix is traveling so far away from her and for such a long time (more than two thousand kilometers, for two long months). The frosted glass is like a mist in front of her, hiding something not known. She imagines the ones who walk into the mist like visitors in dreams: Come on, they say, if you want to know what's here you have to come with us; she shivers, Matías is in some unknown place now, as of this morning any attempt to call him would be in vain. She feels like praying. Not a religious prayer. Just an overwhelming confusion of emotions, or the desire to create an energy that might change the direction of what's going to happen if anything bad were going to happen. Suitcases move along the conveyor belt and into the X-ray machine, bringing to mind the scene she'll be witnessing that afternoon: the casket inching toward the refractory glass door, red reflections coming from the inside, fire like the painted set decoration in a children's play. Her mind wanders. The thought comes back. Felix's journey gets tangled into Matías's journey and it confuses her, overtakes her with a horrific sense of dread. She can't help it, she's crying now. She notices people looking at her. The furnace at the last cremation ceremony she attended in the basement of a funeral home was an exact replica of the oven at the bakery; manufactured by the same company, surely, maybe even the same model, a hygienic bakery oven without all the baroque paraphernalia that often adorn the cremation chambers, a black drape hiding the mouth of the furnace, black curtains opened on the sides, or red ones decorated with gold borders. A stream of classical music plays as the coffin inches toward what looks like a set decoration, drowning out the hiss of the flames from the blast of oxygen when the entry is opened. But the last ceremony didn't have any of that, the chamber door opened and the box moved forward, reflecting the red flames inside and making the sound of crackling wood. The roaring flames were silenced when the door closed again. Misent's crematorium is in the other style: baroque, theatrical. She's already been to several farewells there, with music and without. There were ceremonies with live quartets or quintets playing, friends of the deceased from the municipal band, musicians contracted by relatives. They played Mozart or Bach. She can already more or less imagine the scene she'll confront this afternoon. She'd have liked to choose the music herself (she'd thought of a Coltrane piece Matías used to play in Benalda; wicked, Matías used to call it), but her father already said he'd choose the music himself. I'll listen to the Coltrane, but I don't think it's appropriate, he said when she gave him the CD in the hospital yesterday. Music is another component of her father's dictatorship at home. She trusts that he'll take Matías's tastes into account above his own when choosing the music. But of course he's going to do what he wishes, she thinks, drying her tears. And the gesture frees her. But how to free herself of this tightness in her chest? It's not something you can wipe away with a hankie. She said to Felix: Think carefully now, think about the things you're going to need because once you're through security there's no coming back. Her son seemed uneasy when he heard her say those words. They made her nervous, too, what a ghastly sentence to leave hanging there, quivering in the air. Last night, sitting by Matías, she'd contemplated the idea of someone who's never coming back: all those tubes, the blinking lights, the screens, there was no way back, for days there had been no way back. Stop thinking about that. Get it out of your mind. The baggage begins its journey once the ground attendant sticks a tag around the handle so it won't get lost. Silvia will get back into her car in a few minutes (a car can be a coffin too), she'll buckle her seat belt, and look for the highway access road. It's better to focus attention on specific things: that you haven't gotten much sleep, that you're on edge and still have to pick up your car at the jam-packed temporary lot that the airport authority put into use while the old terminal is being expanded. The temporary lot is inconvenient, the space between cars is tight and hard to navigate, it's far from the terminals, you have to wait for the connecting shuttle. And if that's not bad enough, it's shockingly expensive. Just the thought of having to maneuver through those tight spaces, figure out which exit leads to the access road, drive over a hundred kilometers home or back to the hospital, because she's right on the verge of deciding against swinging by the house. She'll head straight to the hospital, convinced she might come completely undone at home, she might collapse. She's so exhausted. She's afraid of succumbing to it. She has a bottle of Prozac in her bag, she'll take a few and go straight to the hospital, that's what she decides as she approaches the terminal exit. Too bad she didn't see José María, she would've asked him for some coke to help her face the hours ahead. José María always carries a little with him, they're bound by that kind of intimacy that comes with clandestine activity, in some ways an even greater intimacy than what she shares with her husband, or with her friends. To think she has to return to Misent. Misent, a place far removed from anything a person truly has to do in life. Like an insipid theme park, a stupid place for a vacation. There's quality of life, but only relatively. She and Juan decided to stay in Misent after they got married, hoping to find that quality of life—when Federico Brouard first settled in Misent, he too talked up the quality of life there (now he complains bitterly), the sea, the sky, the landscape and climate, the gardens in bloom all year round, flora to the heart's content, Brouard had said—but any time you have to do something out of the ordinary, grab a train or a flight, go somewhere else, the whole experience plummets: it's hard to get out of Misent with the constant traffic jams on the roads that lead in and out; there's no train, there's not even a good bus system, uncontrolled development is crushing the city, half-built structures in use all over the place, construction sites everywhere, it was built for a population only half its size off-season and a fourth of its size in summer. Juan says you have to resign yourself to it, because heaven and hell are promiscuous and always travel in the same coach. What else can you do, he says, though also: Theologians should be analyzing the city, not urban planners. It deserves a postmodern reading of Revelations, of the *Divine Comedy*. Juan says: Misent's recent history works like the parody of a voyage, except backward: it starts in paradise and ends in hell. Silvia teases him, calling him Judeo-Christian. He says that like a good Judeo-Christian he believes in the advent of the beast from Revelations. There's no such thing she says, Revelations is somebody's wild trip, the wild trip of your namesake who was out of his skull from eating and smoking hallucinogenic whatever's in Patmos. Juan jokes: The beast of Revelations isn't coming because it's already here. What's to come has come. Silvia: The only sure thing is what we've already lost— this whole way of life. That's what we can be sure of. And no art, no literature, no history can bring it all back. Saying this, she notices her voice getting reedier: the Misent of her childhood, the nearly deserted beaches with shells and starfish left by the tide, seahorses, dried sponges, the smell of rotting marine grass, algae drying in the sun, decomposing fish; the aroma of iodine and saltpeter; the wilted textures between liquid and solid; life between two worlds, one that enveloped you like an empty bell and one that picked you up, cradled you, and stuck to your skin like a thick oil that's sharply saline: a Misent that no longer exists, it was forced out by all the developing, the necks of building cranes crisscrossing the sky, the half-paved streets. She thinks back to Brouard's words in the local newspaper a few months back, his article they too had signed to denounce urban overexploitation: Juan, Matías, Silvia, environmental groups and some of the city's personalities (half a dozen doctors, teachers, a few random scientists, the four or five local artists). She had given Brouard the idea for the text, saying: We live in a place that is nothing—it's the destruction of what was and the scaffolding of what will be. When Juan takes up the subject, she has a quick response: What do you mean "how would I know"? It's the reigning topic of the Baroque, which is my subject, what I studied, my discipline. What can you say that I don't already know? Paradise lost, the serpent and the apple. We have no idea of what will happen in the future, it's a liquid chemical, a corrosive element that dissolves everything. Being the literary one, Juan, Silvia says to him, remember the verses, "You seek Rome in Rome oh pilgrim! And in Rome itself you cannot find Rome." Quevedo. Yesterday is gone, tomorrow hasn't come yet: that's what art is about, all the arts, nothing less. Juan believes the future is always a complex return of what we think has been extinguished, while Silvia is convinced that you can never know the direction things might take. The zigzag. Which rabid dog might show up, she says. And Juan: Just look backward to figure it out, it's hidden in the traces left behind, look at history's half-buried dead and you'll see fingers start to move, worming their way above the ground. Whenever a period of more or less rational ideas comes to an end, the old superstitions come back again with renewed energy. Look at Islam, we thought it had died out but no, that buried egg was only keeping itself warm beneath the desert sands, incubating. Juan mentions the plotline of those monster flicks so popular during the fifties, the atomic bomb incubates the eggs of animals that had gone extinct millions of years ago. The past is an alien we all carry inside of ourselves, nascent, always ready to burst from our chests, about to escape. Matías was there too and his ideas aligned with Juan's: The instants of light are fleeting, unstable. We don't know how future generations will describe what we're calling progress today. The natural state is darkness: as soon as humankind stops paying attention, darkness returns. The same is true in our private lives. You let your guard down for three or four days without cleaning up, and the dark, the dirty, the prehuman comes to eat you up again. It takes a lot of energy to keep the little flame of civilization burning. In any case, everything that seems dyed-in-the-wool to us now may seem like a big joke to those who come later. Surely it'll be that way. Juan: The worst is always yet to come (Juan loves to flirt with his own pessimism). That conversation was on her mind this morning while exiting Misent, leaving behind the dozens of buildings under construction, backhoes stirring up the earth, stacking the desiccated trunks of uprooted orange trees lying in piles; excavators opening craters (the nearness to death makes one's nerves tense up, turns them into highly sensitive lightning rods that don't miss a single current of energy pulsing through the air, everything catches you, mesmerizes you), and again she played with Quevedo's verse: In Misent itself, Misent you cannot find. Matías teased: Karl Kraus said the Viennese were able to associate the sounds of Mozart's *Requiem* with the sounds of the mortars of war. Same as your father. Mozart's *Requiem* plus mortar fire equals Rubén Bertomeu, only your father's mortar is not exactly a weapon per se, it's concrete. The counterpoint in Rubén's music is the churn of a concrete mixer, that's how he composes his Dies Irae, with a background of gravel and metal. These are the things crossing Silvia's mind this morning, Felix messing around in the back seat, annoyed she wouldn't let him sit up front with her, it's what was on her mind going through the toll booth, crossing that swath of highway that rises up over the fields, the view of the plains from the window extending out between the mountains, a severe profile, and the sea; she contemplates the abandoned plots and the dry, crooked branches of orange trees that look like strands of hair from those exhumed corpses you see in contemporary history books, the mummies of nuns dug up by anarchists when they stormed convents during the Spanish Civil War, a few yellow leaves still sticking to the branches; the fallow gardens, the trunks of fruit trees heaped and ready to be incinerated, arid irrigation ditches that once flowed with water, the westerly winds blowing papers and plastic to and fro, scrap heaps, sacks of dry cement, busted box springs, filthy mattresses, broken toilet seats, cracked sinks; landfills in the city's outskirts that the newspapers describe as being beyond any control, growing like a constellation of tumors, a multiplying metastasis, engorging until they run together and form new ramifications, running on for kilometers; myotomes, an arborescent nervous system swelling thick and compacting. Riffing on the Rubén is Mozart plus mortar joke, Juan compares the suicidal behavior of Misentians with that of the

Viennese between the wars (a pocket version of Vienna, given the huge economic, political, aesthetic, philosophical, and moral differences, he says): One strolls along the Avenida Orts (not quite the Ring, of course), dancing and laughing (there's no Gartenhaus in Misent where suave characters like Karl Kraus go to hunt or hook up, but we do have some pretty spectacular dance clubs: DJ's, Fantomas, Arena, with their fog machines and laser shows), talking spiritedly in cafés (not the Alten, but the Dunasol), in the *Weinstube* (here they're called Pan y Vino, La Vinoteca), and though we lack those thick, fragrant woods (in Misent there's asphalt and spindly shrubs) and the Danube, we do enjoy the gentle sight of the bluest Mediterranean. One dances reggaeton (not the waltz) and toasts while nibbling fattened goose liver (nowadays you can find foie gras in any two-bit restaurant around here and likely there are more one-star Michelin restaurants in the area than in the old imperial city); we don't drink sweet Tokay, but we do have some good muscatel, plenty of champagne, lots of gin, scotch, whatever, but why not make it pétillant, or golden, or both at once, golden and pétillant; or at least luminous and sparkling: effervescence, light, tiny bubbles in the glass. What makes us so like the Viennese is that we're standing at the edge of the abyss. Misent is like the *Titanic* (what Felix de Azúa said Barcelona was in the eighties), though without the golden cutlery—a *Titanic* or whatever name you prefer, that's sinking amidst all the recklessness and ado, a pocket *Titanic*, of course, but one that's leaving the harbor and headed toward becoming a shipwreck: *Auf Wiedersehen, adieu, adios, goodbye,* the ensemble plays and keeps a difficult equilibrium while the ship keels just seconds before it's swallowed by a great wave that engulfs it whole. Did you know that if the ice continues to melt at the poles, everything under construction now will disappear within thirty years; that the sea will have swallowed it back? Juan laughs, punchy now after a few drinks—not

Hungarian Tokay or county muscatel but an excellent single malt scotch. It's the *Titanic* sans grandeur. We have zero intellectual production. So we are as much like the interwar Viennese as an egg is to a chestnut. We're alike only in the cheesy things, that we scratch at the seats of our pants, and a coming storm is going to swallow us whole. Of course in exchange we have these azure skies, a quality of light they only have in little trickles. The Edinburgh flight blinks on the screen for a few minutes beside the word *boarding* then vanishes. Silvia notices the change, plays with the words: You seek the flight, and the flight itself you cannot find. She thinks: You seek that stylish ocean liner passing the Halifax coast on a winter eve and all you find are objects floating adrift among the ice, blue corpses rocking in the current, the ebb and flow of the sea. The sinking of the *Titanic*. End of an illusion. Felix is up there. If he scrunches his face up against the window he'll be able to see the diseased landscape, the buildings packed one on top of the other, the lots, the cranes, the stillness of the shroud-like sea beneath the burning light of noon, the white light, livid, a corpse's light, the light of a morgue, filtered through clouds of desert dust; the dust raised by backhoes rummaging under the earth's skin, the dump trucks tipping debris into a landfill, light like a nightmare, dust like cosmetic powder caking the scrublands, the desiccated trees, the construction sites (in Juan's words: The unexpected always happens, something comes that takes even the prophets by surprise. We're starting to see the Antichrist now, he's among us: his name is Concrete, like the title of a Soviet novel. He's been hidden among us for a century, frolicking like a pet, and we never noticed the little darling has rabies, he's been getting more and more violent, poised to attack as soon as we try to pet him. Silvia argues: No, it's not something that is happening, it's what is already here and doesn't work for us anymore, cement and congestion). In Silvia's mind, the harsh light of the present overlaps the temperate light of her seaside memories, the kind of light that used to cut things into silhouettes, illuminated objects, the picnic basket, the happy pieces of fruit, the vivid colors of the towels as if they contained reflective material, as if a miracle were taking place every day, a kind of transubstantiation. The light of yesterday before the light of this morning. An airplane passes by the other side of the glass, cutting through the air made of an infinitude of little black dots, a pointillist painting, a faded Seurat, inclining, tilting upward and to the left as it takes flight. She can't see the logo on the fuselage to know for certain that it's carrying Felix. It passed by the window diagonally and is no longer there. People shuffle around the parking lot in clusters, between cars, beneath the sun, minimally clad in shorts and colorful short-sleeved shirts, untucked, unbuttoned, many of them with cloth or straw hats to protect them from the sun. Most of the women, even the older ones, are wearing tiny skirts with slits up the sides, their bikini bottoms peeking through as they walk, or panties, a fleshiness that is not always appealing, not gentle on the eyes. Matías died and Felix doesn't know. And his not knowing makes Silvia feel uneasy, because it highlights even more ruthlessly the distance from her son, the fact that they have two separate bodies, two different minds. She thinks too that Juan isn't with her, or Miriam, or her father. Their absence causes pain. Felix will learn about Matías's death when he gets back from Scotland. He couldn't know how much Matías meant to Silvia. Children think they know their parents but by the time they're grown their parents have already lived half a lifetime. Felix—in the best-case scenario—will only catch snippets of the life she's already lived, or his Uncle Matías. *Mon oncle.* Matías and Silvia saw the movie together. He'd taken her. A joke. They laughed so hard at the guests strolling around the garden, skipping from stone to stone by the fountain shaped like a fish, and when the owners heard the front doorbell, they switched the fountain on, the water spurting from the fish's mouth, until they realized they weren't the posh guests they'd been waiting for, but only the baker or butcher: they shut it back off and the water got stuck in the fish's mouth again in a ridiculous, retracting motion. Silvia pulls at her knuckles until she hears them crack. First the right hand, then the left. She's not aware she's doing it, it's a tic that comes when she starts to think she's going to screw things up no matter what. It's an automatic response, her way of relieving anxiety since she was a little girl. The thought that she'll never see Matías again in this life makes her feel so lonely now, it feels like some kind of a mistake. What you can't solve is not a problem. Only worry about the problems you can actually solve. That's what her father used to say when she was younger, one of his directives she tried to infuse with a dose of optimism, even when she saw it as the expression of a kind of interested acquiescence more than anything else. She never believed in the truth of it and began refuting the idea early on. She'd say: What you can't solve is always your biggest problem, Papa. What you can't solve you find a way to get around, one way or another. But why are these things popping into your mind now? She's anxious. A person can be on the verge of a nervous breakdown even though it's barely eleven in the morning—nerves in shreds, trembling hands, as if she hadn't slept in a week: summer drives a person in that direction, heat tenses muscles, nerves, puts the neurons on high alert. The traffic jam to exit the airport, and now she's finally free of the tangle of access roads, free of the spider's web that had held her in the terminal area, now the sight of the jammed highway traffic to her right, the congested exit lanes leading to the general expressway, hasn't been a very stimulating scene. Felix hadn't wanted to go to summer camp in Scotland. It took more than a little coaxing. He wanted to stay, to hang around with his friends. She had to corroborate that none of his friends were staying in Misent over the summer, that Aitor was also going abroad, to Boston, René is in France with his parents, in La Rochelle, and Josema is leaving in a few days for his grandparents' hometown in Maestrazgo. He had known he would be left on his own but tried to be evasive, tried to make excuses. Silvia wasn't sure why, if there was a particular reason he had wanted to stay, or if he was just scared of going so far from home on his own. It scared her too, but she tried not to let it show. At least Felix is tractable and studious, not like Miriam who flunked all but one class and said that her only plans for the summer were devoted fully to relaxing. I'm going to chill, that's what I'm going to do, she said, so unflappably, as if she'd spent months toiling at some grueling task. I'm eighteen, I want to quit studying, take a few months to think about what I want to do for a living. Her peevishness galls Silvia, the tone she uses to express such selfish intentions. And where exactly do you think you're going to work without a high school degree? No clue, Mama, that's why I need a little time to think it over. I guess I'll look for a job in a club, a bar with live music, a friend of mine works in one and she said I could find work there, too. Silvia was on the verge of raising her voice, but collected herself in the knowledge that it's precisely what Miriam was aiming for, to get a rise out of her and drive her nuts, make her lose it, provoke an argument that would end with her stomping out the door, slamming it behind her, and refusing to call for three days and only to say she'd stayed at her friend Erika's house, or Sonia's, or Leticia's. So while trying to swallow her annoyance she teethed out her words: You won't be needing much of a backpack for a trip like that, then. Don't get ideas in your head about a club. Miriam grinned back saying: Guess you haven't processed that I'm legal now (bitch really knows how to poke where it hurts). And Grandpa's giving me a car, so my chances for getting a job are much better, nobody has to drop me off or pick me up; anyway, you won't let me ride with Erika because according to you, scooters aren't safe at night, I could be kidnapped or raped, but now the problem is solved. I'll be safe in my car. Silvia preferred to end the conversation: Go tell that to your father. In the meantime, I suggest you come up with a few alternatives. Let's see what he has to say. Talk to Juan, she decided, he should be home any minute now. She ought to check in and see if he's on his way, share this emptiness that's causing her such distress; and call José María, though she doesn't want to discuss Matías with him. No matter, she has to call José María too, let him know it would be better to postpone their date on Saturday. Tell him: I'll let you know when it's all over, Matías is dead, my son's in the UK, my husband's on the road, my daughter, as usual, is out of control, missing, absorbed into the darkness of the night, sweet bird of youth, who could ever hold you, she thinks. Kneading her hands while squeezing the phone between her shoulder and ear, she realizes she's using the gestures of an old lady, she has the quirks of an old lady, an old lady body, oh, sweet bird of youth. *Sweet Bird of Youth*. She pulls over to the side of the road to make a call. Her father's cell is off. She dials José María's number. She talks to him. She tells him, among other things: José María I miss you. She controls her tone of voice, letting her words trickle out as if from the fingertips of a person sprinkling water over a shirt being ironed. That's how it's done, she thinks, offer but don't give in, keep the self-assured distance while stimulating the closeness of desirability. To be but not to be wholly with him, as if there were nothing bringing them together but pure air, no ties, no pacts, because air is something you can't break. If anything it gently disperses. All a matter of not getting obsessed with whether he's going to break things off, and what would happen if he did. It's always a sort of private cataclysm when a woman her age feels discarded, even if she wasn't really that close or didn't care that much about the person doing the discarding. At first, there were comments that didn't really sink in, though they kept playing out in her head: I've always had a thing for older women, José María said when they first met (he was thirty-two and she was teetering on forty-five). She thinks about José María telling her that he prefers older women, and how right away she felt like asking him: And just how much older do you like them? And involuntarily these words overlap with a conversation from a different time and place: I like older women, but not old ladies. And she gets the inkling that something had happened without her realizing it (she thinks: forty is plenitude, but she doesn't really believe it, she notices the sagging flesh, liver spots, time is whizzing by). She heard her own voice saying: I'm dying to see you, José María (her voice soft and throaty, allowing desire to impregnate their interaction; sweat moistens the skin of her voice, covers it in invisible, microscopic droplets). His voice. She has switched off her phone; she's sitting in her car, parked on the shoulder where the highway widens, a sort of rest area that's empty now except for her, the cars buzzing by on her left. At a certain age it gets harder to substitute one body for another. She's aware of it and feels regret. She thinks: Instead of becoming more lenient with age we become more demanding, desire hems you in even tighter: offering yourself is demeaning, having to go out there and look around. She knows a lot of mature women hang out in bars or dance clubs to offer themselves up, it's easy to be anonymous in Misent, plenty of places for an older woman to kill time unnoticed by the people who live there, places her friends would never frequent. The advantages of living in a city crawling with tourism is that there are places for outsiders and places for insiders, the city splits into classes and there are milieus where people of a certain position would never set foot: places for tourists, and places for the staff. The local television station broadcasts nocturnal messages for people looking to hook up, I want you inside of me, to fuck you, to eat you, online chats are full of mature local women playing at sex, riling up the adolescents who are unsettled by them, thinking the women know things that they haven't learned yet: a kind of sexuality that goes beyond the bedroom, that exposes you, chucks you out into a cold place verging on deviance—coded texting, spur-of-the-moment online dates, off-hours and in marginal places, roadsides, highway exits, service stations, activities at the margins of what society is willing to tolerate. She turns off the phone and can't help desiring him, she desires José María, believing what she just said—I miss you—and excited by the words she whispered, also sheathed in the soft, sweaty tegmen into which her voice had come to rest. All her worries, the goodbyes, the death, it all fell away for a moment and left her alone, gripped by the curling pang of desire: she wants to press up against him, feel him enfold her before she abandons this condition of being an older woman and passes on to the next stage in life. How strange to desire him so intensely when they aren't together (she pictures his body, she craves it, she masturbates thinking about that body, sometimes only one part of his body, and not always the same one: she masturbates thinking about his fingers pinching a nipple, she imagines those same fingers and they pleasure her, his tongue a slithering, slippery creature—all warmth and moisture below), and when they hook up, too: from the second they're together, no matter where, they can never manage to finish their drinks, there's an urgency, recklessly undressing, the tangle of their bodies, and when it's over, afterward, the urge is to leave straightaway, a quick shower, comb through the hair, get out of the room. She stays in bed and smokes a few cigarettes when all she wants to do is to take off. As if the whole point of each encounter was to prove how much she really didn't care for him, his intellect, his face, his dick, all examples of what she despises most, the only reason she's here is to see him kneeling between her legs, submitting, adoring her. Maybe it's panic at the thought: what started as a mature woman at the bar will end up as an old lady in bed. She's afraid to look in the mirror that's beside the bed. Not everything in life can be explained, her father used to say. You have to flee from the inexplicable things; don't dig in places you can't fill up again with cement. Silvia runs her fingers through her hair, looks in the little mirror stuck to the back of the sun visor. Juan's probably home by now. He likes to drive at night. A certain someone who told him he shouldn't drive so late at night or so early in the morning came home once in the early hours to find him already there, waiting for her, lying on the couch reading a magazine or nodding off. Things aren't so far away anymore, the highways are fine, only five hours from El Escorial to Misent, less if you gun it, though Juan would never do that, Juan is scrupulous even in his driving, you'd be hard-pressed to catch him speeding and he's not the type to get killed in a reckless act, she teases him because she loves speed, to feel the car gliding down the highway as if it had entered some soft tunnel, to make sure the car is obeying her. She learned to drive with her father and one of the few things she actually inherited from him is his voracious way of being in a car: bring the vehicle to the limit of its performance, enjoy its features (that's what she thinks. She doesn't realize how many things she actually inherited). If Juan was already at home, he probably would've called her. Though to him, it's as if the cell phone had never been invented. He only uses it occasionally, when it's unavoidable. No such thing as a cell phone, not even a ballpoint pen for that matter, Juan still walks around with stained fingertips. Silvia knows full well how irksome it is to fill in customs forms in an airplane with a fountain pen, inkblots everywhere, only to end up having to ask the flight attendant for another form and a ballpoint pen. Juan the klutz, incapable of doing things the way they're supposed to be done, no variations, like filling in official documents that have boxes to tick; he's hopeless with life's everyday details and yet so particular about knowing the minutiae of other people's lives, their work, like Brouard's for example, about whom he could give an hourly play-by-play. Silvia found his blatant disregard for domestic life comical, when not appalling (and utterly annoying), his pure chaos before the details of everyday life at home, when at work it's the opposite in every other way, he's pure methodology: rewriting every one of his sentences a hundred times, consulting ten sources for every statement. He teases himself: His wife may have a cross to bear, but how lucky to be the tenured professor's secretary, and the on-again, off-again lover of this very thoughtful professor, the velvet-voiced, disciplined keeper of his promises, who records and documents every word he speaks in public, every line he's ever written, a footnote for every page. Exactitude, order, decorum. Juan hates her father's yachting sprees and their entourages, even more than she does. He alludes to the guests as a gang of brazen bon vivants, politicians, and businessmen (some of whom are all three at once). He parodies their conversations, observations, and gestures: We opened a Flor de Pingus the other day and uncorked a Pétrus, so and so brought a Pétrus from France and we imbibed, it was pure heaven, so delicate, such silkiness on the tongue, he says in an affected voice with a bitter edge: brands that fill your gullet and empty your pockets, all their boring discussions on varieties of grapes and vines and tasting trips, when not one of them has a fucking clue. Fancy Eurotrash, guys with overstocked wine cellars full of high-priced Riojas, whose yards are protected by killer dogs. He, Bertomeu's son-in-law, can't stand the sound of them, their racket;

92

it's like fingernails on a blackboard. Juan Mullor sees the world as an intricate machine with a multitude of little wheels and pulleys that need to be left alone, nothing should interfere with the mechanics, no noise: sentimental expressions are counterproductive to the development of intelligence; the gratuitous gesture is noise, as is flattery, even the kissing of children—he would never let his kids fall asleep in the grown-ups' bed, even when they were little. The whole hodgepodge of words and gestures he offhandedly calls lovey-doveyism aggravates him to no end: movies with model parents, soaps or TV series or stories with little lapdogs, sweet animallike creatures and loving grandparents, that kind of trash. No emotional goody-goodies in their home. Silvia isn't either, though she does have a certain contemplative streak. Juan thinks things are beautiful enough when taken on their own terms, there's no use trying to charge them with added significance. He says: Beauty is the countryside in autumn, because that's what it is, the countryside in autumn: the trees hibernate, the temperatures drop, but then along comes the insufferable poetics of the checkered curtains, the chimney, the rug, the crackling firewood giving off sparks, the dog stretched out, ears relaxed, at your feet— the mawkishness creeps in and doesn't let you see things for what they really are, cut to the quick of things, know their cost. Splitting the wood, piling it up—what a pain in the ass, lighting a fire requires effort, being uncomfortable. Sitting in front of the fireplace, the flames scorch your front while your back freezes. Life doesn't give handouts. Juan hates movies that make it all seem so simple. Nothing is ever that easy in life. Everything requires exertion, sweat; anything that's worth it involves effort. Children wake from sleep dazed, it takes an effort for them to get up, their mothers have to make an effort to get them out of bed, rubbing their backs, tugging at their arms, sticking them under the shower and scrubbing them clean (Mom, you're hurting me), and they walk into the cold weather outside to wait for the bus with their heads all wrapped in scarves and hats, off to preschool where they're taught how difficult it really is to learn how to draw letters. Both of their kids—Miriam, who has always been indolent, and Felix—started reading late, which was a source of several arguments between him and Silvia. He never understood the purpose behind the method of learning how to read by drawing little figures, playing, and singing. Of course you end up learning how to do it, but it takes so much longer, he says—and it's sending the wrong message, that everything is easier than it actually is and that life is all about playing and singing. The only thing that kids learn after a whole year of stick figures and puppets is how to watch television, which is what they end up doing anyway. And don't get me started on the idea of letting their imaginations run free like the wind. This generation is quickly becoming a bunch of nutty make-believers who cringe at being in contact with reality. He's equally severe with his mother, his siblings. It's what may have brought her and Juan together at first, a similar education, the embarrassment over expressing certain things, blushing at certain words. Juan's skill for seeing things just as they are, unadorned, can often verge on cruelty. Once, during the toast at a farewell dinner when his brother Tomás was leaving for Yugoslavia and his mother, after a few glasses of wine and doubtless not entirely aware of what she was saying, blubbered on about the dangers her youngest son was going to face (Juan is the second, his sister is the oldest), how agonizing these months were going to be for her, he exclaimed: So Tomás, let's see if you can bring a few medals back like those soldiers in the movies do. Juan couldn't contain himself. He muttered: Or a few bullet holes instead. Silvia heard him and gave him a sharp knee, but he'd said it loud enough for his mother and brother to overhear. An argument ensued in the car on the way home. Can't you see what an idiot he is? The idea to go and enlist, what skin does he have in this war anyway, he contended. But Silvia was livid: It's not about that anymore. There's no way back now, it's done, he's leaving. Whatever happens, he's leaving. And leaving for a war no less, and your mother is suffering and however stupid he was to enlist, he's got to be feeling terrified now. You just wanted to poke him in the eye. Juan: What's there is there, whether I give a name to it or not. And he's going to find it. The bullets, the torture, the bombs. But everyone thinks it's better to let the stupid little boy go out and play with his bellicose toys. Let's get the family together for dinner and drinks, all happy-happy because the little idiot has decided to play at being a soldier, grabbing his gun and running off to war. Let's all pretend to be so pleased and proud. Like this is Wisconsin and the boy is Frank Sinatra in a Technicolor sequence, or better, he's one of those great secondary actors from war films, Audie Murphy, who as far as I remember has never acted in a single movie without a helmet on his head: he's selling an image of being a real-life combatant, an American hero from the Pacific campaign. Oh look there, a Christmas tree decked with glittery balls in the background and "God Bless Misent" playing on the soundtrack. Everyone so joyful, just like in the movies, the idiot is leaving a wife and two kids, and a mother, and a brother, who is me, and a sister, who is mine, to raise a rifle like a real man, a hero, and we all get to live on the edges of our seats for the six months that his mission lasts, all the people who actually work on tenterhooks, paying our taxes and doing the best that we can, now holding our hearts in our fists because of him, as if there is nothing else on our minds. So, we're not supposed to warn the idiot he might be turned into a colander? Is that what you're trying to tell me? That he can destroy my mother and fuck everyone else up (cause we're the ones who have to deal with Mama now more than ever), and we're not supposed to tell him what's in store for him, what he's going to find, what they're going to do to him; not what we're going to do to him ourselves. We aren't the ones who are going to shoot him, we're not going to stick a mine under his boots, that's what the other people will try to do, those neighbors over there he's visiting without an invitation. Silvia: He's on a humanitarian mission. And Juan: Yeah, and they always run off to war with a smile, but it's the image of the next day that I can never get out of my head: that disfigured man begging for spare change sitting on a baby-carriage-cum-vehicle in Otto Dix's drawings, or on a cart heaped with junk, things rummaged in a dumpster; the war's maimed, tin medals hanging from their chests, standing on a wooden leg while rooting through refuse or begging, the expressionist engravings after the Great War. The sinister world of expressionism, war's ugliness, the horror of it, all wars, for however much they show soldiers giving bottles to babies, as if that were all they had to do, as if they were interim nannies or wet nurses—do you remember all those wet nurses in nineteenth-century novels? Those buxom ladies hired by rich ones to breastfeed their children so as not to ruin their own cleavages? Well, sergeants are like wet nurses. They dress them up in a soldier's uniform, teach them how to shoot, arm them to the teeth, and ask them to act like nannies. Silvia: Oh come on, it's not like that anymore. Things have changed. Your attitude is always destructive, never constructive. There's got to be some compromise. Juan: Of course, that's how you always see things. I imagine you take the balanced approach, always well-intentioned, let the other person off the hook, free, the theory of mutual respect: I respect, you respect, we all respect, your culture is respectable, your way of thinking is respectable, your religion is respectable although I don't share it, forgive me. A way of skirting the real problems. Just think well of others, you might be wrong in the end, but you'll be free of any hassles in the meantime. Think that everyone loves you, they want to spoil you rotten, they need you, live and let live.

He and his defense of reason, always dragging the argument back to the same shore, to who does or doesn't love you, to what is the meaning of tenderness, what is love, desire, friendship. Social conventions, knowing how to follow certain codes as if they were traffic signals. Never have expectations, depend only on what you can accomplish on your own (whenever he got onto this track, Silvia would remember Matías's words: This is defeat, now it's a question of surviving. Not fucking things up at the eleventh hour—and what the hell had been the eleventh hour, anyway). Her husband's tone became bitter whenever he talked about culture, about his work as a literature professor: We're not cancer researchers, he'd say, we're not trying to come up with a polio vaccine, or something that will end up saving humanity. We're a whim that rich societies can indulge, while poor ones can barely consider it. We're like escorts, lotus blossoms that open above a nauseating puddle of opulence, we provide entertainment that is barely more refined than what the street girls offer (and less intense). Beauty, sentiment: malarkey—ado, as the comedy goes. We read a book, see a painting, hear a song that moves us so deeply and maybe even stirs up a tear, but then it's over, and we go back to daily life and forget we ever even heard that song. Feelings aren't that strong, that certain, or that lasting. We exaggerate their value. They're closer to the animal, to Pavlov's salivating dogs who hear the noise alerting them that food is on the way. They're drool. Emotion is not the most human of things. The intellect is human, and surely also the capacity to come up with evil for the long term: like what my idiot brother's bosses are doing, fabricating long-term instruments for killing. This is surely the most specifically human thing there is, death on the installment plan, to give it a Céline-like title. In fact, Céline is a perfect example of how the intellect is capable of planning out long-term evil deeds. Has there ever been a better novelist and a worse individual? Even his own

Nazi companions despised him for his baseness, his sadism. He plied the dirty trade of butcher. Juan loves convention, good form, the articulation of codes. He likes when thoughts fit actions like a hand to a kid glove. So, it was up to her to demonstrate how it wasn't so easy. Or even achievable. When all is said and done, bonds between people are based on form—the result of agreements, he said. And her: That's a lie. How can you defend realist literature and be so indifferent to the ideas of content, which is the crux of things. Him: But that's what I'm saying, that's why I defend realism, because I understand realism to be a way of agreeing on a form, a way of defining what is literary. Silvia: Relationships only thrive between people when you are able to go beyond mere convention, when you break them. You argue when something really matters, you resist, there's no room for decorum when you're really connecting with someone, you're looking for truth. That goes for everything. In art, in a person's occupation. And when you fuck, it's not about convention, but truth. Your dick swells, it droops, and there's no way of controlling it (now she has become a physiologist, a partisan of the realism Juan preaches as applied to books and her father as applied to business). Him: Even that has its conventions, its forms. You have to know what the other person wants and adjust the swelling and the drooping to this particular arrangement, because fucking is an arrangement, or it should be, and when something involves two people there have to be rules, and rules are exactly that—form, convention. You just don't want to admit it. You're self-occupied. All you see is what you see through your own eyes. Her: What else should I do? They're the only eyes I have. Juan: Yes, but even a monkey hanging in a tree, or a spider waiting to snag a fly in its web, has to put itself in the place of the other, know how their prey is going to react. And that requires being able to see through the eyes of the other. Self-centeredness may yield results in the short term, but if you can't adapt to this idea of other, you'll eventually end up playing the fool. You become blind. You can't see the bigger drama unfolding around the little scene you're absorbed in, when paying a little more attention might reveal advantageous things, ones that might give you a bit of an advantage, or others that might be detrimental. Something similar happens when you stop using an object, when you stop playing with it and identifying with it, like children do when they think an object is a part of themselves, or when you stop employing it for something, like an adult, and you start seeing it differently, start seeing it from another perspective: you behold it there in front of you but now it's unattached, neither a part of you nor created for you, something that simply reflects your gaze, like a wall. Your vision is reflected by it and returned to you, heightened, because now you're suddenly able to appreciate the complexity of the object, its logic—and not its logic as something that's in service to you, but in service to its own logic. Progress is a by-product of usage, by the way, and not from the time when something is being used, but from the pause that happens when there's activity, the moment when an object is contemplated in itself. It's the crucial passage between what is concrete and what is abstract, according to Marx and Lenin. Producing objects that are useful gives people that feeling of consolation, the certainty that comes from functionality, the operative measure of yield, which people like us—whose tasks can't be measured so easily in terms of utility, whose value is more ambiguous—aren't accustomed to. What appeases us is the moral superiority of artisanship, which offers its own certainties; the artisan can say: I've been able to fix this lock, or adjust that one; I found the perfect balance between firmness and flexibility, to make it reach prime functionality. Artisans have gentle dreams. Christian mythology chose a carpenter to be God's stepfather, not a philosopher or a poet, definitely not a soldier, or a politician, or even a priest. Whenever she would hear his tone wax pedantic, turn self-aggrandizing and patronizing, as if he were addressing his students or, what's worse, Monica, she'd feel like screaming. Academics, they always prefer brilliance to honesty, they reject an idea that doesn't suit them by picking apart some trivial error in a piece of information. They hone in on it like vultures. They prefer success to truth, but then, who doesn't? Occasionally, Silvia could still rally faith in the idea that at forty-something she wasn't too late to make a few changes in her life. When she first met José María, she thought he was the herald of this change. The cost of self-preservation is suffering. That's what her father liked to say. And the exhilaration of her first encounters with José María carried her to the verge of suffering. In that sense, José María fit right into her vague hope for change. At the very beginning. When it was no more than an escapade. At first you tell yourself, once. Only once, you say. But then you do it again, you look for someone and get attached. It turns into something necessary, urgent, but eventually you realize that this thing you now require is not a liberation—it's more like an adornment. Now you put up with two things in order to cope with one of them. Place a foot outside the marriage so that the marriage can continue. Ways of being in the world. Maybe they're just excuses for suffering. The desire for desire. It may not always be an act of generosity to think of others, it may also be a way of escaping oneself. Thinking of others: she forgot to ask Juan when they spoke yesterday if he'd called Brouard to let him know about Matías. Better not forget to ask when she checks in again, in a little while. Anyway, she'll call Brouard herself as soon as she's back in Misent, in case Juan hasn't told him. She'll offer to swing by and pick him up for the cremation ceremony. Silvia knows Matías's death is going to be devastating for Brouard. When she was young, she thought art could help people tackle life's challenges and would have imagined that on a day like today, Brouard would find solace in his books. Now she knows it's usually the opposite; artists are often the edgiest people, and the most vulnerable, and like live magnets they attract what most deeply affects others: art doesn't make people stronger, only more delicate. Her father used to reproach her for not making a real effort to become a painter, since she'd decided against working in the company with him; he wanted her to become what he called "someone" in the art world, but his scolding only served to remind her that she lacked that attribute, being a magnet, knowing how to channel internal and external forces into creativity. She could be a meticulous artisan, but never a true artist. He couldn't understand why she felt incapable of making the extra effort that creativity requires, and couldn't accept that her profession—come more by way of chance than any clear sense of conviction, or calling—fit her nature. Replenish the oils, remove additives, the overlaid paint, the grease, the soot, the candle smoke coating the paintings and frescoes, repair the cracks, the *clivages* brought on by changes in atmosphere, temperature, all of which Silvia attends to as if reestablishing some form of justice; it might sound haughty expressed that way, but she's convinced her work brings restitution, returning things to their proper place. The tasks she performs are largely mechanical by nature, but a restorer is also someone who peels away prejudices, who bares a truth that was hidden under recurring inertias that had devolved into a commonplace. That's how we could discover that Velázquez's *Las Meninas* is not the portrait of a somber court, but the luminous image of rich girls, or that Michelangelo's brawny guys have genitalia. Silvia explained it to Juan when they met: You may not be present in what you're restoring, but you can find yourself in the work you're doing. My father thinks it all boils down to my own fear—that I wasn't able to come into myself, to find what artists call a voice. You've never dared to express your true self is what I read in his disapproving eyes, in his tone of voice on the rare occasions he engages with me when I bring up something related to my work. I think my being at the service of others is what he can't swallow, or worse, that nobody's at my beck and call. To his mind, any daughter of his should have triumphed, in the sense he gives to the word. Miró talked about how a painter should be proud when conceiving a work of art and humble when executing it: extreme pride and extreme humility, that's how Miró described it. It's not that I'm humble, but I never had that extreme sense of pride. I've never thought anything inside of me is worth conveying to humanity, she says, poking fun at herself. My father's idea of success: being grander than everyone else, occupying more square meters, rising higher, using better materials; having the most visible advertisements in the newspapers: in the field of restoration, prestige is limited to a very small circle of professionals. But—she says—I am what I wanted to be. Twenty years later and I'm still convinced there's nothing more magnificent than saving objects ravaged by time, seeing how a piece that was disappearing, about to sink forever into the waters of time, breathes again thanks to a well-wrought restoration, returned to life from the verge of surrender. Silvia loathes people who invest money in objects of dubious artistic value when the world is already full of worthwhile artworks in danger of being lost. Just a few months ago in a nearby town, she had the opportunity to participate in the restoration of a pair of murals by Mariano Salvador Maella in a very poor state, nearly erased, and she saw them from a distance on the first day, thinking they were relatively unexciting academic pastels, but as she moved in, slowly but surely working, dissolving the salt crystals that had split the mortar from the pictorial layer, removing the retouched bits, the additions, the superimposed layers from prior ham-fisted restorations, what emerged when you could see the original colors was a scene of violent nightmares in an audacious combination of colors at once intense and somber, disturbing in composition and brushwork, described by the critics who viewed it as possessing a commanding, Goyaesque intensity. Silvia was deeply satisfied to think that what had been painted way up in the dome and neglected for over two hundred years in that scarcely visited chapel, a humble parish church in a two-bit town, could now be resurrected. Someone had painted nightmares predating Goya's by thirty years and they'd been about to vanish forever. A team of restorers gave them the consideration they'd never received. Of course she'd be deeply moved by an accomplishment like that, who wouldn't? It's why Silvia refers to her work as being corrective, a way of restoring justice, of putting things in their place. The reason her father doesn't appreciate her work, she's sure, isn't because he's shortsighted—her father, so wise in so many other areas—but because he's proud. He behaved unspeakably when she first introduced him to Juan: trying to upset him in order to upset her. Silvia tells it like this: He came to the conclusion that we deserved each other because Juan wasn't what my father would call a writer. To him he's merely a professor, nothing more, *merely* a critic, however prestigious that might be. He eyed him with the same sneering glower usually reserved for me alone. I'd described Juan as a literary type, which he understood to mean novelist or poet, and when he realized that Juan wasn't creative, when Juan introduced himself as a tenured professor of comparative literature (he said it that way to impress him) who was powerless to write a verse or put a sentence in a character's mouth (I have zero creative imagination, he said, laughing), Rubén Bertomeu concluded that his daughter was going to marry someone as unrealized as she was. Her father served up a sarcastic remark, his tongue loosened after a couple of drinks: What this company needs is someone who can make original pieces from scratch. Right now, it's no more than a repair shop. He would have supported her, protected her, even admired her if she'd have become a painter, if she'd engaged in what for him was still something sacred: an artistic career, like what his old friend Brouard had done in literature. Juan took the comment in stride: Like I said Mr. Rubén, I don't have that kind of imagination (he called him that at first, Mr. Rubén, half in jest, half seriously). I'd never be able to invent a character on my own or come up with two lines of dialogue, but I do know how to slice up novels other people write. Not long ago, when Rubén alluded once more to originals made from scratch, Juan responded humorously: Only God—and that British scientist who cloned Dolly—know how to make sheep, but any decent butcher knows how to cut them up scrumptiously so we can eat them. And trust me, Rubén (they've been on intimate terms for a while now), I'm a very skilled butcher. People eat up the novels I carve up for them. And my research helps keep the work of your old friend Brouard alive and relevant, at least for a time: I move him around the web, make sure he gets into library collections. I'm one of the good guys. Professors may not be able to bestow immortality, but we can extend someone's life expectancy. I keep certain works on life support that have been unjustly condemned to oblivion, save them from the horrific Gestapo of time, even if only momentarily. Can't do much more than that. Silvia's sure she pays a price for being a woman, the impossible heir of a construction company (it's no place for women, though he would have liked to see her there, imposing herself; people telling him that his daughter was better than any man, braver, more driven). It's hard for her to believe that she now thinks of her father in these terms, he hadn't always been this way, so Brouard says, Matías too, she had seen it for herself as a girl. Life had hardened him. He can't brag to anyone saying: I did this or I did that; but only: I got rich, and maybe it rouses envy in others, but it's not a big deal, especially because by a certain age you realize that being rich can never make up for what you're lacking, and nothing you have is going to last very long anyway. Whenever he's picked on her every now and then, she wishes she'd had the nerve to say: Just take a look around at all the garbage you've accumulated. It gives you away. All over the municipality there are visual reminders of what you've done. Impossible not to see it. Decades of selling any old crap for a living, hawking his junk as if it were sanctuary and salvation with a seaside view. Juan says of his father-in-law to his friends: He sells peace, like an undertaker. *All the calm of the Mediterranean*, the slogans read on promotional pamphlets, advertising real estate to buyers, unerringly decorated with the hint of a building and lots of green and blue: oh that Mediterranean light and oh that Mediterranean luxury and all the glimmering beauty, and all the sun, and everything is ahead of you and the Mediterranean behind. It's all green, all blue, sky, salt water. As if the buyer were making off with the entire bathtub, from Algeciras to Istanbul, the hot-water tank with a set of gadgets (sun, moon, and stars). The *happiness* package. The promotional photos are as alike as a set of Siamese twins, recently cloned Dollys: the palm trees, a golf course with little white figurines in the distance, squished into the lawns, a cluster of wide-brimmed pine trees, and there in the background, the forever sea. The house you're buying is singular and special, somehow he's made tens of thousands of microhomes vanish into thin air. Photomontages, panoramic views photoshopped, fine-tuned, skewed, conveniently tweaked, full-page ads in the newspapers, in travel magazines, car magazines, yachting and golf magazines, glossy pamphlets devoted to real estate promotion, all used as a hook to attract more and more buyers, more and more future inhabitants (looking a lot like Dayefe, Silvia told him once); virtual images of houses emerging from the green, rising over the green, mounted atop the green, growing in the green before the light blue curtain of sky, the darker blue ribbon of sea in the shade of a palm tree, bougainvillea and flowering hibiscus in the info-graphic garden. I'm doing something else he says, my properties are higher class. That's what he says because people take the bait of his overpriced Top Mediterranean promotions, which Silvia doesn't think are any higher quality than the rest: billboards on Jermyn Street, in Marylebone (lately he's been working the British market more than anywhere else: the Germans have begun relo-cating to the Dalmatian Coast). *Enjoy the Mediterranean. Das ganze Mittelmeer liegt zu seinen Füssen. Entre tout le soleil et le bleu.* Ber-tomeu Top Hills: dip your feet in Mediterranean and enjoy the gift of the sun. He's had relatively few Spanish clients, they're what he calls the wannabe clients: they want to buy, but can't. He has—ac-cording to Silvia—German wannabes, British wannabes, and Dutch ones, too. True, the newest promotions are being adver-tised in foreign luxury magazines. He plays with what he calls American models of marketing, the Dale Carnegie school, things like that: the big concept. Ford, Rockefeller. His favorite line goes like this: I'm my best client, meaning that as a client, I want to at-tract others just like me, my equals: the client is a friend of mine (or so the line goes). He explains it like this: My client can have dinner with me, play golf with me, swim beside me in the pool. The kind of people that are like you, that look like you even though they speak another language; who wear the same brand of polo shirt, drive the same car, watch the same shows, attend the same events. You know exactly what he wants because it's the same as what you want, only articulated in English, in German, or in Dutch. No project comes without a fixed concept. The materi-als don't make a difference, it's the idea, the concept. Only the scaffolding truants care about the materials. The materials have to revolve around an axis, and that axis is the concept, an invisible but solid one. Sure you can lose your head, sell costume jewelry at Tiffany prices, I know. But you can't do that to the type of people

I like to sell my development projects to, they're cultivated folks
with standing. I'd never forgive myself if they thought I was trying
to swindle them. I want to play golf with them, play a game of pool
with them, sail with them, go out for dinner, a soccer game, a concert. To Silvia: Don't judge me. Let me absolve or condemn myself
on my own terms. I know being cynical (yeah, I know that's what
you think) excuses you of nearly everything, Silvia, but it doesn't
forgive you, because forgiveness is something only you can give
yourself. She knows how much he loves to play his scenes, Rubén
Bertomeu is a first-class actor. He has to be, to score all his clients,
the financiers who give him loans. He likes to pretend he's built
up only a half-dozen luxury properties where a few friends are
living (those rich, boorish types he mingles with), ignoring everything he did beforehand: veil the fact that in order to erect what
he calls "his jewels," first he had to build and sell off hundreds of
prefabricated bungalows, built on terrain dubiously rezoned as
residential, along dry riverbeds, gullies, poorly cemented structures uninhabitable for more than a few months a year, and only
thanks to the county's relatively benevolent climate. Silvia understands why her father doesn't like to reflect on himself, doesn't like
to peek into his past; he's pained by the things he thinks are behind him now, and doesn't like anyone to remind him of them. No
doubt he, too, wishes things had been different. These conversations only helped to freeze their already chilly relations. As if they
were both embarrassed by what they were saying, as if they were
both embarrassed to find out what each one thought of the other.
He's unforgiving (forgiveness is something you can only give
yourself: she herself). He periodically reminds her of their conversations when depositing money in the kids' accounts, sending
checks for Christmas or for the summer, whatever excuse he can
find. Buy obliviousness, even buy the distance. For him, there's
always a doughy principle of reality wrapping around everything,

flattening everything, which on the good side miraculously be-
stows him with a pedestrian form of optimism, keeping him vigorous at his seventy years, but which also hides a hideous face on the
underside. Reality. A word meant to explain everything away, to
justify everything. The sprigs Daniele da Volterra used to cover
the genitals of Michelangelo's figures represent the reality of the
times after the painter's death. By their own right, Michelangelo
and Raphael ran with what Perugino, Pinturicchio, and Sodoma
had done: every epoch has its own principles of reality. In Rome,
in Greece, during the Renaissance, bodies were morning fresh,
while in the Baroque, by contrast, the bodies were turbid from
being poorly ventilated, scaly, things to be touched only in the
darkness. In the Baroque, clothing acts as a defense from the fetid,
the filthy, while the Renaissance exalts the beauty of the nude, its
vigor. Ideas impregnate everything, the flesh in the Renaissance
is fresh out of the tub, living; the Baroque flesh is grimy, condemned to death; life in the Baroque, a speedy path to death (this
is the subject Silvia studies so closely with her art professor Elisa,
Matías's friend: still life, ripened fruits, at their climax, about to
begin the process of rotting, *faisandages*). The observer contemplating these bodies didn't see them as either beautiful or horrible
in and of themselves, bodies weren't only a scandalous reproduc-
tion of the flesh. They characterized ideas, doctrines that impregnated reality, that were beyond simple tactile reality. Silvia is
aware that the work of the restorer is to bring an object back to its
own era, which time had tried to lead astray (by liberating the
genitalia of Michelangelo's figures you bring them back to the
time of their painting), the same is true when the worms of decay-
ing bodies, which were being erased by the passage of time, are
renovated on a Baroque piece. Silvia's sculptor friends participated in a fundraising drive to repair the marble veils that cover
the figures in the sinister Chapel of Sansevero in Naples, and she

took part in the restoration of the Chapel of Bones, in Évora, with the thousands of skulls used to build the walls, returning that lugubrious splendor to the reality of its time. It's her job, like it or not, the restorer's job, to be inconspicuous, distance yourself and allow the representation to take place without you. Of course, reality sneaks into everything, sometimes violently, you can't escape it. But what is reality? Saying "reality" is like saying nothing, it speaks of conformity, of dissociating your responsibility from the course of things. The soot of burned or bombarded churches in wars is a salient principle of reality, the seal of a period of time. Not long ago, her friend Helena, the municipal archaeologist, shared with Silvia the work she was overseeing at the time, exhuming and consolidating Roman ruins that were discovered under the old town square: the forum, the remains of Republican baths, together with edifices from Augustan times and others from the Low Empire, whose constructions share materials with the ashlars of the old Visigoth cathedral, everything scrambled up, like a puff pastry, or not a puff pastry but a lasagna with layers and layers that had densified and compacted, poorly baked in time's oven. There were tree trunks piled beneath a protective awning; apparently they were masts used to hold up the tents of the original city, no more than a camp that was razed during Sertorius's wars. Julius Caesar would have been here, Helena said. They found the relics of that battle: weapons, skeletons with broken necks, cranial fractures caused by rocks, ribs broken by a lance, at times the spear tips still embedded in the bone, two thousand years later. Many of the skeletons were missing an arm or a leg, mutilations from older wounds, and others the experts believe were the result of torture. Civilians, or soldiers who served in an army that didn't look after them; the high command, the great leaders, rarely mixed or bothered with the lower-ranking soldiers, Helena said at the end of her briefing. The comment takes her back again to

Matías: she remembers how he railed against the old Communist leaders in Spain who went off to live in exile after the war, how they lived between meetings in Paris, in Moscow, in Prague, in Bucharest, while the clandestine militants inside the country were falling like rabbits into the hands of the police (that's the reality of politics). Apparently, her father had been a militant in the Communist Party for a while, or at least he collaborated; Matías continued in far-left parties until midway through the eighties, when he decided to affiliate with the socialists; he said the socialists were the only left that's possible (though when Silvia—barely a teenager—was with him in Madrid he never stopped whining about them), but eventually he went to live on the mountain and broke his ties with them. Her father never talks about those times, and in truth, she's never felt much like asking about them, either. Too sordid. And some of it is still hovering over the country. When she was young (when she would still get woozy over the smell of oil paints and turpentine) she considered moving—and thought about it again a few years into her marriage, during her first marital crisis—getting out of Misent to find a position as restorer not in Rome, Venice, or Florence, positions that would have been too competitive, but maybe in some other Italian town: retrieve those inspiring ideas of Plato's Republic—beauty and virtue all together—which is what we long for after all. Musing on those restless notions, she tells herself they were youthful ideas, though she remembers being convinced that if she lacked the drive, it was only because she told herself she did: she always second-guessed herself, her own worth. But she corrects herself right away, it wasn't only a question of drive, but also of time. Or in the executive style that Ernesto likes so much: it was a failure of *timing*. She took such a long time thinking it over that suddenly it became too late, and now she's wondering how to break free of the chains holding her to the ground. She feels trapped. Though whenever she tries to imagine the form this desired world would take, she's never been able to articulate an idea precisely. Surely, not knowing what shape or figure to give your desire shows a lack of ambition. You feel the awkwardness of what is around you, the self-disapproval, but can't seem to find a substitute—everything paralyzes you. She plays with the idea of leaving it all behind again, and thinks about her children, her husband, her father, her grandmother, her house, her friends, her books, her furniture, but she doesn't think of José María. Neither running off with him, nor breaking it off. José María is a nowhere, a no-man's-land, a no one instead of a him. He doesn't exist, he's not in her life, he's not outside of it, he's formless, desire without shape, just body, not significant enough for you to lean on, to gain purchase and take a leap. José María is—though it may sound indecorous—her choice of protein (not to be confused with protean), allowing her to fight despair, more dietary supplement than anything ethical or aesthetic. Though by all appearances her relationship with him transgresses her bourgeois lifestyle, it's actually just a form of resignation by a person who never really dared: adaptability, accepting the run-of-the-mill. Being resigned to the idea that no one has the qualities she's looking for and needs; one needs several pieces to put the image of a jigsaw puzzle together. After all, they're more or less veiled forms of surrender and self-denial. The search for the absolute, delegitimized. Leave it all behind and go where, exactly? What place? Her father says the human animal reproduces in the same ugly way everywhere on earth (a joke not without sexual malice). Journeys interrupted. Feints of what will never come because you lack the drive. Matías was a terminus for the teenage Silvia, the end of the line for her inane, interrupted journey. Adolescent fantasies. She finds it all funny now, the memory of it makes her smile, but at the time it was painful. Time plays down youthful experiences: it even neglects them, allows them to disappear. She closes her eyes and remembers: The Chinese merchant boats sailing across the southern waters, solid as homes, light as the clouds that dissipate over the sea. Matías, do you remember the first sentence of the collection of Oriental tales that you gave me? Silvia thinks. Solid and light. Seeing Matías lying on a hospital bed these past few days, her husband teaching in El Escorial, her daughter tramping around nocturnal Misent, Felix packing his bags for summer camp, had been particularly discouraging: the old actor Matías condemned to a death like the rest of us, people who never tried to communicate, never tried to play a role; same as the people who accepted life like docile stable animals being fed and led off to the slaughterhouse. Last night she had felt abandoned and unacknowledged. Now this weight is coming down on her again, here alone, on the shoulder of the road, nobody beside her, just the blanching light outside, menacing as a steel instrument, surrounded by the blazing glints of the cars passing along the highway to her left, and the ones she can see if she looks through the opposite window, at the end of the slope, circulating on the main thruway. The rest of the landscape appears motionless, the plants, the edifices, probably vacant, caked in whitish light. She's paralyzed now, unable to drive, despair like a dull ache that only someone else could relieve, someone else with drive, someone from outside of the pain, or only caught by it tangentially: she feels as though she were at the scene of a bombing, there are bodies buried beneath the rubble, bodies that can't be rescued on their own, requiring the help of someone outside. But there's nobody beside her. Nobody can come and relieve the weight of what's fallen on her, what's holding her paralyzed. Just a few hours ago she couldn't bear the thought that Matías had died without anything happening, but he had died, and it's as if it didn't carry any special meaning.

FEDERICO BROUARD hangs up the phone and the tears come in a wave. Javier observes his face, an uneven surface undergoing a transformation, wrinkles are redistributed, bunching here or smoothing there in successive combinations. He's crying. His shoulders tremble, left bare by the T-shirt he's wearing, the movement makes them look even gaunter. It takes a few minutes to figure out what's going on, what news he'd received that's now making him cry. Javier touches his knee, his shoulder, strokes his head, smoothing the few long hairs, brushing the back of his hand down his cheeks, until Brouard rejects the tenderness with a movement of his head. It takes a moment for Brouard to respond: he stands up, takes a handkerchief from the drawer of the nightstand, blows his nose forcefully, and says: It's what we expected. Matías has passed. Javier isn't sure what to do, how to react to the news. He offers: Would you like me to make you some tea? But Federico responds no, he prefers to be left alone for a little while. It was Juan who called, offering to pick him up if he'd like to attend the cremation ceremony at eight in the evening. But he said no. I didn't think you'd feel up to it, Juan said over the phone, adding that in any case he'd come by as soon as he's back in Misent—he's on the highway now, on his way back from his course in the summer school program at El Escorial—he'll stop by for a visit and they can catch up. I'll swing by on my way to the mortuary, he said. Surely, Juan figures, he wants to avoid running into Rubén at the cremation, though Rubén hadn't even crossed Federico's mind when he said no; he just doesn't want to set foot in the mortuary. He lies back on the bed as Javier steps out of the room, supine, hands crossed over his stomach, legs outstretched. He closes his eyes. Matías, the little one. He was only around six or seven years old when Brouard and Rubén were teenagers. He wants to recall him as a boy but he can't seem to conjure up images from that time, not even with his eyes closed. He tries to imagine an impromptu stage of what's supposed to be the house in Pinar, the garden they played in as kids, but can only rouse a scrappily painted backdrop: a few random plants, the fountain, the little bamboo forest; the wooden planks forming the row of wardrobe doors in the attic, the afternoon light casting honey-colored reflections, disjointed components that don't quite add up to a whole visual scene, sensory, but they're more the concepts he tries to group together, finding connections among them. He tries to focus on Matías but gets distracted thinking sorrowfully of Rubén, he's like the sore edge of a wound, a painful, bright red welt. It's not Rubén's body, not his words or his face that he remembers (he couldn't even if he wanted to), but only the vestiges of something gathering in his imagination, something that had once been a physical presence, palpable, communicative, but that is nowhere now, and yet comes like a hollow, like a resonance: the body of teenage Rubén is an idea, the idea of what was his friend's body and what no longer exists. Rubén is now a bulky individual, awkward, someone who moves with cockiness, flauntingly, his gestures arrogant; that other body no longer exists, or their friendship: that friendship disappeared decades ago. Yet the concepts (the substitutes for what he'd hoped would be memories and feelings) aren't entirely lacking in material, they're more like washed-out stains or residue, more erasures than figures with volume, even the sting they carry is more a dishwatery accumulation of hoary sentiments, a watered-down discomfort instead of something that truly causes pain. Just then, he bursts into tears again. The teenage projects with Rubén, their closeness, their arms brushing against each other while watching a movie, Rubén's hand on his head, on his shoulder, the conversations that lasted till morning, with Rubén in Montoliu's workshop, the artist, who was in a hurry to leave. Architecture, painting, and literature brought together like a weapon, a kind of catapult to lay siege to the Misent that never seemed to pull itself from the grisaille of war. Break that scheme of gray on gray. He still recalls the landscape of Misent at that time, maybe from seeing the pictures of it decorating the walls of bars for so many years, or in local history books and newspapers: Misent during the forties, the fifties: the great, empty port, abandoned except for a few fishing boats roped to the pier in the afternoons. The still visible wreckage of a cargo ship that had sunk during the war. He and Rubén used to swim around the metal hulk, diving from chunks of the hull that rose above the surface of the water. Rubén's body wet and glistening in the summer sun with the brilliance of paper set ablaze, leaving charcoal stains when doused. Every once in a while they'd bring Matías along. They'd tie a vest made of cork to his chest and encourage him to jump in. Misent's streets emptied at dusk, only the lights of a few taverns falling over the sidewalks. The intellectual workshop was going to be the great upheaval that purified the city. Matías followed him and Rubén around from sunlight to shadow, pestering them with questions, sneaking off and reading the books they left hanging around the house. Sometimes the restless kid could be a pain in the neck, snatching for himself whatever Rubén discarded. Montoliu took his own life. Federico counts his losses. His friend Rubén, whom he'd once loved but isn't sure he does anymore, has nothing to do with this person who cruises around Misent behind the tinted windows of a luxury sedan. Montoliu left him so many years ago. Matías left him today. Federico couldn't say which abandonment hurts more. Only Juan is left now, another member of the Bertomeu family, though indirectly. It's as if the Bertomeus had arranged a friend for each stage of his life, only to take them all away. He still has Juan's company (he'll come by later this morning), his tape-recording sessions. Federico worries he'll be left with no one when Juan finishes the biography he's writing, when his research is complete: the Bertomeu family will take away the third friend they'd loaned him. He'll still have Javier, but Javier is a mechanical form of company, as indispensable as the clothes he puts on each morning, but if you don't fill the clothes with yourself, they have no function. He thinks about Matías but it's Rubén who appears again: he pictures him lying atop the metal hull of the sunken ship, he pictures his clipped hair, his neck, his shoulders; in his studio bent over some blueprints, the lines visible between his fingers. So young, and yet his hands are ample, fleshy, the obliging hands of a paterfamilias, from which those straight lines representing future houses radiated confidently. Everything about Rubén exudes a sense of protection, Federico thinks, still lying down, trying to find images behind his closed eyes, a while has passed, more or less half an hour. Finally, he gets up, opens the lower door of his nightstand, shuffles anxiously through the metal and cardboard boxes he keeps there and pulls a pack of Ducados from one of those fabric shoe bags. He's careful to crack the window before lighting up. He looks out over the garden that Javier tends as he takes his first drag, and beyond the garden he sees the clouds of dust kicked up by the machines working the lands bordering the hill. The side of the butte had been cleared already, leaving a stark reddish stain between the silvery green hues of the neighboring terrain, olive tree plantations. Federico closes his eyes for a moment and rests his face against the windowpane, still cool from the cool dawn air (the night had been asphyxiating, the heat only broke at dawn), and as soon as his cheek senses this freshness he's swept back to another time, to a day when he made the same gesture, talking with Matías. Any gesture now would inevitably have taken him back to Matías. He's that absence now that inhabits everything. Back then, Federico had rested his face against the glass and felt the cooling reprieve, saying: I was wrong to come back here (he was sorry for having returned to Misent). The picture and the echo of these words rush back throbbing, vivid, and wrench another sob from him, though also the sense that the gesture and the words are rendered insignificant in the face of Matías's death. Returning to Misent was a mistake, he'd told Matías that afternoon. The haze of his tear-filled eyes blurs the ruddy land, the bustling machines. The fig tree used to be over there in those bald spots left by the machines, and the well, and they used to dry the raisins around there, too. His mother lit up by the oil lamp under the vine arbor that wound around metal columns, where the birds used to nest. You could hear the sound of the little birds nested inside of them, recently hatched, their chirp slightly metallic. The vine arbor, the jasmine climbing the wall, night jasmine; the fragrance of summer nights, the whistle of carbide lamps, the clammy smell of carbide in close proximity to whitewashed walls, the damp walls swept by the sea breeze, the aroma of saltpeter, the smoldering oil of the dangling lamp outside sending its puffs of smoke up to the stars twinkling in the firmament. The scent of muscatel vines permeated the balmy nights, heated for hours under the sun, and of the fruits ripened there (tiny San Juan apples, tasty and sour, pears, fragrant peaches): he loved to drench himself on summer afternoons with the cold water from that well, it was salt-marshy because the dowser had found water buried deep underground, down to the aquifer where salt filtered in from the nearby sea, whose roar travels across the moody autumn nights through pine forests and vineyards, those memories forgotten by all but him now, watching the machines stripping the terrain, now an empty field bordered by a row of buildings, the memory of the paltry vegetable plot cultivated by his grandfather, a poor potter who sold his handmade wares in the streets of Misent, a traveling potter not even a native but born in Belgium; nobody knew how or why he'd shown up here, if he was fleeing, hungry, maybe trying to escape from a war or something, or how he ended up with that foreign name, though it'd served to camouflage the truth of his penury when he was a boy, Brouard the penniless potter who snatched that worthless plot of land where he built his house and workshop and storehouse and for years planted vegetables and a few trees on a rocky hillside overlooking a briny quagmire, a wasteland of rushes and silt that he turned into a vegetable plot and that's now a wasteland again, but whose value at one time had been enough to pull his grandson up and out of hardship; enough to rescue a writer incapable of earning a living by writing; land where they find the remains of poor people with every excavation, who lived there prior to his own version of penury, Almohad workshops and oil presses, the remains of irrigation ditches, potsherds, windmills, modest dwellings, thousand-year-old edifices buried under sediment and time. His mother kept some of the objects they'd found in the land: pieces of pottery, a few oil lamps, a dagger. Federico would joke around with Matías when he'd refused to sell the land, and Matías would say: Your fortress is too close to enemy lines. You better believe that at some point by inhabiting a fortress you'll be forced to defend it, you instigate your neighbor's covetousness, you make them want to possess it; what's more, your neighbor has to worry about you attacking them, too. He wants to seize it away to vanquish you, but also to defend himself against you. For several years that neighbor was Rubén, who'd been buying up the surrounding land. Matías enjoyed poking a little fun: The bad thing is that without a fortress you remain exposed, you're at everyone's mercy. I built my castle on the inside, and have tried to keep it open, unarmed, with the gates wide open. The conquistadors march right past and only regard it with contempt. But you, with your views of the sea like in one of those Sorolla paintings my brother uses in his promotional materials, how could you ever imagine they'd leave you be? Rubén had arisen as the area's land development agent and Federico was eventually obliged to sell him the plot. He and Matías had a good laugh over it all, two alcoholics whose respective doctors forbade any alcohol consumption, and yet there they were in the dining room swimming in whisky, drinking themselves to oblivion again (Javier had gone to spend a little time in Madrid): Squeeze, tighten those screws as far as you can, name your price, more than what it's worth, don't cave, crush the asshole of my brother, Matías hooted. That was three or four years ago. An evening breeze had been drifting in through the window, already nocturnal air, though a ribbon of reddish light held on just behind the mountain. The air came in thin and humid, not as a mass, but a very fine point lace that rose above the sea, already indistinguishable at that hour; it had the texture of tatting, a doily, something spongy and full of little holes, as if it were wafting through holes because it was cool when it grazed the skin in certain spots, though the atmosphere's mass was still sweltering, still carrying the breath of the day. The inkling of a breeze finally perforating the sticky, sweltering mass. It was a gorgeous hour. The remains of the sun ablaze behind the profile of cliffs that looked like a grayish cutout, a stage setting that in a few moments would become a black cutout, darkening against the glow. Matías said: These moments are the only ones that make living here in the summer worth it. But Federico tempers his statement. It's been a typical day in the county, the desert wind gliding across the sea instead of a breeze, then doubling back when it reaches the mountain and plunging vertically as if through a funnel, sweeping the cliffside and swelling along the coastal plain turning Misent into an oven: heavy, boisterous air that brings the dryness of sand, that thankless feel of its grains in one's mouth, a sandpapery

roughness straight from Africa; the wind is what gives these summer evenings that sound of fallen leaves, crackling the way they
do in autumn: leaves that rustle in the trees, palms that sound as
if they'd gone dry and brittle, were on the verge of breaking, broad
fig leaves clattering like wrinkled paper about to tear. Today will
probably be a day like that. Already at this early hour the misty
clouds of dust particles are seeping into everything. Brouard
lights another cigarette. Juan won't bring the tape recorder, they
won't work today. He won't be obliged to tell stories of his childhood. Juan's coming to spend some time with him, to console him
because he knows how great a loss this is for him. At first, Juan's
book was meant to focus on Brouard's narrative work, a strictly
literary project: talk about his books, the characters in his novels,
the stories he had wanted to tell and the ones he hadn't, elements
of style; little by little things got complicated and it ended up
turning into a full-fledged biography including anecdotes, life experiences, temporal sequences, childhood, adolescence, and maturity, etc. Federico finds it immodest to say these things into a
tape recorder: I remember someone's voice, surely one of his
friends, one of his barroom comrades, who shouts at him to knock
it off: Are you nuts, he says, can't you see he's just a kid?, and adds:
Can't you see he's your own kid? I can still hear his voice. I wish I'd
have heard it more often. Someone who'd say: Can't you see he's
just a kid? My father's friend pulls me away and protects my head
with his hands, holding my body against his leg. And I think: To
have had a father like that, I envy the kids this man may have had.
The man picks me up, holds me in his arms. I see my father's back
over his shoulder, leaning against the bar and grabbing his glass,
his back, in a white shirt, his broad, shaven scruff-of-the-neck. A
few months later he's gone. I'm convinced he paid for my mistake,
whatever it was; the one I can't quite place, but that surely has
something to do with my existence, with being the way I am, he

punished himself to atone for a part of my own guilt. Speaking into the microphone he wonders what happened. He'd rejected this memory for so many years, banished it from his mind, and now speaking into the microphone he thinks how one never knows the reasons behind the things that truly matter, that cause concern. He of the broad and shaven scruff must have thought: My son is a victim. He's like me. And thought: They already beat my son up—I beat him—same as they've been beating me my whole life. He'd fought in two wars: in Morocco and in the Civil War, during which he'd suffered and lost both of them. Brouard imagines his father in espadrilles cutting across the rocky terrain, yanking out the thorns that pierced his feet through the soles, inspecting the folds of his clothing for bedbugs and squishing them between his fingernails. Hard to imagine now what he was thinking back then. A medium blinks, eyes rolled back, the whites showing, the fingertips of those gathered held above the round table, that's how people connect with each other in the sessions, the tips of their pinky fingers touching, and eagerly they inquire, anxious to hear the voices of those they've lost, but the room remains silent, the stretcher, the closed windows, the smell of burnt wax mingling with floral aromas or incense that are in fact unpleasant, cloying (the woman had burned herbs, a few scented bundles). But suicides don't answer. Federico talks to the reel-to-reel tape recorder that Juan had placed on the table: I doubt there are more than half a dozen people in Misent who try to remember him, people who have probably gone several years without reminiscing, without giving him a thought or mentioning his name in conversation. Time is the rat that devours everything. A photo in the niche: for all a person may have suffered, there's nothing left, no energy in the air, no force that can move a turbine, no energy to start a motor, nothing. Only he, Federico, still remembers a few things, just a few, though it's a negative energy that this peripheral pain triggers in him, a kind of vacuum that saps his strength. Look at the photo he keeps, he shows it to Juan, who says he could include it as an image in the biography, a photo snapped when that man hadn't yet turned forty, must be thirty-five or thirty-six, he could be my son (Camus commented on this strange feeling: when you see that you're much older than the person who became your father, your father's father). He's unkempt, wearing those rags people used to put on for work, there were no uniforms, no coveralls, nothing like that, just dirty, threadbare pants, a greasy, torn shirt, rags. It surprises me to see how poor he was, how poor we were, not only the clothes, but in other ways that poverty expresses itself: back then he was a laborer, one of so many others, but today he looks like a beggar. It's the only photo I have of him, maybe someone else has another photo without knowing it's him, some local collector of historical memory, some loopy person who conserves old photographs and who bought a few found in a dump, or in a box in some secondhand dealer's window, or on a little table, a photo kept by a son or a grandson, someone who had also died but was a friend of his, my father's friend, or a war buddy from Morocco, from Tafersit, in Dar Drius, in Mount Arruit; or a coworker, or one of the gang who went out to the countryside one day to have lunch and snapped a photo as a souvenir of their outing; someone who still keeps it as a family heirloom, the portrait of a group of soldiers taken during their military service in Africa, or another at the port authority warehouse taken by the people he worked with, posing, some on the ground, sitting, legs spread apart; others squatting behind, resting their hands on the shoulders of those in the first row; or else standing in back. They're all staring into the camera except for one or two of them, caught distracted when the flash went off, chatting, joking around, everyone else looking straight into the camera, which was still something of a rarity; to those men it's still practically unheard of, at once enticing but also a little frightening, like the eyes of a lover watching you from bed while you're still standing there, undressing, and you see desire in their eyes but also the hint of scrutiny, measuring you up, weighing you up, producing a report that can only instill a sense of trepidation. Maybe someone out there hasn't gotten rid of a photo like that yet and can still recognize a relative because he's marked with a circle, or a cross, or because his father pointed a finger at one of their heads, saying, that's your grandfather, may he rest in peace, that's your uncle, but he no longer recognizes the others there beside him, maybe one of them has a hand slipped over the shoulder of the man he knows to be his grandfather, the man whose hand is slipped over his shoulder is smiling in a way that conveys familiarity, camaraderie. Let's say that one of those men in the photograph is him, my father. Nobody knows that, what kind of a job he had, how many children, nobody would be able to write a name below the face. That's the nature of time. When I decided to leave for Madrid, Juan, your father-in-law's father told me that even Adam had to leave paradise to realize he was a man. Time detained, the prolongation of paradise. Time that passes, hell, or simply life. Your father-in-law was convinced that his own father loved me more than him. Your father loved me more than he loved all of you, I told Matías. Federico tenses his lips while resting his face on the windowpane, simulating something akin to a smile. Now, watching the machines stirring in the spittle of mist, he prepares his wording for when Juan asks him if he wants to go to the cremation. He'll say: I won't set foot in a cemetery or a mortuary until I'm taken by force, and that'll be the day I levitate, six angels carrying me through the air on their shoulders, and even then, my feet won't be touching the ground—a lay saint in a procession—may they be six big and burly angels who carry me off. I refuse to set foot in a church even to see works of art, there's enough art in museums, galleries, secular art, ex-cloistered, unconfiscated, recovered with civil dignity in public spaces. I won't set foot in a court, or in front of a justice of the peace, not for weddings, not for baptisms. He'll say that and then start complaining, say he isn't able to sleep, and that looking after his health takes up more and more of his time. Can't you see I'm blocked?, he complains. I spend the day looking for that little paper I had in my hands and can't remember where I left it, my glasses, the fountain pen, the pencil to underline and annotate in books, asking Javier, asking him to help me find them. The rest of the time I try to forget how much my arms ache, my stomach, my dick. You have to transcend pain in order to write, the physical pain of joints, the poky catheter, but there's the other variety, too. Pain gives you nothing, at first it might help you comprehend something else: to realize the human cavern is still a lot darker than you thought, but then, after that, comes the time when it peels off your skin, leaving you naked. Pain does not purify, it does not elevate, like the ascetics preach. Pain doesn't even transform you into an animal. A dog jumps if it's healthy, it gives you its paw, it shakes its tail; and when it's sick, it curls up and whimpers. So let's say that pain turns you into a wounded, sullen animal. It clouds you over. It muddles things up. It blinds you from inside a dark cloud of unpredictable behavior. The heroes or heroines of novels or movies aren't the ones who suffer, it's the villains who suffer. The heroes and heroines are healthy little creatures. Ahab is who suffers. And the tears Ulysses cries by day, before he goes off to tend Calypso by night, are awfully hard to believe. Years earlier, Rubén had said as much of Matías: That nut thinks he's Captain Ahab, he wants to drag us all down to the bottom of the sea, even his mother, chasing after the white whale. But he'd answered Rubén saying that Matías is suffering, he has ideals. Rubén said that Matías's distress was nothing but ego and self-absorption, it was malicious. It's only meant for him, he said, just another property. Evil is goodness failed, Federico told him. God denies absolution for suicides, God can never forgive desperation because it's a representation of himself in an agitated mirror. My father in hell. Won't be long now before I run into him again. Ask him a couple of questions. Demand accountabilities. Federico smiles when talking to Juan: The Bible says despair is a sin against God, a sin against the Holy Spirit. Your hands shaped me and made me. Will you now turn and destroy me? Did you not pour me out like milk and curdle me like cheese? His smile widens now: You like that? That's what I'm writing. The Bible. He bangs the table with his fist and the glass teeters, a few drops of milk splash onto the saucer below and he scribbles out three or four pages on the fly. What kind of a novel would you want me to write, he prays: Lord, turn away from me, if you turn away from me I might be able to write, but you must turn away, that's my prayer. I ask for the pain to mature, grow distant, turn into a medical diagnosis, allow it that level of precision, that lack of emotion typical of a diagnosis, that observation from the outside. But for that to happen you'll have to pull it away a little. Juan remembers Baudelaire's words about artists who hand themselves over like martyrs to feel other peoples' pain in their own flesh, catalyze the experience, distill it in the work. But that type of suffering artist is passé. It's a Christian notion of consecration, communion, crucifixion where sin and pain, all of it, are concentrated into a single point in the universe like a sort of solar panel for gathering energy. The deepest areas of pain would be like the hydrocarbons, oil or gas, condensed energy, fossilized, which art liberates. In reality it's the mystical body of Christ. The electromagnetism of the Church. Its energy sciences. Traditional convents are like solar panels producing energy, the hair shirts tied on by nuns, the lashing, the hours of prayer, the suffering, all positive energy charging the world's great galvanic battery, grace coming down like rain atop a somber Moscow cell and a suffering epileptic in a Dostoyevsky novel, coming down atop a bungalow somewhere deep in the jungle and Conrad's agonizing Kurtz. Brouard picked up a little black notebook and tugged at the ribbon bookmark, opening it to a specific page, and read aloud a sentence about a philosopher and a priest: "In one point only they agreed, which was, in all their discourses on morality, never to mention the word goodness." Like the quote? Let's see if you can figure out whose it is. Who is this disbeliever in culture, religion, and interpretations of the world? Think about it for a minute, yes, you with the excellent memory. Don't know who said it? Juan shakes his heads. Sounds vaguely familiar, he says. It's Fielding, a sentence from *Tom Jones*, Federico answers. I came across it a few nights ago when I was rereading the novel. If only I were twenty-five, thirty years younger and had the strength to read Fielding as if I were reading my own work. But I don't anymore. I read irritably, stripped of pleasure. I admire the novel, but I don't enjoy it. He closes the notebook he'd just read from. I can't seem to pull out of myself. I can't find the path, he says, where's the exit? There's something missing, some mechanism, some gear. If I had cut the wings off the bird she would have been mine forever, she wouldn't have escaped, but she wouldn't have been a bird any longer, and me, it was the bird that I loved. It's a song by the Basque singer and songwriter Mikel Laboa, "Txoria Txori." Ask for a second chance because we let the first one fly away. We wanted a bird that chose to stay with us of its own free will. Why not. But it can't be. He bums another smoke from Juan. The police are currently off patrol right now, he says, alluding to Javier, who is prowling in the far side of the garden, shoveling, raking dead leaves. Make aging meaningful, that's what the psychologists say: at sundown, light sprouts like a flame; in the twilight, a resurrection, an ascension, the Bible and its meteorological examples, God's ire, the lightning bolt ripping across the sky, the thunder that rumbles and wanes until it sinks into the stage box, or the purity of a radiant, Easter-like universe. To have a new life, the diaphanous sky where fluffy-winged angels ascend, what the fuck is that, just tell me, go ahead, living in another body, maybe with a different soul, some other life, the mountains around your home different mountains, silhouetted against a biblical sky rising over you, spinning around you, that, over you, arches like a bell jar of light. Dawn. It's the hour of twilight, and yet a new world is dawning. What kind of shit is that? Who in their right mind falls for expressionist film gimmicks nowadays? All that fuss about consecutive resurrections. All I have left at my age and state of health is to pack the suitcase, Juan. Is that what you want me to write about? Grabbing a suitcase, who cares? Express hope for a world that I'm about to escape from? Like in those old expressionist films, the sky represents the soul that's unexpectedly illuminated by a truth. Well that's not how it works, what it expresses is more a kind of indifference, the indifferent sky, the indifferent light, the indifferent birds who chirp in the morning, chirp in the evening, some even chirp into the night (when I was young and would wake up early to study, all their trilling and merrymaking would aggravate me: fucking birds, let me study I'd scream out the window, they were life. Goethe would have scolded me for having lost my youth among books, turning my back to nature), birds flitting hither and thither, agitated, nervy, they don't offer a smidgen of deeper meaning. Night descends without speaking a word to anyone. Day will rise and you or someone like you will try to make something up about it. I've already made enough up. I'm tired of contriving meanings for things that don't have any. I'm tired of fibbing. It's immoral to write at my age, to add dead leaves to what's no more than a murky forest that someday is going to fall into total darkness. He and Matías had ducked into a café on Avenida Orts for a drink that afternoon they summoned him to the notary to sign the paperwork for the sale of his terrain, and a storm was gathering over the county, four fat drops of rain, more like sludge, the saturated desert dust from its passage across the water; in the notary's office the two Bertomeus eyeballed each other without speaking a word, Matías sat beside Federico in the waiting room, Rubén extended his hand almost as grudgingly as the other party had extended his. Best friends but no longer. Brothers but no longer. A tense silence presided over the entire process. He hadn't the courage to reject Rubén's hand; Matías laughed at him on their way out. One never completely gets over their first crush, isn't that so Federico? Matías, such a stickler for gestures. Remembering him this morning, he thinks: Rereading the prison letters of George Jackson about the Soledad Brothers, the texts written by Carmichael, Malcolm X, the Black Panthers, which I read with him when he was a teenager, when I'd just begun publishing my books. I probably couldn't suffer through the texts now. We lost the avenging impulse of justice. Angela Davis's memoirs already expressed a new form of moderation. We thought they were too disciplined. I used to have copies of those books, but I can't locate them now, they must be somewhere or maybe I lost them in a move. He remembers arguing with Matías: Misfortune that originates in man is called Misery and it can be eradicated; misfortune that originates in the unknown is called Pain and it should be contemplated and explored tremblingly; let us improve what can be improved and reverently accept the rest. Matías copied it out onto a big poster and hung it in the faculty hallway. Then he printed it out onto pamphlets in the shop run by a Vietnamese family. Rubén tried to balance it with a dose of realism: Who would argue against the idea of justice? Of course it's a beautiful concept, Matías, what more beautiful words than the ones used on its behalf? Only it doesn't exist. Matías countered: And what biological law says that someone only becomes an adult when they bury these words, bury these ideas? What asshole put those shitty ideas in our heads? He'd taken the words from something Victor Hugo wrote but had never published in his lifetime. Matías took three or four more notions of romantic exaltation from Hugo, high-minded sentences like: A revolution is a return from the fictitious to the real; or that one that talks about how the natural state of the sky is darkness, night. Now Federico thinks: And how black is that night, Matías? Let us know now that you're there. He's sitting on the bed now, his back resting against the headboard, holding the cigarette in one hand and a scotch in the other, which he throws back before setting the glass on the nightstand and pouring another dose. By the time Juan arrives, at around noon, he'll be soused.

LAST NIGHT he was waiting for her until very late. They'd already raised the lights on the dance floor, two couples were at the end of the bar, but otherwise the Spaniard was alone, hunching over the half of a drink he still had left, no apparent intention of leaving, so Yuri had to sneak her out the back stairway. The Spaniard was leaning on the bar with his elbow, head in hand, sitting on the edge of the stool with his legs crossed as if he were the prostitute. He shooed away the other girls who'd approached him, and told Irina he wouldn't leave before talking to her again. At three thirty in the morning, he'd wanted to go upstairs to the room and spend the rest of the night with her. He'd already given her the money and was expecting to exercise his rights. She said no: Better tomorrow, she said, tonight I need to get some sleep. And he, the Spaniard, Ramón, said: I'll wait for you out in the car. They got to the chalet late, though he still had time to figure out where to hide the money so Traian wouldn't find it. Sometimes it's as if Yuri forgets that all their coming and going, all the commotion they're caught up in, has no other end but making money; it's as if he forgets this from time to time and looks for other things inside of himself, his own inner to and fro. Can someone love and hate the same woman all at once? Traian, Nikolái, Irina, Yuri: they're the base camp, the permanent unit occupying the beach-front chalet that's uncomfortably damp in the winter, but that now enjoys, on these sweltering days, the scarce breeze that flows through the county, the sea, the cool fingers of the sea rustling through the garden rushes, tousling the bougainvillea leaves, rippling the water in the pool, skimming the rooftop, caressing the soft slope, and rising up along the rocky mountainside; a slight breeze, a breath that then relents, leaving behind only heat, the sea distilling a dense breath of mist in these early hours. For the past ten or twelve days, Traian and Nikolái have been coming and going. They sleep elsewhere, in other chalets shared with itinerant people and every once in a while in the rooms at the club with other girls. When that happens, Irina stays there too, and Yuri returns alone, early in the morning, with several hours to think, to observe the plants in the garden, and listen to the coming and going of the waves. When Irina's there, that's all he thinks about. That morning, Yuri had gotten up a few minutes earlier. He had barely slept for the heat (he doesn't like air-conditioning). He hadn't had his coffee yet. As soon as he got up, he went straight into the bathroom, standing below the showerhead. He's been there awhile now, washing up: scrubbing his hair, very short, his ears, his chest, his stomach; when he moves down to his penis, he takes his time slipping back the foreskin and gently washing the folds at the base of the glans. Soaping it up, rubbing attentively, he uses gestures that he slowly realizes are dedicated to her—she's still asleep, surely, she's still sleeping, though he doesn't know for sure. He hadn't dared crack her bedroom door to peek in. It hurts to watch her. He washes gently, soaping the inside of his thighs, his testicles, he leaves the foreskin and slowly washes below the glans, caressing it and thinking about her. An erection stirs as he's washing. He begins masturbating then and there, under the shower's tepid water, but no, he doesn't want to, he controls the desire, he wants to save all his energy for when he's with her, to save his milk, he thinks about that phrase, save his milk for her, but now the erection is relentless. My dick's so hard, he thinks, and this thought makes it even stiffer. He's not sure he'll have the chance to fuck Irina today since Traian will probably spend the day at home. Yesterday he called to say that he'd be by in the morning. He left three days ago. He said: You stay in the house with Irina, and grinned. They both know he shouldn't do that; he shouldn't leave her alone with him; and Yuri is convinced that Traian is dangling her under his nose to see if he can trust him; but Irina isn't Traian's wife after all, his wife is in Moscow and Irina is just a whore who works for him, he likes to know she works for him, but that it's only work. In any case, she's the whore that he fucks, even though she still works in the club. Traian says: I like them better when I know they work for me. When Irina first got there, they'd cruise around in his car for a few days, she'd fuck in the club's master suite—yes, only in the suite, only with Traian's friends, a few special clients. Now she's just one of the rest, though she lives in the chalet and she's still Traian's whore outside the club. But now she goes with anyone, like that idiot Spaniard Ramón who wants to take her out of the club, hook her up with a place outside of Misent, somewhere far away, like Mexico or Brazil. Ramón told her he'd give her a pile of money (Irina promises she didn't say anything to their boss, that the Spaniard gave her the money last night) to prove he's legit, that she can trust him, that he's not all talk (Yuri thinks Traian might not know about the money; but Yuri does know, and he and Irina just stashed it away a little while ago). She tells the Spaniard yes, she'll run off with him, but of course she's not actually planning to go through with it. She tells Yuri about it, saying she wants to stay here because he's here, and if she really wanted to run off with someone, she would want it to be with him, with Yuri; leave the club, find a way to score some cash and take off, the two of them, set up a place of their own somewhere, one of those rural hotels that are so successful in the area, find some quiet, hidden spot up in the mountains, but Yuri's afraid to go through with it. He figures that if she told him about the Spaniard, she might in turn tell Traian about him, saying: Two guys want to take me away from the club, I fuck both of them; she'd tell the boss just to mess with him, to rile him up, to get something out of him; so he'll take her out cruising again, to his businesses: the boss likes to show off the girl that everybody else wants, but only for so long, a few days, and the boss is getting upset now because it's been going on for too long with the Spaniard, it doesn't bother him that they fuck, in fact it excites him: he has no reason to let her fuck other guys; if he wanted, she'd never set foot in the club, and yet he lets her. But later, outside the club, he wants everyone to know that she belongs to him, and to him alone, let the other girls fuck, belong to whomever, or not belong to anyone, they're skilled labor. Skilled labor, Yuri thinks and chuckles, he thinks nobody tells them to rot in hell, bitch, but he doesn't think it's funny (nobody tells him to rot in hell, bitch, either). When their contracts are up, they leave. They argued the other night. But you're you, he screamed at her in the bedroom, and Yuri overheard her response: You don't have to squeeze me too much, I hate it when I can't even breathe. Yuri had gone out for a smoke and was in the garden when he heard them, and now he's sure he'd better not even consider leaving with her, Yuri knows as much, like he knows he shouldn't touch her either, he'd be better off not touching her, but who could resist with Traian making it so easy for him? It's as if the boss got off on it, putting people at risk, letting people fiddle with danger while he watches, it's all part of the game. There's no way he doesn't know they're fucking (what else are they going to do by themselves in the chalet) and yet he acts like he doesn't know and doesn't care. Yuri feels the tepid water spilling over him in the heat of the morning and takes his time, opens his mouth, rinses, and spits a few mouthfuls out, his lips vibrate, and he glimpses himself in the mirror. He measures his body in the mirror that covers one of the bathroom walls. He's strong and fit, and he likes himself in this state of partial erection, though the skin of his abdomen is a little too pale. He's put on a few pounds these last couple of months, going to the gym less, he's drinking, spending a lot of time doing nothing, relaxing on one sofa or another, lying in bed, in a hammock beside the pool. His belly is white and round and he notices it's even starting to droop a little. He looks in the mirror and sucks his gut in several times, passing his hand over the smooth surface that goes from his chest to his groin, he inhales before the mirror, once again sucking his belly in and puffing out his chest, then he scrubs himself down with the sponge, first his torso and next his white butt cheeks now flushed in certain places, he rubs his skin and he grows hazier as the mirror starts steaming up. But he likes to look at himself, he likes his body: he gazes at himself facing the mirror, turns sideways, then twists his head over his shoulder to see himself from behind; now he squeezes his butt cheeks as if they were pushing himself into her, Irina, inside of her; as if he were inside of her and making an effort to go in even deeper. I have blood, strength, he says bringing his dick—bright red—up to her face; he slips the foreskin back and brings the head near her face, opening it between his fingertips, for her to slip the tip of her tongue into the little slit. You enter in me, he says, I have strength, but you're the one who's fucking me. She caresses the head's little red slit with her tongue, she slips her fingers in his mouth while she licks his testicles; with the other hand, she strokes his anus: she spits on her fingers and rubs it softly, again and again; you fuck me, fuck all my holes. He rubs saliva over the little fold of skin, saliva on the tip of his finger that he smooths over the head several times before tensing it between the index and thumb to open the slit a little wider, a tiny vulva that she stabs with the tip of her tongue. I have you inside of my dick, he says. He likes to watch the tip of her tongue licking his little hole, it excites him, quickens him, so he pulls her away brusquely, lays her down, opens her and shoves it inside, everything is rough, there's no tenderness anymore, a half a dozen quick, arrhythmic thrusts, he pushes her, she's fragile—her body is more like Traian's, thin and steely—but her skin is white, white, nearly translucent where her veins are visible, before a bluish interior like an ice-filled lake, like the frozen grottoes you see in the movies, in television documentaries. Her inside is blue, icy, surrounded by a sort of polar aura. She fucks but never surrenders, the deeper you go inside of her the further she wriggles away, that's what Yuri thinks. He sees her further away with every fuck. Irina isn't submissive like the other women Yuri has fucked, she's not submissive like his wife was until she found out through her in-laws what went down in Italy, and picked the phone up only to tell him she never wanted to see him again. Pig, she said. I hope you rot in prison. His wife kicked him out, but she'd done it in a way that lets him know that he was still inside of her. Irina allows herself to be fucked, she needs it for some reason, but he can't quite figure out why, he knows she's aloof and at times he thinks she's so blue, so transparent, he can't hold her too tightly in his arms or she's going to break or melt like an ice sculpture, like those ice swans they put caviar inside, and other times he thinks he can't hold her too tightly because of that icy-cold edge that cuts and can wound you. Yuri consoles himself by thinking she must appreciate how big and strong he is. That's what he thinks she thinks, and the thought gives him confidence. What he doesn't realize is that she thinks he is very big, but also very fragile, and she knows where his chinks are (goof, she called him once in front of Traian: Yuri the goof; she said to the other girls: the big klutz, the lummox, also making fun of him). He doesn't want her to know how his entire body collapses for a gesture of hers, or better yet, in the absence of one. He thinks there's only one thing she knows about him (that he's strong) and that he knows both things about himself (that he's strong and fragile). What he can't imagine is that she knows she's in his hands and that despite all his strength, he's also in hers now. Yuri has been alone since he was a gardener in Italy, where he took care of a house that belonged to a friend of his previous boss. He was the gardener and guardian of that house, watching over the people inside and outside. He was to make sure that the ones inside didn't bother his boss, and that nobody outside bothered them, but there was a teenage girl in the house who liked to stroll in the garden, she'd approach and watch him do the pruning, she'd hang around looking at him, smiling; when her parents were away, she'd skinny-dip in the pool and lie out in the sun with her legs open. Come to find out she was a virgin and when he laid her down behind a shrub, she started to scream. Rape. He wanted to kill himself in prison, kill himself before anyone else killed him. The Russian won't eat, the Russian won't drink, he won't change his clothes or take a shower, he stinks, he won't shave, what's going on? Why is he crying? Why is he so thin, so pale, why doesn't he talk to anyone? Two months of paranoia in prison, thinking anyone could be there to exact payment of the debt incurred when he shunted the young girl behind the shrub and climbed on top of her. He thinks about Yelena, his wife, his little daughter, he'd forgotten about them for a while, he chose the young girl instead and now he'll have to live with that choice for a very long time, maybe forever. When Traian got him out of prison, Yuri realized prison wasn't even the worst of it, or the fear of what the girl's father might have done to him (don't trust anyone, never let down your guard). You fritter ten years away in prison, your wife and children waiting for you, visiting you, they spend time with your brothers, sisters-in-law, for ten years they're still part of your family, they prepare the house to welcome you back. What's so bad is the word that articulates why you are in that prison. Abuse. Rape of a minor. Words are what carry poison. The length of time separating you from your wife is inscribed in the word itself, and that's a lot longer than any jail time. You say: rape, abuse; you say: minor, yes; he did it. And that's it. Nothing can be fixed. Yelena, his wife, heard the words and now she thinks it's best that her two boys don't know who their father is. Or her daughter, Maika, little Maika, whom he barely even knows (she was still in diapers when he left), the boys recognize him, they ask about him, but they'll never see him again, Piotr, and especially Ivan, the one who looks like him, his same cheeks, his feet, his hands, like a little template, the shape of his fingers, his fingernails, the color of his skin, but what really stings is Maika, whom he left when she hadn't yet started to speak, and whose voice he'd like to hear if only once and not over the phone or in a tape recording. Maika will never exist for him, she was just a little lump in diapers, two vaguely familiar clear eyes that reminded him of his own when he looks in the mirror, reminded him of his wife when he thinks about her at night. She'll never exist. Yelena will tell the children: your dad took off, he left for good, he's in heaven with the angels; or probably, he's in a garbage can somewhere with empty coke cans, cardboard, and empty milk cartons, he's not coming back. People don't go looking for souls that are roasting in hell. Mama and Maika don't want to see him again. Mama will find someone else for Maika, a good papa who'll never leave, never push young girls behind shrubs. Sometimes Yuri is certain he'll never see his kids again, but other times he asks Traian to help him bring them to Spain, like he helped him get out of jail. But what's he going to do with three kids in this chalet where he fucks Irina, this chalet where there's coke on the tables and pistols in holsters hanging on hooks. He thinks he wouldn't like Maika to be with Irina. Yuri overhears Traian talking and remains pensive (who isn't aware of death? It's a universal calling). He thinks Irina doesn't know what happened in Italy, doesn't know that Yuri owes everything to Traian, who got him out of prison where he would have rotted to death, where the hired men could have put the hit on him. But Traian spilled it all to Irina and that's why she's messing around with him now, acting like she has no idea about what Traian told her. She knows that if you laze around the pool, flaunt yourself around the house in panties, he'll come; so, the first time they were alone in the chalet, despite it being midwinter, she wore a teeny-weeny sweater that barely reached her belly button to show off her piercing. The metal of it sparkled like the metal of a hook gleaming underwater. She showed it to him that day, do you like it?, she asks, and just like that—as she expected—he's entranced by her piercing, he asks about the one near her belly button, and the one in her nose, how did you get them? Hurt, it must have hurt, don't tell me it didn't, where did they hurt you, which salon was it, where did they hurt my girl? That night he tells her his wife left him, there are no children to look after anymore, you're my only girl now. I have to make sure nobody hurts you now (she also gives up a few details of her past), where did they hurt you, where did they hurt my little girl? Oh baby, let me take some of that pain away, let me lick it softly, stroke it to ease what those nasty people did, how could they, you say you wanted them to? Are you saying you asked for it? And paid them to do it? You weren't scared of getting hurt? What about me, how are you going to pay me to make the pain go away, stop the hurting? They hurt you, I fix you up. It'll be our secret, I'll be your doctor, your sugar daddy, what you never had (she told him she'd never known her father; and this excited him even more, desire and misfortune go hand in hand), show me, show me where those sons of bitches pierced you, and like this, with the tip of my finger I'll cure you, with my breath I'll cure you, with my lips I'll cure you, I'll cure you with my saliva, with my tongue, your daddy, your doctor. What about Traian, does he hurt you? He pierces you too, like all the guys in the club. All those people, all the people coming and going, you're my little girl, neither you nor I has to do this, can't you see we're living in paradise? Paradise is that place on the outskirts, that place where nobody else goes, over there, in the corner, you can see it if you want: that spot in the garden where nobody ever wanders, over there by the oleander, that's paradise, and this bed, that now, this very instant, is both of ours, is paradise too, the hours we spend together and it's both of ours, you and me alone, it's paradise, and especially now that I'm inside of you about to come, it's paradise (from inside herself she emits waves of pleasure that he receives, that occupy the lummox's entire body, causing him to moan and tremble and gasp, paradise), haven't you noticed? Then come the rest, the boss and everyone else, and it's hell, a pigsty, they put their dirty hands on the glasses, the mugs, the frying pan, they walk all over the tiles, put their paws on you, the boss touches you and it's me who has to clean you up later, come on, let's get you cleaned up, let's clean up together, let me soap you up, there, let me see (he sticks his finger in, moves it back and forth). Irina likes playing with Yuri. It's like playing with those little cars that kids like so much, a remote-control car that moves forward when you press a little button, you press it again and it stops on the spot with the sound of screeching rubber. Who doesn't like having a toy, a little animal who obeys you? Yeah, the boss comes by in the afternoon for a roll in the hay, and Irina knows Yuri listens to them, she knows her little animal is suffering and she gets a kick out of it. They talk, and Yuri hears her voice. They're fucking and he hears them moaning, gasping. He hears the banging of the box springs, five minutes of the same noise, then it stops, only to start up again a little while later, a syncopated rhythm telling him things he can't stand to hear. That's hell for him: a place that belongs to other people but is his secret spot too, something hidden, something unbearable inside of him, the noise he makes while fucking you is the hell that I'm burning up in, he says, because the sound lingers, I keep hearing it long afterward, and I hear it in bursts throughout the day, at any moment, when I'm showering, when I'm grilling meat, you can't imagine little girl (grab the cheeks of her ass in his hands, lift it up high and then let it fall, impaling her over and over again: little Irina), you don't notice how they soil everything, you don't notice how clean you and I are, in heaven, and they come to fill us with their garbage. Let's see, show me what they did to you again, how they pierced you, made a hole in you and then stuck it into you, my poor little girl, how could you know what you were asking them to do, they broke it, you know, they broke your skin, they pierced you, they stuck it into you, they hurt you, it's always bad when things get inside, it hurts, show it to me, that's it, what is it, a sapphire, a ruby, tell me what it is, not that it really matters but I want to know the name of what you carry with you, what goes to bed with you, wakes up with you, if it's a red ruby, if it's a blue sapphire, a green emerald, or aquamarine, it could be an aquamarine, things aren't always what they seem because, just imagine, you're the cat and I'm the mouse, and a big one at that, oh yeah, yeah, a hundred kilos plus, but a mouse all the same. Feel my arm, squeeze it, squeeze my biceps, tickle my belly, slide your hand across it, eat me like the cat eats the mouse; lower, slip your hand lower still, but you move your little paw toward me and I scurry here and there and hide so you can't hurt me, I'm in my mouse's den, in my room, a hole in my cheese, and I hear you, I can hear you at night, now he's in, now he's out, and you scratch me, and you hurt me, you hurt me from a distance, I'm on the other side of the house but I can't stand it and walk past the closed door separating me from the bedroom where you're lying with the boss. Your fingernails are sharp, you're playing with me, you moan, you know I'm listening; you gasp and know I'm listening, you make the bedsprings squeak knowing I'm behind the door, looming, I want to hear the bad kitty meowing, because you're such a bad kitty, when he comes the little mouse shudders and he wants to die, he asks kitty to eat him up again, once and for fucking all, make him disappear, swallowed in a single bite, tongue on the sapphire, the aquamarine, the ruby, let me lick it, and me between your teeth, my tongue between your teeth, who did this, who punctured you like that, why did you want that guy to puncture you, oh, but I can't, me, I stroke you, I lick you, slowly I bite, gently, you'll let me nibble you now, won't you?, like this, yes, like this, not a person, but an animal weighing a hundred kilos, licking and moaning, who's crying because it wasn't him, he wasn't the beast who pierced you. Irina, I feel like crying. Poor beast, have you ever heard of an animal that can cry? No, there are none. Same as there's no animal that worries about its future, no animal that cries over its past. It's true, there are none. All I want is to hear you say the name of the person who goes to bed with you and wakes up with you: because hearing it makes me hard. Suck, bite, eat, embrace. He could strangle her if he wanted to, break every bone in her body, and yet it's she who is breaking him, who squeezes and drains him. You've taken every last drop out of me, he tells her when they finish. They're lying on the sofa. The sound of the television can be heard in the background. He'd entered her, he'd been inside of her, felt the heat and suppleness moving her in waves, and now Yuri is tired and brooding. He's so sullen that he doesn't even process the images on the television, instead he sees landscapes, icons, birches, cupolas like golden onions, trunks of trees swept along the Neva among pieces of ice, bleak, black tree trunks being carried nowhere, gusts of wind driving snowflakes into the faces of garden statues in Petrodvorets, of the sphinxes lying along the quays of the Neva. Shards of ice pummel the wild ducks fleeing south, fling shimmering sparks against the bronze cavalier. Yuri's thoughts drift back to his wife and three kids. He thinks about Yelena, his wife; and especially Piotr, Ivan, little Maika whom he doesn't know (he saw her as a newborn) and may never see again. She'll always be a little doll to him, with transparent skin and eyes like little glass marbles, something you can hold in one hand, in the palm of his hand, a face peering at him from a newborn's photo. A piece of colored paper. She'll never be anything. She can't be anything else to him, he forfeited seeing her incarnate, seeing what her little hands and little feet would look like. He'd like to lie down on a reindeer skin beside the ceramic stove, rest the samovar atop the fire and watch the glass mist up from the tea and mingle with the smoke of the cigarette he just lit up, whose pungent odor prickles his nose. He doesn't imagine his house as it really was—a flat in an unremarkable Saint Petersburg neighborhood—but the way Russian houses are depicted in Western movies, not his real house, with its grubby, timeworn staircase that groans underfoot, a third-floor apartment with an ugly door showing locks that have been changed several times and other new ones added, a living room full of rugs bought in the Gostiny Dvor warehouse, an outdated television set, Finnish furniture he'd acquired thanks to the jobs he did for his previous boss, new furniture that doesn't match the rest of the dingy flat. We'll be out of here soon, he told Yelena. Then he left and now he can't ever go back. Now he's thinking about traveling even farther away (always parting, keep on parting, will there ever be a place to stay?), run away with Irina, forget about Saint Petersburg, those flowerpots his wife placed on the other side of the double-paned windows, the heat of the stove; forget the melancholy of the wooden *izba* houses, the birch forests that always show up in Western movies set in Russia. The bad thing about this journey is that it'll only last as long as Traian wants it to. A couple of days. He thinks: Nobody can escape destiny. Exciting days to come, he tells himself, because he's going to enjoy what Irina doesn't know yet, that he's already done what they'd agreed to do some day; Yuri emptied out the safe in the garden, the one Traian never opens, and cleaned it out late last night. It tickles him to imagine the look on her face when he orders a pricey bottle of wine in a restaurant on their trip, or makes reservations in classy hotels. That's why he's smoking now, grinning while she's getting dressed—Traian should be back at any moment. But he's feeling lazy, doesn't like the idea of getting up and getting dressed. He slips his jeans on without underwear, like he's still ready for her. It's normal to wear jean shorts with no underwear in the summertime, exposed flesh, maybe a Speedo. Who cares anyway? He's ready for Irina. She slips into the bathroom. He can hear her in there, moving bottles and cosmetics around. An old cabaret scene comes on TV, the audience hanging over bannisters. Spectators converse, laugh, drink; they watch the girls exposing their backs and shoulders, little bobbed haircuts giving the napes of their necks a wounding simplicity. The girls fan themselves with massive feathers, they wiggle. We see close-ups of their faces, fleshy necks cut by the perfect line of their coifs. The beads, the glinting baubles, all draw attention to the perturbing presence of breasts, and instead of concealing them they only announce their nakedness beneath all the gleam and glitter, the eyes of the sweaty audience dripping with desire. The sequence continues in the suffocating, smoke-filled atmosphere. Perspiring characters mingle among tables. The women are smoking, sitting at the tables with the men, introducing long cigarette holders into half-opened lips, dark lips, elastic, like black latex. Yuri notices how detached their gazes are, how unconcerned with what's happening on stage, and suddenly he feels out of sorts. Everything on the television screen seems indecipherable. He rouses himself and heads to the kitchen where he slices off two pieces of meat and throws them on the grill till they're charred. Raw meat makes him sick; he likes to eat what the boss—who likes his steak well-done, not a drop of blood—calls shoe soles, burnt rubber, Yuri can't stand blood in his steak, what can you say, not even the pink of medium. Why on earth would the boss leave him alone with Irina, he wonders, and expect him not to touch her, it's impossible, impossible not to touch her, even knowing that touching her could bring consequences he does well not to imagine, and she saunters into the kitchen for breakfast in her panties and she does all that breathing at night, tossing and turning in bed: the chalet is not small but if you're not careful you can hear everything, and if you can't sleep you're forced to hear the boss penetrating her, he knows her sounds, her moans. Yuri complains: I don't know how to see things differently, turn them around like he does. You tell him something is this way and he says, oh, so you mean it's that way, and somehow, he sees it all and figures it out and knows why so-and-so did this and not that. Traian says his maternal grandfather was Romanian, a Romanian railroad engineer who escaped into the USSR in 1922 to become a train conductor. He was a true Bolshevik. Back then calling someone a Bolshevik meant he was a straight shooter, fair, honest. The times of the revolution. Today we live in the times of the economy. Traian told us his grandfather used to say that Romanian people are nothing but deadbeat men and raped women. He says: Nowadays the Spaniards fuck them on the sides of highways. But that's nothing new. My dad reminded me of what my grandfather used to say. He said: The Germans have invaded us twice, the Russians, who hasn't vanquished us, who hasn't raped our women. Romania is a corridor through which half of Europe has passed, half of Europe has raped, squatted, and fucked us, shat on us: Greeks, Romans (Trajan and Aurelian were there. Why do you think my grandfather named my father Traian, and why did I inherit the name?), the Goths, the Huns (I don't know if Attila or some relative of his), Mongols, Teutons, Hungarians, Germans, Russians. And yet, my grandfather used to say: Bucharest is beautiful, it has boulevards, not great monuments but gardens on the banks of the Dâmbovița River, a little Paris, a Paris that's a little colder, sultrier, but it could have been more welcoming than Paris, kinder, with its turn-of-the-century houses and parks. I visited it thirty years later. I found it to be a decrepit city, populated with a mixture of ghosts and beggars. You ever been to Bucharest? While Traian spoke, Yuri lost the thread of the conversation. He doesn't understand. My poor grandfather, Traian continues, an engineer of the revolution. He said his soul was red, but no, he hadn't read his Marx properly. We don't have a soul, not even a white one, or red, or black, or brownish-gray or blue, we're like trout, beings without a soul, cold, no light illuminating from within, heating us from inside, we devour each other because we don't have a soul. We swallow each other, same as we swallow trout. Human beings converse and con, work and destroy, but curiously we have no soul. Humans live for a time, produce whatever, then we die. Statistics, that's what we are, monetary value, like fish, like trees, or poultry. Irina hears Traian and laughs. And that laugh takes her away from Traian and back to Yuri. He tries to remember the terrified Irina, remember feeling her saliva or her tears, hot, wet through the fabric of her shirt, his mouth rubbing against her ear as she sobs. Not now, though. Never when Traian is home. Now Traian is drenched in sweat, walking across the yard beneath the already scorching midmorning sun, his white shirt unbuttoned, his chest smooth as a tabletop, his sleeves rolled sloppily above the elbows, his thin, sinewy arms. Traian is slender, with a shock of yellowy-reddish hair that falls over his forehead, he looks like one of those images in a medical textbook, the kind where the person is in movement with one foot forward, one arm bent, but with his skin peeled back: there are only tendons and muscles showing; while Irina, standing under a ray of sunlight filtering through the window in the hall, looks like one of those figures you think on first impression are made of bone, or ivory, but you realize they're made of a phosphorescent substance that when the lights are turned off will glow in the dark, greenish blue. Nikolái, who had been rummaging in

Traian's car, lies down on the sofa to watch an action flick. He's dog-tired, he's been going for fifty hours without a rest (it was a very long party, he said to Yuri laughing), and mutes the television. No need for sound. He doesn't speak Spanish. Just the actors running from one place to another, carrying weapons of all possible calibers. He thinks about America, he thinks how good the stylists are in Hollywood. Real stage sets, first-rate ones, realistic, it's as if you were there, as if you were in San Francisco, in New York, in Chicago during the twenties; that's what he thinks, though he's never been there. He'd like to get a visa and hang out there for a while, the center of it all, where the turbulent river of money flows for real, wander the streets of New York, climb to the top of the skyscrapers, even cross the grimy bridges, travel in the shadow of those huge cement octopuses where tens of lanes crisscross each other and separate beside the dark water of the ports, water filled with bobbing beer cans and floating bits of rotten wood; store things in huge merchant warehouses, empty, abandoned hangars; but he wants to see the weapons more than anything, the perfect reproductions of movie weapons, or real ones, whose brands he knows instantly, and pronounces under his breath while watching the television: some he recognizes because he's seen them in person, even held them; others he's only seen in gun magazines. He watches television while Traian talks with Irina. Yuri went into his room and shut the door. Now Yuri knows he doesn't have her. She belongs to Traian. He closes his eyes and pictures the golden cupolas, the tame water of the canals, the Neva that rolls forward, looking for the sea. He pictures her, a frozen well. For however much he looks at the bluish well of ice, he can't see anything. Emptiness. A dark, hollow cave. Her eyes, like question marks. The seaside chalet, the sound of roaring waves, the breaking tide, coming in through the window all night long, hasn't allowed him to rest. People say the sound of waves is relaxing, but it's not true, it's a sound that drives insomnia, agitating, a stimulant that sharpens nervous tension. Locked in his bedroom now, Yuri can hear them talking, but he can't understand what they're saying and it mortifies him, it forces him to remember that he doesn't have Irina; he hates her now nearly as much as he desires her. He sees her as one of the women in the movie on TV, not the girls bouncing around on stage but the ones escorting the sweaty men, a cigarette holder clasped between latex lips, eyes lost, staring into the distance. There's the ache again, the pressure in his chest. The more you put out, Yuri thinks, the less she seems to need you, the more you give, the less use she has for what you've given. Receiving becomes a daily habit, no longer meaningful. Grab her attention, make her look at you again. Enter her. Children find that strange, and scary: one person entering another, you see, Irina? It's a terrible thing to be inside another person. The thought of it is scary, so scary you want to keep on trying, over and over, just to figure out how it can be done. We're made like that, to keep trying over and over again, so tell me, Yuri, what else can be done with human material, what else to do if we're made of bones, of flesh, of blood coursing and building to an almost unbearable tension that can only be relieved inside of her? Irina likes having a man inside, the moment a man discovers the full charge of pleasure she holds inside of her (boundless sensations, seemingly identical, but never the same), that's when you have them in the palm of your hand, when you drive the little toy car, command the dog, push the mechanism of the music box to hear the melody, push it again to turn it off, and turn it back on whenever you want, knowing you're making them do things they'd never imagined. Yuri would never have considered abandoning Traian, he'd never have thought of emptying the safe hidden in the yard, but yesterday he and Irina opened it to see what was there, and last night, in the small hours while Irina was sleeping, he emptied it out.

TIME TO call Collado. Time to say: Tell me about it, what happened to you, explain it to me, you got in a fight with someone, went on a bender, dropped a lit cigarette somewhere inside the car and the seats caught fire, you passed out in the car, drunk, dropped your cigarette, is that it? Don't tell me you're mixed up in anything, right? The car, the torched car, that's the least of it, the insurance will cover that; and if it doesn't, you scrape your pockets. The important thing is you, that you're okay, wounded, I know, I read it in the newspaper, heard it on the radio, but it's nothing serious, the radio never said it was serious, is that true? You got lucky inside that burning car, thank God, just forget about it and count your blessings, miracles like that don't happen every day, nowadays they just don't happen at all. The police aren't going to lift a finger, they'll write a report and that'll be the end of it, too busy to launch a full investigation of some guy whose car got torched in a field beside a brothel, that's drunk shit, people who can't hold their liquor, turn into vinegar when they drink wine. Hundreds of thousands of them in this country, violent types, some asshole goes ballistic over a whore telling him he doesn't know how to fuck, that she can't find his dick; let her know when he's stuck it in because she couldn't tell herself, she'll just keep on filing her nails. Bitches. Catch one in a bad mood when she's with some insecure creep and she'll curl his ears till he loses it, first they charge him, then they drive him nuts. I'm stuck in traffic now, I'll tune in to the next newscast, see if they've found anything else out, but they won't, what are they going to say, it's just one more car, just another car among many torched every day. In the capital city, Valencia, they incinerate thirty or forty cars a night. Here in

Misent it happens every once in a while, mostly on the weekends, when the drunk kids start daring each other, except this time the car came with a drunk sleeping inside and it nearly caused a tragedy. That's what they'll report, or maybe that you were arguing with someone, and they waited for you at the door looking to get revenge, to teach you a lesson, some drunkards' squabble. Nobody loses sleep over stories like that, or opens an investigation. I'll call you back later this afternoon. Right now I have to get myself out of this traffic jam, turn left as soon as I can to catch the other highway exit. Access to Misent is the same as every day: impossible. Moving the offices outside the city to the chalet in Las Villas was a great idea. Now I can avoid going downtown, which is always congested, more chaotic with each passing day, you can't move around even on the coldest days of winter. I look at my watch. Already past ten thirty. I should turn on my cell phone to see if the hospital called, if there's another call from my daughter or my brother's ex-wives. No. If I connect it, all the work calls will start coming through. I wonder if his body is still there in the hospital, or if they've already transported it to the mortuary. I should've gone by reception to find out. I still can. If I take Avenida Neptuno I can get to the hospital in a few minutes (in Misent, the new streets have nautical names, of marine gods, fish, seas and oceans, birds, or flowers: the kitschy, meaningless street map of a tourist city). If I swing by the hospital, I could make it in and out in a little over half an hour, allow myself to be seen by the widows, check in to see how the funeral parlor staff has prepared the cadaver. But that would be in the best-case scenario where everything worked, not in the middle of tourist season. What're the chances of actually finding a parking space close to the hospital at the end of July? Even if he finds a spot somewhere, he'll have to walk an extra ten or fifteen minutes under the blazing sun. No, not now. I'll head straight to the mortuary a little later, when I'm sure the cadaver is there. It's all the same to Matías now. Rest in peace. Anyway, wherever his body is now, all I can do is let myself be seen by the others. And I really don't care much about the others (the two widows, some friends of Matías who've come down from the village: though I doubt it, nobody's come to visit him these past couple of days), didn't care about them when Matías was alive, either. What do I care if Angela and Lucía see me, or my daughter knows I'd stopped in for a minute, I mean, my daughter won't be there, either. She had to bring her son to the airport and won't be back until the afternoon. But it comes down to something else: visiting a dead brother for the last time, a theme of classic nobility, supreme test of a conscience, especially in such a small family as ours, Matías, my only brother, the little one, who should have survived me if life had followed the rules. Like it or not, I carry him with me, always by my side, he's in the car with me, surrounding me, touching my hands holding the steering wheel, stroking my face, perched atop my head, entering it. The dead brother takes shelter inside, he occupies my body, my breathing feeds him, so does my blood, inside this air-conditioned car. There's a flash of the old days inside the car, a glint that flashes over a cadaver's back: the smell of kitchens, closets, plants; the sunlight of childhood that's always glistening, another joy, the toys (why do the voices from childhood as the poets have described it always come to us in a hollow echo?). The death of a brother brings all of these feelings. I turn at the last roundabout before the long stretch leading to the highway, but I'm discouraged to find this road packed with cars, too. I turn sharply to the right, looking for a shortcut, a way out. The hospital is on the other side, I can see it through the car window, over there at the foot of the mountain. I caught a glimpse of it for just a few seconds, but then it vanished. It's hidden behind orange plantations lining the road and the industrial warehouses under construction. They could be dressing him now, making him up, shaving him. Do they shave the dead? They probably use creams and powders to hide the black hairs of an incipient beard, apparently hair and nails continue to grow for a few days. They used to work on the cadaver in a room behind closed doors, with the family waiting on the other side. Children's morbid curiosity is piqued when a room is closed behind doors: What's going on in there? Tell us what you're doing to Matías? What are you doing to the little one? What are they doing to you on this sunlit morning in Misent, the palm grove powdered with desert dust and looking more like Memphis, not the city where Elvis Presley is buried, but the Memphis of the priests of Anubis, the head of the dog, the chief of the cadaver manipulators, black dog of death? Before, people wanted the details, they were curious about everything taking place, there was a proprietary feeling toward the dead, over their effects, they wanted to know what was being done to the body and what was not, making sure there were no thefts, making sure nobody touched it, as if by touching the body they were taking something away, and now almost the opposite is true, the dead no longer belong to anyone, the relatives look for someone else to take charge, pay someone else to look after the body, they wash their hands of it; the body becomes an object on the last leg of the journey, merchandise; truth is, even before death you begin belonging to nobody: the old man, the old woman, they don't belong to anyone, what we want is someone who will medicate them and clean them up. To the very end. Cleaned, coiffed, shaved. They shaved my grandfather in his bedroom after he died. I was six, maybe seven years old, and I heard one of my uncles tell my father the barber had arrived and was ready to shave him. Ever since, whenever I passed by the neighborhood barbershop, I would imagine that all those men sitting in the chairs were cadavers, their chins pointing up to the ceiling, faces slathered with soapsuds. A barbershop was a place for old people, an antechamber for death, those luminous cloths that would slowly become covered in hair. And the old guys waiting their turn to sit in the barber's chair, they'd tousle my hair, pat the nape of my neck, or pinch my cheek as I walked by. One of them might even draw his face closer with a contorted mouth to give me a kiss. I never understood why my dad let them do that. The barber would put his little machine against my neck, and I'd feel its cold, metallic fingers. With time, the old barbershop became a sort of refuge, with its smell of to-bacco and Floid aftershave, the pleasant heat of damp towels cov-ering the clients' faces. I missed it during my student years in Madrid, and whenever I was home on vacation I made time for a relaxing shave there, eyes closed, warm towels and the smell of Floid. I wonder if they'll shave Matías, if they've shaved him al-ready. I witnessed my brother's agony yesterday, strung up with tubes the doctors said wouldn't help him regain consciousness: unshaven, consumed by disease, Matías looked at least a hundred years old, the little brother who put more kilometers in the body that luck assigned to him than I have put into mine. He may not have been blessed with a long cycle, but you can't say that life wasn't gracious to Matías. To die in his early sixties. To have lived sixty-some years. That's not so bad when you keep in mind that Europe has been through two continental wars and another cou-ple of national ones in the twentieth century alone, fifty or sixty million human beings perished in them, victims of shrapnel, tor-ture, and the viruses spread by war en masse. Sixty years is a pretty acceptable age for death, even for a twentieth-century man. In all the documented millennia of Spanish history, my generation is the fortunate one, the first not to participate in a war. I was grazed by war, caught a glimpse of it as it passed by. My father told me stories of bombs blowing the warehouses to bits in Misent's port during the Civil War: I never stopped talking about it, my father told me once, not so that you wouldn't be afraid, but because talking about it nonstop helped me exorcise my own fear. You'd rest your little face against my chest and close your eyes. I don't remember any of it. Only the things he told me about. The fleeing, the deafening noises, the explosions: all of that was forgotten. My face against my father's white shirt, that I do remember. It's one of my childhood memories. His white shirt, the smell of his cologne. Curiously, I don't remember my mother's breast, I don't ever remember being near it. Paradoxes. In people's biographies, in novels, one reads how the coddling chest is the maternal one, it's the heat of your mother's lap that stays with you, the warmth of your mother's breast; literature is full of stories about suffering mothers, authoritarian fathers, the melancholy of the mother's lap. When I look back, I realize it's the exact opposite of what I remember. Matías never experienced any of that: the fleeing, the explosions, my mother ceaselessly fingering the beads of her rosary and murmuring, all of us huddled with the maids and gardeners in the basement of the house in Pinar. He was born half a dozen years after the end of the bombings and died without ever having experienced war. He only saw it in the movies, in the newspaper, on television. He who so fervently studied the world wars in history books, who ranted on and on about armed conflict and revolution, who years later confessed he'd even hidden a few pistols and supplies to make a bomb at home during the Franco years; he who was prepared to take up the armed struggle, died without knowing the trauma of war. Not bad. *Beatus ille*. A privileged generation. We've experienced times of unrivaled progress and usually can't seem to figure out what to do with these offerings. If we haven't reached full happiness, surely, it's because human beings just don't have it in them. I glance sidelong at the car phone. Still no new messages, aside from the one Silvia left early this morning. I turn it off again. The widows silently control the vagaries of the funeral cortege moving from the hospital to the mortuary. They called ten days ago to let us know that given the state of Matías's health, they would remain in Misent, and Matías's two ex-wives (the second one really an ex-lover: he never married her) showed up together to see the dying man like two board members on the eve of a company's bankruptcy, their business in ruins, holding wake together over the severance package of a corporation in which they'd consecutively invested. Angela and Lucía, in that order, had dealt with Matías's mood swings, his egocentric nature made worse by being a bad drunk. Now they want to know how the last chapter ends in the book of a life in whose pages they've played supporting roles. They hadn't been able to locate Ernesto, Angela and Matías's son. He's off gallivanting somewhere in the US or in Mexico. He left twenty days ago on a two-month trip and has only called his mother once the whole time. I'll tell you all about it another time, this hotel's phone line costs a fortune, he told her. He called from New Orleans and by then he'd already passed through a bunch of cities on the East Coast: New York, Washington, Chicago, Boston. I don't understand why you want to see so many places in such a short period of time, but Ernesto told his mother he'd enjoyed traipsing around the cities on foot (*sic*: traipsing on foot. Silvia had a chuckle over the cheesiness of walking around cities that are built for vehicles and driving around cities built for walking. Silvia doesn't like Ernesto either, obviously). He was en route to California, the Mojave Desert with its monotonous extensions of rocky ground and saguaro cacti like great candelabras and then to Mexico, Guadalajara, Dayefe, Veracruz, Oaxaca, San Cristóbal de las Casas (the last leg of the trip will be harder with all those Zapatistas, Ernesto had said). As Angela read down the list of cities, I was reminded of my own trips to Mexico, even that time I traveled with Collado: images of Tehuantepec, the desolation of Salina Cruz, the empty beach covered with garbage coughed up by the sea, the abandoned port that Porfirio Díaz had built with the grand idea of uniting the Atlantic and Pacific by canal to the north of Panama—some hundreds of kilometers closer than its bigger brother—hoping to revitalize those meager, godforsaken lands, which history shows us remain to this day outside any future development plans. I meandered the muddy streets, little dark-skinned pigs rooting among mountains of garbage; men and women snoozing in the doorways of derelict shanties. Most streets had a gully of wastewater running down the center, the only sewage system. We were waiting for someone to come by plane, by boat, and could never figure out how that fat man actually made it up there for the meeting, the man who gave us cigars in the rickety hotel room with gutted armchairs. Poor Collado's legs were shaking, so were mine, but I tried to conceal it. You're familiar with Mexico, aren't you Uncle? Ernesto asked me before he took off. I cursorily described a few places I'd been to there, thinking the boy is clearly not going to learn the same things I did in Mexico. Your Mexico and mine wouldn't recognize each other if they crossed paths on the street, I thought. Though who can ever tell what people might be hiding. The thought brought a pang of melancholy. If only my first trip to Mexico had been more like my nephew's. The image of a magpie pops to mind, a creature that collects shiny objects it won't share, to learn and then to die, and the whole tangle of yarn coming undone in the air. My nephew told us about his long trip, everything measured, calculated, a strict itinerary, all flights and hotels reserved ahead of time, a program planned to the millimeter several months in advance. Ernesto explained: As long as I'm crossing the pond, I might as well take advantage of every minute. At least catch a glimpse of the vastness, the great American diversity. It'll be an inspiring trip, he said. He talked about extreme contrasts, from above to below, from everything to nothing. It was strange for me to hear him speak like that. How can a trip represent such a romantic experience for a raging capitalist like him, so that he sounds like one of those bogus television journalists who sprinkle a few well-chosen words between one toponym and the next, heavy on the syllables, measured stresses, polishing it off with a couple of superlatives? He came over for a few days before he left, a little over a month ago now, in mid-June. We had dinner beside the pool, but eventually had to retreat inside because a chilly, humid northeasterly picked up giving us all goose bumps. How much longer before those cool, perfumed nights are back; shoulders covered with a cardigan or a towel, and we'll say come on, let's go inside, it's getting chilly. Right now there's still a lot of summer left to get through. Matías hadn't been hospitalized yet and nobody expected his end would come so quickly. Ernesto had gone to say goodbye that same afternoon, before taking off. We knew Matías was in bad shape, the cirrhosis, or whatever it was (until a few days ago none of us had a clear idea of what his illness was, I still don't really know: alcoholism, a variety of abuses) would end up taking a toll sooner rather than later, but there were times when he'd seemed to be in even worse shape. When he finally collapsed (his cleaning woman found him lying on the floor) and was brought down to the hospital in Misent, the doctors said it would be a slow and painful demise, so his exes began making arrangements by asking for recommendations from oncologists and pharmacists, stockpiling relief medicines, opiates, whatever could be prescribed these days: probably the same as always, I imagine, morphine in all its variants and derivatives. Things don't change as much as we like to think. When I was little, the women in Misent used to rub *cascajo* on their breasts, the gummy milk from inside wild poppy pods; a bit of opium to help the children sleep peacefully. Once the children were weaned, they'd graduate to a punch made of grape juice and alcohol, with an egg yolk thrown in to boost nutrients while relaxing them as night wore on: maternal milk with opium, alcohol, and protein. Silvia and Matías's exes had argued through all possible strategies, including sedation. Matías deserved a dignified death, he shouldn't have to suffer, everyone agreed on that. The two pre-widows settled in Misent and together with Silvia argued to have him released from the hospital and brought to Benalda, the place he (they claimed) had chosen to die. I'm convinced the opposite was true; that Matías had chosen Benalda to see if it might help him escape death. He planted his trees, rescued the old crops with a view to recovering. If he could build a forest around him, surely death might pass by without seeing him, without noticing him: it would follow the path to somewhere else. Since death had gone looking for him in Baghdad, he headed to Basra. He wanted to die at home, his niece and the pre-widows contended, oblivious to Matías's real motivation. I told them it was unwise to force a trip like that on a terminal patient. He would receive the best of care in the hospital, it's more hygienic I told them, which to my consternation set off a fiery discussion that was perfectly in vain because not even twenty-four hours later a sudden failure of his immune system carried him to the edge of the abyss and forced them to connect him to a machine in intensive care. Shortly thereafter, in the manner of the French poet who, surrounded by a battalion of doctors all arguing about his diagnosis and treatment, asked them to stop arguing over him. I'll get you all to agree with each other right now, the poet said. And he turned around, put his face to the wall, and died. Matías did something similar: just when he seemed to be recovering from the sepsis and the worst of it, an artery or a vein burst.

The doctors explained it to the imminent widows and my daughter. From what I could gather it was a kind of critical inner varicose vein that ruptured, triggering an uncontrollable hemorrhage. They said he wouldn't last the night, and he didn't. Apparently in these cases the patient bleeds to death quickly and inoperably. In the women's assembly that took place after the prognosis, and during which I sat like a deer in the headlights, my daughter and Lucía suggested trying to locate Ernesto in Mexico (he needs to know, they said, it's his father, the death of a father only happens once in a lifetime) and Ernesto's mother went along with the other two, but in fact she preferred to spare her son the harrowing experience, and focused on the inconveniences: Of course he has to come, to be here, but let's just think it through, because maybe, on second thought, no, it'd be better not to. No matter where he is, it'd take him at least four or five days to get back home, and seeking the help of a consulate would be like trying to move Rome via Santiago, impossible. We could never put the ceremony off for that long. And in the end, we'd be ruining a really significant trip for nothing. Silvia, with her perfect talent for being rude, for poking a finger in the sorest wound, insisted on the idea of a son being made aware that his father is dying. I finally jumped in to say the cadaver would have to be cremated within a few hours. It's summer, I said, we're in the middle of a heat wave. So, what exactly are you suggesting? That we deep-freeze him for a week to see if Ernesto shows up before cremating him? I know it happens that way. But it seems more than a little odd to me. I didn't dare to mention that neither Ernesto nor Matías ever seemed to care that much for each other. The boy had always lived with his mother, never spending more than a weekend at a time with Matías, and the few times father and son got together never seemed especially inspiring. Most of them ended up in high-voltage arguments that began the moment the boy had learned how to speak. Never born of an attempt to reach an understanding, but out of perpetual misunderstanding. And if either of them ever exercised decorum it was Ernesto, probably for that simple human need of constructing a personal narrative around family, having a father, a mother, siblings, uncles and aunts, grandparents. Ernesto loved his books by Friedman and Greenspan, all those free traders from the Chicago school: a role-player who liked games that put what he called—condescendingly—his intelligence to the test, his mental agility; binger of internet chats and forums, manga enthusiast and partisan of the triumph of monetarism, none of it fit well into Matías's way of life. In the family zoo, Ernesto "the Cracker" (that's what Matías liked to call him) plays the role of fledgling financial shark. Even as a little boy he bore a certain swimming-pool air; pale, meaty hands, the hue of an aquarium bottom, overall lack of a firm bone structure. He looked like a toy shark, those gummy candy ones, or those kids' bath time playthings made of spongy foam: *Shark*. Ernesto goes around with his laptop hanging from a shoulder, and once he finds an empty chair he whips the computer out onto his knees, connects to Wi-Fi and checks the stocks of who knows what company, sending and receiving urgent emails. Then his fish air morphs into a lumbering avian air: *Hawk*. Truth is he can never just sit still. The night he came over for dinner he kept pacing the garden, inside the house, nerves like a caged beast, jotting things down in the notebooks he kept pulling out of his jacket pocket, dictating numbers to his co-conversationalists. Silvia always said that Matías and Ernesto are irreconcilable. I'm not so sure. If Matías had been born thirty years later, and instead of becoming a despotic Stalinist shipwrecked first on idealism and then on the beach of ecology and a health food obsession that was supposed to save him in the eleventh hour from cirrhosis (faith, it has to do with the mechanisms of faith, positive vibrations Silvia said), he would surely have been—like his son—a free market shark. He would have incubated the eggs of free trade with the same perseverance as forced collectivization. Silvia, I said to my daughter at some point, Ernesto and your beloved uncle are more alike than you think, I would say they're nearly identical, and the reason they can't seem to get along is because they recognize each other at such an intimate level. Character is transmitted genetically, and it adapts to the roles dealt out by the theater of the world at different periods of time. Life practices what we now call *casting*. Life gives you a part that's suited to you in the seasonal play, and if it proves to be the right fit, you're allowed a more or less harmonious existence. It's essential that you're dropped, *plop*, right onto the stage and that the role you're assigned matches your character, your personality, doing this and that, saying this and that, what you're supposed to do, without skipping a beat before the curtain falls, which *oh*, inevitably falls way too soon. If you can't adjust the part to your particular gifts, then the curtain closing turns very bleak: you finish the play like a dizzy duck. Silvia cringes: If people argue so much because they're so alike and they recognize each other in themselves, then that must be our problem, I assume, that we're identical. No. Not at all. You, my love (I could've said my little dove) are a carbon copy of your mother, I say to tease her. And here we are, assembled together to care for Matías who's never bothered to care for anyone but himself. All right, I get the idea of family codes, rules to abide by even despite the worst kind of relationships, it's all theater too, you pretend not to notice how flimsy the props are, the set, you keep on saying your lines and moving around the stage. Fraternity is a state that obliges the fulfillment of drastic codes of representation. Silvia challenged: He wanted to die in Benalda. But as it fucking happens, I answered, he died in Misent. Silvia charged on: He's not dead yet. We can still bring him there. And I replied: Are you out of your mind? Move Matías and while we're at it, the huge contraption he's strung up to. Bringing Matías down here, only to bring him back up, only to bring them both back down here again, yes, both, him and the contraption, only to bring him over to the crematorium in Misent, because if there's one thing he did leave crystal clear, it's that he wanted to be incinerated (or were you thinking of setting him ablaze with a splash of diesel like they do to cadavers in World War II novels?). Silvia made a gesture to show how insensitive a person she already knew that I was. I pretended not to notice and continued saying: He doesn't know anyone up there. Or am I mistaken to think he was lonelier than a dog in Benalda? How many people from Benalda have come to visit the hospital these days? Silvia, sweetheart (here I should have said "my little lettuce" or "my little cucumber"), what's up with the song and dance, why are you twisting everything around, what are you staging with all the moving around? Let the hospital do its job, the mortuary, the professionals. They're in charge of doing whatever needs to be done. Some primitive tribes follow the custom of having friends and relatives eat the dead person. It's not the worst solution. A more contemporary version, and Matías was himself a bit of a prophet here, would be snorting him; mix the ashes with a few grams of coke and feel it blow through your veins, up to your head, through your body until hey there's Matías, squeezing your bowels. Got a better idea? The only one missing from Matías's harem now is Mama, who never had eyes for anyone else, even though it fell entirely onto my shoulders to care for her when her health took a turn and she was no longer able to look after herself. I was forced to get over my hang-ups, rebuild the relationship, once again confront the rules of biology, or the rules of the tribe. For however much it weighs on both of us, she's my mother, I told my wife, who was skeptical about it. I had to find company for her: Colombians, Peruvians, Ecuadorans, keep tabs on her doctor's visits, check in on her at home and make sure she was being well cared for, while Matías slogged on, watching his mountain tomato plants grow from the town bar, dry-farmed tomatoes obtained from the seeds of a local variety on the verge of extinction; olive trees imported from Tuscany that behave extraordinarily well during oilization (that's how he described it); and a few local varieties: Blanqueta, from the Sierra de Espadán, which produces oils of outstanding quality (my plantation is a forerunner, he used to brag, I'm in the vanguard of agriculture—while I was trying to find someone to wipe the old bag's ass); and on his land (let's not dwell on the origins of that property) he conserved the old Marcona almond trees, which the makers of turrón can apparently never get enough of. Beautiful, oh that's just beautiful, I used to tease Silvia, *le vieux marxiste agronomique*, I'd say each time she came by with news from up-mountain, animated by a zeal that seemed ill-suited to her character, which was closer to *morne*, expressionless. Every time Silvia went up to see Matías she'd come down and go on and on about it, the crops, the oil from an Italian variety they would harvest early in November (Matías didn't last long enough to see the first yield), to preserve its fruity aroma, the slightly bitter, piquant taste, preserve the polyphenols. She told me about baking bread in the house's old oven. Is your uncle still up there?, I'd ask, why doesn't he come down for a visit? At least to say hello to his mother. The *vieja* is constantly complaining about it. You should bring Grandma with you the next time you go up. It'd never even occurred to my mother that Matías should be responsible for taking care of her. Matías has always been irresponsible; in the way that the Spanish Constitution defines the Monarch: ("The person of the King is inviolable and shall not be held accountable"). He's not accountable to anyone, doesn't need to prove anything to anyone. I've tried not to let it get to me, I've tried not to get upset or overly frustrated. When a man reaches my age, he forgoes movement except for the respiratory muscles that keep him alive. Retire, sure, retire. I'm seventy-three years old. It's the natural course. But who? Whom do I give it to, who'll inherit everything? Silvia, the expected heir, refuses the gift. Doesn't want it. Never has. Though I prefer not to broach that subject right now. Silvia joined us when Ernesto came over for dinner last time, and she quoted Speer to me, and honestly, you have to be full of spite to do something like that. She compared the development projects here with the ones Hitler's architect, Speer, did, though not for their grand style but for their social function. I joked to Ernesto: When Speer visited the amphitheater in Verona, he realized that if people of different opinions are congregated in a certain space, they can be brought to share one single opinion, and that's precisely the stadium's purpose, to get rid of the individual. Turn it into a mass. Render worthless what one silly individual might think personally, because the only thing that mattered was the opinion issuing in unison from the multitude. The same thing could be said of that kind of condominium architecture you see along the coast with identical buildings. It's got a collective air, a style that could be called, I don't know, retiree or the eternal summer vacationer, as what Georges Brassens wanted to be on Sète beach: a spectral being, alone and blank, insignificant, aspiring to nothing, expecting nothing more than to delay death for as long as possible. A wintry, dangerous being who couldn't care less about the future of anything. Just making the most of those last rays of sun. I poured a little more wine for myself. Don't strike someone, don't turn the other cheek. Don't think about Silvia. Don't think about Matías. They make my blood boil. Matías never had a free moment for those crops to take care of his mother, never arranged his mountain home for her to spend time there, to breathe the air that was supposedly dry and pure and good for congestion and arthritis. She's your mother, and as long as she's alive you have a duty to her. And that duty is not only toward her, but toward yourself, too. Your mother, your sibling, mothers and siblings, they're life problems, you comply with your biography, deal with what you got when you came into the world. Can't leave an empty column in the accounting book, because leaving empty spaces will end up costing you dearly. They're the kind of spaces that fill up with ghosts that haunt you at night and won't let you sleep. I tried explaining it to Monica: It's not that old age brings a family together, into something tight and close, like a pineapple, but it does bring you in, forces you to realize that you're a part of it, a member, head, heart, hands, feet, or dick, whatever, but a part of it. You represent a function of the body, which is something very different from a pineapple, which is a union of equal parts that makes up a piece of fruit. There's nothing fruitful here, but when an old person dies, it awakens the sleeping child in the old person who is still alive, that's how any family works. She mumbled a complaint: I hate it when you go there, the old man routine. I insisted: I am, Monica, I'm an old man. And cutting to the quick: All I can say is Mama will be staying with us for a little while, just till we find someone trustworthy. I don't want to leave her in just anyone's hands, there are so many shady people out there; you read things, so many stories about it on TV: old-age homes where people are kept in squalid conditions, tied up, even beaten; old folks gagged, tortured. Overpriced facilities where on closer look, you see they're more like *Oliver Twist* asylums or prison camps, a bunch of squalid old people shuffling around, the living dead; and employees who smile at the visiting relatives, but the instant you turn your back to leave, their smiles turn into sneers. You can't trust anyone, I said. And so, I didn't, and I brought Doña Teresa home. It wasn't an easy experience. Monica, within a couple of days, waiting for me with an anxious half smile, like a day laborer after a particularly excruciating shift who endured it only for you;

before taking a breath, before I could take off my jacket and hang it on the rack, she explodes: She's driving me nuts, babe. She was hugging me, kissing me, my shirt wet with her tears. I stroked her hair and thought: You wanted to be a part of this family, right? Well, here it is. She stayed with us for three or four months before we found a female caretaker to keep her company in the house in Pinar; no homes or residencies. But I wanted Monica to know that she has certain obligations, that old age brings the family together and that she, if she wants to be a part of it, needs to take the bad with the good: life is about more than just shopping, hanging out with friends, opening a bottle of champagne for two before jumping into bed. I have them, these obligations, because I'm my mother's son, and by extension Monica does, too, because she's married to me. Monica, all sugar: Sure babe, but your brother could step up a little too, he could help out, he's the one who's managed her, the accounts and all that. That's what you said, you told me so, the apple of her eye and everything, you said it's been that way. Sweetheart, you know what Matías is like. He can't even take care of himself, he's barely accountable for his own things, I answered. And all the fuss these days in the hospital has Monica on edge again. The bedside shifts of the pre-widows and a niece, the brother's visits, constant news on moving the patient to die in Benalda, the shocking stockpile of barbiturates to ensure an easy transition. Monica made sure to remind me a few days later: You shouldn't lose your head over Matías, let yourself get so bent out of shape. He never worried about you. Did he bother to visit when you got your pacemaker? Sitting there in the armchair, letting her stroke the nape of my neck, I replied: I know, darling, but how is the brother not going to be there in the first row, when even the abandoned wives show up? Family affairs. When all's said and done, an ex-wife doesn't mean anything, just someone he fucked for a while; someone he bought furniture with to set up a house; it was very poorly explained, and Monica's eyes gave off sparks of anger; and so, to stoke her anger just a little more, I say: And it would be nice if you could spend a little time there, let the family see we aren't abandoning them. There it is, the rage in her gray-blue eyes ready to explode into blinding splinters. But she paid that visit to the hospital. It was the following day and Monica spent a little time in the hospital room looking askance at the patient, she didn't kiss him or greet the imminent widows with a kiss, but there she was, even if her appearance lasted all of five minutes, truth be told. Long enough for me to pass my tongue over my lips, lick myself down like a cat, my authority on display, and more than anything else, to be able to say for as long as I live: My wife was there. After all, the day my mother dies, little Ernesto will be as much an heir as Silvia to the few things that Mama and Mateo leave behind, and when that day comes they'll be forced to sit down and talk, and that's when it'll be time to tell the economic expert: You weren't at her deathbed, you weren't even at your dying father's deathbed, you went off to travel knowing he was dying, but I was there, and so was my daughter, my daughter was there sweating blood, and my wife was there too (there the rival enters the game with a handicap). His conversation with Monica took place four or five days after Matías was admitted to the hospital; by the end of that same week, his exes were holding their wake over the cadaver. The two of them had arrived together, taking advantage of their summer vacation. They drove together in the same car and parked in front of the house, a sorority of ignominy. Talking to Angela beside Matías's bed that afternoon, I couldn't help but reflect on my brother's art of seduction (I call it something else) and his peculiar taste in women—I said as much to Monica: Explain to me what his first wife, Angela, ever saw in Matías, why she put up with his tantrums, and what the fuck is she doing here, all these years later, since they separated just after the

Cracker was born, the one running around the US and Mexico as we speak, her brain must be wedged in her vagina (that must be it: a woman's brain is in her vagina and you have to thrust hard to reach it, and whoever is able to touch it can do with them whatever they want. If not, you know the tune. I read that somewhere, not the bit about touching it, but that it's located there and that women see the world through it), sitting there dabbing the dying man's forehead with a towel, murmuring things to the nurse, holding his hand, asking him if he's feeling okay, does anything hurt, even though he can't respond and surely can't even hear her; and there's even less of a reason for the second one to have shown up, Lucía, who must still be residually affected by the relationship. He made her to move up to the mountain with him only to turn around and send her home like a package in the mail, empty-handed, Lucía coming down to a bar on the beach in Misent to cry on my shoulder and vent about the tribulations of their relationship (I don't know what he wants, it's as if he only gets off by hurting you, as if he were reenacting some kind of trauma, something inexplicable, he's so self-destructive, she sobbed), a sea of tears, but his con didn't work anymore, like he had conned everyone with his big ideas of revolution and adventure, how he must have strung this one along, I can just imagine, freedom for sure, the freedom of being in the mountains, all the Lord's little wild animals, far from civilization, far from the banks, shops, and hospitals, Lord oh Lord what a load of shit, defining even the desire not to sleep alone as "freedom" (and there, there, I console the poor woman: what do you want me to say, Lucía, I see him at Christmas, because it's an obligation. I've had to deal with his chicanery, too. I lent him the money for his tickets when he went to Madrid; and of course, he never bothered to pay me back). Both women have been here for ten days, representing the Descent from the Cross, the Pietà, the Anointing, and the Holy Burial in a hospital room with an air-conditioning unit that blew out like a Boeing turbine ready to take flight (that unit is about to go any second now, Angela had said; like everything else in this shithole hospital where nothing works, Silvia replied); or conjuring classical mythology, that more brazen, more explicit cosmos (far more realistic, though it may appear paradoxical, all those gods breaking bread together, taking long naps on sofas), in the hospital room of a small coastal town, the exes raised the alter, the Ara, for making offerings to Priapus, arrogant, indifferent, self-contained (isn't that the essence of being a Don Juan, that lazy indifference, that being there and not being there?). Matías lying in bed, blind, deaf, and dumb; an absent god clearly the worse for wear, behind a barrage of tubes, bones perfectly outlined beneath his hairy blue skin; beard stubble more yellow than white like a mask across his face, unconscious; the strength of spilt semen. I would have liked to tell Silvia about it, all the spilt semen and saintly women, but I didn't dare: all I did was corroborate once again how little culture matters, how little it serves to sublimate desire and instinct; it's barely capable of camouflaging them, here are two free women, liberated, feminist, cultivated, one a biologist, the other an English professor, and yet both are tangled in an invisible spider's web, tangled in a thread of semen (or maybe the hope of being cited in a will that nobody is sure exists. Nobody dared to ask while he was still semiconscious). Angela called me before arriving in Misent to ask about a place where she and Lucía could stay during his illness. The two of them, Lucía and Angela, together in a hotel, maybe even the same room, sharing a closet, one's skirts and slacks on a hanger beside the skirts and slacks of the other, a little hotel with seaside views, Las Dunas, Costa Nova. Which hotel would you suggest, Angela asked: stretch out in the sand, take a dip, help with the dying man in Virgen de las Rocas Hospital, care for him, caress him, speak softly in case he still comprehends what's being said around him, console him in his eleventh hour should his consciousness not be altogether lost, then take a dip in the Probatic Pool of the Mediterranean, the River Jordan that heals the ravages and wounds of old Europe, return once again to anoint the cadaver in the perfumed words of love. Are you all right? No need to answer; if you can, if you understand me, just squeeze my hand. The two imminent widows waiting, like in the movies, for the cadaver to squeeze a hand to say yes or no. *Philadelphia, Johnny Got His Gun*. Squeeze my hand if you can hear me, if you understand what I'm saying. Maternal, good-hearted women. There are actresses who specialize in these kinds of roles. Forget for a second that marriage is satanically cruel, it exudes a sulfurous scent of private enterprise, which is exactly what it is. Wills, inheritances, separate properties, patrimonies, legitimate, rightful inheritance, communal assets, free disposition of goods, all that lawyer-fertilizing manure. Matías. The cruel political commissioner. Yet here the widows sit, what a fucking talent for seduction he had, still has, still seducing them right up to the extreme unction. The two of them; and others (among his innumerable victims are Juan, my son-in-law; and Brouard, a former friend who ended up as Matías's friend). Even Silvia, always so petulant, so pugnacious you'd think someone had sown cat's claws into her swaddling clothes, and yet with Matías she'd always suspend her critical faculties. Soft as a cotton ball around him. Uncle Matías's stuffed animal. One of the only people I know who is truly free (that's Silvia talking about him). I know, you'll say it's about ghosts, childhood or teenage fetishes. But it's true, Papa. You've never cared about my feelings. I feed you, I pay your tuition, pay for your whims, take you on trips, show you the world, that's what you believed, but things aren't like that. Kids want something else, besides all that, I'd say even more than that. Matías gave me books like *Moby-Dick* when I was little, Verne, Salgari, *Java Jungle Tales*, *Le Petit Nicolas*, *Quo*

Vadis, I don't know, the artillery of sentiment and imagination a kid needs (he gave her *Quo Vadis*, not *Fabiola*; they read Salgari together, not *Little Women*); and as a teenager *Lord Jim*, *Steppenwolf*, *The Razor's Edge*. Uncle Matías's movies: when I was little, *The 5,000 Fingers of Dr. T*, *All the Brothers Were Valiant*, *Around the World in Eighty Days*. All the stories he told me: they're a part of me. They made me who I am, they've accompanied me my whole life. And he gave that to me. Silvia defines it without meaning to: he gave me the artillery I needed of sentiment and imagination. What I gave her—eating, drinking, dressing, studying, traveling; yes, I took you halfway around the world, I told her—is worth less than a few books, a few movies. The human soul is that irrational. The parable of the vineyard in the Bible: just because you've worked the vines from sunrise to sunset doesn't guarantee you'll be the one who takes home all the denarii. How is it, Lord, that you're more generous with the slothful, with the ones who've shown up late and worked half-heartedly. Matías took her to see old movies, from twenty, thirty years ago. Then he bought her a projector. Uncle Matías showed up six times a year, he brought a book, a copy of some old movie (from where is anyone's guess), or brought her to the movie theater, and that's all it took, *voilà* the girl's education. And she's coveted them her entire life. Matías had the pirate's natural inclination for pillaging, and the talent for brainwashing his comrades, a strong concoction, stimulating, a Molotov cocktail. Koestler or Solzhenitsyn both talk about a variety of this in their novels: *Darkness at Noon*, *The Gulag Archipelago*. The tough Soviet brainwashing, the Chekas. Pol Pot's parentless children. Stockholm Syndrome, as they call it today. A lie repeated a thousand times over. One swallowed it or else. Inspector Matías's books, movies, toys, brainwashing his little niece, the Meccano sets, the puzzles that became the Kremlin domes when finished, or Che's face or Lenin on a dais with his fist held high, waving a red flag, the Soviet stamp albums, the Chinese and Albanian ones, Mao Zedong Ho Chi Minh Enver Hoxha Kim Il-sung, and Silvia asking me a few days ago if I remember the little sailboat Uncle Matías gave her, if the boat is still around somewhere; surely it has to be, up in the attic in some box, maybe an armoire; she remembers having put it in the attic herself, maybe we should ask the girl who comes to clean to look for it, because she wants to recover it, restore it, as a sort of posthumous homage to Matías, put it in a showcase, another lay altar. It was such a nice boat, everything was so carefully reproduced, so lifelike, it opened and had perfectly furnished cabins, the boiler room, the hold with little sacks of coffee, everything reproduced to the millimeter; as if Uncle Matías had ever had anything to do with the merchant marine, with the long journeys narrated in the books he gave her and the movies they went to see, him, Matías, who knew nothing beyond the bar scene of Madrid (he studied literature without ever leaving the bar), drinking holes, pubs, and cafés where people talked about war, colonial armies of occupation and popular guerrilla forces, may a hundred flowers blossom, blossom and erupt into a thousand Vietnams: in Colombia, Bolivia (little Bolivian soldier, little Bolivian soldier, armed with your gun, your American gun, a gift from Mister Nixon to kill your brother), Angola, the streets of Madrid while we polish off what's left of the gin. Bring on the descendants of Túpac Amaru and let them finish us off, but pour me another please, will you; the descendants of Spartacus, the sons of Patrice Lumumba, the grandchildren of the slaves who cut sugarcane and harvested cotton in Saint-Domingue and Louisiana, on the rocks please; come on Malcolm X and Soledad Brothers and pour me another one, yeah, I said on the rocks because the tonic is warm, before shooting a few bullets into our hides; bring on Ho Chi Minh, Che Guevara, all of them aboard Matías's sailboat, peering out the portholes, lying in the perfect miniature replicas of bunks, lounging on those little sacks that really do look as though they were full of coffee. Welcome, all of you, the doors are wide open. Come on in, come on in. Jaume Sisa sang it in Catalan in the seventies: *Oh, benvinguts, passeu, passeu, la casa meva és casa vostra*, though Sisa knew to surround himself with a less troubled crowd: Cinderella, Snow White, Peter Pan. Oh what the fuck. Let 'em all in. Come on. We've been waiting an eternity. Make yourselves comfy, take a load off, here's a free recliner. Matías threw the doors open wide, straight into the living room. When death came looking for him in Baghdad, the coward fled to Basra. Imagine, I was just on my way to Baghdad looking for you, death said. Or was it the other way around, or perhaps not like that at all. I'm not sure, I don't really remember how that story goes. Just the idea that if you run away from death in Baghdad, you'll come face-to-face with death in Basra. For fuck's sake, when's the fucking light going to turn green already? My Silvia (mine?), cat claws, shanghaied, trapped in the spider's web, using teenage tricks to substitute the grisly truth that keeps the spider from snaring her and sucking out her juices: the great ideas, the abstract assertions, they're all fine, and even better when they're lavish, but one has to appreciate the details, my child, I would tell her; it's in the details that everything gets thorny, it gets away from you, won't bite your hook no matter how closely you try to follow the instructions that are in that fishing manual you bought, which bait to use, how much line to let out, where to place the sinkers and buoys to catch your fish, and you get to the beach, take out your rod, and not a single bite all day. That's life. Irregular, arbitrary. Nothing is free of that inconvenience because it's the essence of what is real. Lines in front of the ticket window, quarrels with cab drivers, with bus drivers, long waits in the airports: details are a part of the trip, not accidents of the trip, they're the trip itself. The toy sailboat won't carry you anywhere, just a cruise around the inside of your head.

My yacht will. It will drop you off at the foot of a Greek temple in Sicily and the coves of Ibiza, whose water is blue as Chinese ink, like the Caribbean. Though you'll have to make a little effort yourself, even the most luxurious yacht requires certain inconveniences. The rest are hiding places. Your Uncle Matías doesn't get it, Silvia, the only thing he has to offer is virtual adventures, I told her on more than one occasion. Her latest answer was that Uncle Matías worked the land and there was nothing *virtual* about land. She would defend him, she always defended him: the crops, the fruit, the marmalades, the bread, they're all material things that can be touched, she said, things that have to be made, the fruits of labor. His vineyards don't die, his olive trees don't die, she said, which is the result of his efforts (vines and olives are resistant crops, the county has thousand-year-old olive trees that nobody wastes too much time on, I teased, they've survived everything). Coming to reasonable terms should be an easy thing, but nobody's ever been capable of it in my family. Not today, not thirty years ago: always the ghost of the incredible hovering around, muddling things. During Silvia's difficult teenage years, Matías seemed bent on further destabilizing a confused girl's sentimental drifting. It was a decisive moment in our relationship: I don't understand all the malaise, Silvia, you're twenty years old, where is all this coming from? What is it that you hold against me? What we wanted was to fight—your uncle, Brouard, me, so many of us—against the dictatorship, each in his own way, and not so much a political system; we fought against a closed society more than anything else, I'd say, a prudish and suffocating society that wouldn't let us breathe. But I don't follow you. You say you hate our lifestyles, but can you show me another one we could have lived? It's fine for you to escape reality by jumping down whatever rabbit hole you come across. Reality is always a hassle. But next time you're about to jump down that hole, consider that it might lead somewhere even worse: dirty pans, rotten food in the fridge, cockroaches skittering beside the plate where they're serving your lobster. That's what you'll find underneath all of it, if you insist on going into the kitchen instead of sitting at the table and eating in peace. It's better to enjoy dinner and not worry too much about the ingredients. Silvia had just returned from spending a few days with Matías in Madrid, and made up her mind to leave the French School, to leave Misent altogether. So, what do you want to do? Everyone has to do something in life, plan for some kind of future. Go back to Madrid with your Uncle? And do what, exactly? But she didn't want to do that, either. Sweetheart, Matías goes hunting for freedom by night, in the bars of Madrid, into the wee hours. But freedom doesn't dwell in those kinds of places, Silvita (Papa, stop calling me Silvita!), and it doesn't keep those kinds of hours. For however odd it may seem to you, for however much you don't want to believe it, freedom tucks in early and sleeps a full and uninterrupted eight hours. Freedom is having a job you like that allows the kind of lifestyle you want. Our business is what guarantees your freedom. Have you ever thought to calculate the impossibility of things without it, the traveling to see what we've seen together, learn what you've learned, read what you've read? At that time, Matías had already split from one continent and not yet arrived at the other, he was adrift on the high seas. He was nearing the end of the phase of life that's like a high-risk occupation, from which nobody emerges unscathed (and all that nonsense about gods carrying off the young people they love), he'd yet to learn the advantages of keeping one foot inside and the other outside of the system. It would still be a while before he found the sweet point of communion with his original herbivore, before deciding to start from scratch again in later years, for a third or a fourth iteration: the untold story of why Matías chose to return to the veiled forms of the hippy life he'd sidestepped thanks to Marx and to chemistry and to the abundant exchange of body fluids during phase one. A post-Edenic Adam. Since we can't save ourselves, let's at least save the earth. That was the message. If the content is rotten, ditch it and keep the form. Those random television news clips are so rich, ten or twelve people, an elected politician among them, all dressed in white lab jackets, supposedly doctors, biologists, veterinarians, who proceed to set a bird free, a wounded bird, whose broken leg or wing had been cured at a clinic. The bird, after being cured and observed by the impressive team, was returned it to its habitat, they tell us, though nobody seems too concerned about whether the tens of people waiting and spilling into the hallways of the Virgen de las Rocas Hospital's emergency room will be returned to their habitat any time soon. We take it for granted that birds are part of nature, even though birds are also good builders, good carpenters, they erect fine nests; birds are excellent predators capable of setting traps for their victims, sharp hunters. Despite all the little animals' industry and activity, they're recognized as being part of the natural world, while the human being, even when a brazen slacker who won't get out of bed, who sleeps on piles of straw whose artisanship is far below that of a nest, is not: humans are instruments of harm, even the one over there who's napping while the industrious beaver builds a dam to change the course of a river. We could resolve the problem once and for all with a clean neutron bomb. Now behold Matías in his environmentalist phase. Playing house in his toy kitchen, making little rolls of bread out of clay and baking them in the sun, never soiled by anything, never seeing anything untoward. Little milk-fed lambs (some tobacco and copious amounts of alcohol). These are the stage props for the scene of Matías's later years, when instead of arguing about things like seizing power, or how to destroy oneself the quickest way possible with the junk of pharmacopeia (phase one, or maybe this is already phase two?), or working from inside the system (phase two or was this already phase three?), he was arguing for the rights of animals and plants and our duty as humans to one another. The human being is an animal charged with duties. For the simple sake of argument, Matías and I have quarreled bitterly over things like whether it's more ethical to roast or to fry, or is frying better than simmering. I'd engage him mostly to score a win in front of Silvia and Juan: Look, Matías, I'd say, cooking is not the same as philosophy or literature, you can't use false syllogisms or outrageous metaphors; cooking itself has nothing to do with revolution; it's more about the quantity of products a family unit needs to subsist, in a home; whether you earn enough to provide the daily number of calories your body needs. If you don't, even Father Mariana himself acknowledges the right of insurrection. But that's as far as revolution goes when talking about cuisine. But not for Matías, who showed up after phases one, two, and three. He discovered things in the final phase like the fact that some cuisines have history—which we should respect and preserve—and cuisines without history, that are high-tech, invasive, should be rejected. But what kind of history are we talking about? I argued. Gazpacho is from Andalusia, made from tomatoes and peppers, two varieties of produce that were brought from America; what we call Spanish tortilla is made from potatoes, which the conquistadors imported from the Andes. Neapolitan pizza is a burst of tomato, American tomato in its purest state, *pomo d'oro* introduced by the conquistadors and merchants. But it didn't matter: to him there was an ethics of spice, of cooking times and techniques. Cooking up to a certain point was ethical, but not if you left the pot over the fire for five extra minutes. It was ethical to use cloves in a certain dish; and immoral or hypocritical to use it in others. They squabbled: don't be ridiculous, the choice of spices, how you use the oven or stove, cooking methods, it's all a matter of flavor and taste. Allow us that freedom at the very least,

Matías. Let's suppose I like my meat *saignant*, and you like it well-done: neither one of us is right or wrong historically. But he just kept at it: You can't tell me a filet mignon charred to the texture of a shoe sole is better. There's an ethical responsibility to the product itself, to how you treat it. I know you could care less about these little details. You aren't even able to discern the ethics of a landscape (there it is, touché, the landscape dig, he imagined I'd clutch a hand to my heart at the thrust of his blade, a flower of blood between fingers and white shirt). He explained it as if the product were like a prisoner who shouldn't be oppressed by forced labor. As if a red mullet suffers less when roasted instead of fried; or frying it just so, instead of scorching it to a crisp. Him: It's an ethics of conservation. When we talk about cuisine, we're referring to an entire system of values in which cuisine is only a single aspect. One sees the world in a certain way, and cuisine is part of that perspective. Hamburgers, ketchup, industrial mustard, preservatives, industrial fries cooked in disgusting oils … And I interrupted: Yes, they're revolting, they're bad, God spare us from having to eat them, but they're neither ethical nor immoral, except if you refer to the companies that control the products, which are all American, imperialist, but that's about a system of ownership, it's about capitalism, not cuisine. He shot back a reply: Junk food belongs to the junk world, you can't separate one from the other. Choosing a piece of perfectly ripe fruit and tasting it is like paying tribute to the world, it's a form of respect, and it's a reflection of other values. Me: But what if somebody likes to eat junk food? Him: Then let's talk nutritional value and all that. Me: But where does that put us then? Are we talking cuisine as necessity or pleasure? If I happen to like the taste of ashes and I'm able to derive the protein or whatever's lost when you scorch a steak by other means, why shouldn't I be allowed to fill my mouth with ashes?

Him: Any principle, no matter how abstract, must be resolved in action, by acts; otherwise, it's useless, which means it's immoral, and I think there are ethical principles from which nothing is exempt. Sure, there are culinary principles, I chuckled, knowing how to thicken a sauce, how much butter a good croissant needs, these are culinary principles. Then we have other principles, clearly, we have other principles, one wants revolution, now there's a principle, clearly a desirable one, which is still desirable, I desire it—though it may surprise you—I still want it because I think the world is poorly distributed, but I don't want the Russian kind, or the Chinese, the Cambodian or even the Cuban version, which doesn't mean I'm opposed to revolution in principle. But what a huge distance between principles and acts! Not all ideas unresolved by acts are purely immoral, a good part of them remain potential acts. How many people love humanity—the mother of all principles—but can't stand to be around anyone. Matías moved like a fish in water around the notion of scrambling it all together, it was his natural habitat, he seduced Silvia and he seduced my mother too, I imagine, with that metallic glint of scales in the sun; he kept my mother in thrall right up to the very end. I prefer to think of her as a victim of that idle energy, but she was an interested victim, blinded to the outside, turned inward, into herself, incapable of picking her head up to take an outward glance. It's inconceivable to think she would ever be capable of putting herself in someone else's shoes. She had no problem paying off—with someone else's money—a ventriloquist to help her reaffirm her own beliefs. My mother. Matías used to poke fun at her haughtiness calling it High Flamboyant Gothic: Mama is Gothic, igneous, conceited, convoluted, full of extravagance. But there are ways of getting to know her, like studying a Gothic cathedral: pay special attention to the stereotomy, the stonemasons' work; the shape of the steeples, the proportions of the flying buttresses, the design of the gargoyles, the measurements of the crossing, the apse; the play between bulk and resistance; Rubén, you've never bothered to identify the model, even though you're an architect: Mama's style is Gothic-egotistical. Her insatiable egocentricity touches me. Don't try to convince me it's not moving. She hates anything that obliges her to take a step beyond, and I don't mean a physical step: she'd never, not even out of common courtesy, take that extra step in her ideas to put herself in someone else's place, not for a second. The effort it takes to change an opinion, she won't put up with it: so she defends the opinions she has tooth and nail, immovable. She fights so she won't have to deal with getting outside of herself. Putting yourself in another's skin is a long, jarring journey and, as far as she's concerned, a useless one. In that sense she's the exact opposite of Papa, who was only interested in what was just out of his reach, what he couldn't recognize or have: he was always interested in alterity, it made things worth studying, observing; mechanisms that functioned in ways that were different from what he was accustomed to were deeply fascinating, if only for that reason. His curiosity made him generous. Mama, on the other hand, has always been sure that wherever she looks, she'll never find anything better than what she already has: herself. The rest of the world is no more than a substitute or an inferior imitation of what she already so effortlessly is, naturally. What she can't control is either lacking in something—provoking the apprehension one might feel around someone who is anorexic—or excessive, which she sees like some fat man's beer belly. Matías used to poke fun at Mama and at me, but she only cared about Matías: not her other son, not her grandchildren, not even her husband. She treated Silvia the way they used to treat illegitimate children in those nineteenth-century newspaper serials, with complete disregard (why Silvia so docilely responded to being mistreated is beyond me). Only Matías, the little boy who caught every cold, who read novels aloud to the iron lady. Mama is glacial: she's powdered, self-satisfied, and she's sharp and angular like the towers of a Central European cathedral; better not ruffle her, she'll stab at you with her stingers, other people's problems run right off her the way that water slides from cathedral spires in those cold, rainy climes. Matías would say things like that, yet nobody but him was allowed to stroke her hair (let it down, you look better with your hair down, you look younger), give her a smooch (that cream is working, your skin is really soft), or brush a cheek against hers. His corny *attrezzo* was the only one tolerated at home: the cuddling, the squeezes (though not too much, either); she just let him do whatever he fancied, she gave him free rein at home and outside. He was budget-averse, he used to say, and couldn't care less about family matters, it bored him to tears, yet it was he who kept the family accounts, managed the properties. I do it for her, he would say. Since you have a company, she considers you—and sorry to put it this way—a competitor, she thinks she has to protect herself. You know how selfish she is, and she's staunch about keeping her business separate from yours, I'm just her pencil licker, an ancien régime clerk. Matías the scrivener decides what's retained, what's traded, what's invested, and what's sold; what is expected to make a profit and what goes on the back burner for some vague or, again, some corny reason. When I started my business just out of school, I couldn't convince her to cede the tiniest plot of land for me to develop; first I had a modest studio; then a no less modest real estate development firm. I never asked for handouts or gifts, I only wanted her to sell me the land, cede it, cosign a bank guarantee so I could get a loan. I wanted to step into my own life somehow. I had my degree, I was an architect, splendid, but I had bigger ambitions, I was born for other things, I wanted to control the process from start to finish, to build a house up from its foundations on land that I'd acquired, oversee construction, even get to know the client, the buyer, the person who is going to live there, who would complain if the cable chases aren't done well, if the extractor malfunctions, the joints or the bathroom tiles don't quite fit together; if there's humidity around the drainpipes, or if the air-conditioning is too weak, that's my vocation, to each his own, mine is construction, construction in the full complexity of its mechanics. Some people are good at hanging their feet over a swing and doing backflips, and there you have a trapeze artist. I'm a developer. I like the technical jargon of the forge, I like concrete, shuttering, buttresses, reinforcing rods, steel meshes, floorings, and cinder blocks. I've always known that this is where my gifts lie. We all have a gift for something. That's life. It is what it is, I used to say to Matías, who couldn't wrap his head around the idea that a developer is always more than an architect, no matter what they tell you in books: money always trumps ideas, because money puts them in its service. I used to joke with him: As a developer I'm my own boss, and the owner of my other self, the architect. An architect is the developer's employee. I try to keep the architect in line so the project doesn't get out of control, and to impose the discipline of business, attentiveness to estimates and budgets and compliance with schedules and specifications. I say: This is what I want, this is your budget, plan it out for me; and the architect, my alter ego, goes ahead and does what I say. I exert control over myself, I manage myself. I impose the principle of reality. But Mama wouldn't sell me even a tiny plot of land. She preferred to dispose of her properties by other means, and we're talking privileged properties, land that helped other developers make fabulous profits, plots that were sweet as pears in a pie, little candies, and it's true they were sold long after when I would've needed them most, but back in the day I could've used them, they would've helped me avoid hitting so many potholes in the road; and they were sold only to turn into smokescreens (over time I figured it all out, they turned more into moonshine vapors). So, it fell to me, Teresa Bernia's firstborn son, to pave my own way, find my own path in life; and to my brother, who never had a project that wasn't smoke and mirrors, words spilled over bar tops, over the tables of countless cafés, my brother was put in charge of deciding how to handle the family patrimony. I try to strike it from my mind whenever I stop by the house in Pinar but I can't, whenever I see the maid pushing her wheelchair down the hallway to the black basalt fountain outside, whose four gleaming stone petals hold the moss-covered water, her sitting there under the shadow of the pergola and its twining jasmine and bougainvillea, facing east to look out over the sea, if in fact she looks at anything, drooling, her head bobbing to one side, her hair—scant and gray—pulled into a chignon like some old bumpkin dressed in widow's black. Look at you now, you were always bejeweled before, so fastidious over the tones of blouses and skirts, perfectly coordinated accessories, the exact shade of highlights in your hair; a woman who could annihilate without saying a word—an elevator glance, the curl of an eyebrow, the flutter of lashes—and now her dress, her coiffure, her shoes, her taste, her class, all reduced to an antediluvian hick, what she most despised. At first I couldn't figure out who'd decided to dress her that way and why, in rigorous black, a peasant shawl over her shoulders, hair fixed into a bun, a sort of step backward, a genetic skip back to the origins, three or four generations closer to the embryonic stage, the old family of plebeians who a century and a half ago began caring for the Lord's lands, cultivating his gardens, his muscatel vineyards, grapefruit and orange groves, the big Pinar house on the hill, the pines, the palms, the araucarias; and through a series of convoluted ups and downs, heirs dying without successors, purchases, donations, more or less legitimate appropriations, shady deals, they'd ended up taking everything over themselves. It's not Silvia, not her caregivers, nobody knows. They didn't buy those clothes. Apparently, she chooses them herself by rifling through old chests and closets, nobody knows their origin, who owned them originally, whether they were a maid's, maybe her own mother's. Like a new form of defiance. Silvia can't stand it: We have to persuade Grandmother to change the way she dresses. She looks like a beggar, like one of those Balkan war refugees on television. She's never listened to me, not a day in her life, that's what I told Silvia. And truth be told, I almost prefer seeing her that way, dressed in black. It's as if she were applying some kind of moral discipline to her own self, a corrective worthy of Seneca, a divesting, dressing up in costume only to go naked again, *sic transit gloria mundi*. I feel no mercy or pity for her, not in the least, only a blend of melancholy and—why suppress it—satisfaction; deep down I like it, it's a masochistic form of satisfaction seeing her defeated, a boomerang feeling that turns itself back on me, the defeat that sooner or later is going to catch up with all of us. *Sic transit*. She'd always navigated the body she was given with calculated acumen, for the long circuit, a nearly hundred-year-old ride. She'll turn ninety-four in November. Grilled vegetables, grilled fish with a few drops of olive oil, white meat, nothing fried, bread with a dribbling of extra virgin, fruit, lots of fruit for keeping the skin taut, grapefruit and oranges, loquats, peaches, grapes, lately some avocado, mango, papaya, soursop, other things you find in gourmet shops or the ones that have sprung up to supply the immigrant communities, she asks the maids to bring her things she hears about on the radio, reads about in the newspapers, keeping up with the times, vigilant, a vigilant intelligence (meat, fats, they're mind-numbing, dim the wits, turn you more animal, she told me not long ago, as if she'd just been reading Engels: we are what we eat). Regardless of her attentiveness, I doubt she spent more than fifteen minutes of the past quarter century actually feeling good. Live longer, suffer more. Nobody finds relief in the final years of life, they're bitter years, or in the best-case scenario, mindless ones: bitterness upon bitterness, if not foolishness, dementia, maybe not so bad after all. But that bitterness inside of her has nothing to do with age, it may be the case for other people, but not you. Given the choice, what would you prefer? Surely mindlessness, oblivion. Being strolled around the bougainvillea to look out over the sea and drool, the dusky surface of the reservoir water glistening like a black, petrified flower (the motor no longer spouts the stream of water that I remember). Out of selfishness, she chose a controlled blend of two states, at once vigilant and mindless, a sort of senile dementia that leaves nothing or no one in peace. She'll last an eternity by harassing everyone. The family truth is that none of its members have ever been given over to great feelings of tenderness, love, hope, none of that; at the most decorum and good manners. Kisses were barely suffered at home, hugs scarce, celebrations limited, hardly any crying or laughing together. We've never sung happy birthday to each other—noisy festive scenes—or Christmas carols, or arias in the shower or while shaving. If my father was ever struck by the mood to joke around during dinner, she would respond with a sneer, if he'd try to sneak her a little squeeze, she'd wriggle away, like an animal, like something both hard and flexible, a dried-out organ that folds, both wood and leash, stiff leather, bad-tempered. Leave me alone, calm down. My father's suntanned face expressed joviality, he felt comfortable in his skin, he was easygoing, lacked any vague or mucky sort of guilt complex, which she spent a lifetime trying to inoculate into him. My father was elegant even in his corduroys and a white shirt on his way to hang out or go fishing with the farmhands, see what kind of a catch the morning might bring. He declared himself an Ortegan, Montaignian. In some ways I'm a disciple of Ortega, if only he weren't so full of himself and, at the bottom, rather frivolous; more than anything I'm a not very gifted student of Montaigne, who called himself a liberal. He'd rationalize: I like Ortega's poise. He writes as if he were trying to seduce a woman, which I think is the only thing that really interested him, much more than philosophy. Flirting with the ladies. Not making love to them, but getting them to fall in love with him, which is not the same thing; that they admire him, applaud him the way one applauds a well-coiffed dog standing on its hind legs. Beyond that, no, he wasn't interested in consummation, I can't imagine him with his pants around his knees pushing a woman up against a kitchen stool (he'd giggle like a kid who'd said something naughty. Truly, I could never have imagined my father with his pants around his knees, either: Ortegan). Matías was right where that's concerned. No doubt our father was too lazy to bother (all the fuss of finding a bachelor's pad, a garçon-nière, carving out time for dates, coming up with alibis). His brand of laziness was the exact opposite of Mama's, his was a gen-erous form of laziness, he preferred to relent before going through the hassle of negotiating; throw in the towel before being over-whelmed in battle. Languid even for vice, he was so patrolled and oppressed by his wife he never thought about taking up an activ-ity or developing a vice. It was my mom who kept the accounts with the gardeners and hands, she gave the orders, oversaw the foremen and their work. My father stayed out of it: he joined the workers for lunch whenever one of them caught a hare, a par-tridge, a mallard, or a coot in the marshlands; or if someone hooked a grouper, a turbot, or a dentex (variable forms of para-dise). They were his pals. He never cultivated other friendships. A few cousins came to visit a couple of times a year, distant relatives from Madrid or Barcelona who dropped in on him whenever they came to Misent. He gave a wide berth to city people from his own class. He preferred the solitary life: an even-tempered, refined bourgeois, a Tolstoyan count surrounded by happy servants. We could call his biography *The Story of a Happy Man*, but I never bought it myself, how happy he really was. He was more like a plant that never had enough soil to thrive. He had the germ of happiness, the seed, but I'm convinced he'd always lacked the proper nutrients. There was always a trace of melancholy in his voice when he talked about things. As if his lands, his house, and even his children didn't actually belong to him, weren't parts of the whole, of himself. There was something evanescent in the way he related to things, something not quite solid between him and us. Not that he didn't love us. On the contrary, he was affectionate toward us, but it was a nebulous kind of warmth. Instead of taking long walks, or running around behind us, grabbing us by the shoulders or stroking the napes of our necks, gestures that other parents make with their kids, he gave us books, questioned us about our studies and commented on our answers, more like a professor than a father. There was a sort of spider's web hanging between him and home life, a state of mind that was hard to pinpoint, a matter of character or position. Like I said: he never seemed greatly interested in the opposite sex. He observed women from a distance, in art books, on postcards (Matías and I once found a collection of those so-called artistic postcards in his desk drawer, from the early twentieth century—back then they called a striptease a *tableau artistique*—naked, fleshy women holding bouquets of flowers, or wearing them as garlands on their heads, a foot raised as if they were dancing; bodies that offered themselves up as art objects, not flesh to be touched, flesh that sweats, smells, can be penetrated; that had to be scrubbed and washed). Saying that family life conditioned my father is just another way of talking about my mother. Diligence, vigilance, the precision blade that slices the correct from the incorrect. Given my childhood, a psychiatrist could easily explain why I find Monica's spontaneity so invigorating, so prized. To be married to Monica. To touch, to laugh, to free oneself in one's own home. Give each other raucous kisses. Hear belly laughs from the other room or dive-bar music near the swimming pool, her holding herself against you and pouting because you said no to this or that whim, or something she proposed, the kind of childish things that hadn't been in the house for a long time. It's not that I believe in a second youth, but neither have I used up all my chances of being reasonably happy, of feeling my heart valve still capable of pumping blood, even with the help of a pacemaker. At home it wasn't only considered immodest to touch or kiss each other, but even to open up a little, let down your guard, show concern or happiness. Life was lined by a fabric both elegant and gray. Emotion was the territory of weakness, something to be concealed: one locks oneself in the bathroom to perform certain essential needs that nobody else cares to know about. Jumping for joy over winning some school game is equally vulgar, or shedding a tear because you're sad about losing. The tasteful response is to look the other way, hit another ball with the cue, ask for another drink, tell another joke, not a sarcastic one, not bitter, but an innocuous one, even stupid if possible. Sometimes I wonder if my first wife, Amparo, was a continuation of my mother. Aloof during courtship, but little by little she took the initiative at home, imposing discipline, becoming bossy, good manners the most prized value of coexistence. But Amparo had a benevolent side that softened her strictness and zeal for order. I've often thought it was the proximity to my mother (we lived with her the first few years after we got married; my father had just died, Matías was in Madrid, and Mama felt lonely) that magnified these aspects of Amparo's character, which might otherwise have remained mere bourgeois brushstrokes, rendering them insufferable: that need for a fabric of order to protect daily life. Silvia is a prolongation of her icy paternal grandmother, and her mother's uppity mood in her last years (the feminine zigzags through the family, from one genetic trunk to another). Maybe she wasn't a Gothic cathedral (too extravagant), but a very Bauhaus-like edifice, all angles and cubes falling like lead on a barren field; colorless Mondrian: thin crisscrossed lines made by a knife; a work of art separated from the spectator by a piece of bulletproof glass, security ropes, and an alarm system. I've never felt close to Silvia, despite having tried countless times. I would've loved for her to study architecture, economics, or business administration, whatever would have made it easy for her to work with me in the businesses (I picture Ana Patricia Botín; the daughter of the Lladró family), but my line of work always seemed to make Silvia a little nauseated, too intertwined with despicable elements of the economy. I rifle through the glove compartment for my Davidoff cigarillos for señoritas and light one up cagily, aware the smoke is going to impregnate the car's interior, and the butt in the ashtray will give me away to Monica, proof I'm still smoking (I only smoke a random cigar, though she's convinced I smoke like a fiend behind her back: traces of tobacco, of other women, that's what she's on the lookout for, finding little of either). There will only be a single butt now, but it's enough to condemn me, when before there might have been three or four left in the ashtray. I squeeze the petite cigar between my thumb and index finger beside my ear to make sure it's still fresh, no signs of dryness or the stale crackle (nowadays a box of these Lilliputians lasts only fifteen days, the heat dries them out), and then I light up, relishing that first puff, the smoke inside my mouth, gums tingling, my lips, and a prickle in the eyes from the rising smoke. In just a few hours, Matías, your eyes will sting, too, from the smoke. Silvia and Juan will be there, the two widows, Monica and me.

Nobody else. I doubt Brouard will show up, or Miriam, or any of your neighbors in Benalda. Not a single Benaldan soul bothered to visit the hospital: not even the field hands who helped with the plots. Not one of those lushes you liked to get drunk with, either. So it seems like congratulations are in order. That's some excellent social work, really "laboring for the masses," as the comrades used to say, or as Chairman Mao called it, "moving among the masses like a fish in water." I hope Silvia doesn't get it into her head to bring my mother to the hall, the one with the stained glass window painted in colors with static flames and images of people moving toward a light awaiting them in the background. Just don't, Silvia, you're only going to make her suffer. I must've told her that at least twenty times yesterday. Not a word to your grandmother. There's no greater disruption to the natural order than when a mother loses a son. And a man's mission during the short time he's given to roam the earth is precisely to avoid disruptions like that. To devise methods that give order to things, putting them in their proper places, filing them away. That's what separates humans from animals. Building order: the clock, the calendar, the notebooks with sheets of paper bound by a metal spiral, the folder, the home, a cluster of specialized rooms: kitchen, dining room, bathroom, living room, bedroom. Above all the bedroom: shut disorder into the bedroom, and shut me in the bedroom with Monica. The heat of flesh as an antidote to death. I help build order in my own way, Silvia, I'm a builder, an architect, I organize space. If you bring your grandmother it'll disrupt everything, and though it upsets you, it's barbaric, and goes against nature: an old lady observing her son's imminent cadaver. She could barely look at him the day you brought her to the hospital. She said: And this one? Pointing at the barrage of tubes, why is he so skinny, don't they feed him? (I thought: thank God she's so out of it), and right away, "let's go." And down the hallway she glides in her wheelchair, putting distance between herself and her dying son, come on, come on, help me up, so at ease her entire life with giving orders. Nearly a hundred years old, practically blind and doddering, but boy can she still bark categorical orders to the Ecuadoran nurse. Let's go. She continues gesticulating with her hands, imposing her will threateningly, cawing out demands. Get me out of here. She never actually learned how to speak, only how to give orders. But they come out more like grunts now, words only half-understood. She scolds under her breath at all hours of the day. The Ecuadoran woman complains about how hard it is to understand her, and if she hesitates even for a moment Mama cuffs her with her fists. When I dare naysay her she belts me one, too. I joke around a little to release the steam and say: How long your arms have grown, Mama, glancing at her and back at the Ecuadoran woman: dark herald, barbed, shriveled old lady with a raised fist. A decadent character actress on stage performing a classic tragedy, crying vengeance with a metallic voice—but vengeance for what? Vengeance against whom? I don't know what the Señora is asking for, the Ecuadoran woman moans, constantly pestering me for a raise because she can't take it anymore. It's not worth it, Sir, it's just not worth it. I know she's your mother, but you have no idea what it's like to put up with her all day and all night, twenty-four long hours, she laments, and the trouble she gives at night. I have to fight tooth and nail to get her to keep her diaper on. The worst is when she gets it off. I have to spend hours scrubbing to get rid of that smell; it never goes away. Well, for seventy-odd years I've known what it's like to put up with her. She's done nothing in her life but order people around. She ordered my father around, too. Rubén, and Rubén, and Rubén. Rubén this, Rubén that, you have to do this right this instant, you have to do that, here's the next thing. His entire married life, my father hardly received more than a vocative followed by an onslaught of imperatives. She didn't even have to change the name to bark her orders at me. I used to hear that waterless voice, the same one she used to address my father, the same words. From father to son. Nearly a century of saying the same exact thing. It feels like you came out of a mother, a uterus, but never had a mother who'd hold your hand. I've conjured that painful idea several times, not sure how it popped into my head, as a ready-made phrase, or whether I read it somewhere, in some novel. I've never had a mother who'd hold my hand. Nobody could ever accuse her of not being true to herself. And me, stuck here in my car, I smoke and listen to a CD with the music that I'll probably have to hear again this afternoon at the funeral, Bach; not the music Silvia says Matías would have liked, not what Silvia wanted herself: Silvia wanted to play a few tunes from a Coltrane record, *Live in Seattle*: "Out of This World" and "Body and Soul." She gave me the CD to listen to: the first theme—according to the CD jacket—lasts 24 minutes and 20 seconds; the second one, just over 21 minutes. Either one of the titles and their respective lengths are perfect for the ceremony. Out of the world. Body and soul. I found both of them devilishly boisterous, wholly inappropriate for a funeral, and I'm aware that by saying this, I'm attesting to the fact that each one of us has a different image of what it means to be outside of the world (to me it's more like a melancholic sensation of peace, of silence, not all that dissonant racket); and of the more or less tortuous relationship between body and soul. The length of either one of the Coltrane tracks, I figure, would last more or less as long as the physical-chemical process of combustion by which Matías's eyes, hands, legs, stomach, kidneys, spleen, and liver, and their respective metastases, will be turned to ash, the ashes that Angela and Lucía will take from the hands of a man in a burgundy uniform (the crematorium employees dress like waiters at a catered event), who has carried them over in a closed chalice meant to look like some movie prop tasked with getting Alexander the Great or Cleopatra tipsy, which is precisely why the mortuary uses them, because they confer a sort of classical, Greco-Roman nobility while at the same time maintaining a connection to popular culture through film. Death and the Greek; death and the Roman. The architecture of death has sought these forms because convention considers them immortal. Symbols of eternity. When the idea of paraphernalia on tombs and columbaria seems out-of-date, what's left is the shape of the urn. They don't build funerary monuments like they used to, hardly anyone does, and I don't think anyone cares as much about aesthetics or arrangement anymore. Modern columbaria are insipid cubes lacking soul. Truth is, I've never bothered to think about mortuary architecture up until now. I've visited the cemeteries everyone else goes to because of the famous remains buried there, full of spectacularly dramatic pantheons: Père-Lachaise, Montparnasse, the cemeteries of Genoa, Nice. Hordes of marble skeletons armed with sickles. Stone clepsydras and marble women wearing clingy tunics (following Phidias's wet clothes technique) rise above the sepulchres of bankers, artists, and fathers of the homeland. Mortuary music also follows certain protocols of classical decorum, not necessarily a requiem, but something appropriate. I was at a funeral with people who liked to say they were progressives and found their decision to play Serrat and the Nueva Trova Cubana in dubious taste, petty, showing that tacky, oversentimental style that seems to have overtaken the Left these past few years. Whatever the case, last night when I put Coltrane's music on, I knew for a fact that this wasn't the music we were going to play. Better to look toward the Orient, the red Orient where Matías's spirit wandered in life. I thought of Prokofiev, the cantata in Alexander Nevsky's last battle on the lake, when the camera pans over the cadavers lying on the ice and the mezzo-soprano recites painfully: "Here lies one felled by a wild saber; there lies one impaled by an arrow. From their wounds blood fell like rain on our native soil, on Russian fields. He who fell for Russia in noble death shall be blessed by my kiss on his eyes." A song that shrivels the heart, no doubt about it. Or better, even more along the lines of what Matías wanted to be, is Shostakovich's fifteenth symphony, written when the composer was dying, so sorrowful, so lugubrious. I looked for it this morning before heading out, but couldn't find it. Suddenly it seemed the perfect music for Matías: the composer of a dying revolution's final work, written with a moribund hand. Mortally ill when he wrote it, Shostakovich had lost all faith in the Soviet Union, to which he had devoted the best years of his career (he died a few days after composing it). He was sick of the revolution by then. Just imagine the bitterness he must have felt those two dark and final days with no god to entreat. Since I couldn't find the damn CD in my collection at home (I found it on a few vinyls, but I doubt the mortuary would still have a record player), I chose Bach, who raises the rigor, the classical decorum over life's last gasp to its highest degree. I have it in the car with me now. Matías will be ushered into nothingness by the hand of Bach. The greatest music for transubstantiation (moving from one form of matter to another), or even better, for that completely inconsequential moment, because it no longer means anything to the person who's dead. For him it's all the same, they might as well be singing "La Carmagnole." We're the ones the music is meant to console, Matías, the ones escorting you on this so-called last journey, the journey to nowhere: it spurs us to reflection, helps us distill one of the liquid sentiments we call upon at times like this. You'll depart, attended by the most beautiful thing ever created by a human. Not too bad, even though you could care less. We live and die alone because individuality is insurmountable. Nobody's able to cross that border between a person and the rest of the world (we are me and the rest, and the rest are others around us, near us, but they cannot permeate us; they'll never be us), though a social contract has allowed us to reach a reasonable level of coexistence, keeping us from devouring each other save on rare occasions (in his memoir, Jünger tells of soldiers who would cut off their enemies' viscera and testicles to parade them around: playing into the myth of growing stronger by eating your enemy's virility); and this pact even entails during certain periods the security that we bury each other respectably. Bach: *Weinen, Klagen, Sorgen, Zagen*: weeping, laments, worries, fear; sacred words transubstantiated into music by the spirit of Bach. Matías, you will exit this life wrapped in the most beautiful, the purest thing that any human has ever produced, the fire that purifies and the music of Bach, which disinfects the outside and illuminates the inside. Silvia and Matías's exes will think it's fine—who can't agree to Bach for a funeral—it's fine at home during a rainfall with the water sliding down the windowpanes; it's fine even for a drive at dusk when the landscape seems to contract and shrink back from the side of the road, and in front of you the horizon, a curtain closing over the straight line that leads to the heart of La Mancha; and if they don't like it they can go fuck themselves, they can go play the Coltrane shit later, when the widows and my daughter sneak off to some dive bar to raise a glass to a dead man. Arguing with my daughter sometimes feels like a rekindling of the arguments I used to have with Matías during that stage in his life that I like to call "phase one." They were some tough years (the early seventies), and Matías was convinced that only the callous and uncaring are doomed to survive. He called them philistines, lifting Marx's terminology: the cowards, the stingy, the social climbers, the magpies. In his particular version of the long live death call, everything was meant to burn in a huge inferno. He was more a son of Mao and Nero than of the easygoing Rubén Bertomeu Senior. The red book raised high out on the streets, and may Rome burn on all four sides, Esquiline, Aventine, Quirinal, the seven hills ablaze, the marshy flatlands a sea of flames, and the banks of the Tiber with its reed beds (I can hear the bursting, crackling reeds from my palazzo tonight, licked by the flames on the banks of the river, the noise stretching all the way over here, a pyrotechnic show of dry stalks exploding like fireworks a thousand years before Marco Polo brought gunpowder to Europe). I used to make fun of him. I'd say: I smoke, I drink, I let loose, a little fast life, but no need to burn out, and do it singing the praises of velocity, which is more of a Fascist thing than a Communist one, like Marinetti, or D'Annunzio. Life is too costly an investment to turn it to ashes so quickly: diapers, baby food, kindergarten, schools, universities. It costs a fortune to turn a child into an adult: loads of cod, trout, hake, lentils, rice, garbanzos, and all the big human ideas that go into making dubious scraps of meat more or less palatable: Salisbury steak, meatballs, baloney, salami, supposed heads of boar. It's not very honest for a Marxist to throw it all to the wind indiscriminately. It goes against economic common sense. There must be a better way of getting a return on the investment, of recouping the cost of what took so much to raise. But you want to pick up the asphalt to peek at what's underneath. An extravagant madness. There's nothing but pestilence under there, left by decades of putrescent, poorly treated water. It's a strange syndrome that affects all the spoiled kids who are ready to cast off, cut ties, fly the coop. Let's go burn the museums to the ground. Be the exclusive heirs of history. The Incan emperors executed the chroniclers of their predecessors, and so on down the line, each new emperor writing his own story from scratch, the way it best suited him. It's a destructive urge that's not revolutionary, only selfish. To be the last eye to contemplate the museum. The futurists and surrealists, likewise another bunch of spoiled rich kids, found it irksome that museums were at the disposal of the middle class. What would they think now seeing all those workers' offspring cramming the entrances? These were the subjects we argued about, Matías and me. We hadn't yet begun hurting each other whenever we had one drink too many, the sparks flying from words we rubbed together to wound: we knew each other's triggers and poked at them. Back then we simply enjoyed arguing, and we argued passionately. His petulance still had the sweet fragrance of youth and I hadn't yet associated it with a blatant disregard for whatever wasn't strictly convenient for him, surely inherited from our mother. He harangued me with rousing speeches during those first years of the transition to democracy. All of us were no more than a bunch of traitors, hypocrites bent on masking our true selves. He said: My generation thinks it'll save itself by turning into hermit crabs, symbiotic little animals who protect themselves using abandoned shells, organisms in costume, in camouflage, who saunter around wearing other people's clothes. How far can you go with a phony life, pretending you're someone you're not, poking your ugly, hairy, spiky crab legs out at night when you think nobody is watching? Nowadays, my pals go to parties in rented tuxedos. They smile, but inside they're consumed with envy, they hate the others who own their tuxes. My generation's bile (yes, mine, because yours capitulated right from the start, didn't even bother to fight, so they don't even have a sense of guilt, just of being mediocre) will end up wreaking havoc. You'll see, it'll produce a generation of degenerates. And the ones who've scratched their way to the top are the worst of the lot. Matías could find no reason, in the twilight of his first phase, to adapt to the times: the hermit crab abandons its shell and parades its suppleness around in the raw. What the shell covered was the injustice that begged reparations. Victor Hugo said something similar: revolution is the movement from representation to truth, so let's say it means removing the adorning shell to show yourself butt naked; turn your fragility into something explicit, shine a light on the resentment of the people who were left behind, make the latent violence materialize. Matías was hermetic, too, and haughty like Mama, incapable of empathy, of putting himself in the place of the other. The total opposite of Papa. Papa used to say: I'm like Montaigne because I have a pair of goddamn kidneys that make stones, just as he did, and I feel curiosity for everything that doesn't concern me. He should have mentioned a sense of friendship (the kind that bound Montaigne to La Boétie), the loyalty he felt toward the peculiar friends he surrounded himself with—not a single one from his own social class—and who accompanied him for long days of fishing from dawn, through lunch, and well into the evening. He'd come back with fire in his eyes. I'd never seen him drunk, everything about him sprang from a wisdom that was born of benevolent ordinariness. Whenever he wanted to explain something, he'd say: You know what Montaigne thought of that? And he'd throw out a quote, sometimes totally made up, but probably genuine most of the times, because there was always one of the French thinker's three volumes of essays on his desk; in the mornings he'd lock himself away in his study in the house in Pinar, listening to arias and reading; in the afternoons he'd wander through the orange groves. At the end of winter, he'd always come back with a little branch of orange blossoms in hand. If Brouard was over, my father would come over to greet him, he considered Brouard a poet: Coming from a stroll through paradise, he'd say. Just smell that. And he'd tickle his nose with the blossoms. Life is going to take you far away from this someday, and you'll realize that you've lost paradise. Even if you stay, you'll realize you had paradise and lost it. You have it right now, Federico. Keep the branch and breathe it in. He'd tousle Brouard's hair, give him a little pat on the cheek, look at him earnestly, and show him the affection that he never showed to us. He liked talking to Brouard. Whenever he saw us together, he'd make a point of addressing him. I liked that he liked my friend, but his attentions sparked ambiguous feelings, fed a delicate, glassy substratum that could unintentionally wound if tread upon, it felt as though he considered me incapable of appreciating what for him belonged to the realm of the spiritual, the smell of orange blossom and night jasmine, the afternoon light, the fragrance of the pines, or the sea's iridescence, all the clichés of Mediterranean beauty that my father knew how to convey so well. I sensed he found me somehow unable to distinguish the dark nooks and crannies a man conceals beneath the cover of daily activities. He treated Federico differently, as if embedded in Federico was a magnet capable of attracting the light and fragrance of day, as well as those darker regions we all carry inside; but me, it was as if I lacked such a magnet and that kind of strength, or held none of the nooks and crannies apparently so essential for a teenager yearning to signify by whatever means; nor was I able to locate them below other people's surfaces. After a while, I realized that Federico didn't figure in the chapter on communal property my father shared with my mother, which included Matías and me; and that's what allowed my father to treat him with more openness than he could with his own sons. Federico must've seemed more fragile to him, more helpless in a physical way. He tried to shield him from the kind of social neglect that forced Federico to work odd jobs from when he was seven or eight years old, running errands, delivering things here and there, chores, small tasks on top of what he did to help his mother, which paid for his notebooks, pens, and the books that went into assembling an ever more colorful stage around him—things that would become an essential part of himself. I think my father could sense that energy, that stimulating interior wound that provoked his departure, gave him the extra willpower needed to create a work of his own. From a very young age, Federico knew he had to leave, so as not to confuse himself with the grayness in Misent that asphyxiates the local people who have ambitions beyond their scant prospects, whose inescapable destiny it was to become clerks in a bank or a store, maybe accountants for one of the three or four modest companies that had limped on after the war. This morning his firstborn, Rubén Bertomeu, thinks: If I'd been an adult back then and had seen that fragile boy, fearful, restless, gifted, and underprivileged, who saw the world as if through the eyes of an old man, I might've understood things and treated him like my father did, too. My father said to us: In these lands, one can make paradise last longer, stretch it out a few more years, it takes longer for Peter Pan's ephemeral boat to wear thin as it crosses the sky, to turn into a cloud above the sphere of the sun. It's a matter of symbiosis between geography and consciousness, between landscape and lifestyle. That's the way it is. This land allows you to lie to yourself. Look at how old I am and it's still playing tricks on me, still giving me little slices of paradise (*débris*, he said in the language of Montaigne when he wanted to charge his words with greater depth, or a different category, more Ortegan), like when I'm at sea, or when I'm under the trellis, when I smell that sweet aroma of muscatel at grape-picking season; like now, I've just been strolling through these blossoming orange trees, the fragrance is intoxicating, dizzying, the light is bathing everything in a golden hue, and there's the gift of clean skies on wintry afternoons here on the banks of the Mediterranean, all in perfect harmony, our light isn't like an overexposed photo, as it is in the south, which is a more African light; but neither is it excessively cold, European, which you find beginning with the Ebro and moving upward. Some poet wrote verses about this. Don't look outside: paradise is right here. But to appreciate it you'll surely have to go elsewhere. But you'll return. Some night when you're out, a hundred miles from here, you'll think back on those winter afternoons in Misent, the light, you'll remember us, you'll remember me, your buddy Rubén, won't you my boy? Remember us (he remembered me not entirely benevolently in his novel *The Erratic Will*). Rubén tells me you've dabbled with some verses, that you write stories. You'll have to bring them by one of these days. Brouard did, and my father read them: You write well, keep at it. Being gifted doesn't mean anything; or it means everything if you're careful to add a little discipline. You need drive, you need to know how to resist. He said these things knowing that Federico had lost his father, he'd attended the wake himself; he even interceded on Federico's behalf so his father wouldn't be buried in that rat-infested field beside the brick wall where the suicides were interred, same as he interceded later to get him a scholarship. Federico tucked his chin to his chest. Yes Sir, he said, gently taking back the spiral notebook he'd given my father, who seized the opportunity to give Brouard another, new one. We raced to his house that afternoon. We ran between hundred-year-old pines, beneath the intimidating, haughty spires of cypress trees that lined the road, through the orange groves, till we made it home. I liked his tumbledown house more than mine because his mother made us snacks in the afternoon and let us run around while we ate, or nibble while sitting on a branch in the apple tree, or in the fig tree, and when we finished the snack we could reach out an arm to pick and eat the figs; his mother never imposed any rules. She might venture some warning like be careful, don't get hurt, out of the instinct or the mechanics of motherhood. Poverty seemed to me, in boyhood, the kingdom of the free. Brouard's father hadn't been around much at first, and when he was, it was more as an apparition, a white shirt moving through the vineyard of muscatel grapevines. Then he was no longer. Back then I still had a father who was generous in his own way. Memories of him evoke feelings of peace, like the memory of those years of friendship with Federico. Matías had just moved to Madrid when our father died, and was trying to impose a form of revolutionary honesty on our family, saying: I can't imagine Papa ever kept a lover, with all the fuss it would've required; juggling schedules for dates, getaways, reserving rooms in *mueblés*. Hard to picture him as some Casanova. I doubt he ever had a mistress, though I was witness to a scene when I was barely a teenager and it stuck in my mind; surely it must've been the result of some affair of the heart. I was around ten or eleven years old, and I had walked into our parent's bedroom one afternoon thinking nobody else was there. I'd gone to fetch something, I don't remember what exactly, in that room that was practically off-limits to us kids. It was near dusk because the window to the garden was already open (the windows were kept shut during the day in the summer). He was sitting on the bed, and the light of the setting sun fell across him diagonally; he had his back to the door so he hadn't noticed me come in. It startled me to find him there, in his T-shirt. I was about to close the door gently and make a run for it, but something drew my attention and I hesitated: his naked shoulders were quivering, as if he was mutely coughing, or laughing silently, or choking, so I skirted around the bed until I was in front of him and that's when I saw that he was weeping. His fists were pressed tightly against his eyes and he was sobbing. I tiptoed out of the room and he never noticed I'd been there. Matías must've been just a newborn at the time, and I had so many chances later to ask him about what I'd seen; but I never did, and now I'm glad I kept it to myself, that I never shared it with anyone else. Now the memory is like private property, something that belongs to me alone. Who knows why he was crying, but it showed me how little I really knew him. From time to time I've wondered if Papa was truly as averse as we suspected to the idea of secret dates and hotel reservations. How little we know the ones we're closest to. It's bizarre, Matías is the one who died, and death is the ultimate defeat, we know, yet I feel as though I'm somehow the one who lost; as if he got his way in the end: he failed at whatever he tried in life, and yet to my mind he always figured out how to land on all fours like a cat. A person can work, fight, find a position, earn money, not be in need—finally—of anyone, and yet he's on the wrong side of things, he grew in the wrong direction. And the other one, without contributing a single thing, is somehow better off, he falls on that other side, the right side of things, and lands on his feet. He may grow upward, he may grow downward, but his development seems to have meaning, or purpose. He's been on the right side. I told you so, he laughed. I'm talking about something a person can smell, detect. Like what they say about an actress, the camera either loves her or rejects her. It's like an aura, some people have a light that illuminates from within and others don't. You've always been able to get your way. Even when you lose, you come out ahead (one of our first serious arguments was over what he was doing with Mama's businesses, I was infuriated). He laughed. Back then he was still running around with radicals (the death rattle of phase one, or was it already phase two?), but he managed Mama's bank accounts, her deeds and papers, the apartments, my baby brother, the little apple of her eye. A thumb in every pie; and Mama, who treated everyone else to a piercing glare, moving it up and down like in an elevator, lips drawing a sarcastic smirk (the two Gothic cathedral spires), just melted like ice cream in the sun with him, with her Matías: her little Matty, so docile with him, her little lap dog, and so despotic with the rest of us. And all the while, capitalist money isn't worth anything, it should be thrown away, but what did we want (yes, little brother, me too, what did I aspire to)? I didn't like the world I was about to enter, to make my way in, either. It's hard for young people to identify what it is they want and follow a path, but I knew I wanted something too, even if it was only to build socially protected housing units (construct a Mediterranean Karl-Marx-Hof with palm trees, bougainvillea, and night jasmine on the patio; there were few workers in Misent, and no shortage of poor people and unhealthy housing): or later those kinds of buildings they like to call emblematic milestones (auditoriums, city halls, post offices, courtroom complexes); so the Japanese tourist can say, here's a canonical Bertomeu while reading a guide and pointing at a building the way they do standing before the Gaudí buildings along Barcelona's Paseo de Gracia, clearly I would have loved it; or more modestly, I would've loved to build consummate homes with no greater pretension than that they are well built; and later they may appear in the architectural catalogues as a paradigm of economy and discretion. Someone please write it down: let the building be the star, or even better, let the star be the person who is lucky enough to live in such a luminous building as this—in writing lines like that, they would be referring to my work. One doesn't choose where they'll be obliged to struggle to make way. Puberty, adolescence, it's a stage of life that's as slippery as it is fleeting. Avoid touching the ground to keep from getting dirty. Live in the tree branches like monkeys, or like people in that Verne novel; fly through the air from tree vine to tree vine like Tarzan, Jane, Chita, and Boy, that child born without a prior act of coupling, fruit of pure air. Or Calvino's little Baron who preferred life in the trees, who refused to grow up and dragged his mattress from branch to branch. We turned into boxers, punch-drunk, thanks to an education full of holes and overly demanding. I said so years later: ours was more Disney than philosopher, something between *Peter Pan* and *Lady and the Tramp*, you remember what the little dog Butch said in *Lady and the Tramp*? "When you're footloose and collar-free, you take nothing but the best." That's called falling on the right side, Matías, you're a Disney character, not even, as Silvia pretends, Larry from *The Razor's Edge*. He was more complex, had other doubts, a different texture, other dissatisfactions. Disney's little anarchist dog cheerfully chasing after the chickens in the corral, and when he hears the shots of the farmer behind him, exclaims: Ah, this is living. How exciting to be chasing after little revolutionary chickens, dodging the farmer's shots, all the while seducing the little lady. That's all there is: surely because you're scared of not meeting expectations, of falling short of your own expectations, a demanding education full of holes ends up turning into a time bomb. We knew how insufferable everything out there was at the time, but what was the alternative model you proposed? What was mine? I was the oldest, Matías. Before you became a teenager, I was striving for something too, who wasn't? But what was it? The Soviets' greasy mechanical revolution, the Chinese and their sheaves of rice, the Albanians with their ugly buildings and hot winds whipping down the streets raising clouds of dust; the urban one, the rural one, the town with benevolent classes like a ray of light; the proletarian one, a demanding class with zero sense of humor, men of steel on the march. Which version did we want? I realized I wanted to build houses for people to live in, that's what I wanted to do, build spaces where people could eat, sleep, lounge on the sofa, or stay in bed on their day off. Are you aware of how important that is? Well, that's exactly what I wanted to do, something that's essential to everyone, and not for architectural catalogues, or design prizes, I wanted to earn a living doing it, have a nice sporty car (I like speed, I like to drive), go sailing, fishing, catch the fish myself to cook at home, isn't that important too, Matías? Enjoy what nature has put within arm's reach? I imagine your worst discovery was that democracy puts an end to politics. That was the worst of all. Twenty, thirty years of stomaching Franco and pushing for democracy, only to realize that once it came, it let you know you weren't needed, because democracy is the perfect forum for eradicating politics. And how you despised me. You said things during our dinner-table arguments that should've driven Mama insane, but she just pretended—that way you have of falling on the right side—that she hadn't heard a thing. Revolution is about making latent violence bubble to the fore, you said. The hermit crab theory on the horizon. In the late sixties and early seventies in Madrid, Mama still sent you a monthly allowance that was much more than I could ever have imagined. Years of excitement, those turbulent sixties. You must've sensed the feast of electrifying words wasn't going to last much longer. I remember when you came home during break, we still went out for walks along the beach. It was an excellent time for me, I had just won my first big solo real estate project, finally I was my own boss, and you were talking to me about things remote, which nevertheless seemed designed to hurt me: bringing out the hidden and making it explicit, you called it; what's there, inevitable, and we pretend not to notice, you said. Shed light on the violence lurking behind decorum; bricklayers taking you for a beer and a joke after being handed their weekly envelope with their shitty wages, when what they'd prefer to do is smash you in the kidneys with a steel beam, open your face like a tomato. Those clients who smile when handed a cup of coffee, whom you're about to strap with a twenty-year mortgage, who'd prefer to steal the deeds and enjoy happily what would be within reach if it weren't for you. You handed me that pamphlet. I can still recall its contents: The French invented the guillotine; they spilled blood to be a rich and happy people. By shaving necks for the falling blade, the executioner proved that the necks of the nobles were identical to the necks of the miserable. The North Americans also spilled blood to achieve their constitution, their power, their well-being. And they continue to spill it, inside and outside of their borders, in order to continue being a rich and proud people. So, who can deny the right of the proletariat to shed blood to free itself, to attain their share of happiness? What authority does the bourgeoisie have to send them off to kill and to die for the rest of the world? The proletariat has shed blood in Germany, in France, in Russia, in the African deserts, in the jungles of Asia and Latin America. The proletariat has shed blood whenever the bourgeoisie has sent them to whatever part of the world, and has continued acting as both the butcher and the bellowing ox tied to a pillar where it's given the *coup de grâce*; bloodshed in Vietnam, in Bolivia, Angola, and Nicaragua. They're given gear, a rifle; every once in a while even a gas mask, best-case scenario some boots, and off he goes to kill and to die. But when the proletariat asks to shed blood for its own cause, the right is denied. On whose authority is the proletariat denied the right to continue the work it was trained to do? Later I realized you quoted Malcolm X, nearly word for word: "You didn't come here on the *Mayflower*. You came here on a slave ship—in chains, like a horse, or a cow, or a chicken." Then you left the Communist Party and took up with Direct Action, where the rest of the militants were ten years younger than you; then you participated in a few burglaries to finance the organization and hid—that's what you told me—a few pistols in the Pinar house (end of the sixties, early seventies, years when suddenly things turned violent again). But like I said, I only found out about all that years later, from other discussions we had: Yeah, that's right, me, the person standing in front of you, you told me about faith in armed struggle, that the guns were in your own home, in Mama's home, and you had a small stockpile of explosives in the *bodega*. You've got to be out of your mind, Matías, I told him. I was, you replied, but not anymore. I was still the same undesirable person when we had that conversation, but you'd already held the megaphone to your mouth and led several demonstrations organized by the official party you hated so much, barking out slogans; you'd been photographed by the newspapers beside the secretary of the party hanging posters the first night of the campaign, the same person who a few years earlier, you'd called the great traitor of the working class, saying you worked out of an office in some unspecified headquarters, doing a job supposedly in the realm of politics, but I think you were recruiting political activists you'd worked with into this new alternative: they used you as a lure and surely—same as Mama—gave you a bit of an expense account so you could dangle a piece of bait on the hook, recruit the conscience-stricken, find information on people who still read Malcolm X. That's right, informant, steward of your ex-comrades: *chota*, what the characters in Eloy de la Iglesia's movies call a narc, a fisher of famished little fish who haven't had a piece of flesh near their mouths for a while: you converted them into becoming kings of the steak house, advertisers of Ribera del Duero wine; emperors of haute cuisine, the restaurant with a sommelier and a Michelin star: I've shared tables and flesh with them; I've watched them ascend to the firmament like space rockets. It's strange. I say: Matías and Mama are both equally closed, self-absorbed, and unmoving, and yet you haven't stopped drifting from one place to another. I don't even think you were proud, pride was just your outer shell, your hermit crab casing. All these jumps from one phase to the next must've been humiliating to you. You returned to the land to protect yourself, the land a metaphor for your mother's selfish uterus, while I'm in the ox's little bowels, where it neither rains nor freezes, poor little garbanzo bean. I mentioned it to Brouard once: Matías never wanted to throw himself into the fire or burn; his fire could only be ignited by words pronounced in barrooms, or in the closed meetings of his faithful flock; there was more alcohol in his blood than hemoglobin, more gin than chloride. The words burned in the air for a few seconds and then collapsed and rained like ashes. They were no more than the strategies of the self, of ego.

YOU HAVE to put yourself in his shoes, he used to tell Sarcós, to understand Bertomeu. Then he's answer himself: Sure, I'd love to put myself in Bertomeu's shoes, especially at night when he lies down on Monica. How's that for a house. How's that for a wife, how about that car. It's him who needs to try to understand me for once, someone who's devoted his whole life to working for him, who's taken risks for him and has nothing to show for it; who's dealt consistently with the goons who go around pinching our posts, cement mixers, cable, saws, the compressor; who wrangles deals with the security companies, the clans that send their thugs over to try and scare us into their clutches, all those fights over them stealing our materials—and they aren't some kind of idiot neighbors who pilfer a few sacks of cement only to throw their backs out a couple of times, who lug the sacks off, but within a couple of months are looking to ditch them somewhere because the sacks got wet before they could figure out what to do with them, and now they're just lumps of rock. No, I mean the ones who filch entire machines, the tools, the generators; they blast the wall you'd just raised the day before; next day you show up to find the site empty, they carried off the grappling hooks: the kid you hired as a night watchman is left behind with bruises and a shiner. Grappling hooks are worth ten, twelve euros apiece and they pinched three hundred of them; or they swiped all the wire meshes you'd prepared for the site, or the boilers you were just about to install; they stripped the piping to the boilers, all the copper, or the doors about to be fitted, the security gates, and it's money, serious money you have to add to the home buyer's invoice; you have to factor in the costs because if you don't pay up, if you try to deal with it some other way, you're completely fucked. No choice but to pay up. The extortions depend on the size of the construction project, and on top of it they force you to hire a few members of the gypsy clan and pay for their insurance on site even though they won't lift a finger, they just lounge around all day, plucking their harp strings, and they're probably the only two workers on the entire site with insurance coverage. But that's how it works, and the pair of insured deadbeats keep the people who sent them informed in real time on the materials, the quantities, coming in and going out, and whether the security contract needs to be adjusted or not and everyone complies, the big companies and the little guys, because nobody wants the extra trouble; see, construction already comes with its fair share of conflict and who needs a body riddled with bullets dumped at the foot of your site, or the security guard you hired to get whacked, or leave someone they bumped off themselves right there on your scaffolding, or someone else maybe, a random body from who knows where, now on the third floor dangling from a rope or slumped over on the ground. That's the day you know you're fucked: now you got inspections up the ass, they pull out the magnifying glass, the employment office cartels are on your back, the tax agency mafia—and suddenly you've become suspect. Try to distance yourself from the security mafias and the state starts looking at you sideways; the only way to be considered innocent is if you jump on the bandwagon, pay the clan, jump through their hoops, let them poke a finger up your ass and fondle your prostate. Can't do anything about it, no doubt they slip a little to the inspectors; if not, how else. They'd say they dumped some dead junkie on this one's site because he won't play their game, what an upstanding citizen. Nope, on the contrary, you turn into that suspicious dude, the guy who's getting a kickback for trafficking this or that, though nobody actually believes it, everyone knows what's going down. I'm not saying anything you don't already know, though you came on board when the wind was already in our sails. Bertomeu was already rich and nobody wanted to fuck with him, nobody was jumping through no mafia hoops anymore. So yeah, I'd love to be in his shoes, Sarcós. Why not? No more dealing with the mafia. Stretch out on his bed, climb on top of his wife. Sarcós teased him: You like hookers too much, and gambling—only thing hookers and gambling do is eat you up. They ruin you. Rubén likes to have his own personal whore and not share her with anyone else, the one he keeps at home, and the only place he gambles is on the stock market. That's the sum of his whoring and his gambling, and that's the difference between the two of you, Sarcós had said when Rubén married his current wife. Sarcós was a piece of shit, a chickenshit ogre. Back when Bertomeu was still living with his first wife but already involved with his new one, he said: If all women were whores they'd be easy to handle. But that's not the case. There's my wife, there's my daughter, and there's my mother. I'd almost say and there's Monica, and even though she goes to bed with me, even though she's my lover, or perhaps precisely because she's my lover, for that reason alone, rest assured she's no whore. She's my lover. He met Monica when his wife was sick, and Monica was still working in reception at a hotel in Benidorm (that's what Rubén said. Others say he plucked her out of some roadhouse in southern Alicante, in Elche or in Orihuela). But she's a lady now. Collado has seen her cruising around Misent in her convertible, going to buy expensive cosmetics, getting her hair done in salons in the Almendros resort, picking up food at the gourmet deli on Avenida Orts. A woman can rise like a hot-air balloon. Down in the dregs and ten minutes later you're flying high, watching everything from above. Life doesn't work that way for men: there's a pyramid, a chain of command, a ladder. You can move up fast or slow, but you have to fight for every inch, every stair. Not so for chicks, from low-down to nosebleed in a minute flat. That's the difference between being active or passive. The passive person waits for an opportunity while the active one has to deserve it. It's about whether your organs are on the inside or the outside. What's outside betrays you. Limits you. You can only fuck to the extent that you are able to fuck. You are what you are. There's nothing else. Someone said it once: Despite Napoleon's vast empire and all he conquered, someone told me the only thing he was able to fuck was the vegetable hawker, or something like that. You can only do what you can do, what your body allows. You can't force your body to grow. You can feed it better, take better care of it, nourish it fine—but you can't suddenly sprout a second dick. Your milieu is organized according to what you earn, you may have a bigger bed, but it'll be the same person lying down in it, you may have your dick extended in some clinic, your house may be a palace and you may wear million-dollar suits, but it's still you inside of them, with your dick, with your shit, just you. The old bricklayers used to tell Collado stories of when Rubén visited sites while still working for other people. He got contracts because he charged so little. He thinks: Where did all of your money go? You got rich, but there's hardly anything left now, you're surviving on scraps, patently poorer and still without two dicks. Though one thing is for sure, you can fuck your mother and kill your father. Activities. The options and desires of an active person. Stick it wherever you want. Wives, mothers, all those sayings about wives and mothers, which ones are sluts and which ones aren't. Collado used to tell Sarcós: Men like dirty things. Smut. That's just how it is. We're pigs, we like to poke our flesh into places that have been poked by others, why else would you be obsessed with whores? Why do you think we love married women? To wallow in the same puddle other fellas have wallowed in before. To measure your dick against theirs. You know, Sarcós, I think half of us whore lovers are actually a bit gay. Take me, for instance. You kind of like it better when you know they've fucked someone else before you. If not, why go rooting around in what others have already had? Eat out a whore's pussy that's just had another guy's dick inside. Drinking from the same watering hole, dipping your whisk into the communal cocktail mixer. Collado pictures his mother underneath some bald, scrawny drunk's belly poking at her with a drooling tail. My father, my mother. A couple of pigs. They all are. Every house has a room with a nuptial bed: there's the brothel, the whorehouse, right inside the home. We fuck, we do dirty things, stick our fingers in all the filthy holes and with the sleeping kids nearby. See? No separation between one thing and the other. None. They're all mixed up. Not like our recycled trash nowadays, glass here, batteries here, paper and cardboard there, organic matter in the next can over. There's no recycling, no separating the bad from the worse, it's all mixed up. That's family. Kids drawing little flowers, praying, playing, washing their hands before they eat and brushing their teeth before bed, and their parents holed up in the next room over behind a closed door fucking like dogs, sticking things up each other's asses. Your parents. Cultivated societies design uniforms to hide it all: priests and nuns, the military, judges, soutanes, togas, white coats for doctors and nurses, concealing the body behind a shield of cloth, hiding what's giving the real orders, the body is what rules everything, not health care, not the justice system, not religion. The body. It's unnerving to see a nun undoing a button, or a military man undoing a button that reveals the sad truth that generals wear undies beneath their uniforms. We catch a glimpse of something awkward, like the limp intimacy of a married man, something we'd prefer not to know about. Every button has to be in place, to pass muster as they say in the military, everything ironed and polished, carefully fastened and secure. Be nothing but a uniform. Sarcós laughed at him: Man you're warped in the head like nobody I know. Just fuck, get your rocks off fucking, and call it quits. If you're between a woman's legs and she's giving you life, there's your mamita, kid. Call her mommy while you're fucking her. You can talk to Sarcós like that, he doesn't get offended, he grew up in a facility for orphans and abandoned kids, he never knew his father or mother, they got rid of him; for Sarcós the words mother and father are synonyms for sons of bitches, for john and hooker, no doubt that's what his parents were: that fatigue, that pursuit, that unsafe itinerancy, a fickle mommy who makes big promises and then ditches you—a mother who abandons a boy on the doorstep of a shelter, a convent, throws him into a dumpster with his head wrapped in a plastic bag and takes off after her lover. The wounds the child's head caused on its way out have barely healed and already she's looking for a different head, a brainless head that holds her in thrall, a little head she takes into herself, pleasure and pain all at the same time, and children come only to turn into dead flesh, or worse—Collado thinks—insalubrious flesh like Sarcós, in places that are flushed out, scrubbed, perfumed, prepared with such care, the bordello, the body, the home a bordello, everything volatile, negotiable, this much per piece, that much per hour, what lies hidden behind the buttons of a nun's habit. Sarcós remembers the rites at the institution he grew up in (what they used to call a hospice): Call her Mama and tell her all about the Virgin Mary, about the little card with the depiction of the Virgin Mary, about the lilies, about the flowers that decorated the altar during the month of May, come on, let's all bring flowers to Mary, Our Mother, wildflowers, golden buttons, daisies, poppies, and free yourself from having to know the truth. From knowing the filthiness that lurks behind everything. As the tango goes: The world is and will always be a dirty trick. Get it? That scent of May roses on the Virgin's altar is something you've never been able to forget, isn't that right? How those roses smelled. Roses don't smell like that anymore. How rich the school smelled, how fragrant the church in the month of May when you'd walk in after the children made their offering, how fragrant that classroom, the kids holding their bouquets of freshly cut wildflowers to place before the image of Murillo's *Inmaculada*, what an aroma, the scent of the children with a whiff of excrement, the chalk, the ink and old wood of the desks mingling with that floral aroma, the kind that no longer exists. The perfume of wild roses. Collado listens to Sarcós and thinks how flowers have definitely lost their scent nowadays, even the ones his wife raises in their little front yard. Unscented, artificial roses. Like Europe, artifice, the artificial continent. Everything is grown in nurseries and the essential substances have all been lost. Collado says: A dead continent, mummified (decadence, his father would have said). Everything they call culture is mummified (he hates the word culture, it reminds him of Rubén). A sorcerer's potion to make the dead appear living so they don't start stinking. They say that animals are attracted by smell, and that we are attracted by smell, but the deodorant manufacturers make a fortune. What attracts us if not smell, what is it we're looking for when we stick a tongue into a pussy, or when we lick an asshole? Explain that to me, Sarcós, what compels us to stick our tongues into pussies and assholes. A mixture. A blend of the best and the worst. That's why it's so hard to deal with women, you have to negotiate endlessly, put up with so much precisely because they are a blend, because not all of them are whores. Not exactly whores, or not only whores. It's like they're wrapped in something viscous, something sentimental that you have to rip open before you get to the whore. Otherwise, it'd be simple. It was simple as long as you stayed on script, and didn't ask for anything more. Until then it'd always been so easy for him, but this time he'd wanted more. That's how everything got fucked up. The day he met her nearly a year ago. There in the club. They usually swap out the girls every few weeks, but they kept her on. That first night: Irina. Marina? No, Irina. A pretty name, but it's not your real one. You all have such alluring names. As alluring as these little titties here: soft names, like these tits, like this here, aw no come on, don't move away, let me touch you, have a drink but let me touch you, they're names that don't have wrinkles, hairless names, nothing crooked, nothing ugly, nothing dirty, nothing displeasing. I can poke my finger into you and it comes out spotless, look, let me do it sugar, don't close your legs, look at that clean ass, I can stick my tongue in your mouth, and it's clean. Later they'll call you by another name, Margaret, Ana, Isabel, names you can't find there, right? Any Anas, Margarets, or Isabels there? Must be an Isabel or two, the calendar says that Saint Isabel was a Hungarian queen. Though Hungary falls on this side of things; it belongs to the Austrians and you, you're closer to the Russians—that's it, the Ukraine was Russia, or at least the Soviet Union, right? I'm serious; come on, tell me a few of the local names there, not the ones you use when you're working at the bar, not the slutty names, I want to know some common girls' names from your country, the kind you hear walking down the street, the kind that husbands use when they're fucking them. Imagine, the thought of ordinary names makes me horny, look how hot you are and to think your name might be Lola (Lola is a sweet name, and it's a slutty one too—it could be the name of a whore and also someone who isn't, you could call yourself Lola), or maybe Gloria, Asunción, or maybe you're really an Irina. That's what happened on the first day. And more of the same on the second: Just think, I can call you Lola while I'm riding you. Look, touch it, I get so hard just imagining your name, you'll get me even harder if you say your name is like one from around here, like I could fuck you more

often, not pay to fuck you, but do it for real, so you feel pleasure
like the other day when we spent the night together and you wig-
gled and screamed and pulled my head away with your hands, you
wanted me to stop eating your pussy because you were dying of
pleasure, you were going wild with pleasure, my tongue, my fingers, my dick, you couldn't take it, you pulled my head away, look
how it is, I pay you to pleasure yourself. Men are like that, don't
say you don't pity us, we pay because we don't have anyone to give
pleasure to, because we crave seeing that look on your face when
you're coming, we pay to be able to tell ourselves that we're capable of sexually pleasing someone. So pathetic, isn't it? But you
don't understand me, my confessions, do you, you don't get it, you
don't understand what I'm saying—all you know how to say in
Spanish is drink, dick, suck, and fuck because you just got here a
few months ago, you're new, don't try to fool me, they just brought
you over; though all you girls learn languages like sponges, pick
things up so quick, in a month or two, same as the guys, I watch
the ones working at the building sites with me, or the waiters, who
arrive not knowing anything and within a few months they're
picking it all up, and go figure there are foreigners, Brits and Germans, who've lived their whole lives here, bought a house and
settled for eight or ten years and still have no clue, pronouncing
words as though they were chomping on eggshells, incapable of
putting a sentence together, while you girls start fumbling
through immediately. But hey, here I am, fuck, your tongue's so
hot, bitch, you suck my ear and burn it, you fuck me in the ear, son
of a bitch, daughter of whore; oh, oh not that, not daughter of a
whore?—so you know what it means, don't you now, don't want
me to call you a whore's daughter, but whore is okay, you slutty
whore; but not a daughter of a whore, not that, it has nothing to
do with your mother, she's a saint, embroidering doilies, and those
dainty lace curtains you see decorating the cabin windows in tele-

vision documentaries about farmers in your country, those wooden dwellings with pointy roofs and lace curtains. You're annoyed. Yes, of course you can have another drink—but have it upstairs in the room. Why waste more time here? Let's go upstairs. We'll do a line, you know what a line is, right? Don't tell me you don't, you're all addicted to the stuff, that's how they pull you in, get you started, by the nose like oxen, they stick a ring in your nose and off to work you go, a little bump then all the compulsory fucking. Let me stay. I'll pay to stay the night. Give me a good price and I'll pay for the whole night. But she can't stay. She says they're waiting for her. After they close the club, they wait for her. Really, I can't, she says, stretching her arm out again and giving my dick a squeeze. It's hard, but she can't stay the night. She's learning how to speak now, to explain that they don't like her spending the night with the same client, and especially not two nights in a row. They like that even less. It's not a good idea to disobey these people—they don't like her doing these sorts of things. Not a boyfriend, she says, who knows in what language, but he understands her, now he understands everything she says, she's improving with each day that passes, she says friends that watch over her, protect her. Not that she can't do what she wants mind you, but this is her way. It's my choice to do things this way. They fetch her at five in the morning except for Fridays and Saturdays, when they pick her up at seven or even a little later. He tries to persuade her to make today a special occasion: Just this once, come on. But no, not a special occasion. That's how it goes. He's angry. Come on, let's not argue. Let's fuck. Get up. We'll go for as long as you want. Collado knows he shouldn't parade his coke around, never shit where you eat, but what the hell, they all snort it, don't they?—no nuns or monks around here; what the fuck is life worth if you're the one who has to go to all the trouble and can't enjoy the fruit of his labor? His snorting used to infuriate Rubén. But it might do Rubén some good to have a little chat with his granddaughter. Oh no, nothing. Just that his little pumpkin runs around the clubs snorting her brains out. Collado hangs out in the clubs where the young babes go, not that he's into minors or anything, but he frequents them and sees her there. So why not indulge in a few lines with a friend upstairs. Let life last longer in less time. He remembers the trips with Bertomeu back in the day—the shipments, Madrid, the politicians. All kaput. The horses used to arrive in Barajas at the shipping terminal and cross the Mancha on the way to the ring, the stables. He never could stand the stables, they reminded him too much of the ones at his father's house. All he could think when Rubén put him in charge of them was how life seems hell-bent on bringing precisely what you least desire, and wouldn't it be nice if destiny could spare us the practical jokes. Stop fucking around with us. Getting its nuts off because it's bored. Horses for the hippodrome, but not something that will last a lifetime, things end up being discovered. His job was to watch over the stables. It all flashes through his mind again as he climbs the red velvet neon-lit stairs, as he continues along the more tenuous bluish lighting of the hallway where ghostlike creatures pass in silence. She sits down on the bed and takes off her shoes. That was the first day, the second. Then he gave her his phone number and started showing up in the club almost every night. Party with me, Lola (he keeps calling her Lola though she insists her name is Irina). Party. As in having a good time. Don't mess with me. I can't, too late. You can come back. No, not now. What the fuck? Don't fuck around with me. No games, I won't put up with it from you. Suddenly he notices the music playing. The clients sitting around the bar drinking, making out, grinding, mumbling under their breath, pinching a tit, fondling under skirts so short you can see their skimpy panties underneath, their thongs. They poke around in the panties. Little animals driven by someone, a shepherd, a foreman, the girls;

the clients, animals driven by someone sight unseen who watches every step, every night. Quoted from a calendar: *Yearning born of hatred is the desire to possess and to consume the soul of the person despised, as the lover's desire is to possess the person loved to the very limit.* It's from a bank calendar hanging in the office. He hates her right now, but he can feel the anxiety to possess her growing: him, one more, like the whole lot of them, little animal, asshole. Hatred. They're all the same, he thinks. They pick you clean and then call in the gorillas to throw you out. Poor gorillas out there in the wild, what a tragedy that they have to share a name with those greasy brutes yawning at the door of the club. He chuckles at his own joke. He heard it from Rubén. Yeah, the porkers at the door here are uglier than real gorillas, they're knuckle-draggers. With her in the room now. The little mirror. The curve of her insole as she holds a shoe in her hand, sitting on the bed. He could never remember which music they played, he'd always shown up plastered and let himself be cajoled by the first whore who came along and rubbed up against him, but now he only had eyes for her, and some evenings, buzzed after a third or fourth drink, the craving for her became excruciating. What music was playing that night? Sometimes she'd ignore him, he would watch her talking to other men, luring them toward the stairway and up to the rooms, to the long hallway flanked on either side by lines of doors. Standard room, Jacuzzi, suite, junior suite. Different sizes, different services, some had televisions, round bathtubs, refrigerators stocked with soft drinks and little bottles of alcohol or cava or champagne. Big difference in price. A half hour in one room isn't the same as a half hour in another, the suite costs four times as much, and he likes the suite. He remembered his conversations with Sarcós: whoremongers like us are half fags, we like to eat other people's leftovers. Every whore we fuck is part of an orgy. Lola: I can't be with you all the time; but he saw how other girls beelined to the men they knew, the ones they'd gone upstairs with before, and how they allowed themselves to be taken up again. I don't know what other girls do, I know what I can do, Lola said. He was getting the idea that someone else was jealous. She belonged to someone outside of the club, someone who didn't like her to have regular clients, or any possible competition. At first Ramón Collado thinks he can outsmart her, outmaneuver her; this is his own turf, it's his scene, not hers, but he watches her take others upstairs, others he knows by sight and knows they're richer than him, and that's when he starts thinking about how a body is capital: you can have it all. He thinks: As time goes by and she figures it all out, she'll move further away from him and into someone else's arms, she's too hot to go under the radar, she'll be noticed by some businessman, factory owner, developer, anyone could get a hankering for her, take her off, buy her a flat, marry her. Back in the day nobody would think of marrying a prostitute, but now they do, now there are men who cherry-pick a girl from a club, marry her, and make her a lady. You can see them now, crossing an intersection behind the wheel of an extravagant car, flashing a scornful glance at you, all haughtiness, the newly arrived slut, and she thinks she's better than you, a local, who's worked here their whole life, knows everyone, and now suddenly she's attended to before your wife in the stores, she sends her kids to private schools while yours are stuck in the public system, the piece of shit school with prefab boxes for classrooms, your son is there while hers is learning how to sail, ride horses, play tennis and golf, and spending summers abroad. He hates her even more when his mind wanders off to these places, he feels hatred and love for Lola all mixed together, all tangled up (can't recycle life, Sarcós old pal): to possess her, to own her, but with you being on top, knowing she's no more than a newly arrived slut; but it's dangerous now, she can leave now, she can abandon you, she has her body and if that weren't enough, she's beginning to speak Spanish well, she's picked up the manners, now she can be whatever she wants because her body is like a safe with treasure in it that can be boundless if administered carefully, if spent only little by little. It's always been that way, only now it's more so than ever. Always take that into account with a bimbo. Body trumps class, overcomes it, a little piece of shit student can bring a tenured professor to his miserable knees and a little slut can turn a billionaire banker into a nervous, insomniac wreck. That's what Sarcós said to him, and he responded sarcastically. But Sarcós was right. They hadn't seen each other for ages. Another one of Rubén's victims. He said to Sarcós: don't you dare come around here again. And Sarcós, who was privy to company dirt like no one else, let his jaw drop open like an idiot and didn't say a word. Then clammed right up. But Rubén gave him a hefty tip, that much is true. Sarcós could've sunk the whole thing, sent them all to prison, though it would've been self-inflicting; but it didn't go down like that, he just took a big dump in the security-guard uniform pants he'd bought for himself, not a question as to why Rubén was getting rid of him, no begging, he just walked away, maw agape, shuffling off in reverse without giving his back to Bertomeu like they do in the movies when someone exits an audience with the king. He knew perfectly well what he'd done wrong. It wasn't his bragging about seeing Monica's panties, or her parts beneath the panties whenever she walked around the terrace or when she skinny-dipped in the pool. Bertomeu could give a shit about that sort of thing. She's the lady of the house and Sarcós a nobody. Ladies don't worry about upsetting the hired help. They get naked in front of them like they would the bathroom mirror. They're not worth the trouble. It had to do with his arrangement with the Star Club and with Luna Nueva, and that restaurant, Mediterráneo, where he sidelined peddling the coke that came in with the horses. Rubén went insane. It broke the pact: We know nothing, don't even know what it is. We transport it from one place to another but fully ignore what's inside. We've never seen it. I've never seen it. So that's how Sarcós fell. And Collado falls here, every night, trapped at the bar, every day his eyeballs glued to a phone that only rings when she needs something. Upstairs almost every night, blowing his wad at the bar and in the room, a half hour more, let's hang out another half hour, and she pulls out her wallet, the whole thing a big joke, saying: Pay up baby, as if the little pieces of paper she counts and stuffs away were play money, with no real value. Like a big game. Wait for her at work and wait in vain for her phone calls on her day off. Take her to the restaurant in the cove, out-of-the-way places to eat in peace, walk along the beach with her on winter days, run up behind her and tumble onto the sand. Before long, he was utterly pussy-whipped. And that's when she says she doesn't ever want to see him again. Ramón Collado collapses, and a little while later she calls to say she wants to see him, that she needs his help, can he make a contract at his business for someone in her family who needs a residency permit. And Collado floats up to the heavens again, though it's no easy thing to find homes for her cousins, her uncle yes, with a construction contract; but the aunt, well, maybe, the office cleaning lady, but to do that she needs to show up for at least a month, a month and a half. Lola-Irina says: Aren't you the boss? And he doesn't tell her he isn't; that really he's nothing, that his business is a shitty little joke, a horse stable with fewer than a dozen workers. Irina asks for and then rejects what he gives her. It's always too little, too late. The necklace, the bracelet, the earrings, the suit, she chooses the items, but when he buys them for her it's already too late. No, I don't want anything anymore, it'd be better if you don't come back. He gets angry, he's always angry when he says goodbye, she's constantly putting him on edge, every night she leaves him in a bad mood, sleepless, wishing it were late afternoon already, when she wakes up, to call her. He's called at seven in the evening only to hear her complain, you woke me up. I went to bed really late, and she hangs up on him. He decides to drop her. Never call her again, but she calls him out of the blue with some excuse for getting together again. By now she speaks Spanish very well, almost like a native. They learn fast. It's Lola, she says. He loves that she calls herself Lola, the name he gave her. He gets excited by the voice at the other end of the line. A housewife's name and a whore's, multiple purposes. Good, that's nice. The puddle is stirred. Life cannot be recycled. The best and the worst all mixed up: the good smells, the bad smells. That's sex, he thinks. No recycling. Whatever they say, nobody can take the filth out of him. At times after sex you have to shower immediately. The smell is overpowering. That's why he told Lola that he can't stand it anymore, that he wants her for himself. We have to take off now, he told her. Now. And she acknowledges his proposal for the time being: I have a flat where you can live and then we can get married, or not, whatever you want. Lola: You're already married and I can't just leave. They watch me. Him: Then let's run off. Her: Where to? Collado: Just let my wife try to find me, and let them chase after you. He's thinking Mexico, where Rubén can put him in touch with friends if he wants, friends who work with the Colombians and who don't know the Russian, somewhere in Mexico where nobody can find them. Though he knows it's not possible. He says it, knowing it's impossible. But Lola, who wouldn't even acknowledge him at the club these past few days, says it's time to run off now. For a second, he lets himself think it could happen: talk to Rubén, ask him for a quick loan because she wants to see the cash, show her the money. I won't leave blindly she tells him, but he only has what he has, which is less than ever—in fact, he's been blowing it all on her, by the hour and the half hour; but I'll talk to Rubén who'll spot me the rest, who'll give me a few names, he tells himself, let me know how to get in touch with Gustavo, the Mexican, and the Colombians. The ones Rubén claims he's not dealing with anymore. He scratches my back and I'll return the favor, he thinks. He pretends to believe it, makes the effort. He acts it out, though he can't even swallow his own story. That same day he withdraws the barely fifteen thousand euros in his account, that's all there is (Friday he has to pay his guys), and hands over six as a kind of advance, a promise of more to come (but where would he find more? This is everything he has), and he talks to her about America, making it look as though his wallet were still fat with bills. Go back to the places he's already been—he tells her—where the natural world hasn't disappeared completely, where past and future live together as if they'd been mixed in a blender. Cement and jungle. The airplane and the silent fields of blue agave, that's the north; then there's the *tianguis*, the street markets in the south, the dark jungles full of strange noises. He was in Mexico a few years ago, in Cancún with his wife; but before that he was with Bertomeu in Monterrey, in Guadalajara, in Dayefe, in Tehuantepec, everything there has an aroma, not like in Europe, there it never stops smelling, burnt rubber, corn, the fat of grilled meat, cilantro, he tells her, and there's all the fruit in the world at your fingertips, all the vegetables, meats, he says. But he doesn't mention how on that first trip with Rubén he barely ate a thing: the smell of cilantro like a torment everywhere he went, whenever they laid a dish out before him, tortillas, huevos rancheros, that green smell pestering him like a field tick; he remembers but avoids telling her about the Merced market with its odors of cilantro and rotten fish. The paucity of fish surprised him: how could a large market in the capital of a country with so much coastline be so deprived of decent fish? He missed the market in Misent. It was Rubén who usually went off on the spectacular fruits and vegetables of Mexico, and Rubén, who's normally so

fussy about hygiene, went around touching and squeezing everything while Collado, green-faced and on the verge of throwing up,
fretted over being called a wuss by the locals. That's where the
Colombians had set up the meeting to discuss the horse operation. Better to meet there, said Gustavo, Rubén's man in Mexico.
Got us a nice team of fillies here, too. He whinnied. He guffawed.
He was alluding to the girls in the club: a hundred purebreds. Half
a dozen for us *solo*, later on at the ranch. Half a dozen girls to mix
your drinks, lay out coke, stick their pussies in your face as they
bend over to cut lines. You said strip, they stripped. They did
whatever you asked. Ten toys to play any game you wanted. That
was in Guadalajara. Later, they went to Gustavo's ranch. Rubén
was a bundle of nerves on this leg of the trip. He shoved Collado
into a room and said: Idiot, better not let me catch you snorting
one more line. But I don't want to be rude to Gustavo. You just tell
him you don't have the habit. But Gustavo called him Ramoncito,
Colladín, or Colladito, he said, what a nice kid you have Rubén,
better than a son. Offspring always let you down, let me down, let
everyone down. Rubén was dead set, he told Gustavo that the
Spanish generally preferred alcohol to other substances. Though
Rubén liked his tequila reposado and with sangrita, nice and spicy.
There were tacos, tamales, chiles, and huevos rancheros to accompany the tequila and sangrita, and the coke, and the horses, and
the music and the whores, and a little more of the Jimador, or
better, now a little of the Los Cazadores reposado. No, maybe time
for a whore now. The little harem steadfastly serving more tequila
reposado and sangrita, cutting lines with credit cards, cuddling
with you and stroking the crotch of your pants to check in on your
ongoing hard-on. Eventually everyone stripped down, butt naked.
It was a free-for-all. He doesn't tell Lola the dirty details, he prefers
not to, though at times he thinks telling her might be a good way
to prove himself worthy of her trust; he's seen the world like his

father, though his father never used that expression, he used to say he roamed the world: he'd roamed around the dirty Russian ice. He told him about the frozen, half-buried cadavers, how they'd cry when they warmed up in the sunlight, for a few months a year you could see the poorly interred cadavers cry, and people would say that spring is coming; in Russia springtime makes the dead cry, the peasants would say. He'll tell her about Mexico to show her she's not indispensable to him. He'd stood up to her once, when she tried to throw a wrench into his plans: I don't want to talk to you ever again, he'd said to Lola. He thought he was finally ready to break it off, but he had been lying to himself. He was just pretending. She broke into tears. You cry, you lose, his father used to say. That was true for men. But the opposite was true for women. They shed a few tears and got their way, whatever they wanted. She was on the other end of the phone line, wanting to have her way with him. Who are you running from, he asked her. He'll kill me, she answered. He reassured her, or wanted to reassure her. And she said: I'm not running away from anyone, you'll see. And he thought: Resist the temptation, it's a trap. He fucked her. He paid to fuck her. He looks at the body in front of him, naked, he looks, thinking: the blood will continue to flow through that body's veins after he's dead and gone, blood in the veins, blood racing to certain spots, coursing hard and fast to certain spots for a long time, when he is no longer. Lola's so young. Twenty-two years old. He pays and he suffers. That's life. Pay to suffer. Only with her being there, in front of him, is he able to feel this infinite suffering. Pay to suffer over someone, pay to give someone pleasure. Can you feel it inside you, my love? I feel it, warm, I like it. I have to call Yuri to pick me up and bring me to the club, Lola says over the phone, and he offers: Let me take you, several times he says it, though she rejects his offer, I don't like it, I don't like you hanging out at the club, this is the last day he'll ever fuck her, that night he'll figure it all out when he proposes to her and she laughs at him, he's wasted, he drank too much because of her, worrying about who she's with, what he's doing with her, it's not just work because she's laughing, she's talking, she lingers with a client, she's been on his mind so he drank, he snorted. She gets angry with him: plenty of men have fucked me. Thousands have fucked me. They all get the same treatment. Bring them upstairs, bring them downstairs. She mocks him cruelly. Collado: You shouldn't talk to me like that. You always have a good time with me. It's just tonight, I'm loaded, been doing lines. She says: I try to enjoy my job. Be professional. And today you don't please me. You can't. You bore me. He lobs her bag against the mirror. A few things smash onto the floor. My bag isn't the problem, she shouts, now she's screaming and punching at him. He covers her mouth. He has to shut her up before the gorilla in the hallway comes barging in. Lolairina locks herself in the bathroom and he passes out on the couch. Too wasted. Look, check it out, now I can. He shows it to her, his fat, priapic stiffness that accompanies the coke hangover, won't be coming down for hours, he says. I'll give you the money tomorrow, he says, you keep it as proof, keep the money for the plane tickets safe, for our first few months, I'll bring the rest in a few more days and we'll bolt. He wants her to leave the club the following day. He set up one of the vacant flats in a friend's development for Lola to stay in for a while. Then he'll figure it all out. She pretends not to be the least bit interested in his plans and schemes, contemplates herself in the mirror, lights another cigarette, passes a hand through her hair. You talk too much, she says. The comment stings. Life is the color of creamed spinach without the suffering radiance of naked flesh. Though you have to pay for the flash of lightning that gives you strength. He's over forty and she says she's twenty-two. How does a twenty-two-year-old girl get to know so much? He's got a toe in the grave and she's fucking like there's no tomorrow. Not a good thought to galvanize her desire for running away with him. It's a tough image for him to swallow. Pay for the luxury of that lousy thought, for the image to get stuck in his throat. Bite her, infect her, and carry her to the grave with you, they'll share a coffin, he'll defend her from the fangs of other eager vampires. That body dazzles him, what it's capable of, how it'll ache and weep and yearn for him when he's dead and gone and no longer anything for this body or for any other (but at forty there's still plenty of life ahead). Barely a memory to his kids. That son of a bitch who abandoned us to run off with a Russian or Ukrainian prostitute—no more than a hazy memory. He deserted us, left us with our clueless mother who was only good for grocery shopping, for cooking, ironing. She couldn't do paperwork to save her soul, figure out an electricity bill, deal with taxes, open a bank account. Three useless individuals left to their own devices, two inept teenagers and that utterly useless lady. That lady who would plant herself in front of the toilet and scrub the tiles over and over again to stop herself from crying, the floor tiles, the wall tiles, the sink, the bidet, the bathtub, the toilet bowl, that lady who scraped along on her knees, leaned over the toilet bowl and plunged her fist in for a little scouring, the germs, the virus, the bacteria in hot pursuit. Lady Lysol, Mrs. Clean with Clorox. He thinks: She's my wife and I'm the husband who ran away with a prostitute. I shouldn't feel ashamed; maybe a little shame over the money I'm leaving here tonight. To the wife: Find yourself a maid, a Colombian or a Bulgarian, whatever, to come and help you out, and you really need to fix yourself up a little, find new friends, women with a little more class, hang out with them at the café, the tennis club, get yourself a tennis coach, you'd have fun, and change the way you dress, to which she sullenly answers: Yeah, why don't I just change my look with all that cash you give me, there's so much of it left over to pick myself up a little Loewe, Vuitton, Agatha Ruiz de la Prada, fabulous idea, prance around the tennis court, my little girl, my Anabelén, my Ricardo, oh, others have fathers, there are kids who have fathers. It upsets Collado to think that his kids don't: a father who gets home early, plants a kiss on their foreheads, in the crib, the twin bed, I'll bring you to school tomorrow in the SUV; but Papa Collado isn't like that, and it hurts to admit it: Papa Ramón is always so tired in the morning, so bushed: I don't want to, I swear to God I don't want to run off, but when she calls, I jump, that's how it is now, I can't help it anymore. He calls himself stupid. You start off doing everything for them, you keep the household running. Buy a large-screen TV, buy a stove with a glass-ceramic cooktop, a dryer, a cushy high-quality leather couch, a steam cleaner, and all of it sits there at home like eyewitnesses spying on you, the lady's allies, but slowly your goings-on outside begin to change you. You adapt to the other lifestyle, and this one starts dissolving, the one you meant to safeguard vanishes, because now you belong to the other one, the other life has turned you into something else, it's only natural, you become something else, life becomes something else, you're different, even your body is different. You can tell if a person's a fisherman or a stonemason just by their hands, the way they walk, you can tell if they work in an office, or drive a truck and spend ten hours a day in the cabin; your body adapts to the work you do, to the life you lead. You can spot the undercover agent at the border crossing on first sight, the one with a probing eye, and you know he's sniffed you out too, and both of us try to go unnoticed, it's a reciprocal relationship. The years he spent with Rubén had changed him: your perspective changes, your mind opens, the way you look at things shifts, you still love your kids but don't give a shit about their silly notebooks, their end of semester parties, give even less of a shit about your wife's piddling chores when you're in the middle of an operation, when an excavator could run you over and all your wife cares about are things like her appointment at the hairdresser's and how she's going to be late for your son's year-end school pageant and what's worse you can't even explain to her about what you're do-ing, how you pay for the hairdresser and the kids' private school, they speak English already, Papa, you should have learned English at school, but you didn't go to school, so you don't know anything, you didn't learn anything (he told Sarcós regretfully). He consid-ered breaking it off with her: some days it was goodbye Lola; other days he was running off with her, she'll be his forever; next day he'll never set eyes on her again, be free of her, but ten days of not thinking about her, or hardly thinking about her, keeping himself distracted, finally free, an animal who untethered its legs out of sheer will, who slipped the trap set for him by the crafty hunter, only to fall back again: it's so hard to stay sidetracked, it takes so much effort to stay sidetracked, because everything else is such a fucking bore, the construction site bores you, the accounting bores you, drinking bores you, even hanging around the house, what an epic bore, sitting in the recliner watching *Big Brother* on TV, the wife spouting off about something she heard on the radio, about sharing, about how couples need to communicate, tell each other things, nurture their relationship, all of it a gargantuan bore and what is boredom if not a subtle form of insanity, boredom is the hedge you build around your insanity, a wall like the ones they build around highways to isolate the noise in populated areas, a muffler for insanity to bounce around inside, so it doesn't extend beyond the wall, though it's already there lying in wait, and the second you relax a little it'll scale the glass shards you plastered on top of the wall to protect yourself from her, and trap you again. Collado tries hard to ignore these thoughts and impulses, no, he won't go see her, but the mere fact of her being on his mind again means he's still not out of harm's way, he's still at risk, he said no but it sounded more like a not now, or a not yet, or a not quite yet. He didn't say not ever, which is what he would have said by not responding, remaining silent, silence his sole sanctuary, what does he expect, that she'll fall apart, fall to her knees before him and stop pretending, because it's all been a big performance except for a couple of rare instances of truth, the times they had sex without exchanging money, only for her to realize half an hour later it was something she couldn't allow herself, the ardent tongue, fuck me, not saying pay me, only fuck me, but instantly she rises above him, makes him drool at her feet like a little dog. Playing the role of the lady who lacks for nothing, who could be with someone far better than him, above him, and Collado thinks: Be with him then, go on, but stop calling me, leave me alone, he's sure she won't ever let down her guard with him again, and it's a relief, she'll fall in with others, on other days, other benders, she'll tell someone else to fuck her, coolly, because being with Collado now means she'd have to drop the farce, he makes her confront her need, desire is a need, the gateway to love, it prevents her from going into character, pure character, a doll walking up to the bar, a shard of ice that only melts with cash, everything you have, and she lights a cigarette, slinks a hand through her hair, peeks into the mirror. For months he'd been pleading for the strength to escape her again tomorrow, the way he'd escaped her today. Hang out in the club, ogle the other girls, chat with them, climb the stairs behind one of them to the junior suite, not a single glance her way, fuck the other girl while she's at the bar knowing he's fucking someone else. He pleaded for strength, same as the Pope, the moribund Pope beseeching the Catholics to give him the strength to endure as Pope while he lay dying, not to abandon him to what he really was, a frightened old man on his deathbed. My love, don't let me be what I am. Even he felt compelled to lend a helping hand to the Pope after hearing his radio address, compelled to help bear the cross of his agony. Offer his shoulder to carry it for a while so the Pope could rest. He also asks for strength to continue being what he is not. Economies of the soul. Things went rather well, but lasted only ten, fifteen days; fifteen days without the constant craving to be inside of her. I'm over her, he told himself. It's through. He's not going to see her anymore. It's done, I'm condemned to nothingness, to death, to allowing myself to die, to wanting to die; antieconomy, you're alone because you have no form, because you're air, you move among others without being noticed, without anyone caring to notice you, without anyone being aware you exist: the way his wife was nothing but air to him, he could walk straight through her without seeing her, without noticing her, you're not this or that, and he thinks, it's true, you're nothing. She'd left him whenever she wanted, never raised a finger to ease his pain, the pain she instigated, and one day out of the blue she calls as if nothing—what now, what's she after, I don't owe her anything, but she measured, she weighed. She calculated the consequences of her rebuke to the millimeter and knew how to make it work for her. She called to ask if the money was ready yet. She'd made calculations. Desperate and caught in the net of a wildly tangled life: like one of those aging carnival magicians who's tied up to demonstrate his resourcefulness, his secret means for undoing intricate knots, when, *presto*, just like that reality shifts and imposes itself anew: the clown realizes he lacks the strength; he, who'd insisted on being thrown into the river in a straitjacket, wagering he'd surface a hundred meters downstream just before the bridge, now finds himself tangled, unable to break free: the light inside dowses out, he no longer remembers how he'd gotten free the day before, or simply lacks the strength to do it. The seconds fly by as the certainty of death encroaches; he realizes now that he's going to drown. And Lola takes her time. It's the money. She told him not to wait at the door; not to wait for her by the exit, she says; she'll come, he'll pay her for three hours, not the whole night, no, her boss won't let her spend the whole night, Traian won't tolerate it, he thinks it's a betrayal, a slave running away, slipping the chains. Pay for three hours, she said. And he paid. At five in the morning the room has to be empty. They're coming to pick me up. All he cares about is knowing who. I'll explain everything when we're far away and it's just you and me alone together. How well you speak Spanish now. That's who is coming to pick you up, Collado says, whoever is teaching you how to speak. My clients teach me. My clients are the ones who teach me to speak, she says. And my tongue, I figured out how to use that on my own, nobody had to teach me, she giggles, sticking the tip of it into his ear and pivoting to lick down his body, lower and lower, little by little. A mere flick of the tongue and his body coils, a moan escapes his throat, his eyes roll and close and his own tongue peeks eagerly from behind his lips to point at something in the air. He brought her the cash that night, six thousand euros, and waited in his car, waited for her call to finally pick her up, a short nap in the meantime, arms on the wheel, head on his arms, and woke to the sound of voices in an ambulance rushing him to the hospital. Someone was talking, telling him to do this or that, things he couldn't understand. Now his hands are in bandages and he couldn't call even if he wanted to, he left his cell phone back in the car, likely it's burnt to a crisp— but maybe it's still active, maybe she's trying to call, the number ringing over and over again, a nonexistent cell melted into nothing, or maybe it'll go on ringing as long as the battery lasts. Maybe she's calling, thinking he left her behind and she can't understand why he won't answer, why give her the money, maybe it's a gift before taking off forever. Collado's eyes tear up beneath the bandage around his head. His wife is watching television, distracted, camped out in the chair beside his bed. She told him the kids'll be by to visit after school. He asked the boy to bring him a cell phone. But don't say anything to Mama, he added as soon as she snuck off downstairs for a bite to eat. And the boy replied: But Papa, with what money; and he remembered that the rest of the money he'd withdrawn must still be in his pants, but where are his pants?

SHE SPENT the night thinking about him. She pictured him, heard his voice: The Zayandeh River that flows through the city of Isfahan is the only one that doesn't lead anywhere. Matías explained how the desert swallowed the Zayandeh River, how the sand engulfed it a few kilometers after passing through the embellished city of gleaming cupolas that Silvia had seen in her Wonders of the World sticker album. But there were blue lines leading from the Baltic or the Black Sea to Moscow (the Soviets had turned Moscow into a port of five seas Matías told her), and the blue line of the Seine started at Le Havre, passed through Rouen, crossed Paris, and then died in a splotch of green. Lower the sails so the boat fits below the statue-laden bridges with golden lanterns, turn it into one of those flat, ugly barges that transport gravel and coal. Matías: A boat is meant to carry something, coal, wood, oil, grain. And there are boats that carry only passengers, in which case the passengers are the merchandise. Boats whose cabin walls are dressed in mirrors, with dining rooms and ballrooms and gaming tables covered in green felt. She asked him: Can't I sail to Mexico City on a boat? It'd be difficult to dig a canal all that way, Matías said, imagine the difficulty of pumping sea water to a height of nearly two thousand five hundred kilometers, but you could sail to Hamburg or Leningrad, and Peking too, despite it being so far inland, thousands of kilometers from the nearest coast and in the middle of an ocher-colored plain, but you reach Peking by way of the canals from Shanghai and Nanking. He pointed a finger at Shanghai and Nanking. Marco Polo was surprised when he visited Peking (which at the time was called Cambaluc, and is now called Beijing) to find merchandise there from all over the world. Mexico City was impossible to reach not only because it was far from the sea, but for being at such a high altitude, on a plateau beyond the mountain range where the white tips of volcanoes were visible. Pico de Orizaba she read in the Atlas. And Matías: That's a volcano. If you want to get to Mexico City by sea from Veracruz you have to travel around its perimeter through the Orizaba Valley, which is teeming with exuberant vegetation, and climb vertiginous heights, holding tight onto the mountainsides, the snowcapped volcanoes floating over your head, and then Mexico City is still farther along, on the other side of those peaks. He described the cities in minute detail, as if he were perfectly familiar with them. He explained how in Cuzco the houses were built with solid blocks of stone, in Peking they used ugly bricks (they're covered in soot, everything in Peking was a dreadful blackish color), in Timbuktu they used clay and in other cities, wood (old Moscow burned every summer because the houses and even the nobles' palaces were built from wood, remember how Moscow burns in *War and Peace*? She'd read *War and Peace* in an abridged version for children and she'd seen the movie with its two glamorous leads, Mel Ferrer and Audrey Hepburn, so tall, so thin and elegant). Matías described the stone churches for her, the brick ones, the towers and cupolas, the public buildings, the palaces that had belonged to kings, princes, great merchants, and noble families. Matías the sailor and his ship, Matías the actor, Matías the screenwriter, Matías the film director who'd never written a thing or sailed anywhere, who'd never been behind a camera (Silvia's father called him Matías the Fake), never acted in a play, and only ever traveled to Madrid, Lisbon, and Paris, places everybody's been, but he'd never visited those places he liked to describe as if he'd lived in them, his knowledge came entirely from books or travel pieces in magazines, like everyone else. He hadn't even been to Rome or to Athens. Matías's cities were built from nothing but wind in the throat. By fifteen, Silvia had traveled to more places than Matías in his sixty years of life. But it was he who had the gift of describing them. He talked about what he'd read in the same books that she'd then read, slowly but surely. The boat is a piece of hand-carved wood with four chimneys and a few rods that have pieces of cloth acting as sails, and an even smaller bit of triangular cloth at the top of the mainmast for a flag, a piece of black fabric on which Matías had drawn a red, five-point star. A friend of mine made it, he said, a carpenter, a very good sculptor. It was only a piece of wood but it bobbed beside Silvia in the waves on the beach, in the reservoir in Pinar, like those great white ocean liners from the period between the wars, pitching in the midst of a storm, with its four proud chimneys, its impeccably dressed sailors in blue-and-white uniforms, its salons paneled in oak and mahogany, decked out in marble and rosewood furniture; luxurious liners where people changed their outfits three times a day; light colors in the morning to lounge in deck hammocks with a book, or maybe blue-striped polo shirts for a nautical look; intermediate colors, gray, brown, cream, and loden-green for vermouth and afternoon tea; long gowns for women and suits for men in rigorous black at nightfall, time to call on the dining room and then the ballroom, the cinema, or the casino, a small candy box covered in lightly hued silk. If you open a boat, you'll find all of these things: elegant salons, cabins, storage holds, coal cellars, engine rooms, and boilers. But the wooden boat had no infirmary, someone forgot to make a place for metal cots and stretchers, glass cabinets for medicines and sharp steel instruments. Silvia had experienced a panic attack as she was dozing off the night before: she saw herself searching for the ship's infirmary, getting lost in the hallways, opening doors, peering inside and finding nothing but immense, empty salons behind each door, or cabins full of people looking at her in silence, static, like statues, unblinking, she implored in frantic tears for something she couldn't find the words to describe; all she found were empty spaces and frozen people, but what was she looking for in her nightmare? Where to place the dying Matías? The nightmare carried a sense of dread. She had jolted awake, in a cold sweat despite the air-conditioning. Last night she realized that when considered objectively, a person's death means nothing. The person dying can't offer any secrets. Matías had spent the whole afternoon unconscious: his murmuring, his moaning: physical and chemical acts, all sentient beings die the same way, with the same loss of wakefulness, the same lapse into trance. Rubén left the room and she ran out after him, she couldn't stand the stationary act of watching over a dying man. Angela and Lucía were there when Matías died, but not Silvia. He's gone, he went. She didn't want to be there the moment that last door opened. An image of her trip to Madrid with Matías popped into her mind, with Matías and Angela. They take her to see a movie, to a café, for a stroll together, though she can tell they aren't being entirely sincere, it's a fake performance, a show for her that isn't genuine, that doesn't mimic the truth but instead tries to sweep it under the rug, a way to help her get accustomed to something she can't stomach: her feelings evaporate as she watches them holding hands, kissing each other over the café table, his arms wrapped around both of their shoulders—like mommy, daddy, and the little girl, but in a darker, clammier version, as if they formed a prepubescent triangle, from before the first sexual blush, a relationship of flat bodies without entrances or exits, without protuberances or dark cavities, bodies smooth as Barbie's, before sex makes its categorical entrance into a person's life, complicating everything: little schoolmates, the three of them singing and strolling along the Gran Vía (like a sequence from the movie *On the Town*), but later the two of them disappear into the bedroom and Silvia, from her spot on the fake-leather sofa where she sleeps every night, hears them talking, giggling, the sound of the bedsprings, all of which turns the rest of the day into a bad performance, the height of sham playacting in the worst sense of the word, like in the boleros when they mistake being theatrical with being phony, life is pure drama, bad drama, a con game, self-interested faking of emotions you don't really feel. It's not the kind of theater that helps make sense of life, that raises some moral quandary, but instead the kind with a wily player who seduces with trickery and then forsakes. Angela had been vulgar when she was young. She's refined herself now. Completely transformed. It's off-putting for Silvia to see her dressed in designer clothes, hair flawless, makeup impeccable despite the long nights in the hospital, or maybe it's just that back then vulgarity was the style of the times. As if an entire generation made a spectacle of being vulgar because refinement was reactionary, tacky. Angela would argue with waiters, raise her voice, leave her clothes around the house, even her panties and bras, stick her head in the fridge and shout to Matías asking what was in each one of the containers, like a child asking what's this to get you to say go on, give it a try, take it, it's yours. She ate compulsively, she'd dig through bowls for the pieces that appealed to her and pile them high on her plate in case someone should try to get at them first. If anyone else behaved that way it might've been amusing, Silvia thought, charming even, maybe prompt a bulimia joke, but there was something base in Angela, something grubby. More than twenty years later and the memories are still so vivid. Angela swung from impulse to indolence. When she wasn't eating or drinking compulsively, rolling a joint or snorting (tell her not to look, she's too young, send her to read in her room), she would let herself collapse into the armchair and sit with legs spread-eagle, a dark shadow at the top of her thighs. Bloodstains on her skirt and on the armchair slipcover revealed to Silvia that Angela has her period, and later she'd find a bloody tampon floating in the toilet. She's menstruating and yet at night Silvia can still hear her moaning. They fuck. She thinks: She and Matías fuck even with her period. And she breaks down, sobbing bitterly in this Madrid of her uncle and his little friend, where she'd gone who knows why, hoping to reveal who knows what, obviously something she already knew would be a hard, if not impossible, revelation. She'd already begun to stain a while ago, to use her mother's and the maid's expression, and the sticky, smelly stuff leaking between her legs made her sick, she made herself sick, and to think that Matías wasn't revolted by Angela's blood, that he loves her, he actually loves her, how about that, he's in love with her even though he insults her from time to time, saying: Stop eating so much, you're turning into a cow. And since Silvia knows that he loves that cow, she sobs stretched out on the living room sofa, alone, not sure exactly why, over her uncle, over the man she can't recognize now, crying because her uncle is a vulgar man—a man whom she used to talk to lovingly. What can a man like that possibly do with the feelings Silvia consigned to him? She realizes: It's time for her to leave now, go back to Misent immediately, even though there's nothing there for her either, nothing waiting for her. Matías, who told her all about those sooty, coal-colored houses in Peking, moans while penetrating a sticky hole, that's what came to mind yesterday: the vulgarity of death. The vulgar Matías is what she thinks about at the moment of his death, the one who moans on the other side of the bedroom door in Madrid, the one who now lies in a tangle of tubes, the one whose playacting isn't worth a damn. An unconscious body: troubled, noisy breathing, there's a rattle, there's groaning and choking. An animal stuffed to the gills with morphine. Silvia wants death to deliver some sort of secret, but it doesn't work that way. Moans. There is no secret. My three women are by my side, Angela, Lucía, and you, he'd whispered to her already tubed up and hardly able to speak, unable to raise his head from the pillow. He'd tried to smile. Three women. In Madrid, Silvia wants to save him from that woman who stains the chairs. She surprises him by planting a kiss on his lips, he lets himself be kissed, but when her wet tongue hunts for his, he turns his face away: Love belongs to oneself, it's inside, he says, inside of you. What you admire in other people is a mirror, you see your own feelings reflected in that mirror and it moves you, Silvia, you have to find someone you can share that with. She ran down the hallway to the door, sped down the stairs as fast as she could, then outside; where to go now, Silvia, sobbing alone in the streets of Madrid. She felt like she was in a movie, one she'd already seen; she projected herself into the leading role, which made her want to cry even harder, though it also shaded her pain with a faintly sweeter note, more significant because it had an aesthetic quality now, a figuration of aching beauty. Wandering the streets of a great, unfamiliar city made her feel unique by contrast—she roamed, she turned one direction or another, liked to see how passersby turned their heads when they realized she was crying, like those anonymous people in a movie, the extras on set, and there she was on her own, solitary before her pain; but something started clawing at her, what if he said something to Angela and she'd be forced to confront them both, together, in the tiny living room in the house in Madrid. So she scratched the scene of her drifting through the streets and hurried back to the house, hoping to get there before he'd had a chance to spill a word to the true woman of his life. I'm leaving, I want to go back right now, she said when he opened the bedroom door and found her packing her bags. On the first available train. I'll call my father and ask him to pick me up at the station (the train station is twenty kilometers from Misent). As you get older, you realize the time you wasted is gone, it's irretrievable, you've missed out on all the things you allowed others to live in your place, those experiences you've only lived vicariously. Matías told her something along those lines. It's not love. It's not even the dimmer form of desire that comes from wanting to own or possess something to fill an emptiness, usually an imagined one, and you search for things outside of yourself when they're already there, on the inside. His words sounded to her like some two-bit moral lecture meant to get rid of her, so she wept and trembled and it took her a very long time to forgive him for it. Settled in the passenger seat with her father driving in silence: the façade of the train station moving farther and farther into the distance, the highway empty, Misent in the small hours, dark and hushed, wintry, white crests of waves beneath the heavy lid of clouds, the damp breeze and its aroma of iodine; the all-embracing presence of the sea assaults her nostrils as she opens the car door. At home she went straight to her warm room (they had turned the heat on to welcome her), which felt to her like an empty icebox. She threw herself across her bed and continued to weep till sleep finally came. What's the nature of her relationship with José María? She's never lived vicariously through anyone, nobody's ever said to her let me live through you. She's never said to herself the other doesn't matter, that love arises from oneself alone, like some form of autism in the one who lies dying—you love alone, you die alone; self-involved, the one who is dying and the one who is fucking, not only for one's own pleasure, but also for one's own strength, the body knocking at you is knocking on a bell jar, entering a recipient that's been sealed off hermetically. Maybe it's subjugation and nothing else. Weep, tire yourself out weeping in the cradle here. She wrote letters to Matías but never dared send them, instead she held them over a gas burner till they were nothing but ash. She wrote and torched and cried in that gloomy, wintry Misent where the sea was a thin, icy blade that cut off her passage. What are you working on, what are you up to (Grandma's maid: Silvia spent her days in Pinar, her room at home was saturated by all the thoughts she'd devoted to Matías, evoking that part of her that belonged to him; the sea line at the horizon, always the same backdrop, a different color every day, now reminding her that there were places she would never go, things she would never become, and things she would never experience with him)? She tries to understand Matías in the context of her father and Monica—their difference in age—and then thinks about the age difference between her and José María, applying this perspective to flush out his apprehension when she offered him her saliva like some lumpy sauce. Matías: It's a lie to say the sea is blue, can't you see all the colors it has? Even reds and yellows. The sun-kissed sea, the play of light. When actually, the sea is black, colorless, like everything else. The question of aging came up, it comes up now, that point where aging moves a step beyond and you stop having a choice; an older woman with a boy, a woman rummaging through her purse to pay for drinks, or slipping a bill under the table for the boy to pay himself and fool the waiter's catty squinting when he leaves the change, an image that mortified her. Matías is dead now and she phoned his real women, Angela and Lucía, with no success, the women he possessed when they were on their periods: him embracing you, engulfing you, pushing himself inside of you, the widows—there's something frightening in that word, culling—they carry something of the dead man inside of themselves, not something foreign to them, not an object, things that belong to the dead man's body: fluids, flows, liquids, phlegm, saliva, dissolved inside of you, mingled with your own fluids, penetrating your circulatory system by osmosis, the bundles of muscles, the membranes, that's what makes you a part of someone else, the sex, you leave something of yourself in the other, you carry something of the other in you, and those exchanges grow more sinister now. The dead man brings your cells with him too, you the widow, you're part of the cadaver:

the part of you he carried with him will soon be underground, or turned to ash. But she doesn't want to think about it, she can't, it's better to think about Felix who will soon be looking out the window, a map of what's real unfolding beneath his feet, though he probably won't know how to read it, the plateaus, the verdure of the Basque Country, the plane soaring above the bay of San Sebastián, a delicate example of nature at work, the Cantabrian Sea, a sea when contemplated unencumbered by the rote lessons of a fusty school, one finds is not blue but white, red, yellow, green, steel-gray to emerald, or at times a ghostly gray sheet woven from strips of cloud and drizzle. Silvia had flown this same leg to London from the same airport before, watching through the window the green fields passing below: England is truly green in summer, myriad shades but green nonetheless, an infinite variety of greens. Now Felix will view the endless tapestry that is London and the rows of brick houses emerging from the green, the vast wound that is the Thames glistening in the sun, he'll see it because he's flying into the northern airport with a layover in Luton, and it will all pass before his eyes if he bothers to look out the window. She said: Don't forget to look. She asked the girl at check-in for a window seat and told him not to miss a single detail of the trip: Pull the map from the pouch on the seat back in front of you and follow the flight with the map in hand she said; he listened to her half-heartedly. He'll probably spend the whole time on the screen, watching *Lord of the Rings* or *Return of the Jedi* or playing the game with those little balls you have to drop one by one into the hole. Thinking about Felix, about Juan, who should be arriving in Misent any minute now if he isn't there already; thinking about her father and his quest to find the fountain of youth, the dubious water of eternal youth. Matías, Juan and she have discussed it before: Have you ever noticed how Nazi life spans tend to last a century? All the disgusting things they did! Senseless operations,

placentas, fetuses, pieces of fat ripped out and thrown in the garbage, transfusions of young blood, skin grafts, cannibalism, vam-
pirism. That murky fountain of youth. The notion arrived with
news of the death of one of those nearly immortal Nazis: Jünger,
Riefenstahl, who'd resisted the thump of time for more than a hundred years, lucid up to the very end. Matías brings up all the old
Nazis who'd escaped after the war and found asylum in our county,
she remembers seeing them at the ends of their lives, like vampires under the sun, their leathery skin toasted and hardened like
turtle skin, everyone in Misent saw them, their little Speedos,
their gaunt chests, sinewy muscles, knotty arms, flesh the color of
old tanned and weather-beaten hides taking in the sun like turtles
or lizards. Silvia sees her father now the way she used to see them
back in the day, hunting for the elixir of eternal youth. Monica, his
wife, nearly fifty years younger than he is, a mannequin, her father's friends call her, a perfect mannequin, though when Silvia
talked about her with Matías, when she talks about her with Juan,
she says the best way to describe Monica is to say she isn't even a
body (yes, despite her lovely figure). A body needs a structure, and
it's the brain that provides that structure, the head is what crafts a
rapport among all the different parts, making it a single entity and
not a mere hodgepodge—and in Monica's case her body is missing
that unity, it lacks a unifying pulse. In long conversations with
Brouard and Matías, Silvia explains her father's marriage as the
reemergence of the cannibal that's latent in all of us since primitive times; it's what compels human beings to throw themselves at
each other, licking, sucking, sipping, and biting. Vitality. Her father: tennis, golf, paddle tennis, sailing, swimming, and the spa.
His body is always bronzed, the gold chain like a snake in the
white thicket of chest hair, his belly salient, disconcerted, as if
caught off guard by his contradictory excesses: alternating like a
Scottish shower between a sports regimen (Spartan sessions on

the paddle courts, rigorous exercise programs in the gym) and interminable, copious meals with his associates. It would've seemed pathetic if not for his sheer drive and vigor even at his seventy long years: he's still the company's sole owner, the only one handling the decision-making, it's not that nobody dares make fun of him, it's that nobody dares to look him in the eye, to hold his gaze, to contradict him in person. But time doesn't run backward, toward the past. He's wasting all that energy running backward till he's exhausted, and for what?—to collapse on the endless treadmill that's running counter to your impulses, a band that may seem endless, but it's not, it just comes around again and moves you slowly but surely to that place you'd meant to escape but to which you have no other choice than to return. You're immortal up to a certain point and only for so long; you're young only for so long and up to a certain point. The worst of it comes with his depictions of youthfulness, the eyes, wide with surprise, the little squeals as he tears the wrapping paper from the diamond-studded watch Monica gave to you as a gift because she's a shrewd one, she is, and caught the twinkle in your eye, the way you hesitated for a split second in front of the window on Ree-day-la-pay in Pa-ree, a kid who sees a piece of candy on the other side of the shop window (and she bought it with your own money to boot: How sweet of you, baby). Silvia's words: Papa behaves like he's never read a book in his life, never went to architectural school or hung out in *tertulias* with left-wing intellectuals in the seventies and belonged or partly belonged to the Communist Party (but who wasn't a member back then, he would laugh) or was committed to social architecture, projects like building homes for fishermen, for toy factory workers (before Misent was swamped with tourists), before everything took off economically; as if he'd never argued passionately about things, or bought all those paintings (a magnificent collection of engravings: serigraphs, woodcuts, lithographs: Spanish art that was young in the seventies), which seem ever more unreal, ever more abstract, incongruous stains of color hanging on the walls of his house, increasingly out of place, out of context, with Monica's little boutique bric-a-brac colonizing, multiplying. Overpriced and mindless objects sold in bulk and signed by the ghosts of international luxury, figurines, bags, and suits you can find in airports the world over. Silvia specialized in Baroque and Neoclassical painting and wrote a thesis on the similarities and differences in the portraits of Velázquez and Goya, and when she told Rubén she wanted to work in restoration, her father read the thesis and gave it back beaming: The thesis is excellent, sweetheart. He talked about the advantages of belonging to a happy generation: You have no idea how lucky you are to be able to choose your life à la carte (he thought she would be a great painter, if not an architect or economist). It hadn't been easy to convince his mother of his vocation, that he wanted to be an architect instead of overseeing the crops and managing the family estate. He'd had to fight for it: Happy are the sons and daughters of inconsequential times. There are circumstances that leave a mark, they shape a person's psychology, their character. I was privileged among my generation, though. That's just how it goes. You fight for things and then lose them along the way (this was some twenty years ago: he still talked like that back then, he hadn't fully overcome his guilt over getting rich so quickly). He said: I can't say I don't like what I do, I wouldn't want to do anything else, I don't think I even could. I'd just do the same thing again, only in a different way. Life had forced him into what he calls reality, an attitude that eschews profligate displays of pain or happiness because there'll always be pain somewhere, it's always hovering, and happiness has a very short shelf life. Pragmatism. Silvia's convinced his brand of realism is ingrained in the county's long-standing miseries, the never sufficiently laundered dregs of Francoism, a realism that knocks everything down to ground level. Acquiesce, capitulate to destiny, submit to fatalism, the world is what it is and who am I to change it. We're but spectators to the cataclysms of the world and society. We look on helplessly, like the scientists in a climatological observatory witnessing a devastating hurricane. She closes her eyes and recalls that sentence from the book of stories Matías had given her, only now in order to repudiate it: Hospitable and light. Matías, Chinese merchant ships weren't like that. She smiles. The now mature woman knows the ships were rat-infested and their cabins stank to high heaven. The principle of reality that her father is so fond of: Life is not what you carry around in your head, it's the way things actually are, daughter of mine, he said whenever he felt the need to contribute something to her education, help her alight from what he called her fantasies. Reasoning can't come first, it has to arrive afterward, he said. You're supposed to fill your head with all the things you encounter outside of yourself, material from the exterior. Truth, however, turned more and more into a sludge pit for him—especially since his wife died—a dump site where people root around trying to snatch their fair share, fight for a cut; a matter of taking a cut while fighting as little as possible. Juan says that beneath her father's good-humored façade, where he makes everything seem like a simple exercise in accounting, lies a brutal form of pragmatism, as nihilist as the nineteenth-century Russian anarchists. Nothing exists outside of the puddle of self-interest, it's everyone for him- or herself, Juan said derisively. It all boils down to that. No nonaligned space, no time for truces, nothing on the sideline. She doesn't need to touch that murky bottom to realize the boats her book described had never really existed, that real Chinese merchant ships were floating shitheaps and that Chinese rivers today are like vast sewers spewing industrial scum into the sea. The names of things endure, like ideas we aspire to. Names infuse adventure novels with atmosphere, they bring out—and here she admits Matías has a point—the things we can't express that are inside of us, names of characters, places, cities (though less and less: easy communication, globalization, everything within arm's reach now, everything standardized, which eradicates the sense of wonder—how can you truly be fascinated by a place you can visit for a weekend getaway?): Guangzhou—old Canton—Peking, Shanghai, they're sonorous names full of enigmatic resonances, yet they're just like any other place now: the same ships dock there as the ones that anchor near Valencia's port, built by the same ship owners, consigned by the same shipping companies, Hanjin, MSN, China Shipping... The only novelesque element that remains of these cities are their names, they alone still make us look inside of ourselves in search of the inapprehensible. This mechanism still functions, though surely not for too much longer. The tourist industry still runs on the fascination these names exert over us, their foreignness. But the worlds they represent are losing the qualities that differentiate them, all lackluster now from reusing the same old scraps. Juan mentioned a French novel he'd read before he left for El Escorial, which narrates the vicious fighting that took place between traditional Chinese painters and the techniques and sensibilities introduced by the Jesuits: the tradition of Titian, Caravaggio, of Pozzo, locked in a ruthless struggle against the imperial schools of calligraphy. Each side was bent on imposing their own idea of beauty, and with it the embodiment of their ideas of truth. Power dangled from the tip of a paintbrush. Symbols allow us to express what we otherwise can't, Juan said, and symbols tend to fight against each other, and they fight for dominance. The book is resting now on Silvia's nightstand, waiting to be read. By unifying scraps we've apparently found a way to come to some agreement on concepts of beauty, she thinks, and now symbols can coexist happily together. Divagations. Life seems so hell-bent on proving her father correct, she thinks, snubbing out the butt of the cigarette she'd just finished smoking: You never go wrong when you put yourself into his shoes, she says to herself, when you finally admit the ships described in the book were floating garbage heaps and the names of Asian cities don't really represent anything if not chemical pollution, organic contamination, misery, and the kind of profligacy that goes with their newly discovered capitalism, which exerts a relentless form of violence we could call Mandarinesque or Imperial. According to the newspapers, the old blue-collar neighborhood of Pudong, a symbol of Shanghai's modernity, is now sinking, and I don't mean metaphorically, not commercially or socially— no, physically: it's sinking under the weight of the colossal skyscrapers that were raised atop landfill and river mud. The Gardens of Suzhou, once known as the Chinese Venice, the millenary Empire's prized scenery, are now watered from canals rife with spillage from textile, metallurgical, and chemical companies. Alpinists say you can't take a step around Everest without tripping over a discarded can: the world has become a massive trash heap, an indication of our times and something right up Rubén Bertomeu's alley: admit that now we travel among debris. She recalls something Max Aub wrote, the novelist her husband and Brouard admire so fervently, in the only book of his that she truly likes (the books that they consider his masterpieces she finds tiresome, closer to chapters from history books than novels). Aub writes in one of his first novels, *Geografía*: If you were to travel truly, you would see how everything eventually fades away, and all you'll remember are the sad coasts, all of them alike, and the underwater reefs, nature's submarines, mines of the unfathomable. This dismal vision of the landscape moves her, the reefs like a threatening presence, looming, like hazardous mines, dark submarines. She thinks: Clearly, you have the ability within you to crosshatch and shade the image. Talking like that makes her feel as though something were slipping away, something that might be a part of herself. Over time, the city she hated so intensely as a teenager, Misent, returns to her with melancholy, she misses it: splashing around the crystalline surface of the reservoir, frolicking there with the boat Matías had given her, the motor pumping out cold water. She imagined journeys with an atlas in hand, deserted beaches and cliffs under a dazzling blue sky, the mud-covered walls of the reservoir at her grandmother's house, the sea floor's delicate patterns as seen through a scuba mask, this is the Misent that makes her homesick. Her throat tightens at the childhood reminiscences flooding her memory and she feels sullen, but what isn't gloomy this morning: the cars, metal melting under the sun in the chaotic, jam-packed parking lot. Matías said: You can be free of it all once you have it inside of you. Religion fails you, the beyond, eternity, all that bunk, and then there's politics, the search for happiness, the common good, the universal banquet; and when politics fails you too, and you feel like you've got nothing left at all, when you reach that level of nihilism, only then will your feet finally and for the first time be planted on firm ground; you can appreciate the truth of things now, you gain strength from that nothingness because it's a productive one, it's you and yourself, on your own, with the remains of everything you ever set fire to in your life; the ashes the priest smears on your forehead on the first day of Lent. Then the only thing left to realize is that you belong to the natural world, and when you realize that, you'll want to merge with it, return to what they used to call Mother Earth, identify with the soil, knowing that in the soil dwell preceding lives (something only certain monks, ascetics, and mystics have ever truly understood); discover how to live with the soil, get accustomed to it, feel it, the original clay, let yourself be swathed in it, sink into it little by little. These discussions always struck Silvia as a little forced, even rather truculent. They weren't in character, but he must have found consolation in them. Matías spent his last years in Benalda, only a few kilometers inland, cultivating a garden beside the coastal buzz, watering his plots, roaming the olive orchards, pruning, strolling the terraced hillside where the winter almond trees grow and blossom as early as January, ornamental blossoms like originals copied by Japanese workshop artists, white blossoms, pink blossoms. Silvia pictures him walking through a haze of pink and white blossoms, a botanical tunnel, like a watercolor. Just look at all this beauty here while up there Europe freezes, he says, I transport my own olives to the oil presses in my van, I charge up the oven a few times a week to bake my own bread (it's easy, he taught her how to knead, how to dribble a little oil and a few drops of orange juice into the mass the way he likes it, for a crunchier crust); look at my vegetables, the eggplant, the tomatoes, I have to germinate the tomatoes, prune the olive trees, I've already prepared the tarpaulin sheets to harvest the olives that we pick by hand, it's like milking; boy those eggplants, they're really taking off; why not take a few artichokes back with you; I tried the lettuce this morning; if you come on Tuesday the bread will be fresh from the oven. It's as if she could hear his voice. She walks around the parking lot trying to locate her car and hears his voice; here too, parked in the rest area, with the smell of tobacco saturating the car's interior, there's Matías hawking his goods, touting the benefits of a liniment she's about to buy. A snake-oil salesman: she could laugh at him, find something ridiculous in that bustle Matías liked to disguise as calm. But you could change the angle of sight. What if he already knew he was sick when he retired from his past life and decided to be alone with himself, the long nights spent alone with his affliction, the fear, saving a few olive trees that had been abandoned for decades to the mercy of some future developer who'd build on the land they occupied; planting new ones, pruning the vines that nobody had bothered to cultivate for so many years, sowing seeds, building up a little commerce around it. Juan laughed at him, though he admired him more than he would have admitted: That's not work, it's an aesthetic act, as unproductive as pure leisure, the calling of all failed ideologues: a return to nature, to the good savage, Candide cultivating his lettuce, if possible at the foot of some sumptuous stage backdrop; the crop is the least of it. It's all about the gesture, the scenography, not what's actually being produced. When he was talking to Juan, her father once referred to Matías as the Knight of Stérimberg, a soldier who fought in Jerusalem but tired of all the bloody Crusades, and when he returned, he decided to set up a vineyard on a hillside looking south over the bank of the Rhône River, a spot protected from the blustery winds of the mistral, and called his estate the Hermitage, where a thousand years later they are still producing some of the best wines in the world. Her father loves to read about things like that in the wine magazines he's subscribed to, where he keeps up on the latest trends so he can argue about them with his friends during their bacchanalia. Our very own Knight of Stérimberg, He of the Red Crest, he teasingly called Matías. He said: At least he's not getting anyone into trouble up there, at least not ostensibly. So fine. Let's assume that he's paying his suppliers and charging his clients. Olive trees are a sacred plant after all, and so are vines. Olive trees are more polytheistic, a tree of the classical gods and Olympic athletes, though priests use its oil to anoint cadavers and not athletes; but vines are Christian, they siphon blood from the earth and turn it into Christ's blood, yet the wine certainly flowed in the classical world to perk up their bacchanals. Did you know there's a wine called Le Sang des Cailloux from right there on the Rhône? The blood of stones. A magnificent wine, it got a great rating a few months ago in a tasting done by *Sobremesa* magazine. Matías said that God, in the eleventh hour, had given us a practical conscience, the capacity to more or less get by, the same as ants and bees, but we're not meant to drive ourselves mad questioning the boundless mysteries: the great beyond, the meaning of life, love, justice, revolution, all those highfalutin words that only make us miserable. I'm aware that the best conclusions inevitably come when it's already too late, he said. Yet all it took was a few easy drinks and Matías was back to arguing heatedly about politics, opposing the reclassification of county land; he'd taken his own brother on, lodged appeals aimed at impeding Rubén Bertomeu's development projects, and for several years he flat out refused to speak to him, something had happened that nobody would talk about, but which neither of them seemed able to get over. For the past few years their relationship had been reduced to dinner on Christmas Eve at the Pinar house and little else. I don't argue ideas anymore, Matías said in his own defense, I fight over terrain, I pee on my little patch of land and nobody's allowed to set foot inside my piss line. Over the past few years, he stopped showing up at events, never wanting to absent himself from the terrain he'd peed over. It was all about agriculture now, his little ecological production: supplying a few of the county's restaurants and gourmet shops, selling tomato preserves to the town café and marmalades to the tourists he so vehemently despised but whose money bankrolled his drinking habit. Every now and then he saw Brouard, but no one else. While he still could, he'd drive himself down to the coast for lunch at Brouard's house, or spend the late afternoon chitchatting with him. But now the curtain has fallen for Matías, his rounds have come to an end. The question is whether the different stage sets he built for his show will endure, or if the whole rigging system is going with him, too. Perhaps some kindhearted neighbor will prune the olive trees and vineyards so the next crop isn't lost, or maybe instead take advantage of the untended land and try to make a buck off of it for a while. Ernesto, or whoever his legal heirs are (maybe he left something to Lucía or to Angela) will post a "for sale" sign next year, or the following year at the latest—land for sale, trees drying out, weeds taking over. Everything goes to ruin in a snap. A few months without constant care and the fields grow fallow again, the weeds ubiquitous. Everything we do here—Matías used to say of the planting, of expanding the olive orchard—is no more than a little nuisance, an insect bite, like those welts that torture you at night only to vanish without a mark when you wake up the next day, as if they were the stuff of dreams. Rubén Bertomeu said that knowing Matías as well as he did, it was hard to believe he'd found an iota of peace anywhere: Not in Benalda, not in Kathmandu, not in the Pacific basin. Coasts all look alike, melancholy in the distance, desolate reefs of the quotidian growing like mines set to explode beneath your feet, Silvia glosses and reinterprets the Aub they consider his second-rate work. Brouard defended Matías to the very end: Matías portrayed peace very convincingly, and you can't take that away from him. He performed peace in front of us all. That's to his merit. Not ethics, not art, not even politics are anything but that: coherent performances, interpreting a part while hiding the effort it takes to learn it, interiorizing your character's nature to make the acting appear spontaneous. An actor suffers through the process of memorizing lines so the spectators can experience the story with ease. We find artists who seem to be trying too hard, overly narcissistic. As if truth in art compels the additional lie of something being casual and natural. How strange, Silvia thought, that Juan would argue the idea that performance is not the least important part, being such a staunch defender of the realist novel, even to the point of sectarianism. I'd say the contrary is true, Juan assures her, it's the only thing that matters: the floodlights go up and let the show begin, you memorize a part and recite it effortlessly as if the words just came to you right there on the spot, as if they'd been brewing inside of you, from the folds of your flesh, pure life, then out go the lights, the curtain falls and that's it, that's the code. The flame burns for a time, then it goes out. Haven't the philosophers said that the natural state of the sky is night? Man's job: to perform and illuminate, break the dark normality, the natural muteness, the lack of meaning. Behave using the form of artifice that transmits meaning, illuminate, if only for a brief spell, the darkness, that's what morality is: even civilized life is no more than that. Move around and talk under the spotlights, they're the eyes of the others, the minds of the others. Silvia wonders what kind of play it is that they're performing. What do we really wish to express with all our chattering, our acts, all the coming and going without really ever knowing why? For years, her mother and father went here, went there, let's see this, let's do that. When she was still a girl, a teenager, her mother used to help her father out in the studio, it was a modest space back then, he still wanted to get into architecture, wanted to be a good architect; her mother would look over the blueprints, share her opinions, discuss a few of the projects until late into the night, Rubén asking her to critique them, show him the defects, correct him: This façade lacks verve, this cornice weighs too heavily over the whole, these windows are confusing, they break up the sense of unity, distract the glance. The building lacks elegance, perhaps it's a matter of the molding, hide the abutments and fit the windows farther in so they're more integrated into the façade. Her mother critiqued her father's blueprints, his buildings. He worked through the afternoon and later, after dinner, the two of them would deliberate long into the night. Once in a while, when Silvia would wake up in the middle of the night, she could hear their voices at the end of the hall, the office window lit up, and as soon as her father could skip out, they'd roam around cities looking at buildings for a few days, modern buildings, but mostly older constructions. She was curious about everything, the three of them were curious (surely this was what inspired her own vocation, her inclination toward the arts, though Silvia won't admit it). Piazza Sant'Ignazio. The two of them would observe the Rococo plaza from the church, and then gaze at the church's façade from each one of the plaza's corners. Her father was right that she, Silvia, belonged to a privileged generation. It's been two hundred years since a generation in Spain has lived free of war, whether because of infighting, fighting against hordes, fighting with siblings or the clan living on the other side of the street, it's been a shabby country for a very long time. Peasants and starving artisans, dirty, starving painters and dirty, starving writers, a country of poorly rinsed debris (his mother, *dixit*). You can see in old pictures from the turn of the twentieth century a certain kind of fustiness that continued to exist until not very long ago. Photos from the sixties ooze tackiness too: there's Matías with his heavy, dark-framed plastic glasses, his long, infrequently washed hair matted in its own grease; not to mention photos from the forties and fifties, all those stunted men with sallow, lumpy skin, toothless, bowlegged, transmitting a climate of asphyxia that Silvia finds particularly disturbing. Her mother was gentle: she never could stand Spanish society. Silvia explained it to Juan: I think my father's youthfulness, his curiosity and passion for art, originated with my mother, because to him they weren't as much an aesthetic passion or emotion, as part of a profession that needed to be figured out, controlled, a profession where nothing would be foreign to him, the art of arts, as the classics used to say. That's how it was at the beginning. But then it all began to dissipate. How can it be? During the last trip of their marriage, they traveled a thousand miles to Ronchamp to see Notre-Dame du Haut (poetry in concrete, her father read to Silvia from the guide, trying to tempt her to join them), and a few hundred kilometers more to stand before the Isenheim Altarpiece in Colmar. It's like a million years have passed since then. And now, all the ink has bled into a formless stain on the paper, and she feels mournful for a soul that seems to have dissolved along with it, Silvia tells herself, what a fragile thing a soul is—and what the hell is a soul anyway: nowadays Rubén's studio produces cloned blueprints, photocopied blueprints, cloned models of homes, bungalows, chalets and apartments, photocopies that don't have even a single variation, there's nothing left from what was before. But Rubén Bertomeu has enjoyed extraordinary advantages, too, not only the financial privileges of these past few years, but others, like becoming a widower just in the nick of time, what a close call, just enough to be able to remarry. Matías's words become more sinister on a day like today: to be picking out a wedding tux when it's time to be picking out the one you'll be buried in. It took us two thousand years to get where we are, an eternity to form this single body and its soul, and the luck of social tolerance by which you can register this young woman's body as your exclusive property, with the happy consent of colleagues and friends. And a prenup to boot. It's all yours, no consequences. The coast of tranquility, the coast of fortune. Deliver us oh Lord from our answered prayers, Santa Teresa said. May the gods impede your landing at Ithaca or the coasts of Lazio or wherever the hell you decide to go, Ulysses or Aeneas. That's what Matías said when he heard the news that Rubén was going to marry Monica, someone forty-long years his junior. Instead of retiring, Rubén Bertomeu is taking on even more responsibility, the gorging ogre. What he once prized no longer mattered. He was moving on to something else. On the rare occasions when Rubén broaches the subject with Silvia, he refers to the buildings he admires with a subtle blend of mirthless condescension, the kind of mirthless condescension one uses to address a fool, or a freak. To aspire is to fail. The musicians he admired, the architects who genuinely interested him, they've all slowly but surely become a gang of fools who have idiotically tried to fight against life, who've thrown their lives away instead of realizing that it's about living it. His exact words: Sure, we admire certain illuminated architects, musicians, painters, a few holy beings, but we'd never try to be like them. I'm an architect. I build houses, not monuments. I build houses people buy to live in. I admire people who build extraordinary monuments above all else, but that's not my job and I'm not cut out for it. Listeners appreciate an appearance of ease when an orchestra plays a complicated score by one of the masters, Rubén says, without excesses of emotion, playing the notes without fuss, as if it were the easiest thing in the world: that's how the great orchestra conductors say Beethoven should be performed, and Brahms, Schumann, that's how the work is done well, the music as such, no more than that, without the underscores that most often serve to cover up some deficiency, music should be played without embellishments. A genius is typically some fake who hides his or her deficiencies in bombastic gestures: or who otherwise is driven by public relations instead of the work itself, surrounded by an ever-growing entourage of sycophants and exegetes, which helps bring ever more attention. Someone who flatters the patron, the gallerist, the journalists, the bankers who then reduce their tax burden by hanging a painting on a windowless first floor wall beside the customer service counter; in exchange for financing concerts or sponsoring this or that, your charter as resident genius is to become a piece in their catalogue. Surely geniuses exist, but I'm not familiar with any, and I don't mean personally, I mean I can't identify anything made in the spirit of pure genius. They don't exist today. They're a thing of the past. Genius rises above material limitations, above the enigma of technique, and today the materials and the techniques have already been figured out. Everything is already solved. Sweetheart, he says to Silvia, a contemporary genius is the kind who has a salary and puts food on the table for his family every month. The Peruvians, Ecuadorans, Ukrainians, or Moroccans who cover three, four, ten thousand kilometers across a desert or an ocean, who suffer through hunger and thirst, playing rock paper scissors to see who gets thrown off the overcrowded raft, and finally reach shore to climb a scaffolding or scramble beneath a plastic covering and into the hundred-forty-degree heat of a hothouse in Almeria, who eat only a few scraps to send half their salaries to the children wife in-laws siblings parents they left behind. My scaffoldings are jam-packed with geniuses (get off the soapbox, Papa: this is when Rubén gives a performance, when he puts himself in the workers' shoes, the underpaid, the intellectually challenged. Rubén would reply: There are no underpaid workers in my company, some are paid more, others less, but they're all well paid). He liked to play at looking at the world from a wheelbarrow. He said: It's the time of inventors who make things that simplify our lives, who make us happier, like the one who first put wheels on a bag and invented the shopping trolley, who put a stick on a piece of hard candy so it lasts as long as you want without getting your fingers all dirty and sticky, the lollipop; a genius who invented the mop so people don't have to spend half their lives on their knees on a wet floor. He teases her: Want to know what Le Corbusier said to some clients who complained that the roof was leaking? Of course it leaks. It's a roof. That's what your genius said. An architect knows it shouldn't leak precisely because it's a roof. When Silvia was a girl, her parents took her with them everywhere, they never left her at home, her mother made sure of that; and as a teenager she continued traveling with them even though she could've gone off on her own: trips that were like master classes, in fact for her father they were master classes: to see what he hadn't been able to see the rest of the year, sights that he considered essential, each trip in a better car with a better sound system: driving around Germany listening to Bach, a little Wagner (he particularly likes the *Siegfried Idyll*), Italy with Puccini or Palestrina, France with Couperin, Poulenc, Satie. Auditory sanctuaries. A landscape has its music. Berlin is *The Threepenny Opera*. Paris, Paris is everything. It's the landscape everyone knows, it's in every composer's work. The same goes for Rome with painting, a city that's in every painter's work. All composers have spent time here in Paris. The Couperins in the Marais District. They played the organ in the Church of Saint-Gervais-Saint-Protais. Rubén inherited his love for pairing music to landscape from Grandpa Rubén. California was the only place her father had ever refused to travel. He said: the West Coast is the same as here, only with more money—even cheesier taste, though higher quality. That's where the hell of the ticky-tacky subdivisions started, all the little boxes, the end of the modern city and the dawn of the drab, uniform meaninglessness of life, though it's an idea that gives me plenty of work and feeds you (he said this to his wife and Silvia). I've already been to California without ever having set foot there. I've seen it in my dreams. It shows up in my nightmares. I glimpse it every other night in bad dreams, the prowling nocturnal dogs (Silvia says she should have recorded him back then and slipped it into the car's sound system by surprise; or on the living room stereo, so he could hear himself speak). Driving around Europe: paintings in Siena, mosaics in Ravenna, the Palladian villas in Veneto; Amsterdam: Frans Hals and Vermeer; the altarpieces by Rubens in Antwerp. A full week of mornings in New York taking the subway at Lexington and 59th Street, getting to know every single room of the Met like the back of your hand, African, Australian, and Asian cultures included. It was Silvia's mother, Amparo, who taught him English, who first helped him out by translating books on architecture from the English, who obliged him later to learn the language that became so central to his business. You can't be an architect, a twentieth-century architect, without being able to read English, without speaking it decently, what kind of degrees are they handing out these days (his mother); entire mornings spent in the Vatican, contemplating the paintings at Villa Borghese, the MoMA, the Art Institute of Chicago. Tea under the lime trees in bloom at the Munch Museum in Oslo, their sweet-smelling fragrance wafting along the fresh spring air. See it all. Quote Montaigne, Grandpa's favorite author whose tiny, nineteenth-century leather-bound volumes are in the library at the house in Pinar: the sweetest death is the one that catches me with my ass in the saddle. With my ass in the leather of the driver's seat of a BMW, Mercedes, Volvo. Traveling from one place to another. But now Montaigne (not the old volumes, the old volumes are still in Grandma's house) and Monica, both of them, sleep under the same roof. Montaigne might not have been so averse to the idea, Juan teases, he never turned up his nose at the ways of the flesh. Rest, take a little catnap, and sleep—only sleep—beneath the same roof as your stepmother. Picture her in the nude, her flesh contrasted against the whiteness of the sheets, year-round golden skin as if she were just out of the rotisserie oven, year-round ultraviolet rays, infraultraviolet, naked like one of Titian's reclining Venuses with the musician ogling her, desire in his eyes, his most precious jewel shuttered between the delicate shadows of her thighs. She is taking care of the Monsieur's renal colic, his prostate troubles, the state of his ass, his wishes to piss well, and whether or not Montaigne has expelled that vexing stone. But that's what her father was like when Silvia was a child, a teenager: most of his discretionary income was spent on these trips. Eating through restaurants. Pilgrimages guided by Michelin stars, voyaging from star to star, interstellar explorations from one well-served table to another: dinner in Le Moulin de Mougins, in Les Prés d'Eugénie (*le caneton du potager François à la salade de chicorée*), in La Pyramide de Vienne, in Pic de Valence; trying out Gérard Besson or Senderens in Paris. Winter wandering through Provence, the almond trees in bloom, Roman ruins, Montagne Sainte-Victoire, which Cézanne painted God knows how many times. Culture is what makes human eyes rise from the ground to discern the horizon, what summons the animal to walk on two feet despite the backaches, despite the deformed spinal column, the cervical pain, that's the crux of it all, daughter of mine, her father would say in a solemn tone. She couldn't stand his grandiloquent self-satisfaction (it sounded so provincial back then, though she misses it now). Humans join humanity when they stand on two legs and gaze at the canvas hanging on the museum wall, when they bend to sit in a chair and contemplate the dish that has just been served, admiring for a moment its arrangement, its presentation, bringing the nose a little closer to capture the aromas before breaking it all up with the first charge of the spoon. So long monkey, hello human being. Montaigne accompanied them the whole way through one of their trips to Italy (not Grandpa's volumes, which had been in the library for a century and weren't allowed to leave the house, we brought a little Folio pocket edition) and also Paolo Portoghesi's book *Roma Barocca* and little editions of Robert Graves's *I, Claudius*, and Marguerite Yourcenar's *Memoirs of Hadrian*, from which her mother chose a few pages to read out loud, softly, before the Caravaggios, escaping the heat of the Roman *ferragosto* below the vault of San Luigi dei Francesi, after first visiting the Madonna di Loreto in the Chapel of Cavalletti in Sant'Agostino Church, nearby. Her mother fussed over the tiny print, how hard it was to read, which was only made worse by the sound of the car clattering down the rural roads that her father always preferred to take. He translated: *Every tradition, every cultural expression has a purpose and a history: the choice of using metal plates, of wooden ones (d'étain, de bois) or clay; whether food is boiled or roasted; cooked with butter, with walnut or olive oil; hot or cold, it's all equally good to me.* Wise man. The world is borderless, and the brief time humans have on earth ought to be engaged in soaking up and celebrating diversity. There are a hundred different imaginative solutions for every problem. Her father gave himself plenty of leeway to interpret the Frenchman's writing: Virtue is extraneous to pleasure because it's found in the act of knowing. That's virtue. Its essence is to know, while to feel pleasure is only one form of experience, of knowledge. All forms of gratification, the tingling here and there, belong to the animal order. It's not really even pleasure: we call them pleasures but they are merely stimulants, excitements. Pleasure happens when you begin to postpone, the postponement itself is pleasure; the act appeals to us because it brings us back to our original genetic cause, the animal that's not yet vertical (you hear that Monica, take note of what he thought back then. The animal that hasn't yet learned to stand on its hind legs, that's what my father used to think. He's always been a fucking liar, an embroiler. Referring to him years later, Matías said: Your father the whoremonger. He was already a whoremonger back then). He said: We're drawn to the animal the way dirty dishwater is drawn to the drain (put that one in your cookie jar, Monica, your husband's own words: dirty water circling the hole in the sink). Arguing with friends over which interpretation of *Turandot*'s "Nessun dorma" is the best: Caruso, Tito Schipa, or Mario del Monaco, though we mustn't forget the tenor Antonio Cortis, who they say would've surpassed Caruso had he not been so dead set on remaining a free agent (apparently he'd showed up at the Met in New York too late, when their quota of tenors was already full) and struggling so intensely for his own soul. That was the Rubén Bertomeu of Silvia's teenage years: fighting over whether Barenboim is better than Ashkenazy in the Rondo of the *Waldstein* Sonata, or in the Presto Agitato of "Clair de lune." Whether Van der Rohe of the National Gallery in Berlin is more lucid than Le Corbusier of the Villa Savoie de Poissy. Drinking half a bottle of scotch while pining over the beauty of the Piazza del Campidoglio with Brouard, or the Pantheon's spatial rubrics. Fifteen years have passed since her father's last arguments over architecture: in the nineties, going over construction plans for the German city with her and Juan after the fall of the Berlin Wall, or Foster's HSBC building in Hong Kong—to orient myself, Rubén used to say parodying Blas de Otero, whom he read as a boy and about whom he still liked to argue with Juan and Matías at Christmas Eve dinners. Blas (he called him by his first name, they'd met at some Communist Party assembly back in the day) was a mystic, he said, like his compatriot Unamuno, like Saint John of the Cross. His métier wasn't the result of him being a Communist, but because he was a mystic—just look at (by then her mother was already sick, and she accompanied him only halfheartedly now, pretending not to be in pain while dragging her body from one site to another, furtive movements of a hand to the back, sudden pauses midsentence, a shade of discouragement passing over her countenance) Nouvel's construction by the old Parisian Faculty of Science, the building he designed for the Arabs on the shore of the Seine. Or the renovation project for the Natural Science Museum in the Jardin des Plantes. Silvia can't say whether this version of Rubén Bertomeu was more moral, but he was infinitely more interesting. Amparo, Silvia's mother, planned their last trip herself, and jotted in her notebook the names of three places they'd never seen in France: the Isenheim Altarpiece in Colmar, Notre-Dame du Haut in Ronchamp, and the Royal

Saltworks at Arc-et-Senans, Ledoux's utopian project, an architect with scarcely any constructions to his name, only sketches: dreams, nightmares. *À la recherché de trois bijoux*, she wrote on the first page of the little notebook she carried along with her, though on the trip she barely penned a few stray sentences. She used to write in the car on their earlier trips, on the marble tables in cafés; and at night, Rubén and Silvia already asleep, she would stay up late writing in the hotel room. She liked to jot down notes on everything. And at the slightest discussion she'd go back and consult her notebooks as a source of authority, pulling them out to consult what she'd written while in the field. But that trip didn't go as planned, she was too sick, she lacked the energy to write or maybe she simply figured that what she was writing would no longer serve as a reminder of anything, a document of anything, for her. Rubén asked Silvia to accompany them. Like when you were little, he told her, but she didn't want to, or couldn't. Probably both: she didn't feel like going on that gloomy pilgrimage, the forced bustling here and there to pack the suitcases and pick up the guidebooks, she didn't know what to do with the kids either, with Juan, or with her job. She was working on restoring an altarpiece that had been considered lost during the Civil War and had just been found in a back storeroom in the Cathedral of Valencia, which nobody had entered for decades. A few summers ago, she decided to visit the sites her mother had written about in her notebook. A little homage to her mother, to contemplate the bodies covered in boils and sores on the Isenheim Altar, as they prepared for death five hundred years ago and who now, today, accompany Mama in the bustling underworld, while the person who had accompanied her and gazed with her at all that beauty and horror, the person who took her by the elbow to help her out of the car, who held her by the waist as she walked through museums and churches (while she read pages from their guidebook), that person, her husband, now saunters along the deck of his yacht with a cortege of loutish hangers-on, anchored in the most luxurious slip in Misent's most luxurious marina, drinking overpriced wines, opening tins of sumptuous garbage, gourmet dogshit, bragging distastefully about his trips, the ones he took while holding Mama by the elbow, his arm around her waist. His traveling style is different these days: we were in Berlin last spring to see all the new construction that's going on there, but I got stuck having to bring Monica to Paris. The poor thing, all those ditches, the building sites and scaffolding, all of it was boring her to tears. Monica confirms: Oh, sweetie, what a ghastly place (hearing that slut call me sweetie makes my skin crawl; she could be my daughter for Christ's sake, and I swear to you, Silvia tells Juan, one of these days I'm going to completely lose it), so dingy, a city you can't even enjoy walking around: all empty fields, and talk about ugly houses, there's nothing worth seeing, and those clothes stores, full of punk apparel, God those Germans sure like their black; as if the entire scene weren't dark enough already: long jackets, ankle-length overcoats, floor-length skirts, and black shoes. It's like a tree-filled seminary patio, the whole city a sprawling seminary, a convent, not a great amount of gusto for life there, must be the climate, so gray and overcast, sheets of ice squashing dry weeds all winter long. Just ghastly. The kind of landscape that locks you inside for neverending months of frustration, gotta suck all the energy out of you, must be why they walk around looking like that, sadistic, sinister-looking cannibals. Monica tries to be amusing, but all she does is traffic in stupidity, insensitivity, it's her brand of personal charm, her way of being flirtatious, and Rubén laughs, tells her she's onto something there: Sinister like that Austrian writer who won the Nobel—there's a weird one for you. Gore. The King and Queen of Sweden shaking that bizarre lady's hand, with that face of hers like Dracula's bride; and Monica babbles on and on: There's nothing in Berlin that could be described as elegant, you know, they're so severe in the German countries, there's nothing happy to them, nothing lively to see, it's all sternness, desiccation. Well, then there's Vienna, with the waltzing and the champagne bubbles, the moldings, the gilding, everything all cake and whipped frosting, it's mesmerizing in a way. But it's all make-believe, fantasy, the mask concealing the corrosion, the cellophane wrapper of barrenness and sadness; a disguise for the grayness of everyday, the clammy Central European fog, the scraps of mist clinging to all that white, milky skin. It's like the Germans are afraid of having fun. And that city, Berlin, known for being the capital of Euro cool, the hip scene for avant-garde art, music, and fashion (yeah, but look at the fashion: frumpy clothes with no glamor whatsoever, shabby-chic for rich beggars; and music: a bunch of dissonant noise), but really it's just blasé, and out of tune: endless walking the sprawl no matter where you're going, kilometers without a single fucking store, you can get lost in the woods and rivers, and their lakes and canals. But excuse me, I'm not a bear, so what do I care about rivers and woods. I know it's so ecological, so, so green. As long as you don't think about the sewers, the remnants of war, the cadavers and leftover tanks and bombs that are no doubt buried all over the place. Ecological? So what, who the fuck cares? I'm civilized, a woman. I like my shop windows eventful. I tell Rubén: I remember the photos of the shop windows on your trip to Leningrad before the fall of the Berlin Wall, the sight is enough to cure anyone of communist tendencies: three onions, a pair of socks, and a brown bra. No, don't laugh, I'm pretty sure that's all there was in a shop window on the fanciest boulevard in Leningrad. Tell them, Rubén. Let them hear it from you. And there he goes, like a dummy (idiot, Silvia says), continuing the conversation his wife started: Let your guard down and you run straight into another canal, or a site behind a wall, a wire fence, a place crammed full of cranes, so you turn another direction, and start the whole thing all over again. Then there's another twenty minutes of walking through some field. Monica jumps in again: Where are the Berlin streets like the ones in Paris, a city completed nearly two centuries ago, with kilometer after kilometer of great shopping, left and right, windows giving the landscape color even in the middle of winter, stunning luxury garments, glitter and sequins, moiré patterns, silks, velvets, satins; golds, blues, fuchsia, greens, indigos, the color of burgundy, the color of champagne: the jewels, the furs, the *renards*, that's how you pronounce it, right Rubén? *Renards*, yes, all of it sparkling in the shop windows. There's nothing like that in Berlin. Monica lets us know how much she adores the jewelry shops at Place Vendôme, the boutiques on Rue Sainte-Anne, and Rue de la Paix (her mouth filling with sounds like *ree-day-la-pay* and *plais-vandoum* like all the social-climbing floozies of the world who for two hundred years have been filling their nattering maws with those same sounds to brag about the overpriced gewgaws they bought in one of the stores along those streets and plazas: that's in Silvia's words), on Faubourg Saint-Honoré (*Saynonoray*: making it sound Taiwanese). Monica just loves those fountains flush with nymphs and fauns spitting water from their mouths or the tips of their flutes, Versailles, the Schönbrunn in Vienna (*Shunbrun*: making it sound like a brand of chocolates from the fifties, Silvia says, or maybe something Afro-Cuban like Carpentier's novel: *¡Ecué-Yamba-Ó!*). She likes her façades festooned, covered in flourishes, with caryatids and telamons, a slut's taste, a cocotte, as the classics of erotic novels used to say: lamps with lots of teardrops, curtains with lots of tassels. She continues: Berlin simply lacks the class and luxury of Paris; seriously, it just does. It must've been stylish before, back in its heyday, you can see it in those turn-of-the-century postcards, but not anymore, it's not much of anything anymore, though you can see how they're trying to restore the city and there's a little more flourish to it now, you can see angels and genies and horses and wagons floating in the air over the rooftops (it's a chariot Monica, not a wagon), on top of the domes, but that's rare, mostly everything is stiff and dry, so angular. Rubén, German architecture is angular, isn't it? It's true what I'm saying? The city's directionless and boring. The modern style is plain. And he finds that funny; he who used to talk about Bauhaus and laugh at all the Modernist trimmings, all those trinkets worthy of a Proustian cocotte's garçonnière, now stockpiled in his house; he who was with his queasy, moribund wife in Colmar observing the Isenheim altarpiece back when life still seemed to adhere to some kind of a code, even though its sustenance dangled from a single thread. The Colmar altarpiece: suffering is the only way we can pay ourselves back, Silvia, suffering is a tender for redemption. Her mother preferred not to leave the hotel most of the time, she'd stay in the room reading the guidebooks, marking what she wanted to see the next day and finally reading a few pages of Thomas à Kempis, since illness had brought religion back, or at least mystical forms of it: *Very quickly will there be an end of thee here; take heed therefore how it will be with thee in another world. To-day man is, and to-morrow he will be seen no more. And being removed out of sight, quickly also he is out of mind.* She read and underlined Thomas: *And being removed out of sight, quickly also he is out of mind.* Silvia's main theme, her specialty, that everything is appearance and only appearance, the Baroque recuperated the fleetingness of Thomas, life as decoration, masonry raised over the black hole of nothingness. Life, the delicate colors of flowers, attracting insects so they can both make the most of their brief time on earth. It's a matter of economy. Rubén Bertomeu was annoyed with his wife, he had no patience for mysticism and only tolerated it because he knew she didn't have much time left, but he would've preferred for her to confront death in a different way. His friend Brouard—still his friend at the time—asked who has the authority to tell someone else how to confront death? Authority is gained by experience, being able to say you've been through something and can personally attest that it happens this way or that way, but no one has had the experience of death, so who is an expert on that subject, who has died a few-odd times to have a grounded opinion except movie stars who have clutched their bullet-ridden chests or pulled at their hair a hundred times a day until a director is happy with the scene? Tomorrow this human being is no longer. He or she is leaving before you. The being vanishes, disappears, is removed: Thomas. Her father took her out for lunch to break the news that he was going to marry Monica: I loved your mother more than life itself. I'll never love anyone the way I loved her. But Mama is dead now, Silvia. She died and we're still alive. His eyes were bloodshot. He hiccupped, curling his lips into a pout. The person you love is gone, just like that. One morning she's simply not there anymore. And that loss becomes an obsession, it won't let you be. And then slowly it begins to fade. It withdraws. When he pronounced Monica's name, Silvia got up and left the restaurant without finishing her monkfish *suquet*. Her father wasn't entirely wrong. Someone is no longer there. She no longer exists. It's a presence that vanishes, even in the conversations of the people who were closest to her. It's not always the loved ones who best preserve a person's memory. They loved that person deeply in life, and then they forget about her. It happens. We aren't very good at remembrance. Fucking memory: it's like a traffic cop haphazardly directing cars, letting vehicles pass at a whim, happy-go-lucky, not sweating the city's circulation needs; or maybe the neglect is just a façade meant to hide some secret order of things that we're unaware of, that we can't quite perceive. Silvia could acknowledge that her father had a point, but she couldn't stomach the substitution of her mother, and less so—she says—by someone like that. Doubtless it would have been even worse had her replacement been not only beautiful but also intelligent and cultivated, it would have been a more direct affront to her mother's memory. Silvia didn't want there to be a substitute, period. Her father didn't have an easy time dealing with his wife's newfound devotion the last months of her life, the piousness, the search for sanctity as an expression of fear, the acknowledgment of some design by a higher being, the deliverance to what he called the great beyond. But in her last months, death became a form of repose for her mother, not a lying-on-the-sofa-or-chaise-longue kind of repose, but resting in His arms, Christ's; it was the beginning of a new life with a gentler lover than the one she'd had until then. That's what irritated him, that attitude drove him nuts. As if he was jealous of the other embrace she appeared to desire, as if dying were a form of adultery committed with Thomas's Christ. When she insisted on finally making the trip to Colmar that they'd been putting off, Rubén refused at first; later, he asked Silvia to join them: I think it's creepy, but if you join us it'll be like old times. If you come we'll be able to joke around, you and me, help lighten things up, ease some of the tension. I don't have the strength to travel with your mother on my own, all those kilometers behind the wheel while she looks over the landscape one last time, certain of the meaninglessness of it all, watching the vineyards go by, the forests, the farms, the castles, Thomas in her suitcase, in her bag, in her hands. Now she travels with the guide to the great beyond instead of those travel guidebooks she always used to pack in her suitcase. Can you imagine? But Silvia said no, she couldn't go with them. She had to work, she said, she couldn't leave the kids alone, but he wouldn't take no for an answer. I'm asking you for a favor. It's not a good place to take someone who's ill, the Christ is monstrous, he's massive, his skin is covered in black-and-blue marks, boil-ridden, his hands are deformed like some disgusting, web-footed creature from a mucky lagoon. But she insists on going. She read somewhere that the altarpiece had been painted for a hospital tended by the monks of Saint Anthony, who cared for victims of ergotism (*l'ergot de seigle*, the guide adds), also called Saint Anthony's Fire, apparently a dreadful affliction caused by consuming grains or seeds contaminated with ergot sclerotium fungus that causes horrific gastrointestinal swelling, dropsy, boils, and sores that end in gangrene and death. That's why the symptoms are so precisely rendered in the painted altar: there's a horrendous figure observing the "Temptation of Saint Anthony" from the lower left-hand corner who appears to be one of the army of fiends tormenting and trying to corrupt the Saint, but is also clearly one of the victims of the plague, which became a local pandemic. The monstrous Christ served as consolation, solace, because it offered the afflicted something they could identify with: the body of our Lord had become as repugnant or even more so than our own, they said, he understood and shared their suffering. Unacquainted with these particulars, the altarpiece could seem self-satisfied, even morbid, but once you discover its history and origins, the painting becomes a touching monument to piety, the museum guide explains. Rubén wanted his daughter to join them. Come with us, he insisted up until the very last day. But she didn't, she didn't want to go and wasn't able to. But she still gets emotional thinking about his words: I'm asking you for a favor. Silvia went to Colmar a few years later. She read the little tome and the information it provided. She asked him for it before heading out. She'd tried to justify her mother's intentions two years earlier: surely she feels a need to experience the type of devotion contained within the altarpiece, the comfort it's meant to share, she said. But it only made him angrier: It's morbid. You know what I think? That I'm the only one who doesn't get off on all that carrion. I'm the one who gets depressed over it. There's not much

Thomas can do to get her into heaven. He was never made a saint, and do you know why? Because when they dug up his cadaver, they found he'd nearly scratched his face off in desperation. He'd gouged his fingernails into his face. They'd buried him alive, and when he realized there was no escape, he'd dug his fingernails into his face till they broke off. That's what the priests told us in school. Thomas doesn't have the keys to heaven, he doesn't even know where the path is. He's still trying to scratch his way out of the tomb, he's still looking for that exit, for the air, the fresh air, and he's been at it a few long centuries now. Silvia could never find that story anywhere. She's sure her father made it all up. Her father, the triumph of reason, heir to Grandpa and materialism. Grandpa apparently was more of a quasi-skeptic (she never knew him: Matías had told her more about him than her father ever had); but her father's so-called common sense turned more oppressive and heavier, vulgar materialism as Marx would say; and Matías said: Cement materialism, gravel and sand, concrete, hefty and compact (Mozart and mortar, Juan would say). Eat, drink, fuck, amass wealth, accumulate art, spurred on by a collector's self-indulgence more than any kind of spiritual proclivity, the calculating investor; count shares, inert materials, even more cement, like the stones in the wolf's belly who goes to the river to quench its thirst, weighty stones, open its belly and fill it with stones and stitch it back up again, that's what money has done to your father (in Juan's words). It's not about the money, she tells Juan, it's not the value of the money, the accumulation of wealth, it's that money just never comes on its own, it never just falls from the sky. Money is about what you have to do to make it, how you get it to grow exponentially, the type of people who are involved with it, the people you have to beg, you have to ruin, and what you have to do to keep it; but he's a man who was taught to think, to reason, and now that same man who is supposedly a thinking and reasonable person pretends it's so cute when Monica talks like that, talks to his daughter like that, some homespun cosmopolitan shtick, the happy traveler, the globe-trotter (is Monica a necessary upgrade for this phase one of wealth?); so sweet when she talks like that to his new pals, his yachting buddies, folks who couldn't care less about sloppily clad caryatids in stone tunics and chariots freezing in the winds of Berlin; and the women care even less than the men. What the women do care about is whether that Ordoñez woman really died from snorting too much cocaine like they say, or if Bertin is a perv, he's got that look in his eyes. The ladies who gossip: watch out for that Guillén, he'll be inside you before you know what happened, talk about a lecher, a real dog; or Bartoral has a baby dick. Little? Like a two-month-old's, diaper included! And her father just hoots when he hears them. A while ago, Juan and Silvia refused to ever set foot on that yacht again, you can never be on your own there. Silvia can't stand it: he practically salivates when she mutters her stupidities, as if she were so amusing, as if her vulgar ignorance was instead an enchanting ingenuity, the subtlest charm of Monica's repertoire of charms, it's what balances the size of her tits, what compensates for the roundness of her ass (for however much she takes care of herself now, she's going to end up fat: she's genetically plump); it's her grace, her light touch, her father says, laughing. Maybe he's so mortified that he laughs like that to purge his embarrassment, Silvia says to Juan, who knows, he answers, and who cares, it's probably just cynicism, and cynics don't have aesthetic criteria; and without God, without whatever god you want, art doesn't exist. There's only what serves you (and not who is serving). She told Juan at some point: My mother would have hit the ceiling to see her closets invaded by those skimpy outfits, the see-through fabrics and garish colors;

imagine she came back home to hear some *chunga chunga* playing on the Bang & Olufsen, or the cheap reality stars from *The Apprentice* or those shows about housewives on the extra-flat Cinema-Scope screen, forty inches worth of sleazy talk show celebrities' faces, an ectoplasm of evil arguing over whether this night yes or that night no, as if the life of the country depended on it. My father reading Baudelaire (does he still read him? It's been ages since she's even thought of talking to him about such things, every once in a while he talks literature with Juan, as if reading were a vice he'd given up), reading Mann, and in particular Mann's *Doctor Faustus* (art is ambiguous and music the most ambiguous of them all, yes, Papa, sure, and architecture is the art of all arts, yes, I know, the most categorical art, most inevitable, the dictatorship of the material), lying in the hammock on the porch of the house that they sold over a decade ago, the first house Rubén ever lived in after leaving Pinar, the house where Silvia spent her teenage years: looking up from his book and out across the pines, the araucaria woods, staring at the palm trees whose long branches sway in the midafternoon breeze that's moving in from the sea, reading Hugues, Mumford, Malraux, and Fischer, and now we have Monica with her Knights Templar trash, the Crusades, secrets of the Holy Shroud and the Temple of Jerusalem, *The Da Vinci Code*, the Pyramid of Menkaure, the astronaut of the Palenque Temple. Not a single one of those idiotic notions slips past her, Silvia tells Juan, she has a mean argument for whether it was the Martians who built the great Egyptian pyramids or Lucifer who lent a hand finding architectural solutions to Gothic cathedrals. She brought it up one day: Monica, sweetie, you married an architect, it doesn't suit you to be talking about things like that. She went surface-to-air: I have my opinions and he has his. His buildings won't collapse because I happen to think differently. It's all good. Then there's her self-help books, her diet books, how to digest well, how to care for your skin, trashy books about how to maintain a healthy attitude or keep your husband attracted to you; eat carrots for the carotene, don't forget the vitamin C; eat spinach, it's rich in iron; legumes, they're rich in fiber. Beauty is a body whose pipes are in good working order, a body that keeps the decomposing organic material circulating seamlessly through its system of tubes. I feel great inside since I began eating probiotics, just fabulous, so goes the television ad, and he, her father, is thirsty tonight and drinks once again from your fountain as it moves the pellet of nutrients lightly and effortlessly toward the drain, so the splendor of what you're crafting inside of you, under the terse pallium of your skin, may flourish. Making love revitalizes organic compounds like isoflavones, it ignites the steam engine that burns through polysaccharides, polyunsaturated fats and activates the secretion of dermal tonics. Massage your face with honey, with mango cream, or papaya, with grape-seed pulp or snail slime; bathe in milk, in salt water, in mud, in wine, in chocolate. Whatever the disgusting treatment, whatever the ridiculous but ever so trendy treatment of the day. And there he is lying face up in the hands of an aesthetician, his face smeared with some grease or oil. Elisa, Silvia's art teacher and friend of her parents who died way too young and who dealt with many architects because she wrote for architectural magazines like *AV* and *Casa Viva*, Elisa said it twenty years ago, at the beginning of the Spanish Socialist Party's ascent to power after the death of Franco and the get-rich-quick culture and fast money of those early years, when public architecture became part of the modernization frenzy: Silvia, she'd say, architects tended to marry their daughter's friends until not very long ago, but now they go straight to the friends of their granddaughters. Back then her father was still more or less happily married to a woman who brought guidebooks on their trips and mapped out their routes, who made an itinerary for each city they visited to get the most out of their stay. We've seen so many things in so few days, her mother would say, thank goodness I've jotted everything down in my notebooks, I can only process what I've seen when I write the notes out in a clean version. To me it's the best part of the trip, when I can finally pick up the books, the photo albums, and shuffle through them again while reading my notes at home in the living room. That's when I can travel unencumbered, no long lines or crowds. He could talk and even argue with her over things like whether the Masaccio frescoes in the Brancacci Chapel of Santa Maria del Carmine were better than Benozzo Gozzoli's in the Magi Chapel of the Palazzo Medici Riccardi or if the true summit might be found in Piero della Francesca. Another scene: her mother seated beside the Fontana della Barcaccia, reading from the guidebook on Rome aloud, quoting the song of the African bishop, Fulgentius of Ruspe: *How beautiful Paradise must be if Rome*, he wrote, *which is but a corruptible city, can be so marvelous and grand!* Rome, so stunning that each time Silvia sees it anew she becomes overwhelmed with emotion, the pine trees, the ruins that rise up from the ground and return to her, then collapse on her and go back again to the original dust. The corruptible and dazzling city. Her head fills again with images from the trip to Rome when she was a teenager. Back to San Luigi dei Francesi, Santa Maria del Popolo to see the Caravaggios. He was such a different person then, and you know it, Juan, you've seen him. I fell in love on that trip with Saint Paul in the chapel at Santa Maria del Popolo, tumbled from his horse, but so handsome and so devoted to whatever God or someone else (me) wanted to do with him. Disquieting. I would look at the postcard I bought and feel like masturbating, he was so sweet and so handsome, and he's still so handsome, he's still lying there. The church was under repairs last time we were in Rome, do you remember? I told Miriam: Isn't he so handsome? But Miriam was bored to tears, snapping her gum, looking at everything except what she was supposed to be paying attention to; the laborers had opened a few holes in the floor, apparently they were excavating some of the ancient tombs, the church was full of scaffolding and Saint Paul there in the same chapel, lying on the ground of the painting with his arms thrown open, waiting for me, waiting for the mature woman I'd become who arrives now presenting her children, children who aren't his, poor celibate virgin caught in a static, four-hundred-year fall. Painted saints don't age. We do. When I was young that older man who seemed so gentle excited me, now the little saint, a teenager, shows the same gentleness. A perfect boyfriend for our daughter. He hasn't changed. It's me who's changed, my perceptions have changed, not yours though, Juan, because you saw the painting for the first time on that trip. Saint Paul is the same age as he was when Caravaggio painted him. Silvia continues musing about Rome, thinking about her father. He and Monica still go to concerts frequently; though mostly he goes alone: Silvia imagines him taking advantage of the free days when he runs off to a concert, to go on a bender in Valencia, hit the town, hook up with someone at a favorite spot; maybe he prefers the pickup scene, or calls one of those phone numbers to have an escort sent to the hotel; a visit to one of those high-price whorehouses, she doubts he's changed his old ways; but Monica has no choice but to turn a blind eye (Juan, you realize that's not her real name, right? Her name is Gregoria, her mother calls her Grego—Monica is pure fiction. She had to move heaven and hell to get their marriage officiant to pronounce her fake name for the standard "Do you, Monica, take Rubén as your lawfully wedded husband?" It's not permissible, the good man argued, I don't think it's legal to say it like that if the legal name on your documentation is different). So, what else can he give our dear Grego? It's not like she met him at Mass. She has to know his taste for whoring around, he's been a whoremonger for years. Matías used to call him your father the whoremonger, though maybe now he doesn't indulge as much. He's too old. But that's precisely why, that's the point of it all, he'll pay a prostitute to prove he's still alive. His old pals, Silvia sees them on Avenida Orts sometimes when she's waiting to pay for something in the pharmacy or standing in line at the bank to make a deposit, Macario, José Luis, Andrés, Alfredo, his college buddies. They never bother to ask how her father is. They greet her with a kiss on the cheek, a little chitchat, but never utter his name. Then there's what Brouard thinks of him. Silvia addresses her husband: Yes, Juan, Papa married a set of organs and then put them on display like a taxidermy animal behind a glass vitrine in the natural science museum. The fly that's trapped by the carnivorous plant. Not a drop of the courtesan rhetoric or Provençal poetry: teeth like pearls, lips like rubies, golden hair, emerald eyes or jet black, no, none of that, no wrapping to hide the incriminating evidence. Juan laughs: You sound like some crabby old lady from the Salvation Army. Don't tell me you're becoming devout like your mother, are you? We all sit at the marriage table attracted by the aroma of a tasty meat stew, but we end up preferring Swiss chard.

HE HEARS his footsteps in the hallway, approaching. He'd already overheard Juan talking out in the yard with Javier, so he has a sentence prepared for when he finally walks in: Yeah, yeah, so I'm drunk, what of it? What do you want me to say? I had to drag myself through the morning somehow. Juan is carrying a few books for him to sign, they're a gift for a friend he spent time with in El Escorial over the past few days. He sets them down on the bed before embracing him. It's not a long hug, it lasts only a second. Their conversation kicks right up, both of them skirting the subject of Matías. Federico signs the books; See there?—he says to Juan, holding one of the books up and giving it a shake—You write to get closer to others, so they love you; so they set you down beside their beds when it's time to sleep, on the nightstand; so they clutch you at night as sleep comes down, but in fact the opposite happens. Each book makes you feel lonelier. And you, too, love them a little less after each one. He says it with some conviction, though partly in jest, as he offers Juan a nip of whisky. He opens the drawer in the nightstand, pulls out the bottle of J&B, pours himself half a glass and puts it back, only to pull the bottle out again a second later, as if he suddenly remembers he'd forgotten to do something, and off he shuffles with it in hand. He's able to move around now, to go out, make gestures as he speaks, slap you on the back. He returns with Juan's glass in hand, filled a little over halfway. He must have stashed the bottle in a different hiding place. They keep a close eye, he says, winking, the long arm of the law. Where's the tape recorder? Aren't we going to work today? Write this down: I sought health, and honesty. I assumed that health and honesty were the same thing, and I, with my uncooperative body, absent strength or grace, sickly, sought honesty in health, I thought they belonged to the same semantic field because it seemed that not being physically strong was the kind of sin that I had to cleanse away, someone had to cleanse me of it. Rubén, your father-in-law, was the picture of health. In a way, even though now he's a rotting old man, he is still healthy. Only thing is, I'm not so sure I care about health anymore. I've slowly come to realize that health is the result of a chain of predatory acts. You're healthy because your ancestors have devoured others gladly, because you've devoured whoever has fallen into your clutches, because you only care about yourself, your own digestive system, you shy away from whatever doesn't nourish you, whatever hinders your process of digestion. The trophic cascade. Asceticism without God is nothing, sadomasochism, life without the spectacle of life is nothingness: energy, the will to stay alive, it's all you need, and apparently you only get strong by consuming the strength of others. Blood is only gotten by eating meat. Nature hasn't provided any other nutritional method, whatever the vegetarians try to claim. Oops, forgot the damn rocks, how many you want? You'll have to fetch them yourself in the kitchen, but careful, don't let Javier catch you rummaging in the freezer. He'll know we're bending the happy elbow. I think he counts cubes every time he sees you here, that's how he gauges—rounding up of course—my intake. The patrol is on high alert, you have no idea what a snoop Javier can be. Juan laughs at the way the bottles travel around the house. From the choir stalls to the sewer, he says. And Federico: Javier knows there are bottles stashed all over the place, but he pretends not to, as long as he doesn't have to see them—so you can have all the sauce you want, just promise me that before you leave, you'll go down to the store on the corner and bring back two, three more bottles; come on, be a good boy,

I know you will, the money's there in the desk drawer. My liquor stash has to last till an angel carries a new one in its wings. You're my guardian angel today, my biographer bearing a stash of booze in his wings, my high-proof angel, coconspirator on each swig's survey of infinity. Go on now, get over to the store before the sheriff makes his entrance. Oh the beauty of it all: don't tell me it isn't gorgeous that you can buy a trip to infinitude in a store. The state, the church, theologians of all denominations ought to be financing it. But we digress, back to the idea of health as pure evil. Your father-in-law, Rubén, is health. He'll die, and continue being health. That's why he's secular, a layperson, it's because he's healthy. Go fetch a couple of bottles so we can make ourselves a little sicker, you and me. Illness is a form of saintliness: you're sick, you suffer, you plug yourself into a generator of the sacred, and your pain nourishes the rest. Come on then, fetch the rocks. Pick up the bottles at the bar on the corner. You fly, I buy, we drink together, we explore the gate to infinity together. Okay? Here, take the money. Swiftly, he slips the glass of whisky into the drawer of the nightstand a split second before Javier opens the door and walks in, greeting Juan with a slight nod as he approaches Federico. He touches Federico's forehead. He's carrying a plastic bag, which he holds up to reveal its contents. Bread, pieces of Federico's favorite candy; cookies, potato chips, cereal, a package of boiled ham cold cuts, another with a chunk of cheese, he unwraps a bundle of wax paper to show some slices of salted ham—Ibérico, he says—half a dozen of them, thinly sliced and trimmed. He continues unwrapping little packages, displaying their contents and then placing them on the table beside a carton of orange juice and a few glasses. He says: Go on, have a snack (Juan's name habitually remains unuttered); and addressing Federico: Have a bite, you haven't eaten a thing all morning, I'll prepare a light lunch in a little while. I bought some vegetables and half a chicken to make a broth. Broth, an omelet, a slice of boiled ham. You need to eat something. He pulls the last sweets from the bag, which is empty now: a pack of chocolate cookies, he opens a little package and takes out a piece of candy, a coffee-flavored caramel. Federico has always had a sweet tooth. Javier hands him the caramel when he sees how little success he's having with the slices of ham. But Federico doesn't want it either: Not now, he says. He rejects it with a flick of the wrist. He teases: Tobacco, you should have brought a carton of cigarettes instead. Tobacco and whisky. His voice is gravelly, he flashes a spiteful grin. His breathing sounds like a rock tumbler. When he laughs it's as if he were choking. Javier glances at the ashtray and its pile of cigarette butts, he sniffs at the air and walks out peeved. He'd barely even glanced, disapprovingly, at Juan. Clearly, he's not fond of Juan: the biographer prying into the writer's private life, which he's a part of, too; so, while the biographer noses around the one, he's nosing around him, too, the vicar. The virtue resides in the other. So he imagines the biographer will be smoking out his defects; the obstacles he's placed along the path of the writer's last years, how he's deviated him from it, undermined his vocation, an encumbrance who at the eleventh hour stopped him from taking flight. His footsteps fade down the hallway. With a complicit gesture, Federico asks Juan to bolt the door, quick. The police are on high alert, he says, the snoop abides, and he pulls the glass out of its hiding place in the drawer of the nightstand along with a pack of Ducados and a lighter from under the pillow. He lights a cigarette, sucking at it hard and exaggerating his gestures the way method actors impersonate negative qualities like callousness, two-facedness, Harpagon, Shylock, Torquemada, Tartuffe the Imposter. He says: If Javier comes back, I'll hand you the cig and you act like it's yours, like you're the one smoking. But make him knock before coming in, go on, slide the bolt. Let him know we will protect ourselves from the meddlers, the detectives.

Federico is completely plastered. He's slurring and his ideas have no thread: Keep the guard up. He hates my smoking even worse than my drinking. I smoke in the bathroom with the window open and have to spray something, cologne, to hide the smell. He would've been such an excellent prison guard. His true calling. Be on watch, but not like a predatory animal, no, that's too noble, too virile, attack your prey in the neck and rip; no, he's like a snitch, a fink—all sidelong glances and whispering. Brouard's face transforms into that of a naughty boy who likes to punish adults, who intentionally does the things that will irk them the most (Richmal Crompton's rascally William, or the comic book brothers Zipi and Zape). He continues in the same tone: No love. Not anymore. But what am I going to do without it? Clearly, he's not referring to the tobacco or booze, not even the Pasolinian angel who's been such a nuisance lately, but Javier, the good man Javier. Juan thinks he's being cruel, he shouldn't let Brouard talk like that, he should tell him to go to hell and leave him with the words dangling on his tongue. But he lets him go on: Can you imagine what it'd be like on my own here without him? He's a selfish old man, terrified and selfish in equal parts—Juan thinks—yes, both things at once. Here, he says, pointing at the space outside the window where a steely ray of sunlight filters into the mist, into an infinitude of points of light that break like a blinding spray of foam against a nearby wall, falling to create short strips across the grass. I would've died without him. Slain or given up the ghost, by whatever means, but lifeless. Javier is the punishment God sent to keep me alive a little longer, to drink every last drop from what the priests call the bitter cup. Swallow to the bitter dregs, the priests said. Christ says in the Gospels: Lord, let this cup pass from me, or maybe he says Father instead of Lord. I can't remember. Life, a bitter cup, hard to swallow. The guy there on the cross, dying, moaning, bellowing like a wounded ox, asking his father to leave him to die in peace;

screaming, let this cup pass from me—how troubling, parents, the things they're capable of doing. Saturn and the little boy's body between his teeth. So, I realized that Javier had come to save me from certain death so that I would fulfill the Stations of the Cross, the complete Calvary. I realized who Javier would become for me if I allowed it. The birds soar across the heavens and some of us, the chosen, know how to read the signs, only a few of us are haruspices, augurs, but instead of avoiding the catastrophe we announce it: we deliver ourselves unto it, we fulfill our destiny, be it out of laziness, resignation, or heroism, three words that mean very little and serve to say more or less the same thing. I have a home and I have Javier, who fulfills all the roles embodied in a family tree. Federico falls silent. A few seconds later he raises his glass and says: For Matías (neither one had pronounced his name till then), and takes another swig. His eyes are wet, more from being old and drunk than out of sadness, but that too. Juan thinks how nobody's ever deployed such acts of mercy in writing as he has in his books; that's what it is, it's the sense of mercy that keeps his books relevant, what sustains them, even though Federico claims that not a single one of his novels has endured. Not even a full chapter, he says, maybe a page here or there. Not so bad I guess, it's something, it could be worse, only a smidgen compared to the gargantuan effort it's taken, burning one's life out for a few measly pages hidden inside a mass of seven or eight thousand, a few measly pages that in ten, fifteen years nobody will locate anymore because they're lost among the others that aren't worth a penny. Don't get me wrong, I'm not saying I wouldn't have liked to write something grand, something physically grand I mean: a solid novel, a thousand pages full of pure thought, but I've always known I'm not capable of that, not by education, not by discipline, not by natural intelligence, but my abilities led me toward the short novel, more the consequence of sensibility than erudition or mental order, a novella like the ones that last forever. Can you imagine? To write something like *The Turn of the Screw*, or "Clay," that story in *Dubliners*—that's the title, right? Memory fails me now. Or to write Guy de Maupassant's "Boule de suif." Green, envy. Juan thinks: I've written about this, I'm his biographer, I've covered his novels, I've deployed the tools of comparative literature to analyze them, and I know that only a handful of writers in his generation have been able to get down into the grit of life the way he has, from a place of such compassion. But he's all dried up now, exhausted. Brouard shared a text by Juan Ramón Jiménez a few months ago, a writer who has always been a guide for him, he said. Juan Ramón was your guide?, he poked fun at Federico. His poetics of light shattering against glass? But Federico read him a paragraph: *When will some of the supposedly young Spanish realize that they're praising writers who cut light like paper in cold simulacra of the words they find so precious? They manhandle ideas and mummify them like cadavers and the forms as if they were ruins.* You may not remember them, or you may not have read them, but they are Juan Ramón's words. I was particularly fond of this text when I was young. It animated me. Where's it from?, Juan asked, extending his hand to grab the page he'd never read. I came across it again recently. A poet quoted it in an interview. Now Juan thinks Brouard has a point. He's never been a forensic scientist, he thinks, he's never embalmed cadavers, never mummified. Federico gets excited again: To write the last chapter of *The Idiot*, just imagine that. Even leaving the rest of the novel unwritten. To start at the end and write no more than that single chapter. Juan's editor, Bernardo Alten, spoke with him as recently as a few months ago when they were discussing whether the biography (when he finishes it, whenever that will be: it's expanding, getting more complicated,

Juan told him) should be published in Planeta, the main imprint, instead of in the more specialized essay collection in the exclusively nonfiction imprint, it'd help bring more attention to Brouard's backlist, which has been stagnant for nearly a decade. He told him: He's been able to touch us so deeply without ever striking a false chord, not a shrill note in twenty books, unflagging self-discipline, conscientiousness in every word. He's made us believe that his books are drawn from life itself, straightforward narratives, when he's got to be the most literary author writing today, in full malicious control of his craft. Federico refutes this idea: I doubt there's anyone less gifted than I am at wrestling a thought or an emotion down on paper, at bridging the gap from head to hand: I think it was Kafka who said something along those lines. Even my sentence about ineffectiveness is something I've had to sponge. Kafka could express it that way because what he wrote was a lie. But when I copy him, I write a truth. What he finds the most irritating of all is when they say he has a natural talent for seizing the world and turning it into narrative. The notion of natural talent, of genius, is anathema to him. One searches for an idea and appropriates it by force and eventually pays for the effort with exhaustion. After the interview, Alten, the editor, said to Juan: It's like each book is a purgative of guilt, or an attempt at it. Each new book settles a score with the previous one. There's something illicit about his writing. He keeps killing, he keeps killing himself. He writes against himself, but also against his readers. He defies his readers with each new book, as if he were trying to get rid of them, to banish them from his sight. Make them forsake him, send him to hell once and for all. He can't bear being the brunt of other people's pity, maybe because of the issues with his father, the orphanages and difficulties when he was a child, all of which made him a natural magnet for pity, a victim of other people's pity, and he hated it. Who knows? Federico's soul is by no means a simple thing. Like he just said when addressing the reasons why his father hanged himself: Who knows why and who cares anyway? It's bargain-basement nostalgia. My work, which was supposed to vault me across those dark puddles, hasn't helped me at all, had no repercussions, it's reading material for the happy few who haven't purged me (isn't that the objective after all, to cleanse yourself?), I bet everything on the future; yet the future has brought other subjects, other sensibilities, nothing remotely resembling what I've written. Who knows if it's true, if he believes his own grievances? Brouard says: Who owns the writer, who is able to judge him? Whose world is this? Virgil wrote for Augustus. Racine wrote for Louis XIV. Boris Pilnyak, of *The Naked Year*, and Nikolai Ostrovsky, of *How the Steel was Tempered*, wrote for the proletariat, but us, for whom do we write, for whom have we written; our soul, for whom our soul, whom have we delivered it up to, offered it to, who has tempered our metal (no, we haven't been like steel, more like hollow tin, like the hands of the sinister Popeye in Faulkner's *Sanctuary*)? Juan listens to him and observes himself as if he were someone else, a kind of explorer with a canteen and a pith helmet trying to discover the source of a river, the member of an expedition in search of an ethic where there is no love, an expedition to a hollow left by a sea that had dried out long ago. The scholar specialized in the maestro of a somber generation. He said as much to Brouard one day after a few drinks: I really do belong to a somber generation, yours was a generation of bidets in sordid, rent-by-the-hour apartments, police stations where the moans of detainees could be heard, sodium permanganate injections on the tip of the dick to relieve gonorrhea, but I belong to a different kind of shabbiness, a less evident one, more subtle, a spiderweb that's better hidden, less visible. They taught me to never look at the horizon, the line that delineates the edge of what is yours and tells you that beyond its limit lie other things. Maestro

Brouard, my generation turned forty without lighting a single lantern. It really is a somber generation. You may have chosen the wrong road. But we never had any intention of going anywhere. Stay put. Wait for Godot. Three years ago, when Brouard received his cancer diagnosis, he kept the news from Javier and found a way to argue with him and kick him out: Go on, get out of here. You're young, you're wasting your life and fucking mine over by trying to resolve it. He didn't tell him about the cancer, and certainly not that he'd fallen in love again; he'd been in the process of reengaging with his childhood just as the illness declared itself, and suddenly was interested in health, in pursuing someone else's health. Today he says he's cured of that idea, he says, he doesn't let health sweet-talk him anymore, he's convinced it's the most idiotically cruel form of evil there is. According to Juan it was just a crush: a reencounter with innocence and health, the good-natured health of someone who was holding him in thrall (whom he ended up detesting), because—according to his particular bestiary—he was a mixture of innocent digestions and energy, both born of nature almost spontaneously, nuanced by the civilizing features of the agrarian or of the artisan, or something like that. Strength controlled by the artisan's skill and offered up to the profession. Health, honesty, vigor, kindness, sincerity, hard work, and the tenacity to overcome difficulties—all part of the same semantic field. I just thought he'd lost his reflexes and whatever drew him to that guy, who acted out of a blend of self-interest or curiosity, wasn't going to last very long. And I wasn't wrong. The day came when Brouard finally realized that not only was he ill, but that he'd been ensnared by a poacher's trap and didn't know how to wriggle himself free, because now he's mixing together the scenes of despair with those of contempt, the scenes of extreme need with those of extreme surfeit. He, who seemed comforted by his first years back in Misent, now stood before the window looking out

over a landscape fenced in by an ever-proliferating mass of cranes
and excavators, the mountainsides covered in bald spots where
more and more buildings were being raised. He complained,
knocking his forehead against the window the afternoon he got
back from the notary to sign the sale of the land: Why did I ever
come back, I don't even remember what I was looking for, but
whatever it was, it can't be this. Matías teased him: Know what
Baudelaire said about Poe?: *He was an erratic and heteroclite being,
a planet out of orbit, he was constantly running off from Baltimore to
New York, from New York to Philadelphia, from Philadelphia to Boston, from Boston to Baltimore, from Baltimore to Richmond.* Federico,
let me put it another way: he had a lunatic head and an itchy ass.
The only way to stop being wayward is to focus one's mind, your
mind, that's what you have to restrain, tie it up by the hands and
feet so it stays put for once, otherwise it's out of your mind that
you'll have to go to finally be calm for a while. Whatever it is, wherever it leads, what's truly out of control is your mind. Juan told
him the same thing: You're trying to run away from yourself. That's
impossible, unless you put a bullet in your brain. Then he told
Silvia: I know it's not okay to talk like that to a man his age. Federico: It's not true that literature leads to action, it's more lenitive,
I write about what I see emerging inside of myself, that stench,
nothing sexual, an odor that signals metabolic changes, altera-
tions, the stink of old age, what the scientists know by the physi-
ological-chemical reaction that produces it. Writing about what
comes even before biographical garbage because it's physiological
garbage. My readers. I read what I wrote for them: I will find comfort in my bed; my bed will alleviate my pain. Suckled, nurtured
as a promise, and then abandoned by the roadside, a piece of flesh
that nobody looks after, that boy who drew a house with a pointy
roof and a chimney with a curl of smoke, and underneath it he
wrote the word *house*, and beside that a stick figure atop four lines

under which he wrote the word *dog*. Those days, Juan wrote in his diary: *The thing is that all of it—which is so little, and so fragile— causes him such unease that his daily life is made nearly unbearable (along with inexorable physical decline). Writing becomes disorder for him, it's the crevice through which his private fears seep, the animal who captures the words of the tribe and drags them to its wet, shadowy burrow, its* tanière *as the French say. It's no longer public, no longer publishable. In that shadowy cave, literature loses its role as messenger of societal accord. The novelist is no longer the one who helps construct the narrative, who searches out meaning in the collective, no longer a lay priest, but someone who expresses prior fears, the pains of the pre-accord state.* But now he's not so sure the words he jotted down to work into the epilogue are worth a dime anymore, a lyrical effusion that came after a few drinks with Brouard. Juan had still been fascinated with the possibilities his personality offered. Federico had been alone for a little over a year when Javier—who found out about his prostate cancer—came back from Madrid. Age doesn't matter to me. I like being with you, Javier said, don't you get it? He came back and encouraged Brouard to leave that place, which didn't bring any comfort, and only compounded his pain: Don't worry, it doesn't matter. Let's just pack it up again and take the music elsewhere. Nostalgia for the birthplace became, like a boomerang effect, nostalgia for the Promised Land, only for that nostalgia to prove nothing but a passing state of mind, the great fiasco, ideas that don't correspond with deeds, empty wrappers. Federico said: Even worse are the leftovers of that nostalgia. I act out in life the things I condemn in my books. I don't know how to do in life what I know my characters have to do in my books. You see how literature isn't worth a damn? Matías and Juan held the opposite views: There's never been any other world here. The notion that you came back hoping to find something here is a total lie. You left, and you stayed away because you couldn't stand it here. Same as my brother who couldn't stand it either, who folded flat and submitted to the soil till he became a reptile; same as Montoliu, who couldn't stand it either, who went out to sea so as not to have to look at all this around him anymore; same as me, I left because I couldn't stand it anymore and then came back for a single purpose, for however long it lasts; but you had already forgotten, so you got it in your mind that there had been something here, a handful of distorted childhood memories, but now you don't feel like living in it. You don't feel like living in one place or the other. And what does it really matter, when all is said and done you live at home, with your music and your books. Anywhere you live is going to bother you, whether it's here or in Sevastopol. He stood up for himself: Don't try to tell me that this place is anything like how I remember it. It's not even the place I came back to anymore. Everything's changed. It's as though there were a chopping machine hanging over our heads tearing everything apart. Yes, but what you'd left behind was a lot worse in many ways. Or am I wrong that half the population fled to France, America, or Algiers? You were the one who told me stories about the cruelty endured by the underprivileged class, the ghastly hunger, the political repression, the shabbiness, the incapacity to think freely—wasn't it you who told me all those stories? Isn't that what you've written in your books? It was even worse back then. Nowadays what they're beating to a pulp is the landscape, but back then it was human life, stomachs, skins, and brains. Tally the number of people who weren't forced to emigrate, the ones who stayed, and have a look at them yourself. Talk to the ones who stayed and the ones who left. You know most of their stories. Connecticut, New Jersey, Buenos Aires, Paris, the Swiss Valais, the spinning mills, the auto factories, cleaning, scaffolding, rain, snow, ice, gray skies. It was their lot in life to experience those things. A matter of survival, no more, no less. Stay here and surviving was impossible. A country of the starving, a country of maids, a country of lepers. You can still see the walls of the old leper hospital from the terrace at sunset. Juan eyes them while he's talking and listens to the sound of a small plane fumigating the orange groves with pesticide. It's been running low rounds all morning, narrowly avoiding the house by a few skinny meters, spraying the toxic liquid that attacks the insects' respiratory system, which is clearly not much good for humans, either. The buzz of the small plane over the house drowned out their words for a few seconds as it passed. I don't know where else to go, he complains. Well, you can't blame that on the landscape, or morality, or the economy, or the times we're living in. Juan teases him: All those people who want to live a hundred years, even if they're atrocious ones, and who feel unlucky if they can only live fifty years, even though they're marvelous ones. Remember? You told me that. It's Seneca or Cicero, I can't remember now. You've been lucky, you're the same age as my father-in-law. Federico answers: Your father-in-law is the picture of health, I, on the other hand, am a train wreck. For Rubén, the world is like a carpenter's table, the kind with all those tools hanging within arm's reach, you don't need to stretch too far to grab a tool and put it to use, you know each one's purpose and how to utilize it: your father-in-law is an interesting creature, you can study shades of evil in him, or maybe, as he says, the survival instinct. Clearly my problem is that I came back too late. You could say I was admitted to intensive care, but I had already stopped breathing. You leave too soon to really live, and come back too late, never having lived at all. He becomes serious: It feels like his father had punched him in the face again at the bar. Toothpicks scattered across the floor, the crumpled napkins, the cigarette butts, the gooey stains. He continues: Nobody can bear that kind of unmitigated pain. You need a story in your head to be able to endure that kind of suffering. To give it meaning or imagine it's worth something. Something that cures you, saves you. The pain means it's working, my grandmother used to say whenever she dabbed a wound with a few drops of alcohol, a brush burn from playing outside, a cut from falling down. We can't fathom that something might sting and not be curative, that it just hurts, plain and simple, all pain, no remedy. Christians invented the whole mysticism of the body: my pain won't cure me, but it's good for you. It's a big lie, my pain isn't any good for anyone. We should be proud, look what we've accomplished. Life marches forward in peace, subjected only to the habitual incidents of private life. Never before have we enjoyed so much calm, and yet, never have we felt such a pressing feeling of oppression, either. He was alluding to Matías now, though not by name: We may have entertained absurd notions, impossible ones, but by entertaining them—however mistaken—we could survive, try to be different. By now we've accepted there's no exchange policy here, or that we had no place in whatever exchange was allowed. And it crushed us. It's hard to fall from the idea that you can build the world with your own hands, of having touched the original clay, of having played with it, only to have it taken away. Rubén was the first of us to have capitulated and yet if you take a closer look, he's the only one among us who actually changed anything—he changed everything. Wherever you look, you see what he's changed, everything that's passed through his hands is different than what it was before. We call it devastation, but he changed the world he lives in; and though we think it's for the worse, it must certainly provide him with a sense of security. He's the only great potter among us. Brouard remembers his arguments with Rubén, the last ones, how he grew more obstinate, tenser and more irritated each time: I can't invent something beyond what already exists, we know money is shit and that Switzerland subsists atop a smelly lake of shit, but look how beautiful it is; Lake Geneva, Lucerne, Mont

Blanc high above, all built on shit and how gorgeous they are, don't you think?—who would have all that, who would be like that, all of us wish the whole world could be like that except for a few fanatics, and so you ask me, of course, under those circumstances who was going to produce all of the shit. You're right. But you can't ask me to fix the world that nobody else has been able to fix; it's not something you can ask even of yourself, Federico. It'd be overly prideful. Things move forward at their own pace, nobody can really alter them, you may jump on a moving train and take advantage of its momentum, but you can't stand in the middle of the tracks and expect to stop it. Later, Rubén changed his tone and teased him: So what's your game? How come you're the only penniless writer of your generation? He patted him on the shoulder, drew his face closer, hugged him, gave him a kiss on the cheek. How have you stayed so poor? Federico told Juan about it with a smile. Ask me, go ahead Juan, he said a few months ago, ask me why I was obliged to sell this land to your father-in-law, which I never would've forfeited willingly. I'd have left it as is, barren, or set up a foundation, or maybe gifted it to the city to build a park for children. That's what I would have liked to do. A park, a school, something like that. It's one thing to know we'll never be equipped to enjoy a rational world thanks to our Judeo-Christian education, and something else altogether to be incapable of earning your bread. From the window he could hardly see the water, the glimmering sea was veiled by the noontime mist. Arid desert dust had rained heavily over the county yesterday. The haze had returned today, diffusing the sharp colors, washed out now by an excess of light. Misent was barely visible: a white stain, blurred, a landscape submerged in milk, in pastis blended with water; though here it would be absinthe mixed with water, or *cazalla*, an aniseed liqueur with a splash of cold water. They're the favorite local drinks. Juan combs the shelf for a volume in classical Latin and reads: *The pain in your bladder is agonizing, and you've received unpleasant news, you suffer constant losses; what's worse, you've had to fear for your life, perhaps you ignored all of this when you wanted to reach old age?* He finally got a rise out of Brouard. The same giggling belly as when he was trying to analyze the devastating effects of his recent affair of the heart. So old and so fragile, he laughed at himself at the time: Anyone can break you. A young thing can do in just a few days what time itself had never been able to. Youth, health—they had both made a comeback right when he got news of the prostate cancer and, without saying a word about his doctor's visit, he asked Javier to leave. It's my last chance, he must've thought: looking for himself through the mirror of health, friendship, camaraderie, something new with the perfume of another time, an intoxicating blend, irresistible, look to the future and come face-to-face with the melancholy of what's already passed, the best of what has been, what life had given him, a son who would transmit a few drops of lost health, vigor, who was both son and father all at once, a paternal son, strong and understanding, someone who shows you again the difference between good and evil. Love as a form of faith in the circular nature of life, performing the eternal return. Matías told him: You can have a fling, Federico, a good time, but it's a different matter to fall in love with someone forty years younger, which can happen, let alone fall head over heels without asking yourself how the other person might feel. Him: Javier is thirty years younger than me. And Matías: But that's different. Javier is in love with you. And why wouldn't he love me too?—Brouard said in self-defense. But did he ever say he was? Did he tell you he loved you? That he was in love with you? Matías said, but Brouard skirted the issue: The issue isn't whether one loves me and the other doesn't, it's that I love Javier the way one loves a little pet and I'm in love with the other. I know, I know, such an ugly way of saying it, but that's the way it is. You can't ask me to renounce the last crumb of passion I have left, or to squelch the last flicker of the match that's giving me light. During his time in Madrid, Javier would call Matías in Benalda, and ask him to visit Brouard, check up on him. He's depressed, he told him. He was worried that Federico might do something rash, he used to make sure there was nothing on hand that he could use to hurt himself. He was miserable when I left, depressed. That's why I didn't want to leave for Madrid. I would hear him sobbing at night, Javier told Matías. He could imagine the scene: the new one in Misent, that Pasolinian angel, spending hours drinking with Federico in the living room, looking around the house scornfully, haughtily, like something he'll inherit that's not worth much. The months following Javier's departure were like a long nightmare. The benders, the after-hours clubs at his age, as if he'd decided it was time to burn it all to the ground. Despite the daily chaos, he convinced himself that he would finally reconcile himself to the values he'd known as a young child. It didn't last very long, though. More wild nights, more booze, more coke, all of it thrown into an ever-accelerating blender. The voyeur who watches from a tawdry fake-leather armchair as two bodies tongue-and-groove—see the dirty animal with two backs, you wanna watch, huh? Then watch, see what I do to her, see what she does to me; but afterward, not even that, get out of here, fuck you and get lost, we want to do things we like now and don't want anyone else to see, so, don't let the door hit you in the ass, life lasts two days and now it's night, and him there, seeing the animal's reflection between the rocks in his drink, the spider, the eight-legged creature that rises and falls over the bed, the wounding animal, all that energy squandered over the mattress, the river of health that deposits him on the riverbank, the strength, deposits him on the riverbank of pity, the riverbank of the ailing. Not an ounce of compassion. He talked to Matías about the painter Bacon, whom he'd met in the Cock—an ambiguous bar he said, only to correct himself immediately, smiling, not exactly ambiguous, actually rather explicit—it was just behind the Chicote, with its back to Madrid's Gran Vía. Bacon—Federico told Matías—believed the Christian ethic is a remnant of the Greek ethic and believed that there was no better ethical code for the Western world, although—the painter was always quick to point out—I cannot bear its religious component. Federico glossed Bacon's words bitterly. He said he missed the moral shadings of a faithless Christianity, especially in the public statements of politicians and artists, but even more so in his neighbors. Brouard's language grew more cantankerous as a result of that experience. He grumbled: that kind of pre-Adamism without a sense of guilt. If you take concepts away from people it will prompt genetic regressions. You have to raise concepts as if they were barriers. Save yourself through depiction, credibly perform your part in the play like a good actor. That idea's been lost. It cries at night. If anyone should see you, if anyone should spend a gram of pity on you. The Bible: I am become as sounding brass, or a tinkling cymbal. And though I have the gift of prophecy, and understand all mysteries, and all knowledge; and though I have all faith, so that I could remove mountains, and have not charity, I am nothing. And though I bestow all my goods to feed the poor, and though I give my body to be burned, and have not charity, it profiteth me nothing. He'd stay in bed for entire days, some days because he didn't feel well, other days because he was too lazy to get up. Juan would call to warn that he was on his way over for a visit, but Federico always had an excuse: I'm under the weather, I haven't slept, call me tomorrow. And: I'm not leaving anything that will last, he said to Juan, what book of mine still stands up today? Record the conversation, tell the story of the teenager, the man, who once fought to claim a particle of light for Misent together with Rubén and the painter Montoliu, and how nothing of that is left now. One can be better off in prison than in paradise, it's a matter of character, but also of circumstance. Circumstances weigh. If only Dostoyevsky were here among us, he would explain, explain it all to all of us, explain that life is not always the most important thing. That same man who never used to consider what he needed, only what he owed, now thinks only about himself, or what's more, only about how unfairly someone has treated him, and the injustice he's suffered has become his prevailing metaphor in the world, the game between hunters and prey, you think you're a hunter and you've become the prey, the hunter hunted—today let's party, but don't you see he left you on your own? Don't you see the other one turning around, feeling up the whore, kissing her, sticking his tongue in her mouth? Not even a minute and her hand is kneading his crotch, he's fondling hers. Everyone's in a hurry, there's an end-of-days kind of urgency, the conversation ends and the assault begins. Both of them up to the room, the old goat's paying for it after all, so go ahead and watch, and he stays there, sitting in the armchair drooling, drunk, nodding off a little, tanked up, barely able to fish his credit card out of his wallet to pay, the other one and the girl help him with it, the strand of saliva falling over his chest, his dentures crooked (you should get implants, Javier tells him, and he refuses—what for, I've had more than enough operations for one life already), he and the whore get a kick out of seeing him passed out like that and they give him a pinch—they'd already ripped their clothes off—and laugh as they lick at each other and stop looking his way because now all that matters is what they're doing to each other. And now he, in the worst case, comes to again and sees them fucking, eyelids open, stroking himself to no avail, trying to get hard, while the whore elbows the other, who's just getting down to eating her pussy and she winks at him and says look, Gramps is awake, and he's looking at us. And the other: So you like to watch, huh, then watch, watch how I eat this slut's pussy, watch how I stick my tongue up her cunt, how I suck it down, and there's the sound of sucking, flesh, saliva and fluids, and so he fumbles to zip up his fly and shuffles off, down to the bar to wait an hour or so until the other is sick of fucking—camaraderie, sharing, that's how it ended. Brouard explained to Matías at the start of everything: I like how free young people are, their open-mindedness, he was convinced it celebrated something, health, friendship, camaraderie, the triumph of Apollo, of Bacchus, life had given him a kind of son to help him seize back a little of his youthfulness, and at the same time a father, someone who'd pro-tect him, who came back to the world to acknowledge him, rein-carnated at nearly the same age his father was—so young—when he abandoned him, a new father who'd keep him out of harm's way, teach him about the line between good and evil, a luminous, honed line. Look at it, you can see it clearly, it's right there. From here to there, good. Over on the other side, evil. Not the father who had abandoned him, leaving no more legacy than the mem-ory of his fists, of the kicks he tendered when the boy was splayed across the floor of a grimy bar. But that's not how it goes, the other is not a newly minted father—just a repeat of the father he'd al-ready had, showing up at the bar looking for a good time, where's the fun. This one doesn't punch him; but he abandons him. And though sixty-odd years have passed since then, it feels as though not a single one had, as if life had been held between parentheses, and everything between then and now had been swallowed down into a hole. When he gets back from one of these benders, he locks himself in his room and sobs alone. Javier hears him crying and puts up with all the crankiness until the morning comes when calmly, unperturbed, Federico asks him to leave. You're young, you can make another life, don't waste yours on me, he says. He doesn't mention the cancer, or that he'll need surgery. For the next three or four nights, the sobs that can be heard in the house are

Javier's, until he packs up his things and leaves. In the months that follow, he slinks down the ladder a few more rungs, despairing, wishing he were dead, wishing he could vanish. Juan told Silvia about it: I thought the other one was going to move in, I think Federico expected the other to live with him in his house, to be a substitute for Javier, but it didn't work out that way, Javier left and now he's alone. I don't know who's going to take care of him during his convalescence. Juan wasn't sure how much of his story was true and how much was fabricated. There were days when he wouldn't eat a thing, the house was a disaster, stuff was scattered everywhere, he would hang out at the bar until the small hours, drunk, coked out of his skull, in the company of people forty years younger than him, all laughing at his expense. It seemed like he was waiting for the play to end so he could just be. As if some play was reaching its finale and once it was over all the performers would wriggle out of their selfish disguises: that's when a form of truth would appear, a luminous light. But it wasn't like that. Or it wasn't like that, either. There was no light, no luminous nakedness beneath the disguise. Nature unmasked is somber and its illumination only comes by way of accidental artifice. Beneath the disguise is nothingness. Whenever Juan tried to encourage him: Come outside, why don't you, get a little sun, take a walk on the beach Federico, and he'd answer that he found a kind of peace in the darkness of that dirty house with the blinds down, where night never wholly departed: No, don't raise the blinds. I'm good this way. Plato said we're unhappy beings forever searching for the other half that was ripped from us, but the origin of our unhappiness is consciousness, not mutilation. We seek the state of unconsciousness to rest, and suffer until that silence is located, that repose, that reconciliation with mute nature, we chase after it, we pursue it while making off as though we were running from it. Juan didn't know where Federico scored his drugs: the cocaine, the booze, a whole cabinet of pills and powders. However they got there, the provisions had been interrupted for a while during his hospital stay and for a time afterward, during his recovery. He went through the operation and made the subsequent trips to the hospital for checkups on his own; luckily the chemotherapy cycle was a short one. At least my hair hasn't fallen out yet, he said while vomiting, his hands clutching the toilet bowl. It fell out a little while afterward. It was a clean tumor, the oncologist said, but he had to give up sex. He had a laugh at his own expense: Behold a past without a future, he said to Matías and Juan. It was a joyless laugh, a five-o'clock shadow laugh full of poorly concealed bitterness. He said: Behold the nothingness. He'd only been out of the hospital for fifteen days and already he was hitting the bars, ignoring the doctor's instructions, taking his medicine haphazardly. He whined to Matías, giving the crotch of his pants a good shake, saying: We die by segments, piece by piece. One chunk less. The only thing I notice now is my stomach. It's the only sensation I still feel, a stomachache, and the nape of my neck, the nape of my neck aches after a few hours of reading. Cervical vertebrae, my only nocturnal issue now, and the catheter, which irritates my urethra and causes pain; and the hiatal hernia, a bunch of measly physical nuisances, none of which have a hold on the spiritual side of things, the values that beget desire, hope, exhilaration. The parts of the body that are connected to the invisible, to what is secret and obscure, they've all dried up on me by now, dead, now I'm pure physicality, bad digestion, aching neck and shoulders. No pain in the parts of my body that touch the soul. I have no more soul than a cat, a cat in heat, howling from the urgency of its desire. Juan stopped calling on him, with the excuse of a tight deadline for a commission he'd been given. He couldn't deal with the muted violence, the chaos, the presence of what he sarcastically called the *Teorema* angels, a confused flock of murky beings with murky wings, beating and flapping, all of them wandering from room to room in the house, eating and drinking, inhabiting the spaces, cutting lines of coke on the living room coffee table. He told Silvia: Fine, so he ripped himself to shreds in the books and served himself up on a platter. Let's imagine that's what happened. But that's over. He's a leftover of all that now, an old narcissist who uses me whenever he needs to, who could care less about everything I do or don't do, so long as I resolve his logistical problems, take me here, buy me this, bring me that. If he doesn't feel like going to a checkup he simply doesn't show up; and if he does, he'll call me the night before to drive him there or sometimes even that same morning telling me he needs a ride, and it doesn't bother him at all that he has me running around all day, spending hours in the hospital waiting room. We may have used him as readers, but now he's asking that we waste our time and energy, and I'm not so sure we can allow ourselves to waste it so generously, or at best it's something we'll never approve of or admire. His final novel was published three years ago. Yes, the last one, because I think it's going to be his last, Matías, Juan had said to his friend. Juan had considered the idea of publishing it immoral. You can't do that to yourself. Let it sit for a while. There's no rush. Think it over. He had helped him correct a few things himself, but the core of the novel just wasn't working. He didn't dare insist, though, after the editor sent a fawning letter. Brouard knew best, it was his decision after all—ten years had passed since he published the previous one, and it brought his backlist books once again into bookstore windows, making them current for a while. The editor could tell he needed to be mollified, to be convinced that he hadn't yet disappeared as an author. And he needed the money, he needed it because the advances for his translations were drying up and the royalties from his books had dwindled. Literature professors study his work, students write their theses on it, but nobody actually buys it. He has nothing left to say, Juan told his wife. But she liked the new book. Juan: A confusing story about a lost soul who has lost his sense of discipline and who is utterly incapable of producing what he considers to be good writing: the tightly knit expression of an idea. Silvia: I think it's a tenderhearted book, okay, maybe it's not his best, but you can tell that it was written by someone who takes the time to think deeply about things. Juan, irritated: Who used to think deeply, and who stopped thinking a long time ago. The critics went on again about genius. The Brouard touch. Inertia, pressure from his editors, snobbishness, recollections of his earlier work. Who knows? Well, it got good reviews, Silvia said, the critics approved. And Juan: You mean nobody dared to write a negative review or was in the mood to trash it. Mindlessness, courtesy, mercy, call it what you will, there's a bit of it all thrown in. Matías gave only a lukewarm defense of the novel to Juan and Silvia, though he told Brouard that he liked it, he was moved by it, etc.—in very general terms, largely non-concrete. Juan: The more docile reviewers called him a master of form so they wouldn't have to admit that he had nothing to say. The novel was a commercial failure, the editor never recovered the modest advance. Juan prophesied: His cycle has now closed and the future won't be getting any better. If anything, some random journalist might cover his death. A few obits will come out in the papers. That's all the dead man walking has left. The biographer has already made an appearance, here he is now, his work is nearly done and ready to reveal to humanity the brand of gin he preferred, how many bottles of it he drank, how many joints he smoked with your uncle Matías, the brand of whisky he preferred, whom he slept with, whom he tried to sleep with and couldn't, and if he really was addicted to cocaine till his dying days; if he had to take uppers to be able to write, to get up, to go to bed. How many pills he took and under what circumstances; how many lines, how many cocktails. All the trash we biographers nourish ourselves with, as if the work itself was merely an excuse to forgive the wretch's vices with impunity. Silvia: But the only thing you're interested in is his work. Juan: Precisely the part that's now kaput. That isn't left. It's already on my bookshelves at home. Silvia convinced him to keep at it. Finish the biography. Javier called from Madrid more or less regularly: So? What do you think? How's he doing? Let's just say he wasn't always up front with Javier, depending on the day. He's fine, he said a couple of times. He's a little fucked-up, he admitted once or twice. He never let on about the frenzied, absurd despair, the agitated months when the operating rooms, scalpels, and convalescences all ran together with the benders, colossal benders, and a suicide attempt, which though unconvincing had landed him in the hospital again. Matías had found him. He probably popped the handful of pills knowing that Matías was on his way over. That other shore, Matías, I'm sure now that I'll never reach it again, it's final, the shore of health, I mean. I'm on the other side of the river now, the shore of deformed bodies, the ugly ones, the sexless river, the one that feeds into the wretched, polluting sentiments of pity and compassion; Lourdes or the Ganges, or Fátima, places crawling with the sick, the condemned. He said it with tears in his eyes, the catheter in place, the lull of the barbiturates giving an echo to his voice as if it were coming from somewhere far away. Surely he thought about his Pasolinian angel and the colony of bats, forever distanced from them now, too, his nocturnal Peter Pan, the one who'd been torturing him all those months and who'd now finally vanished. It happens to all of us, Federico, don't think for a minute I don't feel a rush of melancholy seeing all those young things in Benalda. It's called old age. We're all closer to the river of Lourdes now than the beaches of the Caribbean. You have to take it the way it comes, old age, we're paying the piper for the illusion of freedom we believed

in all these years, never tying ourselves down to anyone, to anything, never saying to any one person that we'll love them until
death do us part (I halfway said that to Angela, judicially, civilly,
not very romantically—romanticism obliges the metaphysical impulse of religion), but when all is said and done, at least you have
your books. Not much of me will remain. I doubt the things I've
planted these final years will last for very long. My son will get rid
of it all the day after I'm buried, my young olive groves will soon
be chalets, subdivisions, golf courses, dumping grounds, trash
heaps; all that I planted without really knowing why I was doing
it in the first place. For myself, I suppose. Out of selfishness. To
enjoy it for however long I last, before the *Cracker* inherits it. To
give meaning to something I wouldn't even know how to explain.
Others set sail on a world cruise. I stay here, watching the seasons
pass through the trees, the plants, the eternal death and rebirth
and death again next year. But, Federico answered, you've had
your moments, and you have a son. Matías: Bah, and you've had
yours too, your moments, and maybe even children, who's to say?
You've just forgotten your amorous frenzies, your erotic journey-
ing, forgot all about them; and as far as my son is concerned, he
joked, I couldn't even tell you where Ernesto is now, what he's
doing, and I couldn't care less, a son of mine addicted to the stock
market, not even sex or drugs, something fun: addicted to the
stone-cold screens of the stock index. What can you expect from
that? You've experienced moments of boundless satisfaction,
you've lived your life good and hard, even though you pretend not
to remember anything, people have bought your books, newspapers have written about them, admirers still write you letters every now and again, Silvia's husband is going to publish a Brouardian
summa. Your readers have adored you, they've asked you to sign
their copies of your novels. And if that's not enough, you'll remain
in your books, you'll continue existing through your books long

after any trace of me remains. And Federico: But I'm not in my books, don't you see that? All that's in them is what I've been able to capture, to apprehend, with varying degrees of success. I've remained outside of them. A bug collector isn't in the pages of his or her album. There are moths, crickets, cockroaches, beetles, and butterflies that he or she caught in a net. The book is the dry cocoon that a silkworm leaves behind once it has become a butterfly. The analogy's a little mawkish maybe, but it's pretty spot on. You read books and see yourself in them, you recognize yourself, or you think you recognize yourself and you say, I'm this one, or I'm that one, or I'm that other one over there. Remember how your brother recognized himself in that investment wheeler-dealer character in *The Erratic Will*? I know he got offended. He said he wanted to massacre me, to send over one of those thugs who work for him. Juan told me, and said he's also annoyed that he's writing the biography. But I'm the one who doesn't see himself or recognize himself or find himself in my writing, and I don't know whether this nonbeing is because it's always like that, or maybe it's something genetic, or because my father beat me up and abandoned me and never taught me how to beat anyone else up and abandon them, and with an upbringing like that, you're condemned to always being the victim; or maybe it's because he never picked me up in his arms or carried me piggyback, or on his shoulders, dad's strong, crew-cut head between the boy's fragile legs, no, I never knew what that was like, he never took me by the hand, he never transmitted that thing we don't quite understand but that later we need so much. Or maybe he transmitted his rotten genes that led him to kill himself because he couldn't figure out how to carve up the chunk of life he had left. He hasn't done much since his last novel. Just shut himself away in his room. He'd spend most of the day there and have nothing to show for it, not an article, not a preface, not a conference paper. He rejected all commissions. Juan recorded his series of invectives against literature: Sentimental trash that consoles the weak and cleanses evil. Let them keep my stories, everything I wrote to cure myself, but never could. Matías would tease him saying: Why do you write if you hate literature so much? He responded using that Chaplin line to Claire Bloom in *Limelight*—I thought you said you hated the theater?—I hate the sight of blood, too, but it's in my veins. Don't bother looking for an explanation. It's what's inside of us that we hate the most. They're the very elements that make up our lives, and yet we hate them. Oh, we like the body, it's something miraculous, something sacred, but you rip it open, the sac of guts and blood will gush out along with the remainders of recently swallowed cereal, half-chewed vegetables, chi chi beans, lentils, in a thick, foul-smelling mass. Wars are nothing more than that, ripping enemies open to see what's inside of them. The air of battlefields is impregnated with that sickening stench. It's something all authors of bellicose novels describe. Read Littell, the one who just won the Goncourt; or Ledig, that German who wrote three outstanding novels only to give up writing for forty years, probably because he'd emptied himself of all the rotten things he'd been carrying around inside and wasn't ready to console anyone just yet. Read *Magnet* by our own Ramón Sender. All the great novelists who've told stories of war describe the persistence of this stink, they describe humans as being rotten gut sacs that are better left unopened. The human being. The Catholic Church has nourished itself off of that filth, off the knowledge that we are only that which we hate; that we have the ability to rot away in life. Francis of Borgia accompanies Isabella of Portugal's lifeless body on its way to the mausoleum and when it comes time for him to identify the body, when he sees the contents of that casket after crossing the Castilian desert, he falls to his knees and exclaims: I will never again serve a lord who can die. That's when religion makes an appearance. Or literature: to serve a colorless, odorless, and insipid spirit, to cast aside the genetic compulsion of the original cannibal, who urges you to bite, to bite nipples, flesh, organs, to suck and bite. Literature allows you to fall in love with ghosts who can't be shot or poked, who don't reveal innards and stench. To be elevated above the cannibalistic urge, to fall in love with ghosts who look like bodies, to fall in love with houses, streets, and landscapes that are nothing but words. The Pasolinian angel had stood him in front of the mirror: had forced him to contemplate his nonexistence as a writer whose work, he thinks, is vanishing without a trace; his lean home economy couldn't withstand all the drugs and cheap whores and had taken a sudden nosedive, and the financial pressure had finally forced him to sell the land to Rubén; the image he'd seen in the mirror, above all else, was his age, and his tour through the operating room had multiplied it exponentially. He laughed at his own expense: Following unconditional surrender, disarmament. The boy had gleefully chiseled away at his walls, at everything that'd so delicately sustained him. Eventually I'll forget about him, but how will I ever be able to forget about myself. The damage is done, I've seen myself, he made me look at myself, he said to Matías. Brouard opened the window and rested his face against the glass, peering out at the landscape, that sleepless landscape, unsettling, the city lights, the suburbs, the headlights on the highway, lights flickering in the distance, fading as the reddish hues of the day began imposing themselves, the oranges and the yellows, lights that glimmered at nightfall and faded once again with the coming of the new dawn. Juan found him red-eyed when he stopped by his home in the middle of the afternoon. I haven't slept a wink, he said. On the table the tobacco, the ashtray overflowing with butts, the streaks of saliva and coke across the glass, a little plastic baggie, a bank card. And then: This isn't the place I meant to return to. It was Juan who finally asked Javier to come back: I think he really needs you, he needs someone. Javier showed up prepared to take him away from Misent, take him anywhere else. Packing is the least of it, you can leave your things here, give them away, there's nothing of any value, I'll see to the photos, the keepsakes, what you really want to bring, leave the arrangements to me. I'll call as soon as I have everything ready in Madrid so all you have to do is show up. Javier was a good physical therapist, he never had problems finding work, though when he'd mentioned leaving Misent it wasn't clear they'd be able to afford a roomy flat in Madrid that could fit all his books, with space enough for him to shut himself away to write—it's a question of finance, sure, but you can afford it now that you've sold the land, Javier asserted once more: he should take advantage of having the money now to sell the house, too. With that money they could find something in Madrid, or even better, in nearby Valencia: It'd almost be easier for me to find a good job in Valencia than in Madrid, he said, Valencia is a more affordable city, more reasonably priced, it has a better vibe, it's less stressful, and it offers more opportunities to take part in the life of the city. You can see an art exhibition, a movie when you're in the mood, a concert, take a walk along the wharf in winter, or visit the beach, those priceless days of winter sun, you can sit in the terraces in Malvarrosa in the winter and read the newspaper, look out at the sea, basking in the sunlight. Everything is within arm's reach. Not like in Madrid. Sometimes when Matías went down to Benalda, the few friends he had in Misent would let him in on some of the gossip: when he slipped and fell in the toilet, when he showed up with his fly down, mumbling and slurring, how he was the last one left at the bar, his crotch soaked with piss, and found that half a dozen kids who'd been drinking all the way through the afternoon and into the

night had rung up his tab and stuck him with the bill. He, who was
so proud in other ways, so easily offended, had become so tremen-
dously vulnerable, he just let it all happen. That continued for a
few more months, even once Javier had come back and moved
into the house. Juan found out about it. He told Silvia, too (the
biographer is supposed to know everything, he needs to know the
details in order to silence what he considers opportune), and
ended up regretting having pressured Javier into coming back.
Why does Javier put up with it, why does he remain by his side,
fitting the catheter, attending to his needs, changing his diapers?
He organizes everything, does all the shopping, picks up the mail,
cooks, pays the bills (though Federico is still the only one with
access to the bank account). And for some reason he doesn't live
up to whatever ideal Federico's searching for. Or maybe he does
live up to it and Federico hasn't realized it yet. A good physical
therapist who can knead out a muscle cramp. Maybe he just hasn't
caught on to the fact that his ideal is right there beside him. An
archangel of light, a diurnal Peter Pan. Javier rips open the cookie
wrapper while Juan holds the butt of the Ducados that Federico
handed over to him in a rush, as soon as he heard Javier approaching in the hallway. He considers the man's lack of scruples, a person who for so many people younger than him—Juan
included—had always been a model of honesty, who spent time in
prison during the Franco years, was exiled in Paris and Rome, kept
his distance during the transition, wasn't in cahoots with anyone,
not in the world of power or the world of literature. And look at
him now, how he's behaving over a measly cigarette, how little he
cares that Juan will now have to bear recriminatory glances from
Javier, who thinks he's trying to bother Brouard by smoking in
front of him, because according to his version of things, it bothers
Federico to be around people who smoke, the smell of tobacco
and the sight of the smokers' gestures. But no, on second thought,

he reasons, it's even worse the way he forces Javier into having to fake it, Javier knows perfectly well that Juan is just this morning's accidental accomplice, helping him to get away with smoking his dozen cigarettes. Of course Javier knows who's actually smoking, even though the doctor scolded Brouard at his last checkup: If you continue smoking I will refuse to treat you; and he doesn't even know the worst of it, the massive amounts of alcohol, the coke, because Juan is convinced that one way or another, he's still doing lines at home, that as long as he's still breathing the night angels will figure a way to sneak in as soon as Javier is out of sight, Federico must call them and pay them to appear and disappear, like magic. How can you expect Javier to like me, Silvia? A biographer is an uncomfortable witness. The thing is, Federico incriminates all of us, he turns us all into liars, people who tell half-truths, who wink and gesture behind other people's backs, all of us fibbing to each other to cover up for him. He's a wreck at seventy-something, and yet he's still able to do what he does, if only he'd have taken a little better care of himself, if only he hadn't been so viciously self-destructive, he could've lived a century, Juan tells Silvia (he knows the doctor is pessimistic—the doctor who isn't even aware of the extent of his irregularities: he doesn't think he'll survive to see next summer, maybe he'll even skip the next heat wave). He rejects the chocolate cookie Javier offers. He sticks his hand between the outstretched cookie and his mouth, but Javier insists and brings it closer again. You can hear his shallow breathing, like a death rattle. Juan thinks: He's a dying man. He's the same age as my father-in-law, maybe one or two years older but just over seventy, and yet his health is in steady decline, and by contrast his father-in-law has married a woman nearly half a century younger than him, and is still managing the whole business while Federico is dying, or nearly, burned by the wings of an angel half a century younger than him, being cared for by a nurse thirty years younger than him (Juan thinks: A generation of vampires). He raises his hand between the cookie and his mouth again, and Javier insists, bringing the little cookie up close, saying: Eat, and Brouard finally capitulates, taking a slight nibble and chewing at it listlessly, a tiny morsel, barely a crumb, a quarter of a miniature cookie, munching slowly, then as if in the grips of a sudden wave of nausea, he bends over and pulls a spittoon out from under the bed, makes a few noises in his throat and spits, it's not exactly vomit, but he releases a tremendous round of dry heaves that produces some bile and saliva; taking advantage of the spittoon being out, and after no small amount of difficulty getting to his feet, he fumbles around in the crotch of his pajamas, pulls out his cock, and takes a whiz. The urine spatters on the floor tiles. Juan feels awkward, embarrassed, but he doesn't look away from the shrunken dick. The urine strains its way out, a slow, fragile thread that makes a muted sound when it hits the bottom of the spittoon. Juan looks at the tiny, shriveled dick as he clutches it between two fingers and can't help imagining all the ardent masculine characters in his novels, he thinks about Federico walking away from a club bar, letting his arm fall lightly around some young man's shoulder or else ruffling his hair; all the young, wholesome types he's always seemed to like so much, that he still likes; he imagines that cock drawing close to their flesh, rubbing up against it, penetrating it (Javier kissing it, kissing his liver-spotted hands), sickness and health all jumbled together, searching for each other to find a lost balance, excesses and defects spiraling around each other to find a truth, a perverse order. It's an image of his lies, but also of his truth. The darkened skin and the sad, dark little head awaken something like pity in him, but also a sense of unease. Time and use, he thinks, that's why the purple shade, but the thought disturbs him, an entire life reduced to a piece of skin. All forms of desire, the rapture of love, of suffering, of jealousy, of hatred, of pursuit, of abandonment, all of it concentrated in that dusky little head, in the swath of dark skin he's holding between his fingers. The sight upsets him now. Brouard gives it three quick shakes and winces as if it had hurt, and back into the pajamas the dick goes. Javier picks up the spittoon and heads for the bathroom. He opens the door to the hallway and a warm, clammy current enters the room. A few seconds later, the sound of the spittoon being emptied into the toilet bowl, the flush of the tank. Federico is patting his forehead with a hankie, which he moves across his face. He's perspiring. He has a hard time lying down on the bed, his breathing falters and he wheezes asthmatically. He places the oxygen mask over his mouth, a mask on top of a mask. He breathes in deeply, apprehensively. Juan considers how selfishly he behaves with Javier. Would it really be too much to ask that he go to the toilet instead of expecting Javier to perform these revolting tasks? But who can say what moves people to like or dislike certain things? I'm feeling woozy, vertigo, it's worse than ever, Federico says. What he is right now is pickled, sweating profusely, breathing poorly, as if he were about to choke. Juan thinks: Doesn't he care at all about Javier? What he remembers, what he safeguards, what he stores away? An automaton, a machine that removes the foil wrapper from a packet of cookies and empties the spittoon. He feels like escaping, as if his seeing and knowing, his having seen and having known, somehow makes him an accessory. He detests Federico right now, he wants to quit writing about him, he wishes he'd never met him, never read him. A machine may function better or worse, may break down altogether, but things happen to an animal, an animal feels pain, it suffers, it feels joy, a cat's throaty call announces it's in heat, a dog rollicks and cavorts, wags its tail to high heaven when it hears its owner's car pulling up, you can see an animal suffer or feel exultant, however small it is, however low its place on the food chain, it's not some motorized system that stops functioning: insects writhe when they're squished and one can imagine, like it or not, that in those movements there's something more than the blind inertia of a motor—the mutilation of a machine. Juan has tapes of Federico talking about his house cats: I saw the cat dying and couldn't make it feel better, he said. The cat got sick or ate some poison that the neighbors had left out for the foxes or rats, or ate a rat that had been poisoned, whatever, and for days it was meowing at the door, getting skinnier and skinnier, and the cat would stare at him when he walked by, lying there inert by the door. Federico was troubled by it, so he would talk to the cat, but he couldn't look at it. It was a dreadful sight, he said, the cat was shedding clumps of hair, its skin covered with sores. But it never occurred to him to bring the cat to the veterinarian to see if there was anything that could be done, or to put it down, out if its misery. It happened in the interval when Javier had left. He watched the cat die, but was incapable of picking it up, placing it in a shoebox, and driving over to the nearest animal clinic: I've never been able to touch an animal, how was I supposed to pick that sick cat up, covered in lesions and vomiting nonstop. The cat finally went blind and stopped trying to drink the water he'd set down in front of it. It couldn't see the bowl. I listened to it meowing night and day, I could hear it from my bed, from my desk, but I was paralyzed. The cat lay at the threshold of the door and I had to step over it any time I went in or out of the house, I had to contemplate its suffering, and yet I was powerless to pick it up and take it with me. I simply couldn't. I mean it, I really couldn't. It wouldn't have felt any worse had there been a person there dying instead, he said. Paralyzed. Absorbed in his own feelings, analyzing and testing his limits, once again faced with his inability to react at a critical moment, he was destroyed by guilt but incapable of alleviating the animal's pain. He failed to relieve its suffering and incorporated that pain into himself, took it on like a weight that crushed him, crushed everything around him. Juan, taping the conversation, thinks: I'll save you from the Gestapo of time for a while, I'll write articles and messages about you on the internet, I'll hide you away in shadow-ridden libraries, I'll show your visage to university students during class. The well-intentioned families of Hamburg and Nuremberg, of Munich and occupied Paris, they hid a little Jewish girl in the closet to save her from the final solution. The child suffered for a while, jumping from closet to closet, from cellar to cellar, till it was no longer possible to keep her safely in the house. So, they shuffled her from place to place for a few more days—other flats, cellars, attics—before finally abandoning her in some neutral area, some solitary spot where she wouldn't put anyone else in danger: the following day the girl was detained and shortly afterward, gassed. But we already know that life lasts but an instant, from one day to the next, and she'd been allowed a bit more of life. For a few days the well-intentioned folks had felt like gods, they'd given the girl life, some complementary instants—life after life—spent between sacks of black-market flour and eggs that the lady of the house was able to procure from nearby farms. Something like that.

HE SAYS: I have to get used to staying put, to not moving around (he laughs). I have no other choice. Prepare myself for what's to come. He tells me he doesn't read anything but poetry anymore—it's a matter of economy: more bang for the buck, he explains. Poetry is like those little gadgets they sell on late-night home shopping channels, as-seen-on-TV gadgets throbbing with batteries and chargers that you place on some part of your body and all by themselves, presto, you have muscles again, or they smooth away signs of age and wrinkles, or get rid of your beer belly, no need to lift a finger. Reading poetry allows you to spend a marvelous half hour without having to turn a single page. In literature, poems produce the effect that models do in architecture: you can view the entire building from above, the entire landscape in a single glance, you can even pull the roof up and peek at what's inside the rooms. Novels are getting longer and longer now that everyone uses a computer, and we no longer have to type something up forty times before the final draft: eight-hundred-page novels, nine hundred pages, a thousand pages. Talk about boring. Blame it all on the computer. If you're minimally nimble-fingered, you'll speed along at a good clip and in no time you can correct, rewrite, cut, change, and paste. When I listen to him speak, I think about the Foundation, he likes to spend time talking and talking these days, his voice seems to be taking on a darker timbre, there's less vibration. He gets pickled in secret and then uses me as a surface to bounce his words against. Then days will pass, he won't pick up the phone, or he'll put off the next interview, and when I finally make the trip over to see him, he only answers in whisky-soaked monosyllables. He keeps putting off signing the Foundation documents, though the department knows that all the outstanding issues have been resolved. I told them that by fall the university would receive the donation, and here we are in summer already, and we've gotten no further. Securing the cession is crucial for me. I can't leave things in the hands of whoever Brouard may have assigned as legal heir in his will, whether it be Javier or some other mindless soul who might have gotten him to sign over his estate, since he has no next of kin. There's a lot of material that hasn't been gathered yet, that is stuffed in boxes and folders, papers I've consulted for the book and others I haven't even seen yet. A good part of that material has been salted away (things I'm a little embarrassed to show, more for oversentimentality than for anything scandalous, he says); some of which not even Brouard is aware of, lost in the jumble of domestic chaos: it's a big mess, nothing has been filed in any particular order. Javier takes care of the domestic chores, but everything that has to do with his writing is still left to Federico's hands, which means it's in nobody's hands: his correspondence with Max Aub (he's shown me several letters. Both of them, old Aub and young Federico, griping about everything, this was back in the fifties and sixties of last century. Federico negotiated an exchange of correspondence with Aub's estate, he would return the novelist's letters and in exchange be given the ones he'd sent to Aub, which he's never authorized for publication); there are letters from Alberti (though truth be told, even the doorwoman of the poet's house has letters and drawings from him); from Zavattini: they'd met in the early fifties in Rome. Brouard claims that Zavattini had a strong influence on him, and on other writers like José Ignacio Aldecoa and Carmen Martín Gaite (he has some letters from Gaite where she refers to Zavattini's influence on her writing); also letters from La Capria, the Neapolitan writer he admired so deeply; not long ago he revealed three letters from Claude Simon that had been sent thirty years ago, in response to so many others of his, where Brouard expressed his esteem for *La route des Flandres*: La Capria, Simon, peculiar relationships for a narrator who's been classified as social, as if somehow the adjective were meant to slightly disqualify the writer as such; and there are documents from his forgotten years in Paris, in Rome, in London, in Marrakesh (an awful lot of places to live for a man who's now so sedentary). Their rapport is beginning to wear thin; I'm getting tired of the tumultuous lifestyle he pulls me into, the constant fluctuations in dates and times, the facts he gives and then changes, forcing me to spend weeks amending and adjusting. That's it: once this is over, I'm going into hibernation, I'm going to isolate myself in my study with my books, among people no longer of this world, people who died a long time ago and only come back now as letters on the page, books by people who committed suicide, leaving their fans crestfallen as they thumbed their noses at the world; books by writers who died a natural death, mourned or not by their readers; or who are still alive but living far from the homes of their readers, where they don't bother anyone with their theatrics or antics or fuss, and allow us to treat their books as if their authors were already long-dead and buried. Brouard says that every time he finishes writing a book, he crosses his hands over his chest, he knows he's dead, until he starts a new one. So, he's been a cadaver for several years now. I don't want to die, but I would like to disappear, get the fuck out of here, find somewhere else, far away, though I haven't finished my book yet, Brouard's biography, a chapter of which I read in the course in El Escorial; congratulations, the director of the program said, brilliant, it was a chapter on sex as tragedy in his novels, a desperate search for maimed creatures, asymmetrical beings, an impossible quest, a useless and painful pursuit that's completely contrary to the complacency of our times; Brouard's old-school touch, he's convinced that no form of homosexuality can be experienced harmoniously, happily; I would say that no form of sexuality whatsoever can be lived harmoniously, that not even life itself can be lived harmoniously. But I'm talking about a higher cut of unhappiness, a more somber one, Brouard points out, quoting Genet and Pasolini and company. But how can you say that one person's unhappiness is greater than someone else's? How can you measure something like that, I ask him. Brouard disapproves, though I think it's more in the spirit of being flirtatious. We are nothing, we're with nobody, he laments after a few drinks. And to think I'm just the biographer, a critic, which is not entirely nothing: I'm the bouncer who gets to decide who gets into the club, where inside they're all spinning, seducing, shimmying, and frisking. Meanwhile, I'm there freezing to death at the door, dressed in a uniform with gold braided trimmings, peaked service cap on my head and the authority of the gatekeeper, but I have the privilege of saying: Come on in Sir; or: You're not allowed in, we reserve the right of admission. I may admit you, or I may open my arms wide and bar the door, denying you entrance, but once you're in you become one of the dancers, even though it's me who has to let you in (the vision of the critic as a club bouncer reminds me a little of Reich-Ranicki). Lay me, lay me, lay me down in the shade of a baobab tree in the Congo; a giant sequoia in some vast Canadian forest; a golden stupa in Bangkok; lay me down at the foot of the pine tree at Posillipo to observe the profile of Vesuvius the way it was depicted by Belle Epoque easel painters, the bay of Naples and the spine of Capri like an ancient, ferocious animal frozen midpounce; lay me down in a lamasery in Ho Chi Minh City, is that still what they call Saigon still?, I peek into *Le Monde*'s yearly atlas and there it is, Ho Chi Minh City, are there lamaseries in Ho Chi Minh City? Lay me down on one of their patios to pray for the people who were scorched by napalm bombs, or ripped apart by American soldiers; tortured between one sip of

Coca-Cola and the next, gunned down, split open. If only to prove (despite what Matías, Brouard, or my own father-in-law believed) how religion lasts longer than ideology, lay me down on the patio of a peaceful Buddhist temple with a slight breeze and tiny bells ringing nearby, and in the distance the sound of children's voices reciting their lessons in school, the monks scattering grains on the patio for the pigeons (I had that experience as a tourist in Bangkok a few years ago); become a Buddhist, a Shintoist, a Taoist; rest against the shaft of a broken column and peer out at the blue sea in Epidaurus (the old wine-colored sea that, on the contrary, proves that some ideas last longer than religion), the hills of Crete dusted with olive groves, the cypress trees of Mykonos, while I recite some poems, maybe Hölderlin, Goethe, or Byron, one of those Europeans who preferred the light, the blue, and the perfume of lemon trees, clueless as to where they were, what they were getting into, a wasp's nest, on the shores of that sea of blood that my father-in-law sells by the yard as if it were a heated bathtub; what gate of hell opened when they excavated the old ruins, dug up the mutilated bodies of goddesses and heroes, of athletes and emperors with their laurel-crowned heads. May Anubis Jackal Head bear you on that platter he holds with the entrails of the dead. Of course, I want to be free of it all: finish the book, forget the drooling old sop, his diaper-swollen crotch, the callous codger whose life I had no reason to investigate; only his books, from a distance, to read his books; to forget about that woman who for years has weighed on me like iron on wings, the warp and woof of common interest the only thing holding us together: kids, bank accounts, shared closets, family celebrations. What a sentence, what wingèd words. To fly, or else recoil into my studio like those insects who withdraw into a capsule, a chitin carapace, and live out the dry season unperturbed, I'll encapsulate myself and lie in wait for the next universal flood, wait for the rain with Pléaides tomes on my belly, devour them for nourishment, with a sweet tooth, feeding off of page after page; sink myself down into the Proustian sea, the amniotic fluid, greasy and heavy like the butter of a Norman cow, the thick farce of the lamprey Odette, the pink vagina armed with half a dozen razor-edged teeth, the fleshy trunk where fingers slink, slither, and slide, setting off a wave of vertigo; encapsulate myself in the volumes of Montaigne so carefully preserved at my father-in-law's mother's house in Pinar; the complete works of Tolstoy, Balzac, and Galdós (the great Galdós, whose Spain is cobblestoned with suicides), until the rain comes down and softens once again my stealthy chitin scab. Fly the coop. My sweet Silvia, with your brand-name jeans like sausage casing around your once-tight, ski-slope ass now in free fall and quickly softening, like my own. I'm going to spend some time on me. Write a memoir instead of a biography. I would call it *Between Writers and Women*, a cosmopolitan title, like Paul Morand's, very twenties, an art deco title: the students would appear as Nabokovian butterflies and moths flitting around the most brilliant, the most handsome of tenured professors (the blinding fragility of the moment): and Silvia would have the lead, the role of the eternally whimsical teenager, smoking with a long-stemmed cigarette holder, one of those skullcaps on her head, the kind they used to wear back when the elegant French diplomats jet-setted around the world, her bobbed hair peeking from underneath, cut with switchblade precision at the nape of the neck, wounding sensuality, the brazen neck another sexual organ (Gatsby's Daisy Buchanan, or the stupendous Cyd Charisse in *Singing in the Rain*—a floozy); Miriam, in her silence, a hollow sphinx; and Monica, that permanently exposed vagina as Silvia would say. My women (Mama, my sister, I'd have to deal with them in the introduction), but I don't write about them, I don't even write about my son (a strange clone from who knows where). I spend all my time and energy on Federico Brouard, former maestro to a generation and generous patron, who ended up becoming an unwelcome real estate speculator; he sold the land, he couldn't resist any longer, in a sinking economy. He'd become a symbol of the green resistance, now he's not even that, but who can allow themselves such grand gestures, you need certain conditions for that, not least of all economic ones, and Brouard now lives under an embattled personal economy (you have to be a little wealthier to be innocent, Matías used to say). I've tried to get him gigs, but he's no longer up to taking part in conferences. He used to deliver the same conference paper over and over again, cut here and paste there and half-correct this or that, each new lecture getting more and more confusing. There may have been a time when you could trick others into thinking that a writer could be the potter of the world. That his words offered the performative value of the word of God and simply by saying "light," the sun would shine, along with the moon and the stars. Nowadays we know none of it is true. So now what? The sweet touch of earth. Lay me down in an Alpine field and contemplate the mountainsides from way up high, the jaggedness of the higher altitudes, rocks bitten by glaciers; a little more welcoming down below, the slope softens and the cows are let out to pasture. Clouds hover along the valley bottom and the silence is broken by the church tower bell, ding, dong, ding, counterpointing the clatter of the cattle bells, dong, ding, dong. But my boy the world is round, and up is down, and the world is backward, and what you see down below is what's floating above you and vice versa. You're at the pinnacle because in reality the pinnacle is the point that dips into the abyss; from that pinnacle you see the full emptiness rising higher, millions and millions of miles of abyss decorated with a few dry, scraggy balls, fiery or covered in ice, decorations from the Christmas tree of the abyss, you're below everyone and everything. I have the sentence that will be the heading for Brouard's biography. It's from Baudelaire: *Des hommes qui portent le mot* guignon *écrit en caractères mysterieux dans les plis sinueux de leur front. L'Ange aveugle de l'expiation s'est emparé d'eux et les fouette à tour de bras pour l'édification des autres.* (Though I could have chosen a verse and a half from "Les Petites Vieilles": *Vous qui fûtes la grâce ou qui fûtes la gloire, / Nul ne vous reconnait.*) The job of the biographer. Contemplate the martyrdom of those who expiate the guilt of others inside of themselves. Read Baudelaire, read Dostoyevsky. Contemplate how the martyrs writhe under the whips, how they open the palms of their hands for the nail, how their necks bleed after the executioner has severed their heads. A writer's biography like a Caravaggio painting. Baudelaire wondered whether some sort of diabolical providence existed, one that mapped out from the very crib the unhappiness of the most spiritual ones, and heaved them hostilely toward it like the martyrs of a Roman circus. Vallejo the poet, bullied by everyone, dies in Paris on a spring day during a torrential rain. Who believes in that kind of mysticism anymore? Explain it to the martyr while they're nailing him, flaying and beheading him: what's wrong with you is this or that and this is what is happening. This is what they're doing to you—what do you think?— How well I've come to know you, I know you now, I'm your biographer. And how about you, what do you know about me? Who am I to you? I'm nothing to nobody, Brouard, I'm even nothing to myself. That well-meaning lady who, for as long as she was willing, saved the little Jewish girl whom the Gestapo ended up sending to the gas chamber anyway, or that person who deals with tissues or organs of a body that are connected to the spirit, the soul (the ones Brouard says have died on him). That's my task—but who am I? What kind of a little puppet am I? What hurts me? What makes me suffer? That's right, do you even know? Do you even care? How could you do that to the wide-eyed teenager I was so many years ago, when I read you for the first time and believed there was light in what you wrote, and was so sure you were an indispensable part of reconfiguring a code that'd gone awry? Now that I'm a mature man (if what they say is true of all the rebellious youth of every generation, that maturity is the state prior to putrefaction), I realize you've placed a machine at your service, another one: Javier, a machine for the body; Juan Mullor, a plumber for the system of pipes that lead to your soul. I teach literature, this is the narrator, this is the character, this is the point of view, but tell me, what kind of a profession is it? You took the wrong path. Okay then. What about us? As my father-in-law says to my wife: You've never made a mistake because you never had any intention of getting somewhere. My father-in-law is right. Staying here, under the blinding light of Misent. Waiting for Godot. We've learned how to kill each other in our living rooms because we're tired of not knowing what game to play. We've exchanged your self-righteous, insufferable revolution for a modest brand of domestic violence. We've gone back to the sweetness of private life. With Silvia, with Miriam and with Felix, with my father-in-law, who acts like a victim, condemned to becoming rich, the victim of cruel capitalism that led him there, forced him to renounce anything that doesn't make you rich because what am I supposed to do Juan, the world is what it is: it goes around, so the tango goes, and around (he says copping a melodious Argentine accent). I tell Brouard that my father-in-law spends his mornings running now, and the rest of the day telling us how he lost fifteen kilos in the past few months. It means he's back on the prowl again. He's up at six every morning to go for a walk. And Brouard: That means he's even worse off than I thought. Tell your stepmother-in-law, the one you say is so hot, to double the dosage of bromide in his soup. I say: He won't eat bread, he's done with fats. The only thing he hasn't given up is alcohol, he still likes his wines, his cocktails. And Brouard:

Ah, then the new paramour must be a bartender. I tell my father-in-law that he looks great, but it's not true. His face is gaunt and more recessed, and his empty skin wobbles under his arms. He'll end up at some clinic to get rid of those things. Tuck up the old sac and adjust it to the new measurements, you'll see, I tell Brouard, who laughs spitefully. He relishes every detail I share of my father-in-law's decline. He's insatiable, Brouard would love to see him deteriorate completely, rot away, corrode, all of it at the same time, and may it happen slowly, very slowly. I describe the remodeled house: the combination of record collections and CDs, hers (merengue, vallenato, lambada, reggaeton, garage bands); and how all of that blends with his library, with his record collection (Bach, Brahms, Weill, Shostakovich). He's always been a snob, Brouard says, he likes the high style: with his new wife he expiates his guilt, Brouard jokes, a little humility isn't a bad thing, it'll put his feet on the ground. I tell Brouard how he's called Saura and Tàpies, Torner and Zóbel, Manolo Valdés into stark formation, vigilantes watching over a bizarre mountain of knickknacks: Lladró dolls; Murano crystals: little horses, polychrome mice, tiny elephants; or the jade lions and sauceboats in a splash of vanity, the erstwhile must-have terra-cotta horse, or those huge, visually arresting figures brought from China, the Xi'an Warriors, festooning the house's living room, and there's a black butler in painted ceramic in the foyer, colonial style, a black butler in livery with a red vest and striped trousers holding up a platter for you to deposit a business card on, a very handy decoration for a house on the beach in a town that, in its heyday, was an active port full of exotic merchandise carried in the bellies of merchant ships, the tropical aromas, pepper, coffee, tobacco (you've got to be kidding me, there's a statue of a butler in the foyer? Now that deserves another shot of whisky, he says laughing so hard his belly jiggles, slapping his thighs). I told him about the miniature Copenhagen mermaid, and the hodgepodge of pricey bric-a-brac people buy in airport stores (contemporary shoppers have swapped airports for ports), or in those rich people's souvenir shops in chic hotels. She loves to show off her little silver trinkets, I tell him, and gold ones, a little golden Eiffel Tower, an Empire State Building made of white gold, pointless objects as stupid as they are expensive; how to make it all flow together under the same roof, mix all that stuff together; or not, because instead of mixing, water and oil form layers, strata, there's her stratum and his stratum, superimposed on every corner of the house. Brouard says: Life is what rules over everything in the end, takes it all over, sweeps it from one place to another and you have to ask yourself why, why does the so-called act of life end up depicted in these cheesy objects. And he finishes: Your father-in-law has ended up consuming two full servings of the broth of life. You should hear him talk—I intervene—He uses that kind of brothel verbiage, cutie-pie, little lollypop, gorgeous, sugar, baby doll, it's all about his baby doll; nonstop baby doll this and baby doll that, the telltale sign of someone who frequents strip clubs and cathouses. You see his friends at the bars of the cafés along Avenida Orts, plying a tumbler of whisky and dripping with arm candy, infinitely younger girls, asking for coins to play the slot machines, clutching their purses tight, and the men: hey sugar, you already got all my change little baby doll, ogling the girls with self-satisfied smirks, so pleased to think of them as poor little nieces spending all their uncles' spare change on a day off, but clearly the girls are not their nieces, not their sweeties, not their baby dolls (they're too old and too cynical to have anything like a heart left: not even blood pumping around in there. Hence the pacemakers). Twilight capitalism doesn't believe in the continuity of family, in inheritances and social advances through marriage; as a result: since I believe in nothing, I devour it all, long live bulimia. Federico, yours was the generation that cured the clap with potassium permanganate. Now, when they rape in the battlefields, they use condoms and lubricants. They use latex gloves whenever they have to touch someone, or their greed or fervent desire forces them to touch. And later, in the small hours now, with way too many drinks in my belly, I add: Did you know modern armies still plunder and pillage? The army is and ever will be just that, the army: *à la guerre comme à la guerre*, did you know that, Federico? They relieve the dead of their valuables, cut off their jaws to get at the golden teeth. Oh the joking, the taunting, the wisecracks as they merrily saw the lifeless jaw off for the gold, the smell of beer, same as two thousand years ago. Modernity never passed through there (I heard all about it from my brother, who was in Kosovo with the Spanish troops). There's a smell of burnt bone, like when you leave and forget the chicken in the oven and don't come back until late afternoon (the smell takes several days to dissipate). And we're back to the boy who drew the house with the pointy roof and who wrote the word *house*, then the word *dog*, and who now writes the word *saw*, sweats beer and puts the gold teeth away for safekeeping in a pocket of his jacket. Two thousand years of literature to continue writing about the same thing. You say you want to get out of Misent, but not where you want to go instead. What have they done to everything, you groan, pointing at the cranes that rise up beside the sea, the ones you watch from your house. You say: Not a bad subject for a novel. The war at the end of the world. Or simply the end of the world. *The Last Days of Mankind* as told by Kraus. I think what Brouard has left to write is his own demise. The curtain falls. I tell him: Write about insomnia, about indigestion and the kind of acid reflux that causes a hiatal hernia, and how the burning moves up the throat and there's no position that will alleviate it—fluff up the pillow, straighten your spine a little more, another antacid, another omeprazole—write about how the catheter irritates the urethra, or whether the diaper makes your groin itchy. Write about that, I tell him. A work of narrative is life condensed into a flash, like the night condensing into a dewdrop, the germ of life in the bloody drop that stains the yolk of an egg. Baudelaire's agony or Christ's agon, all the pain of the world concentrated in a few words and arranged in a certain way. Don't giggle, Federico, you know that's how it is. You're drunk, but from the shoulder of a god who carries me, I can see you immolate and burn so that I can be saved. Sacrifice, offering, expiation. The biographer is the one who saps the writer's energy. While you see nothing but loneliness around you, I see you bathed in a ray of livid lunar light. You move around down there, doing your daily chores in front of me, which might seem innocuous, but someone else might define them as terrible: searching inside of yourself, examining what motivates us, what we have inside ourselves, knowing you'll never write another sentence again. A desolate human landscape, surely. You utter a few rambling words between sobs. You say his name two or three times: Matías, you pronounce again. And talk about the peaceful darkness that now enfolds him. What a relief the darkness is, you say. Poor Matías. You grumble over how Javier obliges you to open the windows, air the rooms out. He doesn't allow you the solace of shade. You cry, and I can't do a thing for you. Not even I understand what it is you want to tell me. You're too drunk now and I'm well on my way, too. I hope to God Javier doesn't find us in this condition, I think.

MONICA THINKS about her mother now as she stares at herself in the mirror, her hand frozen midway to her face, clutching a cotton ball—isn't she so thrilled now that she has a brand-new refrigerator, a new flat-screen TV she got for Christmas. Monica likes observing herself like this when she gets up in the morning, lingering in front of the bathroom mirror and scrutinizing herself. Sometimes she'll go through the same routine at night, staying here like this after she fucks Rubén, watching him lying beside her, strong despite his age, compact, but with his guard completely down, vulnerable, incapable of defending himself should she wish to do something to him, Judith and Holofernes, Samson and Delilah, lose his head or lose his strength, which for all intents and purposes is one and the same thing; seeing him like that, subjugated by her, awakens a secret sense of satisfaction. She has subdued him with her strength, a superior strength because it isn't brutal, it's a delicate form of strength; not anything mechanical, but instead that more powerful force they call electricity, not born of muscles, but nerves. This delicate strength is what has subjugated him, drained him. She gets up, stealing across the hallway and into the kitchen where she opens the fridge to serve herself a glass of milk before reentering the room and settling back into the armchair to continue observing him, watching him sleep, his sagging, age-appropriate belly, the muscles of his legs and arms still strong and strapping, though also a bit fallen. She looks at him, contemplates him: perhaps absurdly, she feels a deep attraction to this body through which time—and life—has passed; that's received so many releases of energy before receiving the ones she

offers him. She feels admiration and desire for this man who com-
mands dozens of others, who causes foremen and laborers to
tremble like gladiators in those Roman movies, like mustachioed
circus strongmen, or others who look like elegant, cultivated ex-
ecutives in the style of a Richard Gere, wearing fancy suits, with
laptops hanging from their shoulders and cell phones pinging at
all hours of the day and night. She subjugated him, she gave her
body up like a narcotic and he, obedient, took it and relaxed, he
went to sleep, breathing the deep breath of slumber, like that of a
smoker who won't quit, peacefully but with a hint of agitation too,
all is forgotten but he's still troubled somehow by who knows
what dreams, while she sits and sips her milk daintily, skim milk,
no fat, no intestinal issues please, no filling the skin cells with viscid materials. Humans are the ones who believe in miracles, not
God. Who said that? She read it in some magazine somewhere, or
heard someone say it on television. Rubén says it too. Monica feels
the pulse of her strength, she's her own god now, she places faith
in her strength alone, her own delicate strength and the fluid electricity that runs through a clean system free of obstructions and
fatty materials, connected to her spick-and-span brain, as spick-
and-span as her inner thighs, which she uses to grip his head and
squeezes as if to make it burst, and he moans, her nutcracker
thighs, his head a mature fruit, fragile and clammy, it makes her
shiver to see it there between her two velvety pincers, strength
like silk, like tissue paper: the soft, silky strength of her body becomes power between the sheets, and outside the bedroom, too.
You swipe a no-limit credit card at a shop in Paris and you can be
sure the employee will avert his or her eyes, pretending not to
have noticed and begin fussing over the jewel being placed in a
silk-lined case, a jewel that adds a mere sparkle to your own polished luster, a diminutive part of you, of your personality, which
expresses itself as a complex, nearly endless ensemble: a radiance

that adds to the radiance of your perfectly manicured hands; of your neck garlanded by a little chain of white gold, tiny diamonds sprouting from your earlobes that the employee spies when you stand before him at the glass display cabinet. Monica catches the twinkle in his eye when he sees the little diamonds, his instantaneous appraisal of their sparkly perfection before he looks away again, as if their fire burned, the same cold fire she carries inside of her; that sparkle tells him to direct his hands and his feet only toward the vitrine where the most priceless, the most exclusive merchandise in the store can be found. The coiffure, the exclusive Armani bolero, the Vuitton bag, that's the iridescent glimmer of her personality. She's aware it's not yet a matter of class, it's a substitute for class, an announcement of its arrival, like the clarion call of a courtly procession sounding the annunciation that at the back, the end of the parade, class is advancing, refinement, it's just waiting for the child to be born, her child will arrive with it, with class; she'll carry it in her arms and lead him or her by the arm. It's an inner strength, indistinguishable to almost everyone, it seeks companionship, looks for a way out of itself, encouraged by someone external, who only infrequently comes across that kind of magnetism, encouragement, complicity. When a person is in distress and doesn't prostrate themselves or beg, it's because they have class; when he or she wins and doesn't hoot and laugh at everyone else, but instead keeps their gratification to themselves, behind a mask, that's class, too. Rubén explained it that way. Not laughing when you see him flummoxed, when he doesn't know what to do with your body because he wants all of it at the same time and in every position. When he wants to suck you here and suck you there, all at once, nibble up here and taste down there, all at the same time, and he looks at you, disoriented, and you pretend that you don't notice his bewilderment. When despite the chemistry you notice that he simply can't, and you realize that he's simulating the motions of sex, he's acting it out, don't say a word to him, don't allow your gaze to say, I got you now, even though sex for you at these times is like Easter to the Pope, resurrection. It's essential to begin telling the same yearly story cycle, the same part every day. When the priest officiates Mass he repeats the same ritual every day: This is my body, this is my blood. And the faithful never tire of it, the excitement of faith courses through them every single day. For a young woman, sex is hope. It's what allows you to begin anew next morning, as if the world had just been created. This is my body, this is my blood. The cooking classes, the hairdresser, the mani-pedi, the beauty spa. How splendid are those signs in New York City with the word "parlor" with its nostalgia for the French "parlour": reminiscent of that grand world of the thirties with boudoirs or powder rooms full of stuffed chairs for lounging, where you could gossip with your friend, a peroxide blond, while they touch up your makeup during the interlude of a show given by some black crooner or tap dancer. Mink coats in every sequence of the movie, a great clarity of great ideas, mink, *renard bleu*, not a single swoon in the dressing room, no cut-rate gewgaws, not even to take a dip in the sea: nothing on the skin but a signature bikini and emeralds or diamonds, wear only what's a cut above—even the gangsters learned that lesson; nothing but the finest for their dolls, even if they're floozies: it's a lifestyle that's vanished, which she tries to revive, a form of combat in a world that seems to have lost its moxie (as her father would say), that acts as if any old bauble is fine or even preferred over a real jewel, repudiate that world. Monica thinks back on her mother this morning while the Bertomeu family is grieving, she'd been upset with Rubén for not sharing his pain with her, but now she's overcome with a private joy because yesterday they gave her the results of last week's tests, and they resolve any uneasiness she might have felt. Monica thinks about what her mother will say, what her sister will say, when they find out she's pregnant and having the baby of this terribly older man; more than anything else, though, she thinks about what Silvia and her husband will say about the news that Rubén is soon to be a father again. Tell them: I'm pregnant, all my efforts to watch my figure turned out to be such a waste of time, don't you think? I've already lost it, there's a little bump that has ruined my figure, a curve that will soon begin to bulge; you can't see it yet, but it won't be long, you'll see my ruined figure soon enough, like a Mediterranean amphora in whose concavities a little life is slumbering. Tell him today. This afternoon, at the funeral. Tell him with my rounded, good-girl eyes: God has decided to take one family member and He has given another; isn't that beautiful?—it's so sweet, life is beautiful, it goes on, it endures, it's never-ending. Just look straight at her, at Silvia, look Silvia's husband in the eye, yes, put on an angelic smile and stare squarely into both of their faces, and at little Miriam, just to see how the lines of their faces go sour, how their skin starts to crawl, their lips pull, their pupils dilate (better believe there'll be contained rage), and tell Silvia as we continue the little chat: How could you ever have let your boy fly on his own? I'll never let mine fly alone so little, I'll never let him go anywhere by himself until he's sixteen or seventeen at the earliest, yeah, I mean mine, the one on the way, here, can you feel the little bump? I'm three months, it's still very early but I already notice a few extra pounds. Yeah, I've had to buy everything new this summer, I couldn't button a thing, or get my zippers up; by the end of August I won't fit in a single one of last year's bikinis. It'll have to be loose shirts, guayaberas and saris for a while, what else can I do, I'll have to adapt my tastes to the circumstances. But isn't it amazing that a new Bertomeu should come along just like that, so unexpectedly, just when we lose

Matías? A Bertomeu who will keep his father's last name, your father's, your last name, Silvia, a last name on the verge of extinction. A little brother, aren't you excited, Silvia, that our family name won't die out? That Matías's stuck-up son won't be the only one left bearing it? Monica thinks: Suffer a little, Silvia, put yourself on their level. Not everything is about art, darling. Not everything is about cleaning up the crowns of saints and restoring the shine of the twenty-four-carat gold covered by centuries of grime. I mean, let's really get to the bottom of it, what's really eating at you so much, is it that you can't have any more yourself, is that what you find so upsetting? That they scraped you clean, hollowed you out, left an empty chamber where nobody will be able to spend another night again? Monica doesn't actually believe that's what Silvia finds most disturbing; Silvia never wanted another pregnancy; she already has her little pair of offspring. What's really going to upset her is something else, it's when Monica says: Your dad and I would like to have a set of our own, after the boy, we'll try for her, a little girl, what do you think? Daddy and his little wifey, don't even try to tell me it's the old bugger that gets to you; that you're upset because Rubén is going to be a father again and at his age, like someone said, a father and great-grandfather all at once. That's not it, no, what bothers you is something else, that suddenly this family is filling up with heirs, that's what bothers you, that the absence is becoming presence, the absence being the portion of power that belonged to you at the helm of the succession, and now by losing a slice of that power, part of the money will evaporate right along with it. Monica smiles thinking how much Silvia's disfigurement is going to sting, the amputation: before now she knew what she owned, what her children would get, but now she'll have to share, now she only gets a part of this and a part of that; haggling like everyone else (the ladies at the vegetable stand, the fishmongers in the market, haggling; the gypsies haggle their cheap clothes in the street bazaars, the coarser folk). Being just one more, that's what'll bother her more than anything else, proprietorship, money, knowing she's no longer a sole proprietor, what else? It's always about money, about ownership. Monica follows Rubén's recommendations: Whenever you're stumped about something that's happened, whenever you can't quite understand some event, you can't put two and two together, think money, or better yet, the lack of money, think what you can't do without money while the other person, the one you're worried about or who is so irritating, can do it because he or she has enough money. The issue is that neither Silvia nor her husband Juan likes to talk about these things. Though she's been perfectly aware of it on her own, she's seen it herself, it's not something Rubén needed to explain to her. They use every synonym in the thesaurus, but never the word that actually names the issue, Rubén said about them. Monica swipes her cheek with the little cotton ball. She suspends her hand as moving it below her right eye and observes herself in the mirror, she likes the sight of herself frozen in that pose, such a condensed burst of femininity, like something from the movies, the hotel rooms with art deco furniture, powder rooms with mirrors framed by several rows of light bulbs or fluorescent tubes of light, and there's the woman looking at herself, halted midmovement and staring at herself, a woman putting on makeup looking at a woman putting on makeup, and there it is, the height of femininity. Maternity is another height, though the male has to intercede for that, like it or not, which contaminates everything, lends something macho to the enterprise. Monica is frightened of maternity, those pregnant women who grow a downy fuzz, a little golden beard (worse if it comes in dark, or black) which is not exactly the peach fuzz skin of a little girl, but real hairs, longish ones, like strands of cotton. Maternity makes your face swell, you get a jowl, pimples that erupt, boils, some women get hemorrhoids, so it's clearly a sacrifice, like it or not. Monica is afraid of these things, afraid of the consequences of that sacrifice, but there's also something that comforts her, that helps her lumber her way up that steep and thorn-ridden road to Calvary, she imagines what she can become, she whispers it to herself under her breath, without even opening her mouth, she tells herself using only her thoughts, and she likes to imagine she's talking to Silvia, saying: That's right, Silvia, it's exactly what you imagine, you nailed it, pinned the tail on the donkey, hit the bull's-eye, what helps you deal with all the aggravation is that you feel safe, cared for, tended to; I mean, let's not beat around the bush, you're kept safe by the only thing that can keep one safe these days, that protects everything, that's right, it's tenderness, kindness, a kind of solid tenderness that isn't just a smokescreen of words, but things like medical attention, caregiving, good nutrition, a little layette full of things for when the baby arrives, which brings us back to where we started: tenderness as the positive materialization of money, the healing effect of money. Monica feels strong enough to confront maternity now, she'll make sure the months ahead are a cheerful time of waiting instead of a litany of nuisances. Let's give Rubén the news today. Annunciation: One family member has gone just as we rejoice in knowing that another is on the way; tell her friends, Menchu; and the other grandchildren (she thinks it's fun to be a grandmother, even if only a step-grandmother, it makes her feel like one of those immortal Hollywood goddesses, cosmopolitan, it gives her class: to be young, elegant, a mother and a grandmother, so much like being in a movie), give the news to Miriam and Felix, and to the proud and wraithlike Doña Teresa Bernia; and Silvia, more than anyone else, Silvia; she'll say: I'm going to experience my maternity joyfully, the house will fill up with new objects, fresh bottles of baby cologne, a crib, a bassinet, tiny clothes all folded and ordered, just smell those new clothes, the scent of a baby, as soon as she knows if it's a boy or a girl there will be clothes, new things bought little by little, one day this, another that, in his presence so he doesn't forget, have to get him ready, enthusiastic, Rubén is becoming a father again just like she is becoming a mother; let him develop alongside the child inside of her so when the child arrives, there's a mother and a father eager, ready. Herself, she'd prefer a girl, but considering the larger implications she's desperate for a boy (she'll find out on her own, since Rubén said that if she ever got pregnant, he would want to wait to know the child's sex at birth. It'll be a boy, a boy is on the way, but she'll have to feign ignorance right up to the end; though now she can't fathom how she'll be able to resist spilling the news this evening, she wants to act out the whole scene, to exercise the glory of her power. Let everyone know there's a little one on the way and that it's a boy). To be the mother of Rubén Bertomeu's son, the true little man of the house, because Felix is his daughter's son, and daughters' sons have other families, they belong to another family, because they bear the father's name (Miriam and Felix Mullor). Just wait till daddy sees those two little baby balls, he'll picture them as the rebirth of his own. Let him acknowledge her as the one who's reconstructed his strength and vigor, brought them to fruition in a show of compatibility, a perfect couple: finally, Rubén Bertomeu gets what he's coveted for so long: a son. But why such a sour look on your face, Silvia? Don't you see how right I was? She'd love to tell her: Yes, it's money we're talking about, sweetie. Gobs of money. I told you so.

TALK ABOUT a hot piece of shit, Silvia said to me, you'd have to be nuts to buy one of those bungalows you're building; a few drops of rain and they're certain to flood; that's never been anything but marshland, a big puddle. I loved to tease her about it: I wouldn't buy a house there in a million years. I already bought mine. I have a house. I bought mine in my favorite spot and built it in my own style. I don't build houses to keep them for myself. She doesn't like my luxury developments either, but never sticks her nose up at the stocks that I put in her name, the bonds, the extra money I give them at Christmas, everything that allows them to live beyond their means, beyond what a tenured professor's salary and an art restorer's income would permit, the checks that pass from hand to hand for whatever excuse half a dozen times a year, the deposits into the kids' accounts. Cities have always grown up around corruption, my little cabbage, trust me, they're a consequence of speculation. It's as true today as it was in Haussmann's time (who doesn't love the Paris that grew out of corruption? Who remembers that Paris of narrow streets and wood-beamed houses with pointy roofs? Nowadays it would make an adorable medieval amusement park), or in the times of Augustus. Yeah, Silvia says, but Augustus could tell his countrymen: I found a decrepit Rome built of bricks and gave you a grand one, built of marble—and somehow, I don't think you could say the same thing. I repeat: Marble is like the bread of a sandwich, what's inside is cement; or brick, a material that deserves respect. Even New York made miracles with brick (look at that gorgeous dome on the RCA Building on Lexington. There's something of a *Mudé-jar* influence in the work, don't you think?), the city you like so

340

much was raised above a city that'd been laid to waste: you can see in old photos how New York and its sharp church spires looked like London in the year of the plague, or Hamburg, or Bruges. What happened to all those old turn-of-the-century palaces in New York, the Vanderbilt mansion, where did they go, Silvia? All those Tudor or Second Empire mansions. She decided on a line of work that cares for the relics of the past, as if the past she's caring for hadn't been built at the cost of destroying what came before. She holds art up in tongs that are outside of history; in order not to have to make things from scratch, she decided against becoming a painter, only to restore, which is like being an artist who is—so to speak—unengaged, someone who is and is not an artist all at the same time, who is and is not an artisan, who is and is not proud, because at the end of the day, the work belongs to someone else. You lack the courage to wager on the future, I told her once. I'm the father, you're the daughter and yet you're the one who represents the past. You're hell-bent on the idea that doing good means leaving everything exactly as it was, even worse, exactly the way it was four hundred years ago. You think perfection is somewhere behind us, not ahead. Not because something represents a very particular moment in time, a golden age. No. You believe indiscriminately that everything from some other time, even the darkest things, are worthy of our utmost respect and shouldn't be touched; and beyond being absurd, it isn't even a good idea, it's not even healthy: not aspiring to take a step beyond, to blaze new trails. It won't do: that's quietism, cloistering. Nothing new: you talk about art that other people have made, keep informed about things other people have said about this or that, cite bibliographies, take note of acknowledgments, say this altarpiece belongs to so-and-so and this to someone else. It's like using the excuse of time to mess around with other people's art, repair the damages and strains of time, a job that's alleged to be generous. To glean the secrets of genius: using X-ray vision to see the blunders, the deliberations, unpack the genius until it's no more than a series of techniques you can reproduce, correct, brush over here and there. Feel the furtive pride of saying you know its innards, the metabolism the work exudes because at the end of the day it's not really all that complicated; and to say: you can continue being a genius because I have given you a second life; if it weren't for me, you would no longer exist, a few more years and you would've vanished into the arms of time. You're great because I clean you, I polish you and then publish studies about you, climbing a few more stairs. False modesty. She and her husband. Her husband is just like her. What her husband is doing with Brouard, gutting him out, emptying him, confirming that an author's style is based on a dozen techniques, a few combined formulas, recipes. Juan's strategy with Brouard: now that the whole world is beginning to forget you, let me be generous and revivify you, because I know who you really are and I will let you climb a few more stairs. Save you, Brouard, from the Gestapo of time, that's what he said when I asked what his research meant to accomplish. The Frankenstein complex. Authority residing in the person who resuscitates the already surrendered body. Professors, critics, they analyze novels from their ivory towers, looking down on the novelists, treating them as if they were primal beings, naïve, because they discovered that the emotion in their books, the sense of wonder they imbue, is based on a limited number of artifices, little tricks, ones the novelist may not even be entirely aware of; to describe it in their self-righteous language: narrative techniques, elements of style, voice, metaphorical baggage, a suitcase full of tricks that travel from one book to the next. Not that I wasn't happy when my daughter told me she was going to get a degree in fine art and art history, or when she showed me her first pieces or when she began working in the restoration department. But I liked to joke around with her (now we're barely on speaking terms), restoring is like being at the end of the line, insulating something inside so it can't slip out, what we call the soul, the spirit, genius, and instead you just fix what's already out there (restoration has always seemed like mechanical work to me. Being recognized by experts, receiving invitations to conferences, yeah, all right, you're an authority in your field, but that's not you; you aren't inside of what you're doing). I teased her: Restoration is like doing the artist's laundry. Mopping up after the painter, a cleaning lady for the museum. I was only joking around, but she would shoot me a look meant to slice me in two. Eventually she seized on my words and took advantage of them whenever she had the chance: According to my father, I'm just a restorer, something like a cleaning lady, a specialist in knowing how to mop things up for museums and churches. We do all the cleaning and dusting for the true artists, using high-tech gadgets. We dust the artworks with our brooms, hang them out in the sun and beat them with wicker poles, like rugs. A little sunlight and air to disinfect. We leave them polished and shiny. Like new. A resourceful maid who loves her job. If I'm present she looks at me and says: Isn't that right, Papa? A prime example of pure devotion and lack of ambition. Maybe it has to do with genetics, with Mendel's little colored worms and playful crosses, but it was Matías—not me—who produced the wolf cub, the little shark who is going to continue our lineage and live up to the family name. It was the evanescent Matías who had the supply of masculinity, not me. At the moment of genetic selection, the weightlessness of fantasy turned out to be more potent than the solidity of *béton*. It annoyed me to no end having to listen to that idiot of a nephew, Ernesto, eating at my table and going on about investment funds, the opportunities this season for betting on Gas Natural; a beautiful time to divest your AMC stock and put it into FCC; and even better to play robustly in the energy sector, again

Gas Natural, or buy into Repsol, or the hydroelectric firms, Endesa, Fenosa, and flip them as soon as they spike, which is likely to happen next week. Uncle, it's time to make the jump from the old heft of concrete to the flexibility of pure economy, he said, as if he were talking to a Neanderthal. My nephew's voraciousness, the way he scarfed the appetizers as he was talking—no matter what it was, pistachios, honey-roasted peanuts, slices of dried tuna, salmon, or tuna roe—made me notice the lack of vitality in myself. As if my entire life I'd been worried about trying to hide some faint trace of femininity, something soft that shapes me; and I get to thinking that maybe the teenage Brouard had noticed it back in the day, too, that strength and vulnerability coexisted and masked each other in me. Whenever my train of thought goes there, I start to see Silvia as a phenotype of my secret weakness, but also the expression of that sort of unpleasant, arid strength that's so characteristic of the women on both sides of the family. And I also think it was no coincidence that my granddaughter arrived before my grandson, she's so insolent and swaggering; and my grandson, Felix, fragile and melancholic, a thin and pale version of Hanno Buddenbrook, always on the verge of shattering like glass. The line that runs from my father to me, from me to Silvia, and then to the boy, is a succession of individuals rapidly advancing toward extinction (that expression is reminiscent of a German novel). It's the end of the cycle, the last page of a family tree at the mercy of the autumn wind (Miriam is beyond me, she has some other kind of drive, a woman belonging to some new-fangled family model, the phenotype adapting to the times). Matías killed himself in his own way, and yet he had time to inadvertently produce the successor, or even better the shark, the predator that assures the continuity of a species in which the only survivors are the most ruthless, the fiercest, cruelest, and biggest sons of bitches. We come from that evolution. We're the result of that. Silvia could have made amends with a marriage, she could have widened the limits of her character. But no, my daughter's marriage didn't improve the way the family portrait represents decay and degradation; Juan, her husband, the literary historian, the philologist, the professor who received tenure at such a young age (more astute than ferocious, more wily fox than wolf), who writes the prologues to social novels of the fifties, Martin-Santos, the Goytisolos, Grosso, Ferres; specialist in the possibilities of the proletarian novel, summer school conference presenter: he dabbles in Santander, in El Escorial, in San Diego, in Bologna, always scratching here or there on the hunt for opportune connections, greater academic prestige; conquering pages in university magazines, using the vitality of other people's novels as a lever to raise his own career. In his free time, Juan holes himself up in Federico Brouard's house, the writer who chose to use me as a model for the corrupt main character in one of his novels that half the population of Misent read, winking an eye, everyone convinced it was a portrait of me. My blood boils every time I think about Juan writing his biography: it's as if he were writing the itinerary of a limb that was amputated years ago, or even better, the biography of a gangrene, the portrait of a lesion. He figured a way to prove just how much I lost with that amputation, how badly the sore stank that had spread and festered before they amputated my limb, which is still alive now, thanks to its removal from my body, fucking me over, incorrupt, like Santa Teresa's arm that Franco brought with him everywhere. A biography of Brouard, someone who between one drink and the next is convinced that he has kept our childhood project alive, who has been in his own way like another Matías (yes, he's like you, Matías, though a lot less passionate about other people's property than you were); someone who refused to sell me the property contiguous to mine and to the stables where I kept the horses through those difficult years, land I needed to complete a subdivision plan that I'd been arranging through successive purchases until I was able to form a property development agency (in fact I eventually owned all the land except Brouard's plot). Matías and my old pal Brouard were driving me insane, trying to paralyze the Integrated Development Plan, a rezoning and urban planning project that could have been closed and sold by then, and in whose construction and development I'd already invested millions, but that the judge decided to embargo for months on end. Streets were left half-paved, sidewalks overgrown with weeds and bushes, cement columns left exposed, cranes and scaffolding strewn all over the place, like a ghost neighborhood, all thanks to Brouard, whom the ecologists venerated for months over his refusal to sell, hell-bent on keeping the plots of land as a bunch of desolate fields when they should have already been streets and buildings, gardens, tree-lined groves, which is what they would inevitably become because the land development provisions and approvals were already in place, and because the national guidelines for urban planning are crystal clear on the subject, the terrain was zoned for building and under the control of the real estate developer, regardless of how much Brouard tried to deny it, or Matías Bertomeu, his lawyer, or the judge who ordered the suspension of construction licenses, tried to bar it. And this is precisely the man my daughter's husband is engaged with, his favorite writer, the great renovator of realism. Matías was also part of the whole campaign, out there with his posters, surrounded by green-clad militants, people from radical groups screaming chants against savage urbanism, against crooked developers; Brouard made statements to the press, saying the Integrated Development Plan of the new urban classification system had completely upended the county's land title structure. In only ten years, ownership had gone from being in the hands of small farmers to a mafia made up of twenty corrupt builders (mafia, the

Camorra or 'Ndrangheta, call them what you will, the article said verbatim), Marx already said that capitalism is born by destroying the private property it purportedly defends. Only by sweeping up private property can the primitive accumulation of capital take place. He wrote that in a letter addressed to the local paper that was signed by others, including my brother and my daughter. And there's my son-in-law hanging around in Brouard's house, recording his testimonies, and teaching his work at school. He wanted me to give him some facts and impressions of the writer's childhood and I told him not to bother asking. I told him dryly: The economy is one thing, with its mechanical flows, its pulleys, its unctuous cogs and gears; and another is the free fluidity of art, thought without ligatures, without conditions, isn't that it, Juan? Is that what I should say? When I found out about Juan's idea of writing Brouard's biography, I tried to raise the issue with my daughter, as if I could ever talk seriously with her about anything that concerns me—activities, desires, and aspirations always so far removed from things of the spirit. I don't like the idea, I told her, tell that to your husband. And in the meantime, let me just say that I can't imagine why your husband would want to go digging around in the life of that old flop. But let him know that he's doing me damage. She answered scornfully: You're calling him an old flop? As far as age goes, Papa, he's as old as you, and he's no flop. He's an acclaimed writer. Unless when you say flop you're referring to the fact that he's not rich. Another smirk. She'd washed her hands of it: It has nothing to do with your business, Papa—what am I supposed to do? Juan's been mulling over the idea of a biography for a hundred years. It's not something he came up with to peeve you. Apparently nobody can take a step in this county without treading on your property, without stepping on your toes (that's her way of thinking, as if the land had been gifted to me and I hadn't bought it on the free market; she thinks: there's not a plot of land left that you haven't trampled on). Now the machines are working these lands, on the horse stables, the adjoining plot that belonged to Brouard and took so much effort to obtain. I can see the clouds of dust at the foot of the mountain through the car window. The pestering is over. Brouard. We wanted to do so many things together when we were young. The two of us and our friend Montoliu, the painter. We read tons of books on the function of art, essays on aesthetics (Goldman, Malraux, Read, Lukács, Baudelaire, Hauser, Fischer, the things people read back then), we even edited a chapbook of engravings: I drew a series of geometrical figures, Montoliu painted them, and Brouard wrote a few texts to accompany the engravings, prose poems, everything very avant-garde compared to what was being done at the time—very provocative, you know. Brouard's texts were more existentialist than revolutionary or social, pure youthful angst. The title of the chapbook was *The Shapes of a Landscape That Belongs to Nobody* (that bleak nobody was in homage to our own existential angst), it was a naïve project that caused a bit of a stir in our backward region. A bit of a local scandal that a Bertomeu son would waste time exhibiting shapeless lines together with two misfits, two nobodies. He studied so hard for that? The chapbook was trying to locate the forms that could be found around the county: the ones that belonged to the natural environment (the Montbroch Massif), or those that had grown out of its history: the ruins of walls, coastal lookout towers, silhouettes of boats and sails; outlines of traditional homes, the old stately country homes, some of which dated to the sixteenth century, the uglier modern buildings; the horizontal shapes of the sea, the verticality of palm trees, the opulence of vineyards and orange groves. Everything was expressed conceptually, with straight lines and graduating shades of color. We barely sold a dozen of those chapbooks, we gave the rest of them away, almost as a form of dogmatic affiliation with an idea:

it was all about sharing some good news (let's call it modernity), though eventually most of them ended up forgotten at the bottom of a drawer. I came across a packet of those chapbooks a few years ago when I was rifling through some papers in my old bedroom in Pinar. Shortly afterward, Federico left for Madrid (I'd already been in Madrid a few years, studying architecture, and only came back during vacations: I knew Madrid was a necessary parenthesis), and Montoliu confessed that he couldn't muster the courage to leave home. He spent a few years vagabonding around the county. I would find him sitting by the shore on random days, or run into him at the port where the fishing boats come in with their catch. He always carried a sketchbook with him and would draw, now in a very traditional style, scenes of the fishermen at work, drawings of them unloading the catch, still life sketches of the fish. He'd settle into some corner to draw the old houses of fishermen, palm trees, perspectives of the castle. He told me: I don't have the nerve to go—and anyway, I can't. Nobody is interested in what I do, these vague little sketches. I was born eighty years too late. Even though I'm the painter, you have a much better future as an artist than I do, with your linear drawings, your black-and-white shapes and their geometrical play with color. That's the trouble with not having an imagination, not knowing how to paint what's not in plain sight. If we collaborated, I think between the two of us we could've made one good contemporary painter. It was a big lie. He painted beautifully and had a nearly miraculous capacity for capturing movement, for catching the psychology of the people he sketched in the instant of a gesture, using no more than a few brush strokes. I don't know if anyone ever saved samples of his work. It would be a shame if everything was lost. Montoliu walked into the sea one day and swam out as far as his strength would allow. He left his clothes folded on the beach. It took fifteen days for the cadaver to show up, pecked away by the fish. The fishermen who'd been his models pulled his body out, it had gotten caught in one of the nets that he'd probably sketched at some point, too. I could have stayed in Madrid like Brouard did; I could have stayed in Paris (as Brouard would a few years later); I could have swum out into the sea until I lost my breath like Montoliu, but despite the issues I had with my mother, I was in a position where survival was guaranteed and I had the benefit, or the luck, or the insight, of realizing that an architect is not a prophet, but someone who solves housing issues; someone who materializes a client's idea of well-being. Nowadays any student already knows this, but back then hardly anyone wanted or was able to acknowledge as much. Now I know that the top architect in the world is the one who finds the perfect balance between comfort and the client's financial condition. Though it's true that in order to convince myself of something so basic as that, first I had to silence all the noise inside, all the youthful butterfly dreams. But it's normal, it's the normal process of growing up. Give Peter Pan a kick in the ass. Youth— Dostoyevsky tells us in his novels—finds meaning in the tragic, the violent, in the destructive balloon that bursts and spills garbage over everything below, because that's what the crab-eaten cadaver of beauty at its finest becomes, a pile of garbage; that's what Matías never wanted to admit, while he lived out my own fantasies and those of my friends when he was no more than a curiosity-ridden boy, and stayed very close to Brouard. When I think about it in that light, I'm reminded of that childish vanity, the *désinvolture* that Aznavour sings about in one of his songs, which Pedrito Vidal liked to hum on occasion, that friend of Matías's who went into real estate after his catharsis in Madrid—I'd run into him here and there, he'd hum it on random nights spent drinking at the bar La Dolce Vita, a locale that was never exactly, but also never stopped being, a cathouse, until it finally closed its doors just a few years ago. After hours, last call, both of us soused, Pedrito would get to slurring out those words that talk about being twenty years old when we lived through the night not worrying about the day. *J'ai fait tant de projets qui sont restés en l'air,* he would sing, sullenly, Pedrito, eyes brimming with tears as he drooled over your shoulder pads: *Je précédais du moi toute conversation, et donnais mon avis, que je voulais le bon, pour critiquer le monde avec désinvolture.* It's the song that describes our twenties, when we squandered time thinking we could stop its flow, he explains the same thing to me every time. We ran around so hard and so fast that we ended up exhausting ourselves, Pedrito laments (his real estate blitzes must be the result of that exhaustion). It seems like yesterday. Our twenties, when they wouldn't allow us *rien de vraiment précis,* he sobs, filling my ear with his spit and drivel. If he really wants to be a pain in the ass, he'll sing it to the bitter end. Yeah, Pedrito, right, the lyrics fit your generation like a glove, you bet, for your generation and my brother Matías's. But not my generation, we never had the chance to chase after dreams. Come to think of it, someone needs tell Pedrito about Matías. Call him and give him the news, let him know the time of the cremation ceremony. It's been a while since I've run into him, though I know he's still working in Misent because I see his ad campaigns on the billboards along the highway, and in magazines and newspapers. Give Pedrito a call and let him know you're dead, Matías, somebody has to do it. Your comrade, the one who remembers that Aznavour song you used to sing like an anthem. Young people are the same everywhere, it's only in adulthood that the differences begin to manifest themselves, and it's how we deal with the original disquiet that differentiates us, how we approach that crossroads at the end of our adolescence. The time we lost. Impossible to recover. Not knowing for sure whether we won or lost. It's hard to imagine any other way to grow up that doesn't require wasting so much time in the urge *pour critiquer le monde avec désinvolture,* with the ego on the

sleeve, like a badge, like a flag and objective, though life always
ends up displacing it to the margins. And my clueless son-in-law:
one of the people who prefer to remain ignorant of the true origins of their things. We've all sprung from an original magma, we
met in the same crater with similar water, but then life channels
us along without our having much say in the matter. We do things,
but there's some mechanism, something that's stronger than our
efforts to move in the current. I said as much to Matías once and
also to my daughter: When ideas get in the way of seeing reality
for what it is, they aren't ideas, they're lies. Just tell that to Silvia:
There are mechanisms that've been in place for eternity. Young
people always try to invite adults to participate in their confusion,
their boundless novelty: they've only just begun to discover the
world. But the world was discovered a long time ago. Grown-ups
know that, we know. And you're old enough now, you're in your
forties, you should have discernment, let it be your daughter who
talks to me that way now. Not you, you can't be talking to me like
that anymore. You shouldn't. Don't take that away from her, it's her
space. It's her turn now, yours is over. Give her room; she won't
know where to go if you don't, which card to play. You're over
forty now and you know that in the nonprofit stores, those fair-
trade ones, you might buy little trinkets and scraps, but for the
things that really matter, the serious articles, the good canned fish
and mollusks, good coffee, tea, the home appliances and car, all of
that, big or little, the items on which you gamble your well-being,
your life, you cherry-pick your brands. You buy necklaces in the
Place Vendôme, in Van Cleef, in Reza's (which I think belongs to
the son of the previous Shah of Iran), in Chaumet, where I buy
them for Monica. And if possible you buy the watch in Geneva, in
Zurich. And you stay at the Hôtel Beau-Rivage, or the Hôtel de
Genève on the shore of the lake, in one of those hotels Sissi stayed
in, the one (Beau-Rivage?) where her bloody clothes are kept in

the hall, the bloody handkerchief, the little shirt she was wearing when that loony anarchist stabbed her with a stiletto so fucking sharp that the poor girl didn't even notice he'd just killed her. You don't take your watch to be repaired by your little NGO buddies, you don't buy noble pieces of jewelry from that kindly man you met in Thailand who invited you to his home after he sold you that costume necklace, where the kids were playing in the foul waters of the canal. No. You buy your necklaces from a tedious, sallow-skinned gentleman dressed in rigorous, funereal black, because a genuine necklace is a serious thing. When you're wearing a precious necklace the last thing you do is waste your time thinking about the hepatic man who sold it to you. You pay no attention to him even when you're buying it. The man vanishes before the preciousness of the merchandise. The only thing your eyes have registered during the transaction is the piece of jewelry. But since we're talking about wasting time, why am I wasting it now saying the obvious? Nobody can expect me to go back to a path I already traveled when I was meant to, when it was my time to, Silvia, not you, not your children, not your husband. Not even tyrants are able to do that. You can't face execution twice. By law you can receive a life sentence for each person you snuffed out, but they can only apply it once. The convict walks on the other ninety-nine murders to the anger and frustration of judges, executioners, and the victims' families. If you live thirty more years and read a few more books, your positions might just move a bit closer to mine, because like I said, at your age you should be handing them over to your daughter now. It's a shame I won't be around to experience it, to enjoy you when you're more understanding and if I may, my little cabbage, a bit more humane. How I would have loved to enjoy you. I know time is ticking away for you. I know it's getting late. You make me feel the same way I felt when my father would give advice to Brouard in front of me: as if you were telling me that

I lack those little hollowed spaces where the soul resides; that I'm
like some sort of vacant, unfurnished, ramshackle salon. Apparently everyone just takes it for granted. I think I take it for granted
myself sometimes, too, the idea that I'm unfurnished and vacant
inside. You can't learn it, Silvia, and I can't teach it to you, even if
I wanted to, I can't. That's life. One accumulates knowledge like a
magpie, listens to thousands of records, and over the course of a
lifetime, reads book after book, sees hundreds of television programs, sifts through millions of magazines, and one ponders, gath-
ers information, and then dies, and surely if he or she has a shred
of lucidity left at the end, reflects on all the time that's been lost.
And indeed the time that was lost is also what was won, earned.
Whether you're talking about lumpen trash or the elite, it's all one
and the same, there's very little separating them, a few thin degrees in the aperture of an angle, fewer driblets of cologne, a different brand. Like that tiny scrap of genome that separates man
from monkey, or even less, from rat or fly, just a tiny, nearly imperceptible deviation. But the deviation is there. You can't avoid it.
Nearly indistinguishable and yet decisive, it happens in an instant
my child, all the hustle and bustle of life. You die, and that tiny
deviation in the angle vanishes along with you. My grandchildren
are on the same path as their parents. I guess it's normal, a sign of
the times. But nowadays the ideal, the lie a person makes up in his
or her head, has nothing to do with that arsenal of romantic values
of dedication or sacrifice anymore, all the things nineteenth-century Spanish Republican literature picked up on and were cultivated by the anti-Francoists of my and Matías's generations: now
it's all about self-centeredness, what people want to possess, consume, campaigns designed by big advertising agencies. As ideals
they are far bleaker, though who knows, perhaps they're less harm-
ful too, and strange as it may seem a little closer to me, at least I
find them more understandable. One thing I've learned is that one

is not necessarily in control of one's deeds. That's what I tried to explain, Silvia. Same as in nature, there are cycles in humanity, movements everyone sees taking place but that nobody can figure out how to avoid. I remember that popular story from when Matías was eight or ten years old, I dedicated it to him on his birthday from a local radio station, a common practice at the time. It's the story of two rabbits who argue bitterly over whether the barking of the dogs that are getting closer is the sound of grey-hounds or beagles. They are distracted by the intensity of their argument, and the dogs finally catch up to them and gobble them down. Greyhounds or beagles, what does it matter? In either case, you're lunch. It's as if we don't know how to live in the absence of a threat. I think I hear the sound of dogs getting closer and closer. And here we are fighting over whether they're greyhounds or beagles. If the great banquet isn't to be celebrated on earth, more and more people seem set on celebrating it in heaven. Sometimes I see my wife's eleventh-hour piousness as a sort of precursor to this. And closer to the ground there's the inexorable insignificance of daily life. Miriam: Grandpa, I'm getting my driver's license now since I turned eighteen. So I want a car. I picked it out already. It's a blue Hyundai. She brought me an ad she'd clipped from the Sunday newspaper supplement. This one, but in electric blue. I close my eyes. I tell her: As soon as you finish school. Your mother tells me you only passed two classes. And it reminds me of when I was eighteen, twenty (*Où sont-ils à présent, à présent, mes vingt ans*: I know practically the whole song by heart too, I have it in my glove compartment, sung by Milva, not Aznavour. I get teary-eyed every time I listen to it too, so I try not to: *Je restais perdu ne sachant où aller, les yeux cherchant le ciel, mais le cœur mis en terre*). I remember the long nights with Brouard and Montoliu when we were teen-agers, talking till the sun came up; our own version of *désinvolture*. Greyhounds or beagles: the signs are discouraging, like Traian calling me to talk about Collado, my former colleague, and demanding that I do something about him; I, obedient, am forced to oblige. One never fully cancels a commitment, a pact. I know Collado likes to go around saying he's still associated with me, mostly to show off, to see if it helps him open accounts in the warehouses, secure materials with ninety-day billing, when all of Misent knows that nobody'll lend to him. He chose to follow his true vocation years ago. It's my fault, maybe, for not teaching him properly; his fault for continuing to use the shortcut that was only meant to get us out of a pinch. Collado's amalgam of pigheadedness and lack of conscientiousness is also a precursor to this new generation, like a twenty-first-century young person *avant la lettre*. It's like playing—excuse the pun—Russian roulette, I told him so many times. Collado doesn't have a business in his head, he has a shroud that's getting thicker and thicker and more tightly woven all the time, and it's going to be hard to get free of it, untangle himself. He scrapes along, begs for favors, can't even keep a single full-time worker in his volatile business whose only assets include three or four vans bearing his logo, business cards with his name embossed, and a few random advertisements in a local real estate magazine. Drink up till you see the bottom of the glass, fill it back up, throw back some more till you see the bottom again: there's no remission that way, Collado. That way you're lost. The bottom of the glass is the end of the road. You're a trapped rat. Get it? In Morocco they put glass bottles in the holes of those squat toilets they like to call "Turkish" so rats can't climb up through them. A rat will try to bite from the dregs of shit, it'll dig at the glass, trying to claw a way to the outside. That's you, clawing at the bottom of the drinking glass, impotent, trapped by the sparkly glass and gin. You can't find your way out, you can't pull yourself out of all the shit. We did some things in order to do others, not because we'd lost our bearings. You can't allow yourself to succumb to the head rush of stepping off the trail, trying to go it alone, as if it were like mountaineering, bungee jumping, cross-country, whatever the fuck they call the trendy adventure sport of the day. Our shortcut was never meant to become a thrilling adventure sport. We went off-trail to tie our shoelaces and then we jumped back onto the trail again. That's it. Run along the same trail as everyone else but with proper footwear, tied laces, the curve of the shoe hugging the foot. That's the only reason we went off-road: to get back on again. Collado never got that into his head, more beef than brains, as usual. Nature hardly ever provides the brains to go along with all that brawn, or the intelligence to know how to focus it, maybe because the two energies together—strength and intelligence— would be an explosive mix, it's a matter of natural balance; why not keep faith in the wisdom of nature. Traian, the Russian, sniffed him out as cannon fodder from the get-go. He may have thrown him some work early on, odd jobs in friends' chalets and the like, but decided to get rid of him pretty quickly because he felt he couldn't trust Collado. He reminded me about it this morning, in the café: He sticks his nose places he shouldn't, he said. One has to know how to wait. He wasn't specific about the nature of the trouble Collado was mixed up in. I have no idea how he's involved with you, Traian, and if he still is. I haven't heard from Collado in months (I lied, I didn't want Traian to know that he'd called me a few days ago, panicky, scared, it would only complicate things). I'm just keeping my house in order, running my businesses, you know that. The Russian denied having anything to do with Collado, too. He's just a pest, he said. I pushed it a little further: He's a good-for-nothing (I'm sorry to have said that about poor Collado, but I've been ill at ease lately, and disappointed that he'd put me in that situation, apprehensive, I don't want him to open a book I closed a long time ago over a page I've already read). Anyway, Traian is no model of discretion and neither are his cronies, whatever he has to say to me, and I figured that out slowly but surely and in the nick of time, thanks to Guillén. Regarding Collado, I told Traian: You have a shotgun wedding to a woman you don't love and impose on your life a beginning and an end all at the same time. Everyone does the same thing. They marry out of pessimism (as I was uttering the phrase, I realized that I had read it ages ago in the old bachelor Baroja's work—marrying out of pessimism—something I had considered for several nights after deciding to marry a second time, I didn't want to be blinded by the fear of being alone), and if you marry because you believe you're not good for anything else, you're doomed: you have children you don't want, a wife who scrapes your nerves raw, and a house you really prefer not to be in. The drinks, the bordellos, the drinking buddies, the gaming tables, the bars, anything's better than being at home. And there you have it. That's Collado in a nutshell. Collado is no luminary, but he has been astute, he had a quick mind, good reflexes, what in soccer jargon they call an excellent short dribble. But he's pitiful now. His body is swollen, bloated, but the worst of it is his mind, a brain floating in fat and alcohol. Mama would have said the son of a poor alcoholic is doomed by social genetics to become a poor alcoholic (she used the word bum; she'd say: A poor bum; with all the cutting social accusation the word carries, one of Mama's favorite expressions whenever she wanted to stress class differences). Collado's mind has a single track, which is set on getting away from home and poking his dick into anything that is not his wife. Traian told me: You tell him to stay away. Why does he chase after a whore who doesn't belong to him? The place is full of Russians, Romanians, women from Ukraine hunting for Spaniards to give them citizenship, women nobody would miss if they leave the club. But he screwed up. He went after the one who's off-limits. I gathered that Traian is behind the club, Lovers, and that Collado, as always, is

falling in love with whores, and this time it's one who belongs to
Traian and his friends. It didn't seem like too big a deal to me. But
it forced me to take stock in how I was partially to blame, not
because of what Sarcós the brute might do to Collado the chump
(teach him a lesson) on my orders, but for something I'd done: I
was guilty for having gotten out of all that in the nick of time, a
hundred years ago, and apparently Traian had come to remind me
that we still owe each other certain favors; maybe not even that:
more like that we owe each other a little courtesy, a little consideration, like a married couple who separates but stays in touch and
takes care that the other is relatively happy in his or her new life.
But I was guilty of something else, something more tangible:
though it's an unavoidable guilt, because that's the way a father has
to behave, fight for the good of his family without anyone being
the wiser about how, you can't stain what comes after you, or
touch the pages of the future with greasy fingers, those blank, pris-
tine pages upon which anything can yet be written. Write—for my
daughter and son-in-law—about the time when the work wasn't
enough. You, Juan, so enamored of realist literature, so fond of
Balzac, how is it possible that you can't figure out that what's going
on in your home is just like a Balzac novel, cookie-cutter plot:
there's a dark shadow hovering over the origin of your family fortune. That's literary realism. Don't look away. Or do you think
those narratives are a bunch of lies? You've dedicated your life to
studying a lie? Behind every fortune there's a crime, isn't that what
your beloved Balzac says? Marx, an avid reader of Balzac by the
way, said the same thing. Years later, Lenin, who'd read both of
them, would say the same thing: Marx and Balzac; so you marry
the heiress to the fortune but don't want to lug around that dowry
of guilt. And you're an expert on social literature? The foundations of this house with its panoramic views of the bay, the gulf of
Valencia, this privileged house where you can shuffle out onto the

deck in pajamas and take in the first light of dawn as it glides across the sea's rump, that moment the tourist brochures call the Spanish sunrise, the palm trees, the jacarandas, the bougainvillea, jasmine, and lady of the night, the blue sheet of the pool: these things, turned into fixed assets, are always raised from materials whose names are best left unvoiced, sensitive materials, resting on the back of some little animal that squirms and retracts when you poke it with a stick. Say to Juan: I was already working for you before I ever laid eyes on you, when you were still crawling on all fours around your parents' patio, because it's not about the people, it's about codes, positions inside of a family system. Systems, groups. I worked so that my daughter, my grandchildren, and you could all be happy. Do you know of a way forward that doesn't take into consideration a future that goes beyond yourself? It's the only way. Set a goal that's way out in front of you—haven't you seen those mechanical hares they use with racing dogs? Can't let the anxiety of unpaid loans overwhelm you, Tax Agency penalties, workplace inspections, don't go burying yourself alive so that people look at you first with pity, and then retire their glance whenever you walk by. Though one can never entirely break free. Traian asked me to save Collado from himself this morning. But how do you do something like that, how do you save someone from themselves? It's not easy. Some people are attracted to trouble the way dirty water is attracted to the drain. Admit everything to my son-in-law and daughter. But how do you explain something like that? Like a Catholic confessing his sins through the latticework of a wooden confessional, on my knees, head modestly bowed, chin lowered to my chest, eyes clouded by a veil of tears; or the contrary, a couple of authoritarian fist-bangs on the table, puffing up with an adventurer's spirit of self-importance, as though you're dictating memoirs to a secretary at the end of your life. List it off as some wild, youthful escapade: attach our name to

things that had nothing to do with us, storing substances produced and distributed by others. Guillén kept adjusting the risk
assessment for his businesses, but there he is, with a luxury hotel,
a golf club, bungalows: everyone knows how business has been.
Our parents told us stories of hardship during the war, the cold,
the fleas and lice, but they never told us about the people whose
faces they smashed up against a wall to put a bullet in the base of
their skulls. They did that. The war was like that. Only when they
had to kill the chicken or the rabbit at home did they say they
preferred not to see it, or, on the contrary, they'd create some ploy
to keep the family in the dark to kill the little animal, and would
talk about some outsider who must've done terrible things in the
past, compelled by hunger, duty, avarice, or terror, things that are
better left forgotten. And what's with all the fuss anyway? It
doesn't make it any easier. We needed discipline for what we did,
the same kind of discipline a musician needs who wants to play at
a concert level, or a hard-training athlete hoping to break a record.
High expectations, well-focused effort, control. Qualities are
worth very little without discipline. For example: Collado has applied his qualities toward destroying himself—risk-taking for the
thrill of the risk—while Guillén has played and still plays with an
eye on the future; notions of the past and the future are irrelevant
to Collado. He married out of pessimism, he only finds pleasure
in incinerating everything, including himself. Everybody has their
own problems. Thousands of millions of humans roam the earth
and no two bodies are the same, no two ways of thinking are the
same. It seems impossible. Apparently, there are only twenty-odd
features that allow us to recognize a person by sight, and yet we're
able to differentiate someone from among the thousands of millions of people on earth, the infinite combination of a handful of
features. We recognize a school friend in the distance, an office
colleague, a neighbor, and we call out to them by name from the

throng of people strolling around some city or town that's located thousands of kilometers away from where we are accustomed to seeing them. We call out to them and they come, they recognize our voice, they recognize our features and approach us calling our name in return. Guillén, with all his *bonhomie*, his grand gestures, his bear hugs, is stealthy inside, he works more from a place of silence—despite the guffaws and the soft smacks on the back he gives out left and right—and his way of thinking is in the long term (despite his endless flitting from flower to flower, his apparent haste to get places). Clearly it's something that's in a person's genetic code and is unavoidable. Guillén is in up to his neck, he keeps pulling a string that mysteriously gives and gives and never seems to break. He grows along with the skein, while Collado gets all tangled up in it, he asphyxiates. Guillén is all about keeping his business private and his public life active, even frenetic. You can hear Guillén as a guest on radio talk shows, he's interviewed in local newspapers addressing issues like sustainable growth, environmental quality, how to juggle ecology and tourism. You can watch his face go red on local television, ever more broken blood vessels on his nose, there he is beside the mayor, the yacht club president, at fundraising dinners organized by NGOs, by the soccer team, the association of holiday celebrations. If you go to a business dinner there he is; show up at a party, an event, whatever, there's Guillén in the front row. He's here and he's there and he sneaks off at night to meet the Russian's lawyer in a subdivision tucked away somewhere discreet, or an agent of the Colombians. Such an intense social life begs the use of untraceable telephones, frequency jammers, passwords, fake names for phone conversations, and attending clandestine meetings. The truth of things. Life is like that in Misent, though who can say how long it will last. And while the economy seems to loom so large, shocking, it's really nothing but a stage set, it's the front curtain that hides the stage through which a stealthy animal moves, unseen, so inconspicuous it doesn't even have a name, because it's not power, though it participates in power; it's not money, though it derives nourishment from money; it's not even prestige, though it's equally incorporeal. It's the axis around which the great wheel turns. It is, if I may, the stoking gust, the steam that makes the boiler boil, it's what you can't see, nobody sees, because it's pure energy. Something nobody's ever interested in. People go to the theater to see a spectacle, a play, and not to spy on the work of lighting designers and stage engineers. You take a cruise to play tennis on the deck courts, take a dip in the pool, sit on a stool and order a gin and tonic at the bar, dress up for a formal dinner—not to be distracted by the engine stokers. Only in Fellini movies do passengers sneak down to sing opera in the engine rooms while the T-shirted stokers shovel coal, and it can be so beautiful, so moving, really it can, but it's not real. I remember arguing with Guillén when we broke off our relationship: That's it, each one is the way he is, I've already done what I needed to do, but you haven't, you want the whole thing, that's the road you're taking; it may be how I got started, but I shifted gears, I'm in third gear now (the Bronsel Beach promotion hadn't even begun yet, that's where I made the real money: that urban development project is to me what I call shifting into fourth), and haven't yet bought the Aldana parcels to build the exclusively upscale golf course (shift into fifth, direct; then came the automatic gears), and I don't even need to keep a foot on the pedal anymore, things are moving along on their own, the money is accumulating on cruise control now, no hysterics; the money is making money without fluctuations, no fits and starts, only an even-keeled flow, that cruising speed announced by the flight captain to the passengers once the plane has

been airborne for a little while; I don't need to bring anything in
from the outside: what I meant was nothing that has to be un-
loaded from airplanes, ships, nothing of what was brought in with
the horses during those two interminable years, the origin of everything, and the briefcases Traian dropped off at the law firm
nearly every month, buying silence, putting apartments in the
names of people nobody knew, entire buildings, entire subdivisions—the bricks of the ex–Soviet Union demolished, dismantled,
taken apart stone by stone, ground down, turned to gold and sunk
into the coastal quagmires. That's when the more legitimate work
got started, though it was no less dangerous: credit lines that
didn't come through, the moment that nearly everything was em-
bargoed, the moment you received a call from the Tax Agency and
they began naming companies that you're familiar with but you
had to pretend that you're not, talk about it, tell them about it, the
swan-dive moment of vertigo that will stay with you the rest of
your life, that you can remember and recount over and over again,
at cocktail parties, at dinners, at the bar; you can tell the whore
about it who listens before going upstairs to do what you're paying
her to do; tell your grandchildren, the children of your grandchildren who will be here before too long. Live long enough to meet
them (Miriam turned eighteen just a few months ago, so what's
my gift, Grandpa? A car? All my girlfriends have cars. Nothing too
sporty: just a small one, cute, in electric blue. A Hyundai. With all
your cabbage—that's how they talk nowadays: your cabbage). Let
her know that Grandpa Rubén was nearly bankrupted because
your Grammy (that's what they call their great-grandmother; I'm
Gramps and my mother Grammy: as if my mother and I were
some sort of incestuous couple tangled together in the great
equalizer and ice-cold nuptial bed of senectitude, which straddles
years so easily, relatives linked by family names, bonds of the tribe
and the classes: fucking dotage. As a child, your elder is the person

in the grade just above you, even though he or she may only be a few months or a year older. But as one ages, so goes the tango, twenty years turns into nothing: my mother an old lady, me an old man: to Miriam and Felix, grandpa and great-grandma are huddled together in that sullied snow flurry of old age), so yeah, Grammy showed no interest in what I was doing, never even bothered to ask, she put her money in the bank, invested in financial instruments from the state, bonds, whatever was guaranteed, and kept her lands from drying up, fields and groves that scarcely yielded enough to cover their upkeep, to pay for the trickle irrigation system they needed, the phytosanitary treatments, powders against the Mediterranean insects, against the leaf miners, pruning, herbicides, machinery, harvesting costs, packaging, and transport. She said she wasn't interested in anything that had to do with cement, with profits, with multiplying the value of those ruinous lands by ten, by a hundred, by a thousand, in a single shot, lands she ultimately defended in vain because after all that effort they ended up as barren fields of dried-out trees and weeds that would become, inevitably, parcels, then apartment blocks, bungalows, chalets; parcels like the rest of them, prime for subdividing, developing, building, but by then I no longer wanted to buy them because I didn't need them anymore. I told her as much at the time: Now that it's raining cats and dogs, thundering and lightning, the hailstones are crushing the oranges, the grapefruit, I've got shelter, a roof over my head. I'd needed them before, back in the day, that plot of land had gleamed virgin in the aerial photos in the midst of all those built-up areas, the perfect lines of orange trees outlining the house, the little pine forest, the palm trees, the araucarias, an oasis in the desert of cement in the aerial photos of tourist brochures used by the Generalitat, or City Hall, that graced the windows of real estate offices, but by the time Matías and Mama offered me the land, I didn't want it anymore. I told them I had better projects to invest in elsewhere, because they hadn't even offered me the land with the benefits of being a coproprietor, they wanted an appreciated value, they wanted me to pay as much as any other buyer once it'd been reappraised at an astronomical level, and now wasn't a buyer's market. I told them as much, it's time to sell, not to buy, so I sent them off to negotiate with someone else, to humiliate themselves haggling with Bataller, with Guillén, with Dondavi, with Maestre, with Rofersa, and all the rest of the local builders. I don't want it, I told them. I already took care of what I had to do on my own. I'd been forced to sink my hand in up to my elbow, find a way to get started, get some purchase to move upward, hydrogen, helium, other gases that make an air balloon rise and soar, because at the start there's only one factor to take into account even before you decide on a direction, and that's how to rise; without ascending, without touching the sky and looking down at the earth, the checkered hankie of the earth, there's no voyage possible, so you've got to rise, even if only a few lengths of your palm, a few meters, because the sky, after all, begins a few handbreadths above your head, but you've got to notice you're up there looking down at things from on high, a few meters is enough, and that's when you feel like you can finally choose the right direction; but that egotistical, Gothic spire of my mother had denied me from taking flight. Hermetic, airtight. Blind stone, deaf, mute. Insensitive stone quarried from God knows where. Proof there's not a single fault line in that compact structure, not a single fissure for the sentimental waters to seep through. The god was unnameable, the one who said let there be light, *fiat*, and there was light, who said open, and the earth was split into two parts, and the cleft was filled with the blue waters of the pool, the abyss with condominiums that sprouted from the ground and in whose walls air-conditioning units began to purr; kitchen ovens and glass-ceramic cooktops flared in the honeycomb cells of everything now on the rise, every hollow space packed with life, concavities bursting with children squealing as they ran down the stairs of their homes carrying inflatable tubes, plastic fins, and goggles: oh the joy of seaside vacations. All that Mediterranean blue, all that Mediterranean grace. My God, what would bus drivers in major European cities do if it weren't for the Mediterranean, all the office workers, the secretaries, the welders, the butchers, what would all those modest folk do if there was no Mediterranean on the horizon of their sad working lives. What would the millionaires do, who like to sail atop a silky sea, and swim and pack their clothes? I'm so familiar with this subject it bores me to tears now. Everything can become idiotically transparent now (despite what Guillén thinks). Children watch whales mating behind the glass of an aquarium, or sharks filing their teeth before their morning splash, the world in a fish bowl where everything takes place in plain sight, like in the house on that television program, *Big Brother*, or the Island of whatchamacallit, it's all out there, in plain sight, the huge fishbowl world, the sharks swimming above the visitors at the oceanography institute, baring their teeth to kids who couldn't be bothered to be scared by them. There's something infantile in that need for transparency, as if societies—same as homes; public life is, after all, a displacement of private life—didn't need their dark recesses, the areas where future energy is accumulating. We, ourselves, our own bodies, have walls of glass. All you have to do is press a button and all our guts show up on a screen. My daughter loves to scrunch up her nose when I light a cigar after lunch, so she can probe Monica: Has Papa done his yearly triglyceride count yet? What about sugar, urea, cholesterol? He's devouring those pig's feet like a, well, pig; the hare pâté, that goopy tripe, so greasy, so spicy, such heavy foods. How is your uric acid count, your glucose, your cholesterol? Are you keeping track, Papa? She looks at Monica: Is he keeping track?

His face looks really red. As if she needs to say anything to Monica, who has blind faith in the value of nutrition and spends the entire day pestering me about probiotics and the antioxidants in kiwi and loquat (it's as if Silvia were reminding her precisely so that she'll harass me even more). It's getting harder by the day to have a whisky at home, I'm fine, I can drive perfectly well with a whisky down the hatch, whatever the live-in nutritionist has to say about it, I can keep a Mercedes 600 going two hundred and thirty kilometers an hour in a perfectly straight line, for as far as the eye can see, flawless reflexes, awash in that thrill of gravity when it starts easing up. I can do it just fine, but they won't let me. It's getting more and more difficult to smoke a good cigar in a restaurant after lunch without a perforating glare from someone at a nearby table, or a waiter coming to tell you the house has set up a separate room for that kind of thing, which used to excite everyone. Or else straight to the sir, would you kindly do us the favor of putting your cigar out, smoking is not allowed inside. Women used to go wild when their lips met yours, smelling of the cigar you'd just put out, men envied the expensive, rare aroma your suit gave off when you sat down at the boardroom table closing the business year. Now that same thing is a cause for apprehension, even pity. As if you were the *Bounty*, and you'd run aground, and your ship's ribs are rotting away on shore while the transatlantic ocean liner of the world continues its voyage to calmer and bluer seas. I ask my son-in-law: So, Juan, has my daughter been successful at taking your tobacco away altogether? And Juan, laughing: I sneak smokes in the bathroom with the window open so the boss won't catch me. Silvia shoots him an icy glare. And I vent: Nowadays people ring up that hotline the government installed for people trying to kick the habit: Is a truck driver allowed to smoke in the cabin while on the road? Can parents smoke at home in the presence of a minor? Gum, a choking hazard; short-sleeved shirts can cause fatal skin cancer. The radio says they're going to force fat kids to eat diet foods in schools (in the US they give bad grades each month for obesity), and ban ads for fast-food restaurants if they contain too many calories, the state pretending to make paternal gestures when it's really become a spy. The new generations of newspaper readers, of radio listeners, with their virgin eyes and ears, who consider this the beginning of history and not its end, will analyze these things when their own day comes around. History begins today for all of them, right when it's over for you, Matías. Night falls in Paris and there's a delicate piece of orange porcelain on the horizon announcing that soon the sun will rise over Peking. No reconstruction carries the glimmer of truth. In *Memoirs of Hadrian*—which I read to Silvia and my wife before the Caravaggios at San Luigi dei Francesi—there's a discussion about that exhilarating interval when the old gods have died and the new gods haven't arrived yet. Flourishing times when humanity rises up on its own two feet, but also terrible times because their suffering bears little consolation. The old gods of the county are still shaking their death rattles: Gimeno keeps feeding rubles into the washing machine, which come out as dollars for Traian, and the politicians and their friend, Bolroy, the city councilor, are getting more gluttonous by the day since they're in cahoots with Guillén, another mechanism for laundering dollarubles: they keep doing business with him, they cover for Guillén, and we all know opportunities are optional, either for you or for me, two bodies cannot occupy a single space. Guillén negotiates with the politicians, who behave as though they'd landed from another planet and divvied the earth up with a sword, eyes blindfolded like the statues representing justice, though nobody's really duped, everyone knows that justice doesn't wear a blindfold in real life, and she decides: Here there will be such and such an amount of buildable land, here green areas, here sports facilities, this for social use, tertiary use, depending on who's the proprietor; and each one of the actions benefits Guillén and Bolroy, because Guillén and his associates still receive injections of cash from outside sources, what Traian and the Russians, the Colombians, bring in under the table (Guillén told me he broke off relations with them, but it's not so easy to hide that he's still dealing with them in some capacity, there's too much of a stink of money amidst the scaffolding). This is what I wanted to explain to Matías from the start, my brother who always grasped the mechanisms perfectly when he read about them in a sociology book, but refused to see them materializing before his very eyes, look, look at it carefully: you're watching the model described by Marx and his ilk in motion, the praxis of your theoretical model. It's fascinating. Mercury the thief is king of the world. Don't you get it, Matías? And Matías would come looking for me with a downcast expression: he's a child, a child who used to hide in the ironing room to read books behind a hammock whenever he got angry over being unfairly scolded. Edmond Dantès the avenger. Matías the self-centered dandy who pretends not to understand that beyond the scope of the model, there's nothing. What the hell was that man with real leadership skills doing in a bar in Benalda with three retirees, a gin and tonic in hand, and his eyes lost in the direction of a pinup calendar covered with silicone tits; Matías, looking in the mirror that reflected his own despair, the crests of soccer teams dangling on the wall behind the counter, the emblems of Valencia or Barça painted or embroidered on little triangular flags. On this last day of the world (today we'll live out the epilogue to his world, the cold ashes of anticlimax), even that dingy bar would be like falling on the right side, it had an air of being a gateway to the future of humanity. What can you do? Life slips through our fingers like water. I should turn my cell phone back on, it's probably full of messages already and people in the office are going to start pestering me now, about work or giving their condolences. Connect even if only for a second, call my daughter or, even better, Angela, to find out whether they've transferred Matías to the funeral parlor yet. I didn't want to be there for his last breath. I couldn't handle it. I left. Surely if Matías had a shred of consciousness left he wouldn't have wanted me there, either, in his last seconds of life. The widows and my daughter were whispering, talking under their breath on this of the glass while I thought: Don't let him hear me, don't let him remember me right now. I said a quick goodbye, my brother scratching through the shadows, entering my bedroom, his cadaverous body opening a cold space between Monica's body and my own. That's when I thought I needed to hold her tight, take a few sleeping pills, not melatonin, which I've been taking lately, it has no effect, I wanted something stronger, zolpidem or lorazepam, and to fall asleep holding Monica, my legs tangled in hers, flesh to flesh, flesh against death, heat against death and its ghosts. The doctor's words rang again in my mind: He's clinically dead. And suddenly I'm overwhelmed by emotion. My vision goes blurry, my mouth shrinks and contracts into a series of frowns. I continue frowning inside the car, barely able to make out the traffic on my left. Where the fuck is this sorrow welling from, this aching. I close and open my eyes several times, not at a normal blinking pace, nothing soft like that; it's more a desire to shut something, like you close and open a box, keep the lid down for a minute and then pull it up again; sink into the coolness of the shadows and back into the light, as if rising from an immersion in the sea; let the drops of water vanish, let your eyes see anew, a wobbly image at first, refracted from the water, then it grows sharper little by little, you see everything so clearly now, you breathe deeply, filling your lungs, thinking you could have drowned down there. Your lungs fill with iodized air hovering just above the water, you bathe yourself in the sunlight. Matías. You're laid out there on a sheet, a metal table, a piece of marble. As if there was still time. I say: brother; I say: mother, while I think: I was in her uterus for months but I don't remember her breasts, her hands, I had a mother who never held my hand. Do you realize that, Matías? I've never held her hand, I hold her hand in her dementia, in her bitter nonbeing. Eyes closed, head resting on the back of the seat. Arms on the steering wheel now, head sunk between them. If anyone is watching from the highway, they'll think I'm asleep, a fatigued driver who stopped for a snooze. She worked her way in between us, asked for her share of us, same as she did with our father, community property, guardianship. Mama. Genetics, biography. Who's lord over oneself, one's movements, one's desires. Darwin or Marx. The unsolvable dilemma, perennial, useless. But always coming back. My brother is dead: I think about it, I say it out loud, I sob, I repeat it, and I don't know why I'm sobbing, or why I say it, why I give a name to it, yet hearing myself say his name brings me back to the child who learned his first letters of the alphabet with a piece of chalk gliding over the surface of a blackboard. An old man dies and awakens the child who's still alive: I can see myself writing my first letters. What was it that we could never become: I go back to the blackboard, the chalk, the inkwell fixed in the little hole in the desk, suffering again, as if I were trying to learn a text by heart that I would have to recite before the teacher but couldn't pronounce a single word. When I was little I liked to recite verses I'd copied from the literature textbook. I liked to recite them on the beach. I continued doing it throughout my teenage years, especially on stormy days. Matías was afraid of lightning and he'd go hide in the closet, in the ironing room, and read there (no doubt he prayed, too), but I preferred to jump on my bike and ride to the shore and recite my verses. I'd go alone or sometimes Brouard would join me: if we went together, we'd shout out the verses as loud as we could against the sound of the crashing waves that inevitably drowned out our voices, we saw Marlon Brando doing the same thing years later when he let off steam against the clamor of the Paris metro. I liked to bring Matías with me on those blue summer days, grab his hand, goggles and fins in tow, hold his hand in mine as we walked down the path, hold his hand under the water: show him the caves, the fish, the seagrass meadows, the underwater flowers, the sponges, the urchins. All the dazzling things of Misent that remained hidden, he discovered them all with me, holding my hand, his little hand in mine. The angel of life passed over us so swiftly, moving like a comet across the country from east to west, a few meager sparks of its tail signaling to us that it was already on the other side, beginning its journey across the ocean, on its way to who knows where (*hier encore, j'avais vingt ans*). The oblivion of forgotten things. Forget life. Return to oblivion. Demolitions Bertomeu. May no single monument remain standing to commemorate any of it. Matías, now that you'll be mere ashes moving through an oven, now that you have time there in the tedium we call nothingness, why not pick up a copy of the Blue Guide to Rome and read the part about the tombs on the Via Appia, unscathed despite the ravages of time (who's not ravaged by the passage of time?), proud sepulchres among cypress trees, like arrows gazing up toward the heavens, symbols of eternity, of what endures, that notion so despised by contemporary society, mother of ephemeral architecture, of ephemeral ideas and lives. In Rome, Eurysaces the Baker had someone build a monumental oven near Porta Maggiore that would serve as a tomb for himself and his wife: tourists still go there to visit it, and archaeologists study its funerary architecture as a tribute to his profession, that of baking: even a baker can aspire to eternity; and Gaius Cestius Epulo had a pyramid built that we can still view on the Via Ostiensis, in commemoration of his work in the East, where he suffered but remained forever identified with those lands. Read what the guidebooks say about the tombs of military men still remembered so many centuries later, or the tombs of kings, and even of rich flour merchants. Outrageous, it seems to us now. There's life beyond the last gasp. They'll spread your ashes, Matías, and no symbols will remain, not the sickle, not the hammer, not the five-pointed star emerging from the east you were so sure would be strong as a diamond but turned out to be a mere illusion, a feint of sunlight dissolving in the air, a mirror that reflects nothing. A vampire's face has no reflection in the mirror—remember that film? We saw it together. You must have been eight or ten. It frightened you. You stuck tight by my side. Not marble, not basalt, not porphyry, not lapis lazuli. None of that: just ashes in a funeral parlor with colorful stained glass windows depicting a multitude moving toward a light painted in little pieces of red glass, a sunset over a façade that nonetheless looks eastward, what does it matter anyway, measly representations, theme-park style, architecture without truth, mere decoration. You're just one more, a little donkey who wants to eat in green pastures but doesn't know how to get there, who brays because it got lost in the burrs and can't find a way out, who perceives that dusk is falling quickly, night is coming. It brays alarmed but the herder can't hear it, though the braying tickles the salivary glands of a wolf nearby: solitary ashes below the trunk of a carob tree among the waning purity of the countryside whose harvest didn't arrive in time to cure your infection, or spread over the sea that's been contaminated by the sin of tourism (wasn't Montaigne a tourist? Wasn't Goethe? And Byron? And before them, Ibn Khaldun, Ibn Battuta, Ptolemy, and Herodotus: tourists), ashes commingled with the barren lands of the mountain, fields left fallow and stubble-strewn, olive trees nobody bothers to prune because it makes no difference, they're all awaiting the land surveyors to measure and assess, awaiting the architects; get the backhoes in to excavate, get rid of the thousand-year-old rocks. "I want to be Providence, because the thing that I know which is finest, greatest, and most sublime in the world is to reward and to punish." Remember that? It's Edmond Dantès. My father wept. I see his back, sitting on the bed, now I see his face, fists pressed tightly against his eyes. He doesn't see me. How long has it been, where are those tears today, and so what do you think, does that mean they were useless? They fulfilled the purpose they were meant to fulfill at the time, fleeting as everything is, and they were his alone, and mine. Something legitimate, something we both inherited. They evaporated, but why should that stop me from listening to Bach? Because one day my ears will turn to dust and all the Bach I've listened to will lie with my mortal remains and turn to dust along with me? Because the Brahms *Klaviersonate* that I just turned on right now—played by Anatol Ugorski, in the middle of this traffic jam, when I'm not sure whether to continue onto the highway or turn around and go back home—will one day be dust in the dust of my ears? I'm supposed to forgo listening to them over that puny detail? Because they're going to turn to dust? I know that. The philosophers told us. As soon as I'm gone, the world will cease to exist, all the commotion will cease to exist, and the cruelty will be redeemed. But the selfsame principle of life is built upon that relativism. The evidence that you are here and then you aren't, that you exist and then you don't. Grab the fruit and take a bite, let the juice drench your mouth. That mouthful is what counts. Life is that, the squandering, my child, my daughter. The explosion of excess that the universe consents. The pure arbitrary consumption of energy.

Trophic levels (and tropisms). Silvia: You're going a little over-board this time, don't you think Papa? It's impossible to say any-thing to you. But I'm just teasing, boy are you losing your sense of humor with each passing day, she tells me. And I respond: Don't even try to convince me that you're just teasing, just getting a little rise out of me. That what you really mean is to cheer me up, to revitalize me; provoke a reaction. A little apathy is a natural state for someone my age, I'd wager even medicinal. Don't worry about me. I'm all about moving forward, every stone builds a wall, every piece of wood feeds a fire, I know that, I tell myself that every day, it's my work, my vocation, and when the last centimeter of ground is filled in, the beaches, the plains, the mountains, when it's all built up and there's no room left for a needle in the pincushion of this backwater you seem so concerned about, I'll bid farewell if it starts worrying me too, and still have breath in me. But for the time being, it keeps me driven. What else? I'm lucky that way. I enjoy good health at seventy-three (including pacemaker, triglyc-erides, and cholesterol—I have another day left: I live it), thanks to my pact as Mephistopheles's aide-de-camp, so what do you want, should I beg forgiveness for that? From whom? If I were poor and sick, would I deserve a different treatment, to be re-spected, admired? Is that what you're trying to tell me? The county is full of grifters who have ruined their lives and now plead for justice, suckers who got swindled when what they really wanted to do was swindle someone else but couldn't quite figure out how to do it, so, are they any better? Worry about yourself. Not me. Get a load of my seventy-odd years. I don't wear them poorly. I sleep like a baby, wake up in a good mood, I eat nearly everything I want, though I'm a little more careful since I got the pacemaker; I smoke a cigar every now and then, have a drink or two, what else could I ask for? The years I have left can still be good ones. And you have some of the best ones ahead of you. You'll see, maturity, common sense. The paradise of the forties. Once I'd dug up the treasure chest (I don't have much mercy on myself as you can see, I don't think I'm better than I am, and I'm way too old to deal with all of that anymore, I talked it over with Matías, with Brouard, with the painter Montoliu, with your mother, I've been arguing the case for nearly thirty years, I even argued with myself the other day and found a way to reconcile me with my other self: money is the only thing that allows us a glint in the fleeting reflection of divine radiance), if I wanted to, my little pigeon, my soul's little cabbage, sweet slice of my heart, I could jump over to the other side, live beside a natural park, some protected lands like the ones you care so much about, though if I were to go someplace I think it would be one of those buzzing honeycombs that are so disturbing to you, but that you seem to jump at the chance to visit whenever you can, places where one can find the full package of civilization in our time, the best that life can offer: New York, London, or Paris, a city that smells like withering lilacs, you can stay in a hotel and in a few steps have anything you want within arm's length. Yep, I'd prefer to hole myself up in one of those boutique hotels in the center of Paris where anything the most refined person could desire is within a radius of two hundred meters: delicatessens, wine stores, cheese shops, the best chefs, movie theaters, painting, music, fashion. Or if you prefer, we could go a little more austere, why not? A modern-day Spartan, a present-day monk, sure, I'm willing to give it a try: off to Rome. My final days, doing nothing more than loafing in a hotel room in Rome, reclining on my bed reading books, or sipping Campari with a slice of orange on the Rosati terrace, squinting in the sweet autumn sunlight contemplating the symmetry of the domes of the Piazza del Popolo, relishing a tasty fettuccine, or spaghetti all'Amatriciana, delicious tripe (*trippa alla Romana*), and greasy bits of animal cooked in tomato sauces (*coda alla vaccinara*) in Checchino's; debone a succulent bird in Il Convivio, wash it down with one of those potent Sicilian wines, the fifteen-degree wines that leave a film of velvet in your mouth and get your blood tingling; or a trendy super-Tuscan variety (a Sassicaia or an Ornellaia). Eat, drink, read, contemplate architecture, painting: spend my days zipping here and there to see Raphaels, Michelangelos, Caravaggios like we did on those trips with your mother; perfect afternoons in the Pantheon breathing in space instead of air, an architect's dream, hours on end contemplating—through the oculus—how the rain falls over the most beautiful platter in the world; or get off the major tourist routes to have a look at paintings and mosaics that are a little off the beaten path. San Lorenzo, San Clemente, I Quatri Coronati, mysterious churches that tourists don't visit as much because they're considered second-rate. So, see, I can go to some of the places you go. Imagine. Rome, the old wasp's nest that Augustus filled with brick and marble: marble as pure adornment, don't forget, it's the Wonder Bread of the sandwich; the ham, the meat, was almost always—and still is—cement or brick. I have the impression it means nothing to you and yet well-laid brickwork can be so beautiful: it resists time better than stone, it's more flexible, it can be molded, it pulsates and even more stunningly, brickwork carries the fingerprints of the hands that placed it, their skill is incorporated, their knowledge, their soul, it has a soul. Like human flesh, an inhabiting spirit animates brickwork, a dust that slowly breaks down into dust again, architecture that becomes geology. It's a shame we don't use it more often these days. Though at my age, I realize I could be on my way to a place where not even that hollow-brick barrier closing my niche will be visible to me, bearing someone's fingerprints, someone's know-how, a piece of someone's soul following me into my vibrant nothingness. Have you ever noticed the bricklayer's artisanship in funeral ceremonies, when he mixes the mortar and smears it over the rows of hollow bricks to close off the burial niche in the presence of twenty-odd relatives and friends of the deceased? Nobody moves a muscle till the trowel comes to rest, everyone held in thrall by its movements. It gets me every time I've had to observe the scene: it's the best antidote for grief, a protection from that menacing stitch of nihilism you feel every time a loved one or someone you've spent time with dies. The twenty-some grief-stricken friends and relatives watch the bricklayer working, his task evolving like a sober and elegant ballet, an athlete performing precise movements, unfolding a genuine piece of art, because isn't art supposed to be the blend of craft and performance? He prepares the mortar, measures the opening, places the hollow bricks in balanced rows, applies it and smooths down the surface. His work announces that life goes on. People who take good care of themselves nowadays, who keep an eye on their cholesterol, their glucose levels, blood pressure, prostate, colon; people who are careful and blessed with a little bit of luck can live to be a hundred these days, but in my case I have a little extra mileage tacked on to my seventy-odd years. When you rent a car you pay for the number of days you'll be keeping it and the number of kilometers you'll travel. Here I am with my body, this rental vehicle, a machine in decent condition, what can I say, I've put a lot of mileage on it, done a lot of cruising around. And believe me, I'm paying a high price for that extra mileage, lugging these extra kilos around, but more than anything else it's the kilometers, the heaps and heaps of them, an infinity of kilometers, an infinity of Havana cigars, of booze, tons of filet mignon, of T-bones and rib eyes, of truly greasy, peppery tripe, grouper straight from the sea, tasty shrimp, lobster on the grill or in a bisque-y rice, or thermidor. They say all of these gorgeous things sit like lead inside of the body, all those foodie meals, all that gastronomic glory, it weighs you down. The counterbalance to all that earthly beauty: sugar, cholesterol, uric acid, saturated fats, unsaturated fats, polyunsaturated fats, triglycerides, transaminases, who knows what else. All the verbiage they punish you with in the press and on television. Yeah, I bet it's heavy. Too heavy. But the heart, kept well-oiled by the good mechanics, keeps on ticking. So have a look, see for yourself, see how well I keep myself in shape, it's miraculous really, despite a little extra heft and my pacemaker, maybe not angelic, but fit, a good example of an early-twenty-first-century, seventy-year-old human male. If Silvia had her way, I would have closed the cycle of life when my wife died; stayed circling around my condition as widower, round and round in a perpetual state of grief. I should have blocked off spaces, closed doors. That was my daughter's project for me, maybe it was a place where she thought we might encounter each other again. She's never forgiven my refusal to believe that the only thing that matters has already happened, is of the past; whereas I believe the only thing that matters is precisely what's left to experience, what's happening now. The day the nearly hundred-year-old lady went to see her dying son. A cadaver ready to be cooked, already marinated, salted, and seasoned, looks without feeling at another cadaver in the process of being cooked. The old woman didn't shed a single tear. As if she'd completely sealed off the corridor, the one that always leads me back to childhood and turns me into a sentimental schmuck. We maneuvered her chair to go up in the hospital's freight elevator, pushed her down the hallway, brought her to sit in front of the bed, on the other side of the glass. Where is he?—she asked. That's him?—she said disdainfully, as if she were in front of some migrant worker who was asking for an advance on his wages. It was hard to recognize him behind the mask, with the tubes everywhere. She stared at him for ten minutes and then asked to be taken out of there with that voice she has now, that bossy croak. And that's it. That's all there was to it. Silvia got what she wanted. I encouraged the idea of letting her think Matías was still on the mountain, Saint John in Patmos; Simeon Stylites sitting atop his column like Napoleon in the Place Vendôme, looking down at the world from on high, looking at the display windows of the jewelry stores from above, the multimillion-dollar clients who come and go at the Ritz with their designer suitcases in tow, the porters with their old-fashioned, gold-braided livery. Everything there is old-fashioned and yet so contemporary, too. Silvia was unwavering. Nature creates defense mechanisms that help a person overcome the death of a father or a mother. But nothing for that, Silvia. There is no genome that anticipates the death of a child. It's outside of the natural order. It's a signal that the gods have abandoned you, for whatever reason. Priam slips in his son's blood before stepping in his own. The death of a child is always the highest point of tragedy. The death of a parent leaves behind a halo of peace, the sensation of a cycle completed, nature imposing its norms, its rites, but the death of a child makes the gods stagger and fall. But oh, she got it into her head and the old woman was forced to contemplate the dying son. Another right exercised. I would've liked for a family to offer some sense of respite, of goodwill. Not have to keep fighting over what should have been mine, with those who should be mine. Economics is a remarkably nervous activity, and construction even more so—it's probably the best metaphor for capitalism. Growing also means destroying and that's not my fault: to grow means to not stop growing, and to build means you don't stop destroying. You destroy something to build something else. The people who terraced the land for crops—didn't they destroy things? They ruined the mountains. Nowadays you call it dry architecture, dry-stone architecture, you venerate it, a sacred thing, you want UNESCO to declare the thousand-year-old dry-stone architecture a cultural

heritage, but originally it meant the destruction of the primitive
Mediterranean forests, the original maquis, the evergreen thickets
and small trees along the shores. They've been destroying this
land for thousands of years. There's not a corner of it that hasn't
been spoiled. Take Misent, for instance. Just read the newspapers.
Here they destroy a Roman villa in the process of building something or other, there they destroy an Almohad hammam, a wall
from the Caliphate, and they've already destroyed half a dozen
fonduks (the newspapers say this was a merchant city in the
twelfth century: it traded with Alexandria, Tunisia, and Sicily).
That's what the specialized newspapers say, the ones we builders
print. As if in order to build the hammam or the Caliphate wall
they hadn't already destroyed the wall or the temple that came
before. In which stratum does truth reside? At which layer should
humanity have detained itself in order to be authentic? The Russian, the hyperactivity of insomnia: his eyes were glassy this morning, he reeked of booze and that bitter, distilled odor that cocaine
leaves in sweat, clearly, he hadn't slept. No doubt he's still trafficking in this or that with Guillén, that's what I thought when I saw
him. And how capitalism and cocaine also have a lot in common.
Construction and cocaine have a lot in common, beyond the sudden plumping of certain bank accounts. There's the hyperactivity,
the doggedness of trying to fight against time. Capitalism and cocaine, the twenty-four-seven frenzy. The backhoes have been at it
for three days now, excavating where the stables had been and the
skeletons of the horses have begun showing up. The laborers arranged the skulls in a corner of the terrain and they piled them
like sculptures with bones of ivory, all spattered with clay and
iron-oxide stains from the earth, soil as thick and dense as coagu-
lated blood. The company that owned the horse stables vanished
without a trace. It was such a long time ago. Guillén, Bolroy, me,

there were half a dozen owners. Even Collado held a stake. I think I gave him shares myself. Right now my thoughts wander to when I was young, an aspiring artist, and how I ended up becoming the creator of that outdoor sculpture garden, its combination of the uprooted trunks of orange trees and horse bones: the shapes of torment, vegetable and animal in the process of becoming mineral; described that way, it takes on something of the epic, the red earth rising like a murky veil over the machines, in keeping with the latest trends in art, those avant-garde installation pieces, artists who ask the morgue for cadavers to build their installations, human organs in formaldehyde, pig heads, offal, mummified bodies, dissected. These bones coming to light belong to my secret architecture, the scraps of hide hardened and cured by the passage of time. I would like to stop by Brouard's house, which I can see from here, from the lane that merges onto the highway that I've decided not to take, there's his house at the foot of the mountain, the cloud of dust released by the backhoes behind it; sit down with Brouard, light a cigarillo with him (does he still smoke?), talk as if time hadn't passed at all, as if my father was still encouraging his writing; put forward a moral question, ask him who's the best, discuss the idea of moral decline with him, the clinamen, the difference between stiff Democritus and flexible Epicurus, the types of things we cared about when we were young; talk to him about how Matías burned through both health and money at the same time; describe in minute detail the papers my mother and Matías signed behind my back. Go see Brouard: The main character of his best novel, the unscrupulous speculator from *The Erratic Will*, a visit with the author, a performance in the vein of Pirandello, Unamuno, to talk, reason, argue, confront; let the character defend himself and explain to the author that he hasn't been an erratic being (talk to him about the hollowness as the center of the character, the unfurnished space where the echoes of footsteps can be heard). Brouard, where did our twenties go? What happened to them? Memories overwhelm me, such a rush of them, and all at once I feel like crying, not out of anger, but the pure desire just to weep, here, awash in this white light that stains everything and illuminates it shamelessly, sun that's not the source of life, but a blanching punishment. But it's late now, it's already late. The ring from the glass on the bar's wooden countertop, on the zinc, liquor and tonic—that's it, right Matías? The pact of the just. It's as if I were the baby instead of the older brother. That's it, right Mama? The nights I spent sobbing. Random hours of the day, I'd close the office door and cry. I'd mull the excruciating phrase over and over again in my mind: I spent months in utero, but my mother would never hold my hand. I read that sentence somewhere else, too, in some novel; or maybe not, maybe it's just an idea of mine, something that stuck with me, an absence that becomes words. I might be able to understand Matías, but never my mother, what compelled her to do these things, was it because I listened to music? Or so that he, Matías, would stroke her hair on winter evenings, untie it so her hair falls over her shoulders, or help her settle a little cluster of jasmine in her décolletage and say to her, Oh my, just look at how pretty you are? Here come, those old tears are returning now, here, where I am, stopped on the side of the road, awash in the whitish light, the mist, the cars driving by on my left, the landscape that's been my cage, where I've prowled for so many years—what's before me, surrounding me, all of it caught in the scintillating white powder, blinding and sticky. I'm crying from a despair that's inconsolable. Nothing can alleviate it now, I cry over the hollowness that's inside of me, I cry and can't get out of myself, from a heartache, a despair that nobody else can reach, my arms on the steering wheel, my head on my arms, the tears wetting the skin of my arms, cured skin, covered in liver spots, wrinkly turtle skin that no cream will ever make smooth again. *Hier encore, j'avais vingt ans.* Everything rewinds to seventy years ago, everything that's inside of me returns there, but to an immature state, precooked. Beneath the wrapper of skin, amidst the bony carcass, the circulatory streams and the conduits that turn meat and vegetables into a paste, the passage of time hasn't changed anything, or maybe it's changed everything without changing anything—let's just say everything's been left intact but cold, like a potage taken between meals that has lost its flavor, its grace, everything the same, the same stew, only now in that viscous state, runny, when something is consumed too many hours after being cooked. The sea off in the distance, a laminate of molten metal. And the two words (Matías, Mama), together, united, intertwined; and with them other words from long ago, a warm, familial wave that rises and falls and rises again. There's biscuit ice cream in the freezer, there's chocolate in the jicara, there's perfumed soap in the dish in the bathroom, there's black bitumen in the drawer where the shoe polish is kept. I can smell the bitumen, the ink, the chalk. Words carry it all back, they bring the smell, they bring the color, they bring the taste. They don't actually contain anything, but they carry them, they bring their representation to another place. They carry the lie that you are able to salvage something; but no, they're only cunning words that make you see without seeing, smell without smelling. The smell on your hands, the morning chill, the scarf, the gloves. Tie your scarf around your face before you go out, and put your coat on— not my mother, the maid, tugging at my coat and saying: Wrap your scarf around your mouth. Matías was still in the crib back then, swaddled in white cloths. Be Providence. Impart Justice. Separate good from evil. I see Brouard's house and below it the lands that are now mine, where the backhoes are digging, uprooting the trees under whose branches we used to play together, and a hundred meters farther along, what's left of the warehouse and stables, the red-stained skeletons of the horses that had been buried there. Brouard. The injustice of time, Matías, I don't know if you've finally realized that in the end, time always places things where they don't belong. Your Providence. Mama. Some women are seduced by the unproductive, words that skate over acts without ever touching them, or that have little to do with them, the purring that floats above the reality of the world like sticky green slime, big ideas that glide over life like ectoplasm. Maybe her sole motivation was to hear the music of Matías's words: What have you done today? Let me see now, you look gorgeous, that cream really does the trick, makes your skin so soft. Could that be the only reason? I close my eyes here in my car and smell the bitumen, I hear the voices: there's perfumed soap in the dish, the maid says, there's chocolate in the jicara, ice cream in the fridge. Next to Brouard's house are buried horse skeletons the workers have begun digging up and stacking into heaps, the materials of my secret architecture that a backhoe has brought to light, the shreds of dried-out hide, bones covered in clay mud. They shine in the sun covered in that oxide-rich red clay, transitional colors, earthy, like a Tàpies painting, dense materials, complex, midway between painting, pottery, and sculpture. The perfect materials for one of those installations contemporary artists are so fond of building. And you too, Matías, now you're an installation piece worthy of a contemporary art museum, laid out on a sheet, on a metal table, on a slab of marble.

Winter scene in Misent

*Night. The beach is dark and silent this time of year. No light is coming
from the apartment windows looking out over the beach, the sounds
of the splashing tide are barely audible, as if the sea were composed of a
substance denser than water. A slightly phosphorescent crest is all that
allows you to distinguish the uncertain line separating liquid from
solid, the spot where the waves meet the sand. Following this line,
southward, the city lights appear, and others that ascend the sides of the
mountains, forming rosaries in certain stretches, concentrating then
dispersing. A few hundred meters of the area have not yet been developed, where the sand draws the threaded outline of a string of dunes,
looking tonight like the whitish stains on the dark backdrop of an X-
ray. In the stillness of the air, all that can be heard is the sea's heavy
breathing, and over that sound, nearby, a very slight nervous rasping.
The full moon rises between two clouds, illuminating the scene, turning the landscape into a negative of itself: the earth a dark smudge,
and the sea a shimmering stain that glows like molten steel along the
wide strip of the horizon, and that sharpens itself at the edge of the
sand where the phosphorescent specks and strands of waves glint and
glimmer, coming in and out, one over the other. As the moon continues
to rise in the firmament, a slight breeze picks up. As if the darkness had
held it captive and the light has set it free. The clicking and crepitat-
ing of the reeds that grow on this side of the dunes can be heard more
sharply now. If the observer raises her eyes toward the origin of the
sound, she will find the silhouette of a dog, and the glint of its eyes like
a spark that's immediately dowsed by a cloud stealing over the moon*

again. Out at sea the thick stain forms once more, like pitch, cover-
ing the entire horizon, while the profile of the coast is outlined by the
orange-tinged reflection of the lights. The breeze has died down and the
air is still again, and in this lull a sickly sweet smell is released into the
air from where the dog is digging, the smell of old carrion.

THE END
BENIARBEIG, FEBRUARY 2007

(Valerie Miles, Calella de Palafrugell,
August 28, 2019 – Barcelona, June 6, 2021)